TRICKSTER'S POINT

A NOVEL

WILLIAM KENT KRUEGER

ATRIA PAPERBACK

New York   London   Toronto   Sydney   New Delhi

ATRIA PAPERBACK

A Division of Simon & Schuster, Inc.
1230 Avenue of the Americas
New York, NY 10020

First Atria Paperback edition May 2013

ATRIA PAPERBACK and colophon are trademarks of Simon & Schuster, Inc.

For information about special discounts for bulk purchases, please
contact Simon & Schuster Special Sales at 1-866-506-1949 or
business@simonandschuster.com.

The Simon & Schuster Speakers Bureau can bring authors to your
live event. For more information or to book an event contact
the Simon & Schuster Speakers Bureau at 1-866-248-3049
or visit our website at www.simonspeakers.com.

Designed by Davina Mock-Maniscalco

Manufactured in the United States of America

20   19   18   17   16

The Library of Congress has cataloged the hardcover edition as follows:

Krueger, William Kent.
    Trickster's point : a novel / by William Kent Krueger.—1st Atria Books hardcover ed.
      p. cm.
    1. O'Connor, Cork (Fictitious character)—Fiction. 2. Private investigators—
Minnesota—Fiction. 3. Murder—Investigation—Fiction. I. Title.
    PS3561.R766T75 2012
    813'.54—dc 23   2012021489

ISBN 978-1-4516-4567-5
ISBN 978-1-4516-4571-2 (pbk)
ISBN 978-1-4516-4573-6 (ebook)

For Joanna MacKenzie and Alec MacDonald,
two of my brightest guiding stars

PROLOGUE

The dying don't easily become the dead.

Even with an arrow in his heart, Jubal Little took three hours to die. Politician that he was, most of that time he couldn't stop talking. At first, he talked about the arrow. Not how it got there—he believed he knew the answer to that—but arguing with Cork over whether to try to pull it out or push it through. Corcoran O'Connor did neither. Then he talked about the past, a long and convoluted rambling punctuated by moments of astonishing self-awareness. He admitted he'd made mistakes. He told Cork things he swore he'd never told anyone else, told them in a way that made Cork feel uncomfortably like Jubal's confessor. Finally he talked about what lay ahead. He wasn't afraid to die, he said. And he said that he understood the situation, understood why Cork had put that arrow in his heart.

He died sitting up, his back against hard rock, his big body gray in the long shadow cast by the imposing monolith known as Trickster's Point. If the political polls were correct, in just a few days Jubal Little would have won a landslide victory as the new governor of Minnesota. Cork had known Jubal Little all his life and, for some of those years, had thought of him as a best friend. Even so, he'd planned to mark his ballot for another man on election day. Partly it was because Jubal wanted different things for Minnesota and the North Country and the Ojibwe than Cork wanted. But mostly it was because Jubal Little was absolutely capable of murder, and Cork O'Connor was the only one who knew it.

CHAPTER 1

The walls of the interrogation room of the Tamarack County Sheriff's Department were dull gray and completely bare. There were no windows. It was furnished with two chairs and a plain wooden table nudged into a corner. The subject of an interview sat in a straight-back chair with four legs that rested firmly on the floor. The interviewer's chair had rollers, which allowed movement toward or away from the subject. On the ceiling was what appeared to be a smoke detector but, in reality, concealed a video camera and microphone that fed to a monitor and recording system in the room next door. The interview room was lit from above by diffuse fluorescent lighting that illuminated without glare. Everything had been designed to be free from any distraction that might draw the subject's focus away from the interviewer and the questions. Cork knew this because he'd had the room constructed during his own tenure as sheriff of Tamarack County.

Although he wore no watch and there was nothing in the room that would have clued him about time, Cork knew it was late afternoon. Around five o'clock, more or less. Captain Ed Larson had removed his own watch, a standard procedure when questioning a suspect in the interview room. Timelessness was part of the protocol for keeping the subject focused only on what was happening inside the small box created by those four bare walls. This was Cork's third round of questioning about the death of Jubal Little that day and was the most formal so far.

The first interview had taken place at Trickster's Point while the techs were processing the crime scene. It had been Sheriff Marsha Dross herself who'd asked the questions. Cork was pretty sure nobody really thought then that he'd killed Jubal Little. Marsha was just trying to get a good sense of what had gone down. It wasn't until he told her that he'd sat for three hours while Jubal died that she gave him a look of incomprehension, then of suspicion.

The second interview had been conducted an hour and a half later in her office back at the department. Ed Larson had been present for that one. He was in charge of major crimes investigation for Tamarack County. He'd let Marsha ask the questions—more of them this time and more probing—and had mostly observed. At the end of that round, he'd asked if Cork was hungry and would like something to eat or drink. Cork wanted nothing, but he said yes anyway.

While the food was coming, they moved to the interview room, just Larson and Cork this time, but Cork knew that Dross would be watching on the monitor next door.

Deputy Azevedo brought in the meal. He looked at Cork as if he didn't know him at all, though they'd been acquainted for years.

"On the table," Larson told him, and the deputy set the tray down and left. "Go ahead and eat, Cork," Larson said. "I just want to look over a few of my notes."

He pulled a small notepad from the inside pocket of his sport coat. Larson always looked and dressed more like a college professor than a cop. He had gold wire-rim glasses and wore honest to God tweed jackets with patches on the elbows. He was nearing sixty, more than a half dozen years older than Cork, and still had an enviable head of hair that was a distinguished silver-black. He was already on the force when Cork first joined as a deputy more than twenty years before. They'd become friends, and Cork had a great deal of respect for him and his abilities. As soon as Cork was elected sheriff, he'd put Larson in charge of investigating major crimes.

While Cork sat at the table and ate, Larson pretended to go over his notes. Cork knew that, in reality, Larson was more interested in his appetite, knew that people who'd committed a violent crime were often so troubled by what they'd done that they couldn't eat. So Cork made as if he hadn't had a bite of food in a month and rammed down every crumb of his cheeseburger and gulped every drop of coffee.

"Thanks," he said when he'd finished.

Larson looked up from his notepad and, with his index finger, eased his glasses a quarter of an inch higher on the bridge of his nose. It was a gesture he sometimes made unconsciously when he was about to do something that was uncomfortable for him. "Cork, I know you know the drill. I've got to make sure that you understand your rights."

"Miranda," Cork said.

"Miranda," Larson acknowledged and went through the litany.

"It's official then?" Cork said.

"What's official?"

"I'm officially a suspect."

Larson squinted, a look of pain. "In my shoes, how would you see it?"

"I've been in your shoes. And I know how I'd see it, Ed. If our situations were reversed, I wouldn't believe for a moment that you'd killed Jubal Little."

"Tell me why, if I were in your shoes, I would have waited three hours before trying to get him some help."

"I wasn't trying to get him help. He was already dead when I left him."

"Okay, so why didn't you go for help as soon as you understood the seriousness of the situation?"

"I've told you. Jubal asked me to stay."

"Because he was afraid?"

"Jubal?" Cork shook his head. "No, not Jubal. Never Jubal."

"You were his only hope of surviving, and yet he insisted that you stay. I don't understand."

"He knew he was going to die, and he didn't want to die alone."

"You couldn't have carried him out?"

"He hurt whenever I tried to move him, hurt a lot. It was that broadhead arrow tip tearing him up inside. I didn't want to give him any more pain. If I'd tried to carry him out, he would simply have died sooner."

"So you just sat there and watched him go?"

"No. I listened to him. I think that was the main reason he didn't want me to leave. He wouldn't have had anyone to talk to. You know how politicians are."

Larson gave a startled look that quickly turned critical. "There's nothing humorous in this situation, Cork."

"I'm not sure Jubal saw it that way. The last thing he did on this earth was smile, Ed."

He could see that Larson didn't believe him. Probably he didn't believe a lot of what Cork had said so far.

"Did you have your cell phone with you?"

Cork shook his head. "We were out there to get away from a world of phone calls. But even if I'd taken my cell phone, it wouldn't have mattered."

"Why?"

"Coverage is hit and miss up there. But around Trickster's Point, especially, nothing gets through."

"And why's that?"

Cork shrugged. "Ask the Ojibwe, and they'd tell you it's just Nanaboozhoo messing with you."

"Nanaboozhoo?"

"The Trickster. That's his territory."

Larson stared at him. His face reminded Cork of a ceramic doll with all the features painted on and none of them capable of moving. Larson looked down at his notes. "You had breakfast at Johnny's Pinewood Broiler before you headed out. You had a cheese omelet, and Jubal Little had cakes and eggs over easy. When you left, you both spent a few minutes standing out on the sidewalk, arguing."

Cork said, "Did you find Heidi or did she come looking for you?"

He was talking about Heidi Steger, their waitress at the Broiler that morning.

Larson didn't answer but said instead, "What did you argue about?"

"We didn't argue. It was more like a heated discussion."

"What did you discuss, then, so heatedly?"

"Politics, Ed. Just politics."

Larson maintained his ceramic doll face for a long moment, and Cork, in that same long moment, returned his steady gaze.

"Okay," Larson finally went on. "You said he talked a lot as he was dying. What did he talk about?"

"First he talked about that arrow, whether to try to remove it. Jubal wanted to, I didn't. Then I tried to leave to get help. Jubal wanted me to stay. After that, he talked about life. Or I should say his life. It was so Jubal of him, but understandable under the circumstances. He had a lot of regrets. Toward the end, he was in and out of consciousness. When he was awake, he mostly rambled. It was hard to make much sense of anything."

"Did he say who'd shot him?"

"He didn't have to. We both knew who he believed it was."

"Who was that?"

"He thought it was me."

"He thought you were trying to kill him?"

"He thought I'd shot him by accident." Which was the only lie Cork had told in any of the interviews that day.

"Did you?"

"No."

"You meant to shoot him with that arrow?"

Cork refrained from smiling at the obvious and shallow trap and told him once again, "It wasn't me who shot Jubal."

"Who then?"

"I don't know."

"Did you see anyone else?"

"No."

"Hear anyone else?"

"No."

"So, as far as you know, you were both alone out there?"

"Clearly not. Whoever shot that arrow was out there with us."

In the beginning, Larson had positioned his chair near to Cork, making the interrogation a more intimate affair, just between the two of them. Between friends, maybe. Now he backed off a couple of feet and asked, rather indifferently, "Do you consider yourself a good bow hunter, Cork?"

"Fair to middling."

"When you hunt, you're a purist, right? You do still-stalking. No deer blind. You actually track the animal on foot."

"That's right."

"I'm guessing you'd have to be tuned in to all the sounds around you, wouldn't you? Reading all the signs?"

Cork understood the thrust of Larson's questions. If there was someone else at Trickster's Point with them, why didn't Cork know it?

"Must take incredible stealth," Larson said.

"That all depends on what you're after," Cork replied.

"You were after white-tail deer, weren't you?"

Cork said, "Ed, what I was really after is something you can't understand, and if I say it, you'll misconstrue my meaning."

"I'll do my best to understand." He promised with such earnest appeal that Cork knew he was telling the truth.

So Cork offered his own truth in return. He said, "I was hunting Jubal Little."

CHAPTER 2

Violence took Jubal Little out of Cork's life, but violence was also the way he'd entered it.

Nearly forty years earlier, when Cork was twelve years old and in the sixth grade, the baby boom in Aurora, as it probably had everywhere, resulted in the overcrowding of the town's elementary school. To deal with the situation on a temporary basis, the school board arranged for a couple of annex trailers to be placed on the grounds of the junior high, which was the only school-owned property with space available. The annexes were used to house the two sixth-grade classes. As a result, those kids who normally would have been the cocks of the walk in that final elementary year became, instead, the focus of abuse by many of the older junior high students, with whom the sixth graders shared the cafeteria, gymnasium, restrooms, and playing field. Worst among the tormentors was Donner Bigby, whom everyone called Bigs because of his size. He was a strawberry blond and had a massive upper torso. His intimidating physique came from both genes and working summers with the logging crews his father sent into the Superior National Forest to cut timber on tracts leased from the federal government. Bigby chewed tobacco, drank beer, and swore like a lumberjack. When he strutted down the hallways or across the school grounds, most kids—Cork included—gave him a judiciously wide berth.

The children of the Iron Lake Ojibwe attended school in Aurora and were bused in from the reservation. Three of the reservation kids were in the sixth grade with Cork. Because his grandmother was true-blood Iron Lake Ojibwe and he spent a lot of time on the rez, Cork was acquainted with them: Peter LaPointe, Winona Crane, and her twin brother, Willie. He knew Winona especially well, because he'd had a crush on her forever. She was smart and pretty and a little wild. She played the guitar and made up her own songs and sang beautifully. She had long black hair and eyes like shiny chips of wet flint that, if she wanted, could cut you with a glance. She was fiercely protective of Willie, who'd been born with cerebral palsy and who walked with a slow, awkward gait and spoke with some difficulty.

It wasn't at all surprising that Willie turned out to be a perfect target for the abuse of Donner Bigby.

Most days after school, Winona and her brother hopped on the bus and rode the fifteen miles to the rez, where they lived with a variety of relatives. Their father was dead, killed in a car wreck caused by a drunken driver—him. Their mother was an unreliable caregiver at best, and very often gone. Just gone. For weeks or even months. Sometimes they stayed with their grandmother, sometimes with an aunt or uncle. Their uncle Leonard Killdeer worked at the BearPaw Brewery, which sat next to Sam's Place, the Quonset hut turned burger joint on Iron Lake. Whenever they stayed with Leonard, they would walk to the brewery after school to meet him when his shift ended. On those days, Cork often accompanied them on the pretext of visiting his family's good friend Sam Winter Moon, who owned Sam's Place. Though he liked Willie just fine—they both shared a passion for Marvel Comics—Winona was the real reason Cork went along.

A couple of weeks after the start of school that fall, as the trio passed through Grant Park on their way to the brewery, Willie haltingly detailing the exploits of the Hulk in a recent issue and Winona quiet and distant and beautiful at his side, three figures materialized from the picnic pavilion and blocked their way.

"Well if it isn't the spaz and his keepers," Donner Bigby said. A cigarette dangled from the corner of his mouth in a kind of perverted homage, perhaps, to James Dean. The two kids with him Cork knew, but distantly. Vinnie Mariucci was tall and as thin as jerky, and everyone called him Specs because he wore glasses. Ray Novak was almost as huge as Bigby. They were high school guys, and they hung with Bigby because he was, in fact, their age. He was in the seventh grade because he'd been held back twice over the years. Academically and socially, he was a mess. In a later, more enlightened day, he might have been diagnosed as dyslexic and having ADD, but at that time he was just seen as unteachable, both disinterested in education and defiant of authority.

Cork smelled beer, though he saw no evidence of their drinking. He felt his stomach tighten, and he tried to speak in a calm voice. "Come on, we're not bothering you."

"Look, O'Connor, just being on the same planet with Spaz here bugs me. I don't like watching him walk."

"Fine," Cork said. "We're leaving and you won't have to watch."

"Don't call him Spaz," Winona said, low and threatening.

"Winona," Cork cautioned.

"How about Retard then?" Bigby offered and laughed. His cohorts laughed, too.

"I'm . . . not . . . retarded," Willie managed to get out. His speech, normally a little difficult, was further strained and was hard even for Cork to understand.

"*Inotarded,*" Bigby said, mimicking Willie.

As the son of the Tamarack County sheriff, Cork felt on his shoulders the onerous weight of doing the right thing. Which meant taking on Donner Bigby, who was a head taller and thirty or forty pounds heavier and who probably knew more about how to beat the living crap out of a kid than anyone Cork could think of. He considered simply trying to talk his way past Bigby, and hustling Willie and Winona along with him, but Winona killed any hope of an easy escape. She stepped up to Bigby and slugged him. She caught him in the ribs, and he made a little *ooph* sound, but he didn't budge an inch. Before she could withdraw her hand, he caught her arm by the wrist and twisted. Winona cried out and went down on her knees. Willie tried to go after Bigby, but Specs stepped in and shoved him, and Willie went sprawling.

Beyond thought now, Cork lowered his shoulder and barreled into Bigby. He knocked the kid off balance, and they both went down. He attempted to wrestle the bigger boy under him, but it was like trying to get the best of a rhino. Bigby was on top in the blink of an eye, sitting astraddle Cork and pinning him to the ground, helpless. Cork saw the big right fist, an agate-colored ball of bony knuckle, draw back, and then he saw stars.

As his perception cleared, he was aware that Bigby's weight no longer held him down. He opened his eyes and rolled his head to the side and saw Bigby trapped in a hammerlock, his thick upper arms useless and his chin forced down to his chest. The kid who'd put him in this precarious position was every bit as large and powerful as Bigby, and he was a stranger.

"Stay back or I'll break his neck," the kid ordered Specs and Novak, who stood looking ready to jump in.

"You goddamn son of a bitch!" Bigby cried and tried in vain to shake himself loose. The kid gave Bigby's head a further nudge, and Bigby grunted painfully and went slack.

"Are you through bothering people?" the kid asked.

When he got no reply, the kid bent Bigby's neck so sharply that even Cork was afraid he'd break Bigby's neck.

"Yes," Bigby shouted. "I'm through."

The kid released his grip and shoved Bigby away, all in one fluid motion. Bigby stumbled, and his pals caught him. He shook them off and straightened up, but it was clear to Cork that the move was painful to him.

"I'm not finished with you," Bigby said.

The stranger opened his arms as if in welcome. "Anytime," he said.

"Let's go." Bigby turned and walked away, trying to square his shoulders in a last-ditch effort at some dignity.

Cork finally noticed Winona, who stood with her arm around Willie, and who was not watching Bigby and his cohorts at all. Her eyes were on the stranger, and what was in them was something Cork would have sold his soul for.

"You okay?" the big kid said to Winona and Willie.

Willie nodded, and Winona said, "Yes, thanks."

The kid looked at Cork. "You're going to have yourself a shiner."

Cork felt his left eye and winced at the tenderness there. "What's your name?" he asked.

"Little," the huge kid said.

Cork laughed. "You're kidding me."

"Jubal Little."

"I'm Cork. This is Winona and Willie."

Jubal nodded at them but seemed to take no significant notice.

"You're new," Cork said.

"Just moved here," Jubal replied.

"What grade are you in?" Winona asked.

"Seventh."

Cork was astonished because the kid was like no other seventh grader he'd ever seen. "How old are you?"

"Thirteen."

"Is that like in elephant years or something?" Cork asked.

Jubal shrugged easily. "I've always been big for my age." He looked where Bigby and the others were exiting the park. "You have any more trouble with those guys, let me know."

"We're heading to Sam's Place for something to eat," Winona said. "You want to come?"

Jubal shook his head. "No, thanks. Got things to do." He turned to leave.

"See you," Cork said.

"Yeah," Jubal replied, without any particular enthusiasm. He didn't even look back, just lifted his hand in a brief farewell.

As Jubal Little walked away, Cork had a realization. This new kid had just stepped in to save his ass and Winona's and Willie's, and yet it wasn't especially significant to Jubal Little in any way. It was as if such an action was perfectly ordinary for him.

They didn't talk much after that. There was a darkness in Willie's face, and Cork figured he was fuming at the things Bigby had said. Winona stared into the distance, preoccupied, Cork was pretty sure, with thoughts of Jubal Little. In his own thinking, Cork was divided. On the one hand, because he'd been totally useless at handling Bigby, he was glad Jubal Little had intervened. On the other, his pride had taken a hard beating, and Jubal Little was a part of that.

After she saw his face, his mother gave him an ice pack but didn't press him for answers. When his father came home that night, he asked, "What's up with the eye?"

"Accident," Cork told him.

His father said, "The kind where your face falls into somebody else's fist?"

"I can take care of it."

His father considered, then nodded. "Something like this can get taken care of in a lot of ways. You won't let it get out of hand?"

"No, sir."

"All right." He'd removed his leather jacket with the Tamarack County Sheriff's emblem on the right shoulder and hung it in the closet. "I was thinking maybe we could toss the old pigskin before dinner. What do you say?"

Through his open window that night as he lay in bed, Cork heard his parents talking as they rocked in the porch swing. Although he couldn't hear most of the words, he could tell from the tone of her voice that his mother was concerned. His father said something about Cork's "raccoon eye" and sounded reassuring. Cork didn't want them worrying about him. And the truth was that he believed there was nothing for them to be concerned about. Jubal Little had made certain of that. The problem was Cork couldn't decide exactly how he felt about it, particularly when he recalled the look in Winona Crane's eyes as she stared at her rescuer. He went to sleep that night hurting in a lot of ways that had nothing to do with his shiner.

CHAPTER 3

Although science said otherwise, Cork knew absolutely that the human heart was enormous. Inside that organ, which was only the size of a man's fist, was enough room to fit everything a person could possibly love, and then some. Cork's own heart held more treasures than he could easily name. But one that always stood in the forefront was Sam's Place.

The old Quonset hut sat on the shore of Iron Lake, at the end of a road that ran from the edge of the small town of Aurora across an open meadow and over a long, straight hillock topped by the railway bed of the Burlington Northern tracks. To the north stood the abandoned BearPaw Brewery. A hundred yards south grew a copse of poplar trees that surrounded the ruins of a small foundry built more than a century before. The meadow stretched nearly a quarter mile, and terminated at Grant Park. Except for Sam's Place and the half acre around it, the land was held in trust by Tamarack County, given as a gift by a wealthy developer named Hugh Parmer, with the stipulation that all the undeveloped property be left in its natural state. Parmer had meant it as a memorial to Jo O'Connor, Cork's beloved wife, who'd been gone from their lives three years now.

When Cork pulled into the parking lot of Sam's Place, there was only one other vehicle: the Subaru that belonged to his daughter Jenny. It was evening, and the sky was charcoal with overcast. The weather forecast was for snow flurries, and Cork, when he got out of his Land Rover, felt the cold kiss of a flake against his cheek. The sheriff's department had kept and bagged as evidence his hunting jacket, which was stained with Jubal Little's blood. Even though he was chilled, he stood awhile before going inside, staring down the shoreline of the lake into the gloom of descending night. Well beyond the poplars stood the tall pine trees of Grant Park, black now in the dim light, brooding sentries looking down on the place where he'd first met Jubal Little.

In all that had occurred that day, Cork hadn't allowed himself to feel the loss of the man who'd been his friend since boyhood. He'd been intent at first on simply comforting Jubal as he died. Then he'd been involved in explanations. Now, alone, he tried to understand how he felt. Frankly, he was confused. Jubal Little was an easy man to like, but anyone who'd been close to him knew that he was a difficult man to love. The reason was simple. In the end, in Jubal's heart, there was room enough only for Jubal.

"Dad?"

Cork broke off his reverie and looked toward the Quonset hut, where his sixteen-year-old son, Stephen, stood in the open doorway, framed by the warm light from inside.

"You okay?" Stephen called.

"Yeah," Cork replied. "I'll be right in."

The Quonset hut had been erected during the Second World War, and when the war ended had sat idle for some time, until it was purchased by an Ojibwe named Sam Winter Moon. Sam had divided the structure into two parts. In the front, he'd cut serving windows and installed a propane grill, a deep-fry well, a walk-in freezer, an ice-milk machine, and a food prep area. In the back, which was separated by a wall that Sam had constructed himself, was a living area, complete with a small kitchen and a bathroom with a shower. In the summer, Sam lived in the hut and ran his burger operation. Over the years, he developed a following of both locals and returning tourists, for whom a visit to Tamarack County wouldn't be complete without a stop at Sam's Place. Summers in high school, Cork had worked for Sam, and much of what he knew about what it was to be a man he'd learned from this friend and mentor. On Sam's death, the property had passed to Cork, who'd done his best to honor Sam Winter Moon's legacy. Now Cork's children were involved in the enterprise as well.

He stepped into the Quonset hut and found Stephen entertaining Waaboo, Cork's grandson, who was nearly two.

"Where's Jenny?" Cork asked.

Stephen nodded toward the door in the room's back wall. "Closing up," he said. "I offered, but she told me she'd do it if I kept this little guy occupied."

Waaboo was not the child's legal name. Legally, he was Aaron Smalldog O'Connor, but his Ojibwe name was Waaboozoons, which meant "little rabbit," and he was called Waaboo, for short. He was a wonder of a child, whose Ojibwe blood was apparent in his black hair and dark eyes, in the shading of his skin and the bone structure of his face. He bore a clear scar on his upper lip where surgery had closed a terrible cleft, a genetic defect. He was not Jenny's by birth, but in her heart, in the hearts of all the O'Connors, he took up a great deal of real estate.

Waaboo smiled when he saw Cork, and he said, "Baa-baa," which was his word for "Grandpapa."

Cork lifted his grandson and swung him around, much to Waaboo's delight.

"You're home early," Stephen said.

"You haven't heard?" Cork put Waaboo down, and the child toddled toward a big stuffed toy bear that lay on the floor.

"Heard what?"

Cork was relieved that word of Jubal Little hadn't spread. Dross and her people had, for the moment, done a good job of containment. But it wouldn't last long. Something like this, it would go public quickly, and the jackals of the media would quickly gather to feed.

"Jubal Little's dead," Cork said.

"What? How?"

"Someone killed him."

"Who?"

"I don't know."

The door to Sam's Place opened, and Jenny came in, bringing with her the smell of deep-fry. She was twenty-five, a willowy young woman with white-blond hair, ice blue eyes, and a face in which the cares of motherhood were just beginning to etch a few faint lines. She'd become a parent through extraordinary circumstances that had involved the brutal death of the child's birth mother. Jenny's intervention had saved Waaboo's life, and little Waaboo had, in a way, saved hers. She'd been trained as a journalist but had chosen to put her career on hold while she adjusted to these new circumstances. At the moment, she helped manage Sam's Place, wrote short stories, and devoted the rest of her time to Waaboo.

"Thought we weren't going to see you tonight," she said, heading toward her son, who'd wrapped his arms around the big bear and had rolled the stuffed animal on top of him. "Thought you and our next governor were going to hang out and do manly things together."

"Jubal Little's dead," Stephen told her.

She stopped in bending to lift her son and shot her father a startled look. "How?"

Cork explained what had happened.

"You sat there for three hours while he died?" Jenny had the same look that Cork had seen on Dross's face and Larson's, a look void of comprehension. "Why didn't you go get help?"

He was tired of explaining, and he said, "At the time, staying with Jubal seemed best."

"Was it an accident?" Stephen asked.

Cork shook his head.

Jenny said, "Why so sure?"

"Because what the sheriff's people don't know but will figure out pretty soon is that the arrow that killed him may well have been one of mine."

"How do you know that?"

"I make my own arrows, Jenny. My fletching pattern is unique. When I saw the fletching on the arrow in Jubal's heart, I knew where it came from. Or where it was supposed to look like it came from."

"Somebody's what—trying to frame you?" Stephen asked.

"That's sure how it looks."

"Does the sheriff think you did it?"

"At the moment, I'm the only suspect on the horizon."

Jenny said, "Do you have a lawyer?"

"I called Leon Papakee. He got there in the middle of my interview with Ed Larson. I'm afraid he was a little late for damage control."

"You let them question you without a lawyer?" Jenny seemed astonished.

"I know," Cork said. "It's strange how, when you're on the other side of things, you're not as smart as you think you'll be." He shrugged. "Maybe I was still a little in shock, I don't know. I said more than I should have, and unless I can figure out who fired that arrow, I'll probably regret it."

Stephen had dark almond eyes, the eyes of his Ojibwe ancestors, and they were hard with concern. "What are you going to do, Dad?"

"I need some time to think, and I need a little advice. I'm heading out to talk to Henry Meloux. Look, I don't think things will blow up tonight, but if they do, we'll be getting calls at the house. Don't talk to anyone, okay?"

"Sure," Jenny said. "We'll see you later tonight?"

"Morning, more likely," Cork said.

To which Jenny smiled. "While you're out there, say hello to Rainy for us."

CHAPTER 4

Cork drove north out of Aurora, along the shoreline of Iron Lake. Dark had fallen completely. At the edges of the headlight glare, the trees—pine and spruce and birch and poplar—were like stark walls hemming him in. Although he'd tried his best to hide it from his children, he was worried. Not only had someone killed Jubal Little but they'd also done their best to make it look as if Cork was guilty of the crime. The evidence was slight at the moment, and nothing that would convict him, if it came to that, but he had no idea how carefully the murder had been planned and what other evidence might have been created or planted that would point his way.

After several miles, he turned off the main highway onto a gravel county road, which he followed until he came to a double-trunk birch tree off to the right. The tree marked the beginning of the long trail that led to Crow Point, where Meloux's cabin stood. Cork parked his Land Rover, pulled a flashlight from his glove box, got out, and locked the doors. If there'd been any kind of decent moon, he could have seen his way without the flashlight, but the overcast was solid and the night pitch black, and he flipped the switch and followed the bright, slender beam into the woods.

The hike was less than two miles, much of it through the Superior National Forest, on a footpath worn over the years by the feet of many who, like Cork, sought out the old man for advice and healing. Henry Meloux was a Mide, a member of the Grand Medicine Society. Although in his nineties, he was a tough old bird full of wisdom, compassion, humor, honesty, and, very often, gas. Cork had been in the old man's company when Meloux let loose farts that could have felled a moose.

Cork had been along the footpath hundreds of times in his life, and it was always a journey he made with a great deal of expectation. Meloux knew things. He understood the complexities and conundrums of the human heart. He had his finger on the pulse of all that occurred on the rez. He knew about the natural world, what healed and what harmed. And he was in touch with the realm that could not be seen with the eye, the realm of the *manidoog*, or spirits, who dwelled in the vast forests of the great Northwoods.

What exactly Cork hoped to receive from Meloux on this trip, he couldn't say. But in the past, whatever the old man offered had almost always turned out to be pretty much what Cork needed. And that was one of the reasons he was making his way through the woods on that dark night.

The other reason was Rainy Bisonette.

Rainy was Meloux's great-niece, a public health nurse who'd come to Crow Point more than a year earlier to care for the old man during a mysterious illness. She'd come hoping as well to learn the secrets of healing that had been revealed to Meloux across his lifetime. She was headstrong, and she and Cork had had a rough time of it at first. That had changed. These days, Rainy was usually the reason Cork made this journey.

The air smelled of late fall, the wet-earth odor of leaves decomposing. This time of year always reminded Cork of death, and not just because winter was hard on the horizon. Autumn was the season in which his father and, much later, his wife had been lost to him, both taken through violence. Now, in this same season, Jubal Little was gone and, like the others, gone violently.

Cork was deep in thought and thoughtlessly following the

beam of the flashlight when he became aware of a tingling at the nape of his neck and along his spine. He snapped back into the moment and had the overwhelming sense that he was being tracked. Someone was following him, or perhaps pacing him on one side of the trail or the other. He couldn't say why he felt this. Had he heard the tiny, bonelike crack of a foot snapping a twig on the ground, or the sound of a body sliding through brush? He stopped and swung the light into the woods all around, then shot it down the path behind him. Nothing. He listened intently, but that, too, proved useless.

He wondered if his imagination was running wild, if he was simply being paranoid. On the other hand, someone that day had tracked him and Jubal in the woods without either of them knowing. Someone had been able to commit murder and slip away without being seen or heard. Was this person right now watching Cork from some dark vantage? Was another arrow, soundless in its flight, about to hit its mark?

"Jesus, Cork," he said out loud. "Get hold of yourself."

In the wet, heavy air of the enormous dark, his voice sounded weak, offering him little comfort.

He was relieved when he finally broke from the trees and saw, across the open meadow on Crow Point, the welcoming lantern light that shone through the windows of Meloux's cabin. A cold wind had come up, and it ran through the pines at his back with a sound like the rush of floodwater. He was a dozen yards into the meadow when he heard the voice, and he spun, swinging the flashlight beam as if it were a saber hacking at the dark. As before, it illuminated nothing but forest.

Cork called out, "Who's there?" knowing, even as he spoke, that it was useless. If it was only his imagination, no one was there to reply. And if someone had actually tracked him this far, why would they reveal themselves now? Yet he was certain he'd heard someone speak.

He retreated from the wall of forest and turned his back to the trees only when he was fifty yards away, a distance that, especially in the dark, would challenge even the best of bow hunters. He jogged the rest of the way and didn't feel entirely safe until Meloux's door was opened to him.

Rainy Bisonette was a lovely woman, though not pretty in a fashionable way. She never wore makeup or tried to hide the gray streak in her long, black hair. Her hands were callused and her nails clipped short. Rather than lithe or willowy, she looked strong. Cork thought of her as substantial, although he would never have said so out loud because it didn't sound at all complimentary. In his own mind, what it meant was that Rainy, in her intelligence, her compassion, her humor, her enjoyment of life, was pretty much everything a man could ask for, and a great deal more. He thought himself lucky to have found her.

Rainy put together coffee in a blue enamel pot. She set it on the iron cookstove at the center of the cabin's single room. While it brewed, she gave Cork a big piece of corn bread left over from dinner, buttered and topped with blackberry jam that she'd made herself, and that he gratefully devoured.

The room was simply furnished, mostly with things Meloux had made over the years. A table and three chairs of birchwood. A bunk with a thin mattress whose ticking was straw mixed with dried herbs that the old Mide chose for their fragrance and their particular power. A sink with a hand pump, and above it a few cupboards. The walls were hung with items that harked back across all the years of Meloux's life—a toboggan, a deer-prong pipe, snowshoes whose frames were made of white ash and whose bindings were leather, a gun rack that held an old Remington. There was also, tacked to the wall, a page from an old Skelly gas calendar, July 1957, with a photo of a fine-figured woman in very tight shorts bending over the engine of a Packard to check the oil. It had been there as long as Cork had been coming to Meloux's cabin. What it meant to the old man, why he'd held on to it all these years, Cork had no idea. It was just another of the mysteries, large and small, that were Meloux.

Meloux sat at the old birchwood table. In his youth, he'd stood nearly six feet tall, but he was smaller now, or looked it. His hair hung long and white over his bony shoulders. His face was like a parched desert floor, sunbaked and fractured by countless lines. His eyes were enigmas. They were dark brown, and there was in them the look of ancient wisdom; yet at the same time they seemed to hold an impish glint, suggesting that the old man, at any moment now, was going to spring on you an unexpected and delightful surprise. He'd brought out one of his pipes, this one a simple thing decades old, carved from a small stone block that had been quarried at Pipestone in southwestern Minnesota. From a leather pouch he took a pinch of tobacco, sprinkled a bit on the tabletop as an offering to the spirits, filled the pipe bowl, and they smoked together in silence. Cork was eager to speak with his old friend, but he was also cognizant of tradition and waited patiently until, at last, Meloux said, "Wiisigamaiingan."

Which was the Ojibwe name Meloux had long ago given to Jubal Little. It meant "coyote."

"You've already heard?" Cork said. He looked to Rainy, who'd given no indication she knew about the trouble that day. Then he said with understanding, "The rez telegraph."

Rainy said, "Isaiah Broom came to tell us."

"News he didn't mind bringing, I'm sure," Cork said.

"A lot of Ojibwe were disappointed in Jubal Little, but that doesn't mean we're happy the man's dead."

"You were with him." Meloux set the pipe on the table. "Do you want to talk about it?"

He did, of course. Unburdening was part of what had brought him. He told them about the day, told them how he'd stayed those long hours in the shadow of Trickster's Point as, ragged breath by ragged breath, Jubal Little had lost his hold on life.

"Three hours?" Rainy said. "With an arrow in his heart? Oh, Cork, that had to be awful."

She put her hand over his on the tabletop, the calluses of her palms across his knuckles. He took comfort in that familiar roughness.

"Three hours." Meloux squinted so that he considered Cork through dark slits. "That is a long time to watch a man die."

"I didn't have a choice, Henry."

"There is always a choice."

"He asked me to stay."

"You could still have chosen to go."

"He would have been alone."

"But he might now be alive."

"You don't know that, Henry." He spoke harshly but understood it wasn't Meloux he was angry at. In all the questioning by Dross and Larson, Cork had firmly maintained that he'd stayed because it was what Jubal wanted and because the wound was so terrible he couldn't imagine the man would live long. In his own mind, however, he wasn't at all certain of the soundness of his thinking or the truth of his motive.

"And that is something you can never know either, Corcoran O'Connor." The old man's face relaxed, and in Meloux's warm almond eyes, Cork saw great compassion. "Your going or your staying is not what killed Wiisigamaiingan. That was the arrow. There is no way to know what the outcome might have been if you had made a different choice. Shake hands with your decision and move on."

"Was it an accident of some kind?" Rainy asked.

"No accident," Cork said. "Someone meant to kill him, I'm sure."

"How do you know that?"

"Because it was planned. They stole one of my arrows and used it to murder Jubal. Either that or they made an arrow in the same way I do so that it would look like I'd killed him."

"Who would do that?"

"I have no idea. They were pretty crafty with the arrow, so I'm thinking there may be other evidence they've arranged to point in my direction."

"You didn't see who shot the arrow?"

"No." Cork looked to Meloux. "Sam Winter Moon taught me to hunt in the old way, Henry. He taught a lot of men to hunt that way."

Meloux was clearly already ahead of Cork. "You are a good hunter. You read the ground, and you listen to the air. Yet you did not see the man who shot the arrow. So you want to know who else Sam Winter Moon taught to hunt in the old way. You want to know who could hide himself from you so good."

"If Sam were here, I'd ask him. But he's not, so I'm hoping you might know."

The room was lit with light from a kerosene lantern in the center of the table. The shadows of Cork and Rainy and Meloux fell against the walls, and when Meloux shook his head, his shadow self did the same.

"Sam Winter Moon taught many," he said.

"Some of them have already walked the Path of Souls, Henry. And some have grown too old to hunt that way. And some no longer live on the rez. I want to know who's still here. And of those, I want to know who's good enough to hide from me."

Meloux had made his chairs long ago. They were sturdy pieces, but so old that they creaked easily under the weight of those who sat in them. Meloux's chair complained as he leaned back and studied Cork's face and gave the issue long, patient thought.

"It would not necessarily take such an expert to hide from you," Meloux said at last. "A hunter is only as good as his mind will let him be. You were distracted today."

Cork realized that the old Mide, in his mysterious way, had divined an important concern. "Jubal and I had kind of a falling-out, and we were both pretty upset."

"Over what?" Rainy asked.

"It doesn't matter. But Henry's right. I was distracted."

"So maybe it was not such a good hunter you did not see," Meloux said.

Cork was disappointed. He'd believed he might have a way of narrowing the field of suspects, but Meloux's insight cast a deep shadow of doubt over the possibility.

Then Cork thought of something else.

"I believe somebody followed me here, Henry. They were pretty good because most of the way I only had the sense of their presence, nothing really solid to give them away."

"Most of the way?" Rainy said.

"At the end, when I came onto Crow Point, I'm almost certain I heard a voice say something to me from the woods."

"Did you see anyone?"

"No."

In the lantern light, Meloux's dark eyes burned with a little flame of intrigue. "And what did this voice without a body say, Corcoran O'Connor?"

"Just one word, Henry."

Meloux blinked and waited patiently.

"Traitor," Cork finally replied.

CHAPTER 5

After he first met Jubal Little that day in Grant Park with Winona and Willie Crane, Cork had almost nothing to do with the new kid in town. Jubal was a grade ahead, and their paths seldom crossed in a way that allowed the kind of interaction that might have led to friendship. Whenever the opportunity did arise, Jubal seemed completely uninterested in pursuing it. That was fine with Cork; he had plenty of friends. Still, Jubal Little, in his size and the assuredness of his bearing, stood out in a way that couldn't be ignored. And whenever Cork was with Winona and Willie Crane and they spotted Jubal, he couldn't miss how Winona's gaze fixed on the big, distant figure.

In a small town, people talked, and he knew a few things about Jubal. He knew that the older boy had come with his mother from the West, though from where exactly seemed a bit of a mystery. Although there was clearly Indian in Jubal's blood, his mother didn't look Indian at all. And while Cork knew that looks alone didn't tell the whole genetic story, he figured that it was probably Jubal's father from whom the son had inherited his appearance. But Jubal had arrived in Aurora without a father, and no one, as far as Cork knew, understood the why of that situation.

Jubal's mother worked as a waitress at Johnny's Pinewood Broiler. She was pleasant and pretty, a slender blonde with a ready smile but with eyes that always seemed a little sad. On Friday nights, Cork's family often ate at the Broiler, taking advantage of the best all-you-can-eat fish fry in the whole North Country. Whenever Jubal's mother waited on them, Cork found her immensely likable. His father said she lived with her widowed sister on the west side of town, and his mother said that she often ran into her in the library. Jubal's mom was, apparently, a voracious reader. One evening at the Broiler, Cork told her that he knew Jubal, and she seemed oddly pleased, as if happy to hear that Jubal might have a friend. Cork didn't tell her that they weren't close.

But for tragedy, he and Jubal might have gone their whole lives living in the same town with no real relationship. In the fall of Cork's seventh-grade year, however, his father was killed, shot down in the line of duty. And that changed everything.

Liam O'Connor died in October, and for a very long time afterward, Cork's world lay under a constant gray overcast. He held his grief inside, however, and outwardly went about his days as if losing a father was something he knew how to handle. Partly it was because people were awkward around him, especially his friends, who behaved toward him in a way that made him feel as if he had a terrible illness of some kind. And partly it was because he had no idea at all how to wrap his understanding around so stunning a loss. His mother tried to help, but because she had her own grief to deal with, he didn't want to burden her any further. In his own mind, he was the man of the house now, and he had to step up to his responsibilities. Almost every night, he stuffed his face into his pillow and wept, smothering the sound so that no one would hear.

The truth, which he didn't understand until much later, was that he kept his grief deep inside because he didn't want to give it up. He was afraid that to let go of his grief would be to let go of his father forever.

Aurora Junior High School had a flag football team, and Cork was on it. After his father died, Cork continued to play. He was tall for his age and lean. He was also fast and elusive and was tapped to play end. The team's quarterback was Jubal Little, who had a powerful arm and a natural feel for strategy. Games were played on Friday afternoons, usually immediately after school. Two weeks after Cork watched his father's coffin lowered into the earth, the team played its final game of that season in the town of Virginia, an hour bus ride from Aurora.

Cork always remembered that afternoon as overcast, which may or may not have been true. The teams were pretty evenly matched, but with less than a minute left to go, Aurora was behind by a touchdown. Jubal had moved the ball within scoring distance. In the huddle, he looked to Cork and said, "Can you get free?"

Cork said he could.

At the snap, Cork gave an inside fake to the kid who defended him, then cut for the corner of the end zone. A safety moved to cover, closing quickly. When Cork looked back, Jubal had already lofted the ball in his direction. Crossing the line of the end zone, he had two steps on his opponent. His hands were up and the ball sailed into them. Then it slipped free. Cork tried to readjust, turning in midstride, bobbling the ball. In the next instant, it was in the hands of the Virginia safety, and the game was over.

No one blamed him openly, and the coach, a decent man named Porter, told them they'd played a hell of a game and had nothing to be ashamed of. The bus ride home was quiet, and when they arrived at the junior high and disembarked, Cork walked away alone.

He didn't hear Jubal Little coming up behind him, but the big kid was suddenly at his side.

"Mind if I walk with you?" Jubal asked.

Cork shrugged. "I was thinking of going to Sam's Place to get a burger."

"I could use a bite," Jubal said.

They walked a bit without talking. It was evening by then, the sky a gloomy gray-blue. The town was quiet, and their sneakers slapped softly on the pavement.

"It was a good season," Jubal finally said.

"I wish it had ended better."

Jubal laughed. "It was just a game, and a pretty good one."

"I lost it for us."

"Bullshit. We had plenty of chances to win it. They just played a little better today. Next time it'll be different."

"I hope so."

"You're good," Jubal said. "Don't sell yourself short."

When they got to Sam's Place, Sam Winter Moon greeted Cork through the serving window with "*Boozhoo,*" a common Ojibwe greeting. "So how'd it go?"

"We lost," Cork said.

"But we played a good game," Jubal tossed in.

"Well there you go." Sam smiled at Jubal. "*Boozhoo.* I've seen you around, but I haven't caught your name."

"Jubal Little."

"Sam Winter Moon." He stuck his hand through the open serving window, and Jubal took it. "Tell you what. Dinner's on me today. What'll you guys have?"

They sat at the picnic table under a big red pine near the shoreline, and each of them ate a Sam's Super and a chocolate shake.

"What does *boozhoo* mean?" Jubal asked.

"It's kind of like saying 'howdy.' Sam thinks you're Ojibwe. You look Indian."

In a way, Cork meant it as an opening, hoping Jubal might say something about his past.

"You seem to know him pretty well," Jubal said.

"My father and him were good friends."

"I'm sorry about your father."

"Yeah, thanks." Cork bit into his burger and swung his eyes out across the lake. The evening was windless, the water flat and empty.

"I lost my father, too," Jubal said.

"When?"

"Couple of years ago."

"I'm sorry."

"You get over it," Jubal said with an unconvincing shrug.

Cork wanted to ask how it had happened but thought maybe that was stepping across a line.

A car drove up to Sam's Place, and a bunch of high school kids piled out. Donner Bigby was among them. Jubal stopped eating and watched the small crowd gather at the serving window and order. Bigby noticed them and said something to the others. A lot of eyes swung their way.

Jubal said quietly, "Bigs ever bother Winona Crane and her brother?"

"Not that I know of," Cork said. "You fixed him pretty good that day in Grant Park."

Jubal eyed Bigby. "Guy like that, it's just a matter of time before you have to fix him again."

Bigby and the others took their food and drove away. Cork and Jubal stood up from the picnic table and got ready to leave. The light was almost gone from the sky. A flight of Canada geese coming from the north swung in a loose V over Iron Lake and came to rest on the water, which was gunmetal gray and looked cold. It was nearing the end of October, and already Cork could sense winter in the air. But he felt a little better at that moment, a little more connected, and he knew it was because of Jubal.

"I gotta get home," Jubal said.

"Me, too."

"I'm thinking of putting together a touch football game tomorrow. You interested? You could use the practice." Jubal gave him an easy grin.

"Sure," Cork said. "Thanks."

In the dusk, they went their separate ways, Jubal to his fatherless home and Cork to his.

CHAPTER 6

The summer before Jubal Little died, Cork and several members of the Iron Lake Ojibwe had helped Rainy Bisonette build a tiny cabin of her own on Crow Point, thirty yards east of Meloux's, set against a line of aspen that ran along the shore of Iron Lake. Before that, she'd slept on a cot in her great-uncle's cabin. When she decided that she would stay with the old Mide indefinitely in order to learn all she could from him about healing, word had spread across the rez, and folks had gathered in the meadow to give her a little place of her own for privacy.

By the time Jubal Little was dead, Cork knew the inside of Rainy's cabin well. She'd furnished it simply: a bed with a small stand next to it where a kerosene lantern sat so that she could read at night before sleeping; a table and two chairs; an open shelving unit of honey-colored maple that Cork had built for her himself and that held her folded clothing; and a small, cast-iron boxwood stove that provided heat. A wealth of books stood stacked knee-high against one wall. (Cork had promised that he would spend some time during the coming winter building her a substantial bookcase.) Above the bed, she'd hung three photographs of herself with her children, who were now grown. The room still smelled as if the pine walls were newly cut and planed, and whenever Cork spent the night with Rainy he went to sleep and woke with a fragrance that was, to him, the breath of heaven.

They didn't make love that night but lay together under the soft, heavy quilt and talked.

"Why would someone kill him?" Rainy asked. Her cheek was against his shoulder, and her warm breath ghosted over his bare skin.

"You didn't know him," Cork said.

"And if I did, I wouldn't have to ask?"

"He was a complicated guy. A lot of good in him, and that's what he showed most people. But there was a dark side to Jubal he didn't like people to see."

"But you saw it?"

"Oh yeah."

"And yet you were still friends."

Cork said, "I don't know."

"You weren't?"

"We were best friends when we were kids, but people change. We changed."

"I don't think the essence of who we are changes much, Cork."

She was right. Who Jubal was at heart, Jubal had always been. "When we were kids," Cork said, "it was easy to overlook."

"What was he like as a kid?"

"Like I said, complicated. He had a reputation for not tolerating bullies. He went to the mat for a lot of kids who couldn't defend themselves."

"I heard you were that way, too." She kissed his shoulder.

"Yeah, but when Jubal stepped into a situation, he could back it up. Me, as often as not, I got my face pushed in."

"It didn't stop you from trying."

"I did it because I thought I had an obligation. It was what I thought my father would have done, or would have wanted me to do. Jubal did it because he could. In a way, it was his form of bullying. He just bullied the bullies."

"You're right," she said. "Complicated." A wind had come up, and the cabin creaked, and Rainy listened for a moment. "What else?"

"You couldn't always believe what he told you."

"He lied?"

"Not exactly. He was kind of a politician even back then. He said things in a way that led you down one track while the absolute truth lay in the track next to it. You were always going in the right direction, just not necessarily on the right path. Do you see?"

"Not really."

"His father, for example. He told me he'd lost his father, and the way he said it made me believe his father was dead, but that wasn't true."

"We all know about his father."

"Sure, now. Jubal's been trading on what happened for years. But it was a big secret for him then, and you can understand why."

Something tapped the window, and they both fell silent.

"An aspen branch," Rainy said. "The wind." Then she said, "Tell me more."

When Cork was fourteen, the summer before he entered high school, he began working for Sam Winter Moon. Sam usually hired high school kids to give him a hand during the season, and Cork became one of them. Because the business Sam ran in the old Quonset hut was not about making a lot of money—he was very Ojibwe in his approach to wealth; what you made you shared—Sam Winter Moon was a peach of a boss, and a lot of kids in Aurora, white and Ojibwe, got their introduction to the working world at Sam's Place.

Cork had been on the roster at Sam's for a month when Jubal Little asked if there might be a chance he could work there, too.

"My mom needs some money," Jubal explained. "I thought maybe I could help."

Cork understood. His own mother had begun to let out one

of the upstairs bedrooms, and there'd been strangers in the house, summer people up to enjoy the season. It was uncomfortable, but a financial necessity. He talked to Sam, explained to him about Jubal's father being dead and his mother needing extra money, and Sam was congenially accommodating.

Jubal wasn't only a quick study; he also very soon became the favorite of customers. He had an easy, assured manner and assumed a brash familiarity with everyone that still somehow never quite crossed the line beyond politeness. Folks responded to him in the way they might have a cheeky but beloved cousin.

On Jubal's first day of work, Sam spoke to him in Ojibwe.

Jubal gave him a blank stare in response.

"*Anishinaabe indaaw?*" Sam said again, which, Cork knew, meant "Are you one of The People?"

Cork said, "He's not Indian, Sam."

"No?"

Sam laid his dark eyes on Jubal, who held steady under their gaze, smiled amiably, and said, "Nope. I'm all American."

Sam nodded and replied gently, "So am I, son."

It was a good summer, working with Jubal. Cork had many friends, but he began to think of Jubal as the best of them. They fished together on Iron Lake, and floated down Mercy Creek in inner tubes, played baseball, and went to the Rialto Theater on Saturday nights when they weren't working at Sam's Place. They biked the ten miles to the Ojibwe reservation on the far side of Iron Lake to visit Cork's grandmother Dilsey, who lived at the edge of Allouette, the larger of the two rez communities, and who took an immediate liking to Jubal. Whenever they were in Allouette, Cork kept an eye out for Winona Crane, who'd begun to dominate his thinking in a way that made him intense and nervous. Occasionally he'd run into her in town with Willie, and whenever he first caught sight of her, dark-eyed and willowy, his heart always did a little ballet leap.

One day in late August, Cork invited Jubal to go ricing. This was an annual, seasonal tradition for the Anishinaabeg,

one Cork loved being a part of. His mother took them to Allouette in her station wagon and dropped them in front of George
LeDuc's general store, which also functioned as the town's post
office. That day, LeDuc had turned operation of the store over to
his wife. He greeted them both with a hearty *"Anish na?"* which
meant "How are you?" He didn't wait for an answer but said to
Jubal, "I'm betting I can get a good day's work from you."

"Yes, sir," Jubal said.

LeDuc was black-bear big. He had a long ponytail, a broad,
honest face, and dark eyes that danced nimbly over the boys and
were full of good humor. "Sir?" He laughed. " 'Preciate your
manners, but you can call me George. Let's go, boys."

They piled into LeDuc's dusty, black Chevy pickup and
headed east on an old logging road, which nature had almost entirely reclaimed. While they bounced along through high weeds
and timothy grass that nearly hid the track, LeDuc explained to
Jubal the importance of wild rice to The People. In the old times,
he said, it was their primary source of food, and the gathering of
rice, which he called *manomin,* was vital to their survival.

"We begin in August, *manominigizis,* the month of rice,"
he told Jubal. "We'll keep at it until probably November. Right
now, the best place for ricing is going to be in shallow lakes with
muddy bottoms. Later, we'll harvest the big lakes. Today, we're
headed to Nagamowin. That's what we call it on the rez anyway.
It means 'singing.' On a map, you'll find it called Mud Lake. We
named it first, but white people make all the maps."

They parked among tamaracks on the shore of the lake,
which was a little over half a mile long and a quarter of a mile
wide, full of tall green stalks. LeDuc had Cork and Jubal help
him pull the canoe from the back of the pickup. The frame—
ribs and planking, rails and deck, thwarts and seats—was constructed of wood: white cedar, white spruce, and ash. The hull
was khaki-colored marine canvas. They cradled it on their shoulders, carried it to the water, and waded in. Cork understood immediately why, on maps, the lake was called Mud. He sank to

his calves in goo that sucked hard at his sneakers. LeDuc gave the signal, and they flipped the canoe onto the lake. He returned to the truck and came back with a long pole, forked at one end, and with four smoothed sticks, each about three feet in length. Cork knew that the pole was made from tamarack wood so that it would be strong and light. The sticks were made of cedar, for the same reason.

"Here," LeDuc said and handed each boy a pair of the sticks. "Those are knockers, Jubal, for harvesting the rice. Cork'll show you how. Let's get started."

LeDuc took the long pole and a place in the stern. Cork and Jubal spaced themselves out ahead of him. LeDuc began to pole them across the water and slid into the nearest patch of rice stalks, whose tops stood a couple of feet above the gunwales of the canoe.

"I use a forked push pole so I won't hurt the roots of the plants," LeDuc explained to Jubal. "Show him how to harvest, Cork."

Jubal watched as Cork reached out to the right with one of the sticks and bent the stalks there quickly over the gunwale. With the other stick, he knocked the ripe grains free, and they scattered across the bottom of the canoe. He released the stalks, which sprang upright again, and he immediately turned to the left to repeat the process. LeDuc poled smoothly through the rice bed, while Cork swung his arms left and right, harvesting.

"It's important not to harm the stalks," Cork said. "And you've got to let some of the grains drop into the water to keep the beds growing. Now you try."

As with everything Cork would ever see him attempt, Jubal was a natural.

They spent the day on Nagamowin, and it was clear to Cork why the Anishinaabeg of the Iron Lake Reservation had given the lake that name. The air was full of song. The calls of red-winged blackbirds, warblers, dark-eyed juncos, sparrows, and meadowlarks mixed with the music of the wind across the wild rice reeds and the drumbeat of the knock sticks. Cork loved harvesting because, under a blazing sun, atop the cool indigo water, within the pale jade walls of the rice beds, he forgot, for a while, all the cares of the world he'd left behind.

They weren't the only ones ricing that day. In a small, wooden rowboat, three other Ojibwe worked the beds at the south end of the lake. A few times they came within hailing distance, but not a word passed between them. Cork could see who was in the boat: Winona Crane; her brother, Willie; and Willie's best friend, Isaiah Broom. LeDuc had brought along a cooler full of sandwiches made of bologna—what folks on the rez called "Indian steak"—and lemonade in a big glass jar. At lunchtime, he signaled the three kids, who came and joined them on the shoreline. They'd brought their own meal, which was canned tuna, cheese, and crackers. And they'd brought something else. Beer. They didn't pull out any cans or bottles, but Cork could smell the yeasty scent on Winona's breath. If LeDuc noticed, he didn't say anything.

Willie had grown taller but was thin as a sapling. His muscles still seemed at odds with his brain's attempt to control them, and his speech was still difficult to catch. Isaiah Broom was a kid every bit as huge as Jubal Little, but clumsy as a big-shoed circus clown, something he would never outgrow. He was clearly love-addled. Every time he looked at Winona, his brown eyes went dopey and hopeless. Cork understood. He was still hopelessly in love with Winona, too. She didn't pay any particular attention to either of them. At this point in her life, she was working on acquiring the wrong kind of reputation. She and Willie had continued to be passed from one relative to another, and she was growing into a beautiful young woman with a wild streak that stood out in neon. "Just like her mother" was what a lot of people on the rez said. She was in and out of trouble, nothing serious yet, but Cork feared that bad things might be on the horizon for her.

There was a powerful energy at work during the shoreline

lunch that day, something unspoken but palpable, and it flowed between Winona Crane and Jubal Little. They barely looked at each other, and that, in itself, was a dead giveaway to Cork. They were two of the most striking people he knew—Winona with her flowing black hair and soft, tawny skin and fawn eyes; and Jubal with his big, chiseled body and good looks and easy grace—yet it was as if, over that long hour of lunch, they didn't exist for each other.

When they separated to return to their work, Cork watched closely. Jubal, though he did his best to fight it, couldn't help looking over his shoulder at Winona Crane, who was eyeing him from a safer distance.

That Winona preferred Jubal—hell, what girl wouldn't?—stung Cork, and he found himself envying his friend. It was something that he often felt and that he fought against, but there it was. Jubal had been blessed in so many ways, with good looks and an incredible build and an easy way with people that won them over instantly. Compared to him, Cork felt small and unimportant. But where Winona was concerned, Cork thought maybe there was hope. He could see clearly that neither Jubal nor Winona was prepared to acknowledge how they felt, so he held to the naïve belief that as long as it went unspoken, the attraction might pass, and Winona's eyes would someday open to what Cork had to offer, smaller offerings maybe, but given with a full heart.

Late that afternoon, they returned to LeDuc's store. From the bed of the pickup, Cork, Jubal, and George unloaded burlap sacks filled with the wild rice that would eventually be dried, parched, hulled, winnowed, and shared. George gave them Big Chief grape sodas, and Cork called his mother to come and get them. While they waited, Cork and Jubal strolled through Allouette toward the shoreline, where the broad, sparkling blue of Iron Lake stretched away to the west.

"Winona's something," Cork said. "But if she doesn't watch herself, she's headed for trouble." It was a warning to Jubal,

whose own reputation in Aurora was sterling. But Cork didn't
fool himself. A good part of his motivation was to plant a kernel
of doubt in Jubal's mind that might keep him from turning his
attention to Winona.

Jubal stared absently at the sky. "I guess."

"We worry about her."

"We?" Jubal said.

"Those of us who are Shinnobs."

"Shinnobs?"

"It's short for Anishinaabeg." Cork said it as if being Ojibwe
set him and Winona apart from Jubal, put Jubal on the outside
of an intimate connection that he and Winona shared but Jubal
never could.

Jubal suddenly broke away and stomped angrily to the edge
of the water.

Cork caught up quickly and said to his friend's back, "You
okay?"

"What is it with you and being Indian?"

"What do you mean?"

"Jesus, just look at this place." Jubal pointed toward the gathering of mostly BIA-built homes and trailers that was Allouette,
where many of the streets were still unpaved and a lot of the
yards were covered with skeletal dandelion stalks that stood in
grass long unmowed, and where rusting cars, tireless, sat up on
cinder blocks. "Who'd want to live in a place like this? And look
at you. You don't even look Indian." Jubal picked up a rock and
flung it at the water as if the lake had insulted him.

"I'm only a quarter Ojibwe," Cork said. "But look at you.
You could pass for Indian in a heartbeat."

"That's because I am, stupid."

The admission hit Cork like the rock Jubal had thrown at the
lake. "What?"

"My name's not Little. It's Littlewolf. Jubal Littlewolf. My
mother changed it after we left Montana. She didn't want anyone to know."

"I don't get it."

Jubal picked up another rock and another, taking out his anger on the lake.

"You tell anyone what I'm about to tell you," he said, facing Cork with a fistful of stones, "and I'll break you into pieces."

"I won't say a word, I swear."

Jubal turned away and stared where the sunlight danced on blue water with a lightness that seemed to mock his dark mood. "My old man's not dead."

"Where is he?"

"In prison. Deer Lodge. That's in Montana."

"What for?"

"Manslaughter." With a grunt as if it pained him, Jubal wildly cast stone after stone, which the lake swallowed with barely a ripple.

"He killed someone?"

"That's what *manslaughter* means, stupid."

"I'm not stupid." Cork waited a minute for Jubal to empty his hands, then asked cautiously, "Why?"

Jubal finally sat down on the shoreline, and Cork sat down beside him. The day was hot, but an easy wind blew out of the west and skated across the lake and cooled them. Jubal pulled a long blade of wild grass from the ground and viciously tore it apart, bit by bit, as he spoke.

"My dad's Blackfeet, full blood. He's a carpenter. Builds houses and stuff. Built houses," Jubal corrected himself. "Four years ago my aunt Chrissy, that's his sister, she was . . . well, she was raped . . . by three white cowboys. It was in a town called Mosby way the hell out in the eastern part of the state. She was working in a bar there. The Mosby cops, they wouldn't do anything about it. I guess the cowboys talked like it was some kind of joke. My dad went out there, and when he came back one of the cowboys was dead and the other two were in the hospital, beat up real bad. They arrested him, and at his trial, he said he was just doing what the law wouldn't. What the white man's law wouldn't. There were lots of people in Mosby who swore Aunt Chrissy was drunk and acting slutty and asking for it. Me, I didn't believe it for a minute. I never saw her like that. They were lying through their teeth. But that frigging jury, they convicted my father, and he'll be in Deer Lodge until he's an old man."

Jubal finished torturing the blade of grass and pulled another.

"It was a big deal in Montana. Reporters crawling all over us all the time, even after the trial was done. We got letters and calls. Some of them were from people who thought my dad got a raw deal, but a lot of them were just stupid assholes saying dirty, hurtful things to my mom. We were living in Bozeman. Got to where we couldn't walk down the street without being stared at, so Mom decided she had to do something. We moved to Denver for a while, and she changed her name. And mine. It was pretty hard for her, I guess, all alone, so we moved up here because we could live with my aunt. She made me promise never to talk about what happened in Montana."

They were both quiet a long time. Jubal tore at the blade of wild grass until there was nothing left.

"I guess I understand why you told me he was dead."

"I never actually said he was dead," Jubal shot back defensively. "Whenever anybody asks, I just say I lost him and let them think what they want. But he's as good as dead."

"You don't ever talk to him?"

"Why would I?"

"He's your dad."

"He should've thought about that before he went off and killed a man."

"He probably didn't plan on killing anybody."

"What difference does that make? He should've stayed home where he belonged, and then he'd still be with us." Jubal yanked a handful of wild grass and heaved it as if throwing another stone at the lake, but the blades went nowhere, just fluttered to the ground at his feet.

"So," Cork said, trying to find slightly different ground to cover, to give Jubal room to move away from his anger. "Why Little? Why not your mom's maiden name or something?"

Jubal finally cracked a smile. "Her maiden name's Krupfelter. I told her I'd never be a Krupfelter. We compromised with Little."

"Why not Wolf? That's kind of cool."

Jubal stood up, rose to his full height, and grinned down at Cork. "I like the look on people's faces when I tell them my name is Little."

Cork's mother came to get them, and they rode back to Aurora. Although the sky stayed blue and Jubal had brightened, it still felt to Cork as if they were under a cloud the whole way. Jubal asked to be dropped off on Center Street, and there they separated, each kid heading toward a home where the sound of a man's voice was a rare thing now.

That night, as he lay in bed, Cork thought about Jubal's father and Jubal's anger. The truth was that, after his own dad died, Cork was sometimes angry with him, too. There were still moments when, in his thinking, he held onto a little stone of bitterness, wondering uselessly why his father chose to have a job in which he wore a gun on his belt every day. But Jubal's dad had worn a carpenter's belt, and what had hung from it had been a hammer, and, in the end, this hadn't made any difference. Jubal's father had been lost, too.

CHAPTER 7

Rainy held him. The wind had grown stronger, and the little cabin creaked around them as they huddled together under her quilt. They both smelled of sage and cedar, which Rainy had burned and blown over Cork to cleanse his spirit. Strands of her long hair lay fallen across his chest. Whenever she moved her head, Cork felt as if the lightest of fingers were trailing over his heart.

"Jubal was ashamed of being Blackfeet," she said. "I understand. When we were growing up—you, me, him—if you were Indian, more often than not you were looked on as ignorant and savage. Or worse, someone to be pitied and condescended to."

"He got over it," Cork said.

He felt her sigh. "In a big way, I'd say."

A gust of wind threw what sounded like a handful of sand against the window in the cabin's western wall.

"Must be sleeting," Cork said.

"I'm glad you didn't try to drive home tonight." She kissed his shoulder, then was quiet, listening. "Do you really think someone followed you here?"

"I could have sworn I heard a voice out there in the woods."

"Traitor," Rainy said. "What does it mean?"

"If it was real, I don't know. If I only imagined it, then I'm probably crazy. Crazy with guilt, maybe."

"Why? You didn't kill him," she said.

"Before he died, he told me things, things he swore he'd never told anyone. Secrets, Rainy. Some of them were about me and him. Some were about him and Winona. Some about Camilla. Jubal's whole life seemed to be about secrets, things he knew but couldn't share. Or was afraid to."

"Why afraid?"

"Just too revealing for a man as powerful as Jubal, I guess."

"Even the secrets about you and him?"

"That was maybe the weirdest thing of all. He said all his life he'd envied me. All his life, he'd tried to best me. And in the end, it was me who'd bested him."

"He envied you?"

"I know. I don't get it either."

"What did he mean, that in the end you'd bested him?"

"Again, I don't know, Rainy. Those three hours with Jubal were confusing. He rambled. He did a lot of reminiscing about when we were kids. He spilled his guts, all those transgressions and regrets. And then, at the last, he died with a smile on his lips."

"Maybe you were his confessor."

"Maybe. The oddest thing of all, though, came near the very end. He said a name he'd never mentioned to me before. Rhiannon."

"Who's Rhiannon?"

"Beats me, but she was clearly important to Jubal. By then, he was out of his head most of the time. These were his words as I heard them, which wasn't very clear, because he was speaking barely above a whisper by then: 'Rhiannon. The worst sin of all. God will send me to hell because of her. Pray for me. Oh, Jesus, pray for me.'"

"What did you say?"

"I told him I'd pray for him, but that I didn't believe in hell. He went quiet again and his eyes went unfocused. A few minutes later he said, clear as a bell, 'I can see it. My God, it's beautiful.' He looked me in the eye, Rainy, and for that moment, he was there with me, I mean really there. He said, 'This pain, all this pain. It's nothing, Cork.' Then he smiled. And then he died."

The wind ran around the cabin and threw sleet as it passed. Rainy propped herself up on her arm and stared at him in the dark.

"Rosebud," she said.

"Rosebud?"

"The sled in *Citizen Kane.*"

"That movie always put me to sleep."

"You've got a Rosebud here. It's the last name he said, so it must be very important to him, don't you think?"

"Honest to God, Rainy, I don't know what to think."

A knock came at the cabin door, unexpected and surprising, and it startled them.

Rainy called out, "Who is it?" but received no response.

Cork said to her quietly, "Meloux?"

"He's not deaf. He'd answer me."

Cork threw back the quilt and swung his legs off Rainy's bed. He was dressed only in boxer shorts. The cabin floor was ice against his bare soles. He crept to the door, stood a moment listening, then swung the door wide. The wind rushed in, a bitter shove against his body, full of sleet pellets that peppered his face and chest. He squinted at the night, but without a moon or any stars to shed light, the dark was impenetrable.

"Anybody?" Rainy called to him.

"No one," Cork said.

"Come to bed then."

He stepped back to close the door. That's when he noticed the arrow. It was lodged approximately in the place where, if the pine door had been an upright man, the razor-sharp broadhead tip would have pierced his heart. Cork pulled it free from the wood, took one last look into the night, then shut out the wind and the cold.

"Would you mind lighting your lantern?" he asked as he came toward the bed.

"What is it?" She sat up and turned to the nightstand.

Cork heard the scratch of a match head over the strike strip of the box, and a flame bloomed in her hand. She lit the lantern and adjusted the wick. Cork sat on the edge of the bed, cradling the arrow in his hands.

"That was the knock?" Rainy asked.

"Guess so."

"A hunting arrow?"

Cork nodded. "And look here." He ran his index finger across a word printed finely and delicately in white paint along the length of the gray carbon-composition shaft.

"What does it say?"

Cork held it close to her so that she could see for herself.

"Traitor," she read out loud.

His perplexity and concern must have been obvious, because Rainy put a warm, reassuring hand on his arm. "It's disturbing, I know. But there's an upside. At least it proves you're not crazy."

Cork woke to the hoarse barking of Walleye, Meloux's old yellow dog. He opened his eyes, saw the gray of that morning seeping through Rainy's windows, and realized he was alone in bed. He got up, pulled on his socks, and went to the nearest window. Outside, dingy-looking clouds hung wet and heavy over the North Country. The ground on Crow Point was salted with sleet pellets. Walleye sat on his haunches, his attention focused on the outhouse that stood twenty yards north of Meloux's cabin. As Cork watched, the old Mide emerged from the tiny structure and, instead of heading back to his own cabin, came toward Rainy's. Walleye followed behind.

Cork took his pants from the chair where he'd laid them folded the night before and slipped them on. He was buttoning his flannel shirt when the old man entered without knocking.

"I was beginning to think you were going to hibernate this winter, Corcoran O'Connor." Meloux walked to the empty chair at Rainy's table and sat while Cork drew on his boots. Walleye had come in, too, and flopped at Meloux's feet. "Rainy told me about your visitor last night."

"I wouldn't exactly call it a visit, Henry."

"What would you call it?"

"A warning, maybe."

Cork took the arrow from the stand where he'd put it in the night and handed it to Meloux, who looked it over carefully.

"A warning, you say? About something you have done or something you should not do?" the old Mide asked.

"You tell me, Henry."

"If I could tell you, Corcoran O'Connor, I would not have asked."

Cork sat down across the table. "Have you given any more consideration to what we talked about last night?"

Meloux reached into the pocket of the plaid mackinaw he wore and pulled out a creased sheet of paper, which he handed to Cork, who unfolded it and laid it on the tabletop. Meloux had written on it in pencil.

"You asked about those Sam Winter Moon taught to hunt in the old way and who were still alive and still on the reservation. Those are all I could think of, but it is not everyone."

"You've forgotten some?"

The old man seemed mildly irritated by his suggestion. "I may not see so good anymore, Corcoran O'Connor, but my brain is still as sharp as the head of that arrow."

Cork had no doubt it was true, but there the similarity ended, for in the sharpness of the old man's brain there was no sinister purpose.

"Though we were good friends, Sam Winter Moon did not share everything with me or with others," Meloux explained. "He was a man who, for his own reasons, sometimes kept secrets." The old Mide gave Cork a penetrating look. "Who does not?"

Cork slowly went down Meloux's list of names. The handwriting was small and precise. Meloux had been taught at the Indian school in Flandreau, South Dakota, where the administrators and teachers had done their best to pry the Indian out of him and fill the void with all things white. They'd done a poor job of it. Meloux had, indeed, learned from them but, for the most part, not the lessons they'd intended.

The names on Meloux's list were all familiar to Cork, and, for almost all of them, he could see neither the reason nor the twisted moral fiber that would result in sending an arrow into Jubal Little's heart. But there were two possibilities that did stand out. The first was Isaiah Broom, the man who'd brought the news of Jubal's death to Crow Point. All his life, Broom had been an agitator and activist on behalf of the Iron Lake Ojibwe and, during Jubal Little's gubernatorial campaign, had been an outspoken opponent. Cork had seen raging anger in the huge Shinnob enough times to believe he might be capable of murder.

The other name was Winona Crane.

"Winona hunts in the old way?" he asked.

"Sam Winter Moon told me that she was as good a hunter as he had ever taught."

The door opened, and Rainy stepped in, bringing with her not only the wet chill from outside but also the good smell of freshly baked biscuits. "Breakfast's ready," she said brightly.

After they'd eaten, Meloux said, "When you told me last night about the voice from the woods, I thought maybe it was a *manidoo.*" He was speaking of the spirits that, in his unique understanding, filled the world around him. "But it was not a *manidoo* who came knocking last night with that arrow. I have been out already this morning, looking."

"Did you find tracks?"

"None that these old eyes could see."

Through Meloux's windows, Cork observed that the clouds

seemed to be hanging lower and lower, and he knew that very soon they could deliver icy rain or more sleet or even snow, so that whatever tracks there might be would be obscured. "I'll have a look myself."

"Mind if I come?" Rainy asked.

"Go," Meloux said to her before Cork had a chance to respond. "From me, you learn to heal. From Corcoran O'Connor, you learn to hunt."

"I don't intend to shoot anyone, Uncle Henry," Rainy told him.

"Not today, perhaps," the old man said with an enigmatic smile. He waved them out. "I will clean the dishes."

Cork and Rainy pulled on their coats and stepped outside. The wind was up again, and the air was damp and held a sharp chill. The temperature, Cork figured, was just above freezing. This kind of weather was harder on him than the most bitter winter blows. The damp wind seemed to push right through his outerwear and drove spikes of wet cold into all the bones of his body. He flipped his coat collar up and drew on his gloves and snugged his cap more firmly on his head. Though she zipped her own coat up to the neck, Rainy seemed less bothered by the weather.

"Where do we begin?" she asked.

Cork said, "The door of your cabin faces west. That's where the arrow came from. Let's head that way and see what we find."

He made a long arc in front of the cabin five yards out, moved another five yards distant and walked another arc in the opposite direction. In this way, he moved farther and farther from the cabin, studying the meadow for signs. All he found was evidence of Meloux's attempt at tracking. There'd been no hard freeze yet that season, and last night's sleet had mostly melted, so the ground was clear and soft. He knew that if there had been anything, even Meloux, with his bad eyes, would have found it.

"What exactly are you looking for?" Rainy asked. "Footprints?"

"Not just a print, although that would be helpful. The meadow grass is long and dead, so if someone had walked here there'd be stalks bent or broken. If someone knew what they were doing and didn't want to leave a trail, they wouldn't have come into the meadow."

"Why are you looking here then?"

"Eliminating possibilities."

Rainy pointed to the west. Fifty yards distant stood a tall rock outcropping in a roughly semicircular shape. Beyond it lay the fire ring where Meloux often conducted ceremonies of one kind or another. "If I were going to shoot an arrow from some-place that wouldn't leave a trace, I'd shoot from those rocks."

Cork said, "That would be my first choice, too."

"Then why aren't we looking there?"

He stopped and turned to her. She wore a gray wool cap that she'd knitted herself. Her black hair was done in a long braid that disappeared beneath the back collar of her coat, but loose wisps fluttered about her face in the wind, dancing restlessly across the tawny skin of her cheeks. Her eyes were the color of cherry-wood, and were intense with her desire to understand and to learn. In that moment, out of all context of his purpose that morning, Cork was struck by how beautiful she was to him. He cupped her face in his gloved hands and kissed her and felt how soft her lips were against his own and, despite all the cold that drove against them, how warm they were.

She seemed caught by surprise. "What was that for?"

"Appreciation," he said.

She smiled. "I like being appreciated. But what for?"

"Just being here," he said. "I like being with you. I like not being alone in this."

She reached up and touched his cheek. "I love you, Cork O'Connor. I'm happy being the one who makes you not alone."

Cork felt another kind of kiss against his face, the wet kiss of snow. He looked up and saw flakes beginning to fall.

"Okay," he said, returning of necessity to their task, "the rocks would be my choice for shooting the arrow, but it's an incredibly difficult shot. First of all, it's more than fifty yards away. The odds of hitting the door from that distance aren't great. And when you factor in the dark . . ." He shook his head.

"Night-vision goggles?"

"Maybe," he said. "Or a nightscope of some kind mounted on the bow. They have them. But think about the wind. It's stiff this morning, but it was even stronger last night. It would take a phenomenal bow hunter to pull off that shot. Even Jubal Little, who was the best I ever saw, would have been hard-pressed."

Rainy looked up at the slant of snowflakes the wind was shoving out of the sky. "We should take a look pretty quick, shouldn't we?"

There was a path from Meloux's cabin to the rocks, and they followed it. As they walked, Cork studied the ground, which was worn bare from the passage of countless feet, but he saw nothing of interest. The path cut through the rocks, and as soon as they were on the other side, Cork and Rainy were hit by the smell of char. Black ash lay deep inside the stone circle of the fire ring, and around the circle sat sections of wood cut for sitting. It was an area that had a sacred feel to Cork. He'd seen great healing occur there. But it was also a place that, on more than one occasion, had been the scene of violent death. Meloux consecrated and reconsecrated the ground, and Cork had come to accept that it reflected the way of life as Kitchimanidoo had created it, of dark side by side with light, of peace cheek and jowl with conflict.

Almost immediately he found something.

"Here," he said, pointing to the rock outcropping on the east side.

Rainy looked where he'd indicated but shook her head. "I don't see anything."

Cork ran his index finger along a faint line of dirt across the slope of a rock. "A boot left this. My guess would be as someone climbed to the top for a shot at your door."

Cork ascended the outcropping, looking for another sign.

"Anything?" Rainy called from below.

"No." He came back down.

"How can you be sure it was left last night?"

He took off his glove and touched the line of dirt. "Still damp," he said. He turned. "There's going to be evidence of that boot somewhere on the ground."

Rainy said, "I see all kinds of tracks here."

"Old tracks," Cork said.

Beyond the fire ring, a dozen yards to the west, lay the shore of Iron Lake, which was lined with aspens whose branches had gone bare with the season. The lake surface was choppy in the wind, and the low clouds seemed to breathe gray into the water. Cork walked to where fallen aspen leaves covered the lakeshore.

"Here," he said and knelt. "Do you see?"

Rainy stood beside him and looked at the short stalk of wild oat that he indicated. "It's broken," she said.

"Broken in one place, yes, but creased in two others," Cork pointed out. "The stalk broke under the weight of the boot, which forced it down. Then the boot pressed it into the ground and created these two creases on either side of the sole. The distance between the two creases gives us an indication of the width of the boot. It's good sized. Makes me think it's a man."

"How do you know that's not an old track?"

"Damp dirt on the stalk, just like on the rock over there." Then Cork nodded toward the lake. "And you can see faintly where his boots have pressed into those fallen aspen leaves."

Rainy said, "He came from the lake."

Cork nodded. "Probably by canoe, since we didn't hear a motor."

"But you heard him speak in the woods before you got here."

Cork shrugged. "Maybe Henry was right and that was a *manidoo*. But it's more likely that whoever it was knew I'd be coming here and arrived ahead of me and hid until I came down the trail and then followed me. It's someone who knew I'd come here." He nodded with a grudging admiration. "A good hunter knows the pattern of his quarry."

"So, someone who knows you well?"

"Not necessarily. We haven't been exactly covert in our relationship, Rainy. It's pretty common knowledge, at least on the rez. And long before you came to Crow Point, I was out here all the time looking to Henry for advice, spiritual and otherwise."

"You think this might have been a Shinnob?"

"I didn't say that."

"Is it the same person who killed Jubal Little?"

"It could be, but if you were the murderer, would you keep offering clues that might lead back to you? And if you'd spent a lot of time trying to point the finger of guilt somewhere else, why muddy the waters with something like this?"

"So, two different people, you think?"

"I can't say that at this point either. I don't know my quarry yet, so I don't know his pattern."

"His? You're sure it's not a woman?"

"If it is, she has awfully large feet."

"If I were a woman and wanted to throw you off, I might wear big boots. Just a thought."

"A good one," Cork allowed.

Rainy offered him a sad little smile. "You really have no idea what's going on, do you?"

"Nope. Do you?"

"I can tell you two things. The murderer is someone who didn't particularly care for Jubal Little. And it's someone who doesn't particularly care for you. Implicating you kills two birds with one stone, you see?"

Cork stared at the restless gray water of Iron Lake. The wind was out of the west, carrying snow like ash from a distant fire. Despite his coat and gloves and cap, he was cold to the bone. "Jubal's murder was well planned," he said. "The killer knew we'd be hunting at Trickster's Point, probably had known for a while. He probably knew that eventually Jubal and I would separate, and maybe even knew where. If I understood how that was possible, I'm betting I'd be pretty close to figuring out who it was."

"It's got to be someone who knows you, Cork. Someone who knows you pretty well," Rainy said. This understanding clearly troubled her.

"There's a positive side," Cork replied in a voice as cold as that late autumn wind. "I know them, too."

CHAPTER 8

Cork said good-bye to Rainy and Meloux and walked back to his Land Rover. It was Sunday morning. He glanced at his watch. A few minutes before ten. The bell would be ringing at St. Agnes, calling the faithful to Mass. He wondered if Jenny and Waaboo and Stephen were going that morning. Usually they all went together, which Cork enjoyed very much. He didn't think of himself as particularly devout, but church was something that they did as a family, and in Cork's life, family, even more than God, took center stage. God was generally a distant ideal, but a hug from one of his children or the sound of Waaboo's giggling were things wonderfully real to him and blessedly comforting and, in their way, sacred.

The wind had died. The temperature had risen a few degrees, and the snow had turned to a light drizzle that, every so often, dripped off the bill of his cap. The woods, as he walked the trail, were still and quiet. Although the air was filled with the scent of evergreen, it was the smell of wet earth that he noticed, of all the summer growth that was dead now, of leaves gone gold or red or brown and fallen and lay wet and rotting, becoming again the earth from which they sprang. Usually, when he walked this familiar trail, his heart was light, but now all he could think about was death. Cork felt overwhelmed by the weight of all those in his history whom he'd loved and who'd died violently. His father, his good friend Sam Winter Moon, his wife, and now Jubal Little.

He stopped and wondered: Had he really loved Jubal?

In the first spring after Cork's father died, Sam Winter Moon had given Cork a gift, a recurve bow that Sam had made himself. Cork had rifle-hunted with his father, but that was something so many in the North Country did. There were bow hunters as well, but not many men hunted as Sam Winter Moon did, stalking in the old way, and Cork had heard of no one who equaled Sam's prowess with a bow. He longed to learn, but his father had once told him that Sam had to make the offer. It was not a skill he shared lightly. And it was one he shared only with those in whom the blood of The People ran. When Sam gave Cork that beautiful, handmade recurve bow, Cork understood it was the invitation he'd been waiting for.

All that spring and through the summer, Sam Winter Moon taught him the way of the bow. Sam had a cabin on the Iron Lake Reservation, and whenever he could get away from his burger joint, he and Cork would head out to the cabin, where Sam had a workbench and tools—nocking pliers, a broadhead wrench, a fletching stripper and fletching jig, taper tools, an arrow saw. Sam taught Cork the proper way to make and true an arrow, splice feathers for fletching, and although he used manufactured broadhead tips for his hunting, how to make an arrowhead from a chunk of flint. First he taught Cork to shoot at stationary targets, usually a hay bale on which Sam painted circles and a bull's-eye. Once Cork was able to group the arrows tightly, Sam set up a moving target, a stuffed rabbit he'd affixed to the center of a short two-by-four board mounted on tricycle wheels, which he pulled in rapid jerks across the yard while Cork attempted to send an arrow into its heart. He tossed small burlap pillows stuffed with dried grass into the air to simulate the sudden flight of a game bird. He taught Cork how to move care-fully, soundlessly through the forest, and the signs to watch for as he stalked. Finally, in the fall, they began to hunt small game. Cork was clumsy at first, but Sam was patient, and eventually Cork's arrows began to find their marks. In that first year, they didn't hunt large game, but Cork continued to bring down any-thing edible, and to offer to the elders of the Iron Lake Ojibwe more rabbit, grouse, wild turkey, and duck than they'd probably had since before the white man came.

The next fall, he and Sam hunted white-tail deer. It was chal-lenging in a way that rifle hunting with his father had never been. To kill a deer required that he be almost close enough to hear it breathing. It was a shockingly intimate experience, and after he'd brought down his first buck, he understood why it was necessary for his own spirit that he sing to the spirit of the an-imal he'd killed, that he explain the violence and promise the beautiful creature that his body would feed The People, and they would be grateful.

In the spring of his freshman year, Cork ran track for Aurora High School. He was tall and had long legs, and his specialty was hurdles. Jubal was on the track team, too, and whatever Jubal did—and he could do just about anything—he did well. The one thing he refused to do was run hurdles. Cork understood that it was, in a way, a gift Jubal was offering him.

Cork wanted to offer something in return, something impor-tant, and he asked Sam Winter Moon if he'd be willing to teach Jubal how to hunt in the old way. He knew that it was a skill Jubal wanted desperately to learn, but Cork had so far refused to ask Sam to teach him. He'd refused for two reasons, both purely selfish. First, if Sam agreed to teach Jubal Little, Jubal would un-doubtedly become better at it than Cork. And second—and more important—it meant that Cork would have to share with Jubal the man who now, in many ways, filled the gap left when Cork's father died. In his own mind, however, Cork had begun to think of Jubal as a brother, and so he finally decided to offer this gift. But Sam said no.

"It's something I share with Shinnobs," he told Cork.

"What if Jubal was Indian but not Shinnob?" Cork asked.

Sam shrugged. "Doesn't matter. That boy's white." Then Cork saw a little glint in Sam's dark eyes. "But if he was Indian, I suppose I might."

Cork talked to Jubal, who was reluctant to share the secret of his blood, even with Sam Winter Moon. Cork told him that he suspected Sam already knew, and Jubal seemed taken aback.

"You said something to him," Jubal accused.

"No, honest I didn't. But if you told him, he'd keep your secret, I know he would. And he'd teach you to hunt like he does, I swear."

In the end, Jubal agreed, and when he'd told Sam the truth of his past, Winter Moon said, "The white man took almost everything from us and gave us in return mostly disease and alcohol. But there's one thing he can't take from us unless we let him, and that's our dignity, Jubal. There's a great heritage in being Indian. I'll teach you to hunt in the old way, but in return, I want you to begin to think of yourself in a different way. Accept that the blood of your Blackfeet father flows in you, and be proud of that, even if you don't say a word about it to anyone. Deal?"

Jubal thought it over and nodded seriously. And that, as it turned out, led to the first time Cork had seen murder in Jubal Little's eyes.

In the fall a few weeks before Cork turned sixteen, he went hunting in the old way with Jubal Little and Sam Winter Moon. They drove in Sam's old pickup to an area on the eastern edge of the rez, where the backsides of the Sawtooth Mountains were visible in the distance. It was an area well known to the Ojibwe, an area in which big bucks were often taken.

The day was overcast and wet and cool. They followed a rutted dirt road over bogland where the tamaracks were gold and stood out like lit torches. They wove through birch stands barren of leaves, with bone white trunks and branches. Sam Winter Moon suddenly braked to a complete stop, then backed up. He swung his pickup onto the grass at the side of the road and, without a word, got out. Cork and Jubal got out, too, and followed. Sam walked down a little spur of road, almost invisible beneath the tall overgrowth of weeds. Cork saw what his own eyes had missed initially but Sam's had not, an outline where the passage of tires had crushed down the weeds. They came to a black pickup, a newer model, parked behind a thicket of wild blackberry that made it invisible from the road.

Sam said quietly, "Know any skins on the rez who can afford a new pickup?" He walked carefully around the vehicle, studying the ground. "This way," he said and began to follow the trail left by those who'd come in the truck.

Cork realized that Jubal was carrying his bow and quiver of arrows, which he must have pulled from the bed of Sam's pickup when they got out. Since it wasn't deer they were hunting at the moment, Cork wasn't sure why Jubal had done this, but he quickly forgot about it as he became intent on reading the signs of the trail. Wherever the ground was soft and bare of cover, three distinct sets of tracks were visible. Two sets were large—men. One was much smaller—a child. They followed nearly a mile, up a ridge, and as they approached the crest, they heard voices ahead. Cork and Jubal looked toward Sam, who nodded for them to keep moving toward the noise. In a couple of minutes, they came to a meadow full of wild grass and sumac, with three figures at the center, dressed in camouflage and standing over a killed white-tail buck. Cork recognized them immediately: Donner Bigby; his little brother, Lester; and their father, an enormous and brutal-looking man whose name was Clarence but whom everyone called Buzz because of his logging work with chain saws. Bigs and his father held compound bows. Lester, who was maybe eight or nine at the time, held a hunting knife. The blade looked huge in his small hand. He was crying.

"I don't want to cut him, Daddy," Lester said.

"Your brother and me did all the work of bringing him down," his father said. "The least you can do is help us dress him."

"Make a man out of you," Bigs said with a laugh.

"I don't want to," Lester cried. He looked down at the deer. "I don't want him to be dead."

"He's not Bambi, for Christ's sake," Bigs said.

"Cut him open like I told you," their father said.

But Lester just stood there, crying. Buzz Bigby grabbed the knife from his son's hand and slapped the boy across the face. Lester tumbled to the ground.

"Hey, Pop, leave him alone," Donner said.

"You want some of this?" Bigby held up the open palm with which he'd sent Lester sprawling.

Donner lowered his eyes and didn't reply.

Bigby looked down at his younger son and spit. "Shut up and be a man, or the next thing I give you will be the toe of my boot."

Lester retreated in a crawl but finally brought himself under control, and the sobs subsided.

"Stand up."

He did as he was told. His father handed him the knife. The boy took it and knelt beside the deer.

Cork and Jubal and Sam had hidden themselves among the birch at the edge of the meadow. Sam whispered, "Stay here."

He left the tree cover and walked toward the Bigbys. "*Anin,*" he cried out in Ojibwe greeting.

Buzz Bigby swung around to face him, and Cork saw that he brought his bow to the ready. Bigs, seeing his father's response, did the same, and went a step further. He drew an arrow from his quiver and nocked it on his bowstring.

"What do you want?" the elder Bigby said.

"Thing is this. You're on Indian land, but you don't look very Indian to me." Sam had halted a dozen steps away from the Bigbys. "It's against the law for you to hunt on our land."

"Hell, you got more deer'n you'll ever need to feed your-selves," Bigby said.

"That's not the point."

"Well, here's my point," Bigby said. "Me and my boys are gonna take this buck back to my truck, and we're gonna haul it home, and we're gonna mount them antlers on my wall, and there ain't a thing in the world you're gonna be able to do to stop us. What do you say to that?"

Jubal drew an arrow from his quiver and laid the shaft over the arrow rest and fit the nock into the bowstring. Cork wanted to ask him what the hell he thought he was doing. Would he really shoot Bigs or Mr. Bigby or Lester?

Sam said, "If you do that, I'll report you to the sheriff."

"He's white. Think he'll care about what goes on out here?"

"I haven't finished. I'll also report you to Rusty Benay. He's the game warden in these parts, and he's half Indian. He'll see to it that you never get another deer license, or any kind of license for that matter."

"He can't do that," Bigby said, but not with certainty.

"Is this deer worth that chance?" Sam replied.

Bigby weighed his response, and while he did, Donner slowly edged away from the others, as if to clear himself a space in order to send an arrow into Sam Winter Moon if necessary. In that same time, Jubal raised his own bow, drew back the string, and sighted.

"Jesus, Jubal," Cork whispered. "Put it down."

If he heard, Jubal gave no indication. He held the bow steady, as if it were only an inanimate target he was aiming at, not Donner Bigby's heart.

Cork became abnormally aware of everything around him. The smell of wet tree bark, the kiss of the autumn air against his face, the look of the clouds running like gray wolves across the sky, the feel of the very ground through the soles of his boots, the easy breathing of Jubal Little, the metal taste in his own mouth. He would experience this hypersensitivity several times over the years to come, usually in a situation when a human life was at stake.

He thought of tackling Jubal but was afraid that a move like that might cause the arrow to be fired accidentally.

In the blink of an eye, Cork made his decision. He stepped from the trees and called out, "Hey, Sam, we were wondering where you went. Me and the guys." He walked to the center of the clearing, where all the eyes had turned his way. "Hey, Bigs," he said easily. "Hello, Mr. Bigby. Hey, Lester." He looked down at the deer, as if only just becoming aware of it. "You know, you can't keep that buck. We're on reservation land here. But the elders, they'll be grateful for all the jerky and deer sausage we'll be able to make from it. Thanks a lot. Or as the Ojibwe say, *migwech*. I'll go get the other guys, and we can take it from here."

He spoke fast and friendly, as if he and the Bigbys were pals. And he smiled easily, though his heart was kicking like a mule.

Buzz Bigby took his measure and finally nodded. He looked at Sam. "The buck's yours. Come on, boys, let's pack it in."

The Bigbys left, returning the way they'd come. Cork wondered if Jubal would make his presence known to them, but when he looked where Jubal had been, he could see nothing. Jubal appeared again once the Bigbys were well and truly gone. He'd returned the arrow to his quiver. He walked to the center of the clearing and stood with Cork and Sam, looking at the great buck that Bigs and his father had brought down. There were two arrows in the animal. Cork could tell from the line of blood across the wild grass that the buck had run here after being hit, had fallen, and died. But it probably hadn't run far, because both arrows had been well-placed heart shots.

"Let's dress him," Sam said.

Jubal said with satisfaction, "Bigs and his old man are going home empty-handed today."

"No," Sam said. "They'll take the memory of this day home, and they'll feed on it a lot longer than they would've fed on the meat of this deer, and it'll always taste bitter to them. My advice? Around the Bigbys, you guys watch yourselves."

CHAPTER 9

By the time Cork broke from the woods on his return from Crow Point, the drizzle had ended, but it left a damp chill in the air. A white Dodge pickup was parked behind Cork's Land Rover, and a figure stood waiting there. It took Cork only a moment to recognize Sheriff Marsha Dross. She wasn't dressed in her department uniform. She wore jeans and a sage-colored turtleneck under a suede jacket. She'd dropped the tailgate and had set a big steel thermos of coffee at the edge of the pickup bed. She was drinking from the thermos cup as Cork approached.

"Got me under constant surveillance now?" he asked.

She held the cup near her mouth, and the coffee sent steamy tendrils up against her lips. She blew to cool it. "I just came to tell you that I got a call from the governor early this morning. He requested that I allow the BCA to be involved in the investigation of Jubal Little's death."

She was talking about the Bureau of Criminal Apprehension, the division of the Minnesota Department of Public Safety that functioned, in many ways, very much like the Federal Bureau of Investigation. Cork had worked often with their agents over the years, both when he wore the Tamarack County Sheriff's Department uniform and afterward.

"Want coffee?" Dross asked. She poured some into a bright red mug she'd clearly brought for just this purpose and handed it to Cork.

"How'd you know where to find me?" he asked.

"I stopped by your house. Jenny told me. How are Henry and Rainy?"

"Worried." Cork sipped the coffee. Dross liked her brew strong, which was just fine with him. On that cold, gray morning, it seemed to warm him all the way to his toenails.

"As well they should be. This is serious, Cork. You're going to be in the media spotlight, at least here in Minnesota. It would be national news except for the collapse of that dam in Colorado, so you may have got a break in an odd but sad way."

"Dam break?"

"You haven't heard?"

"I've been on Crow Point since yesterday."

"Big dam broke last night in the mountains near Boulder, Colorado. Floodwater swept down a canyon, wiped out several towns. The death toll is estimated in the hundreds. It's a huge catastrophe. Jubal Little may be news in Minnesota, but he's not front page anywhere else."

That was the kind of luck that didn't leave Cork feeling any better.

Dross went on. "When I talked to the governor, he asked for the details of Little's death. I gave them to him as we know them, and told him it looked like a hunting accident."

"It wasn't an accident, Marsha."

"I know, and it's too bad. Because it was your arrow in his heart, Cork." Dross watched his face for a reaction. "You didn't tell us that when we questioned you yesterday."

"I knew you'd find out soon enough. And once you knew, you might be reluctant to let me go."

"Your fingerprints and Jubal's are the only ones on that arrow. Did you shoot it?"

Cork laid his cup on the bed of the pickup and turned fully to the sheriff. "Do you think I did?"

Dross, implacable for a moment, held his gaze, then said, "You know as well as I do that anyone is capable of anything under the right circumstances."

"Even cold-blooded murder?"

"Is that what it was?"

"You didn't answer my question. Do you really think I shot that arrow?"

Dross reached into her cup, plucked something from the surface of the coffee, and looked at it closely. "Tick," she said with amazement. "I thought they'd all be long dead by now." She flicked it away and gave Cork the same scrutinizing look she'd just given the bug. "Three hours, Cork. You waited three hours before going to get help."

"I didn't go to get help, Marsha. Like I told you yesterday, Jubal was beyond help when I left him."

"My point, more or less."

"I stayed because he asked me to stay."

"Going might have saved him."

"Or left him to die alone. He didn't want to go that way. We finished here?" Cork tossed the rest of his coffee onto the ground in a gesture of irritation.

"I haven't answered your question yet," she said.

"I figured you weren't going to."

"Anyone who knows you wouldn't believe that you killed Jubal Little, Cork. But there's going to be a lot of pressure on us to come up with someone, and right now, we've got no one else to consider. So for a while, as far as the media's concerned, you're the bull's-eye. It'll be rough." Dross poured herself a little more coffee, and the steam crawled over the rim as if the cup were a tiny witch's cauldron. "How could someone have got one of your arrows?"

"I don't know, Marsha. I'm working on that one."

"My first guess would be that it's someone who knows you well."

"Sobering thought," Cork replied, but it was exactly what he thought, too. "Marsha, does the name Rhiannon mean anything to you?"

She squinted, thought. "Nope. Should it?"

"Not necessarily."

"Is it important?"

"Probably not."

Dross glanced at her watch. "Ed and I are holding a press conference in an hour. We'll be announcing that the BCA's been asked to help with the investigation, and we'll introduce Agent Phil Holter, who's been tapped to lead the BCA team. We're still calling it a hunting accident, but that won't matter. By noon, you're going to be big news, and everything we do in this case is going to be watched, and whatever passes between us after that will be official." She reached out a hand. "Good luck, Cork."

She sounded like someone sending a man off to war.

When he hit the outskirts of Aurora, Cork called home on his cell phone. Stephen answered.

"There are some cars and vans parked outside," he told his father. "They've knocked on the door, and the phone's rung a few times."

"You haven't talked to any of them?"

"Like you told us, Dad, we've kept our mouths shut."

"All right. I'm going to park on Willow Street and come in the back way."

He passed Gooseberry Lane and glanced down the street where he'd lived quietly for most of his life. If he'd been asked, he could have recited the history of every house on his block and the lineage of most of the families who occupied them. The street wasn't crowded the way he'd feared, but he saw a couple of vans topped with broadcast antennae and, despite the drizzle, lots of people milling about on the sidewalk in front of his house. He went a block farther and turned onto Willow Street, where he parked. He walked to the Quayles' house, whose backyard abutted his own. He cut through the side yard and along a line of bare lilac bushes. Few people in Aurora had fences, and he crossed onto his property without difficulty. He hustled through the yard, across his patio, and to the back door, angry that he had to enter his own home like some kind of thief but grateful that he hadn't been spotted. Stephen had been watching for him and had the door open.

"Baa-baa," Waaboo cried when he saw his grandfather come in. He dropped the stuffed alligator he'd been holding, ran across the dining room, and wrapped his arms around Cork's leg. Cork bent, lifted his grandson, and swung him around so that Waaboo laughed with delight. It was the best sound Cork had heard that day.

Jenny stepped from the kitchen, wiping her hands on a dish towel, and Trixie padded along behind her. The dog came to Cork, her tail wagging briskly in welcome, and Cork bent and ruffed her fur. Waaboo reached down to grab at an ear, but Trixie, who was used to the child, slipped away and sat on her haunches well out of reach.

"Any trouble?" Jenny asked.

"I don't think anybody saw me," he said.

"We've kept the curtains closed, but—" She was cut off by the insistent ring of the phone. She strolled to the stand beside the staircase and checked caller ID. "Them," she said simply.

Cork put Waaboo down, and the toddler went immediately for Trixie. Then Cork strode to a front window and drew the curtain aside just enough to see out. He'd have been happier seeing no one, but at least it wasn't a media feeding frenzy. He thought of the dead in Colorado, and knew that the national media, like hungry crows, would flock to the bigger kill. He turned back to his children. "Sam's Place?"

"Judy opened this morning," Jenny said. "I talked to her a few minutes ago. There were a couple of enterprising reporters waiting, hoping, I guess, that you or one of us might show up."

Cork said, "Maybe I ought to hold a press conference there. We could sell a ton of burgers afterward."

"Seriously, Dad, what are you going to do?" Stephen pressed him.

"The first thing is head back to Trickster's Point."

"What for?"

"Maybe I can find something Marsha's people couldn't."

"Like what?"

"I'm hoping I'll know it when I see it. I left our canoe, so I need to pick that up anyway."

"Can I go?" Stephen asked.

"You're on the schedule at Sam's Place at noon," Jenny reminded him.

"I'll call Gordy, get him to cover for me. Okay, Dad?"

Cork thought it over and agreed. There was no reason Stephen couldn't go along, and it would get him away from the craziness that was going to be their lives for a while now. Cork wished he could get them all away while he dealt with the situation, but he wasn't sure how to do that or if they'd even go.

"You and our little guy will be all right?" he asked Jenny.

"I think we'll go to Sam's Place and spend the day. Maybe by this evening the vultures will have flown."

"If you need me, call my cell. I won't get a signal up at Trickster's Point, but leave a message, and I'll get back to you as soon as I'm in range."

While Stephen got himself ready, Cork made peanut butter and jelly sandwiches, wrapped them, and put them in a knapsack along with some bottled water. When everything was ready, he kissed Jenny good-bye and gave Waaboo a big, gentle hug.

"Take care of your mommy," he instructed seriously.

Waaboo said happily, "Bye-bye, Baa-baa."

CHAPTER 10

They drove out of Aurora, along the southern shoreline of Iron Lake, then swung north toward Allouette.

When Cork was a boy, Allouette had been a collection of mostly BIA-built homes and trailers, with only a couple of the two dozen streets actually paved. There'd been an old, rotting community center, which had housed the offices of the tribal government, and also a small gymnasium, where the kids could play basketball, and where powwows and community celebrations were sometimes held and the jingle dancers and the drummers practiced. Across the street was LeDuc's general store and next to that a small café called the Boozhoo. A block away was Alf Johnson's Sinclair gas station, a two-pump operation that also sold tackle and live bait and beer. The dock on the shore of Iron Lake was a rickety old thing, and the boats tied up there were generally a sad-looking fleet of secondhand dinghies and rowboats mounted with sputtering outboards.

But Allouette had changed. There was a new, much larger community center designed by an Ojibwe architect and built entirely by Ojibwe contractors and laborers. It held not only a gymnasium and the tribal government offices but also a tribal-run preschool, a health clinic, and a number of new tribal-operated community services. The streets were paved, and every house had access to new water and sewer systems. There were burgeoning new businesses. LeDuc's store had been updated, and next to it was the Mocha Moose, a coffee and sandwich shop that was the darling of Sarah LeDuc. Alf Johnson's station was now a multipump Food 'N Fuel, and beyond it was a large new marina where a number of fine-looking Ojibwe-owned craft lay moored.

The whole reservation was changing. It had always been a hodgepodge of land owned by individual Ojibwe, or held in trust by the tribe, or leased to the federal government or private parties, or owned outright by whites, who, very soon after the earliest treaty signings, had purchased allotments for a song from Shinnobs who didn't understand the reality of what they were giving away. Recently, the Anishinaabeg had begun a movement—the Iron Lake Initiative—for the purpose of reacquiring all the land that had originally been theirs by treaty. The land that had once belonged to The People was coming back to them.

This reflection of recent affluence was the direct result of the Chippewa Grand Casino, which had been constructed south of Aurora several years earlier and which was owned and operated by the Iron Lake Band of Ojibwe.

Cork had mixed feelings about all this. He was very glad to see the Anishinaabeg—the people of his blood—finally able to do for themselves what the government on every level had failed to do. He was glad to see the optimism and enterprise that came with the casino gambling, which the Indians called "the new buffalo." He was encouraged by the flaring of a new fire of Anishinaabe pride in a culture rich in history and wisdom and knowledge and unique tradition. But all this came at a price. In its early days, the Chippewa Grand had seen a good deal of corruption among its management. Oversight of bookkeeping and profits was always questionable, and true and fair distribution of the income was an issue of great and heated discussion among folks on the rez. One of the underlying values of the Ojibwe culture had always been a lack of interest in stockpiling wealth. What you had, you shared, and it was the sharing that was esteemed, not the having. Now, no matter how much people were given in casino allotments, it never seemed enough. Dealing with this sudden influx of money wasn't always an easy affair for someone raised on nothing and less than nothing. If, for example, you were disposed to drinking, you probably drank more. If you were into drugs, you plunged deeper. If you'd been given to coveting the things you saw in other people's houses—particularly the homes of white people on television sitcoms and dramas—you bought items you didn't need or didn't know how to use or didn't even really understand the purpose of, and they accumulated and forced you to buy a bigger home or a longer trailer, and despite all you had, you still weren't happy.

Welcome to the white man's world, Cork thought.

Although there was an official state forest trail to Trickster's Point, it was a five-mile hike. Cork had always preferred the more direct route, a two-mile paddle by canoe across Lake Nanaboozhoo. A couple of miles outside Allouette, he turned onto an old logging road that cut northeast through the reservation. The road was seldom used and had become more a memory of road. But two parallel lines of bent and broken undergrowth showed where, a day earlier, he'd twice driven his Land Rover, first with Jubal Little sitting where Stephen now sat, and then alone.

The logging road ended abruptly in a clearing full of sumac that had gone bare weeks earlier. Cork parked, and he and Stephen got out and made their way across the clearing to the shore of Lake Nanaboozhoo. There was a natural, sandy landing where Cork's canoe lay tipped, with two paddles leaning against the hull. Stephen took the bow and Cork the stern. They lifted the canoe, righted it, and set it in the water. Stephen grabbed a paddle and a place in the bow. Cork took the stern, and they shoved onto the flat gray of the lake.

Its shape was a long, ragged arc with a lot of rocky inlets and small, wild islands. The southern half lay within the Iron Lake Reservation. The northern half was part of the Superior National Forest. The whole body of water sat only a stone's throw from the area known as the Boundary Waters, a vast, unspoiled stretch of wilderness that went far beyond the Canadian border. Under the overcast sky, the pines along the lakeshore seemed dense and brooding, and the water ahead looked nearly black and cold and depthless.

An Ojibwe legend explained the lake. There was once a maiden so beautiful she believed that no man was worthy of her. She spent long hours gazing at herself in the clear water of a small pond near her village. Every young man who saw her fell immediately in love with her and tried to make her his wife. But the haughty maiden's heart was ice, and the suitors were cruelly dismissed. They left with broken hearts and great lamentations. Nanaboozhoo, the trickster spirit, heard their cries and decided to teach the maiden a lesson. He disguised himself as an Ojibwe warrior, the most handsome young man anyone had ever seen. He appeared to the maiden as she sat gazing into the pond. The moment she saw his reflection beside her own, she fell deeply in love. She gave herself to Nanaboozhoo, body and soul. Their mating was so wild that it caused the ground around them to be pushed into hills, and so passionate that it melted the maiden's icy heart, which created a small lake among the hills. Afterward, she fell asleep. When she awoke, she found that Nanaboozhoo had abandoned her, and she was alone. She began to weep and wept so long and so hard that the small lake became the very big lake the Ojibwe named to honor the trickster.

After half an hour, Cork and Stephen came around a long, pine-covered finger of land whose tip pointed northeast. From there they could see, rising on the far side of the lake, a rocky ridge capped with aspens. At the eastern end of that ridge, separated from the rest of the formation by a gap of roughly fifty yards, rose a solitary pinnacle that towered a hundred feet above the trees around it.

In the bow, Stephen nodded toward the pinnacle and said, "*Niinag*," an Ojibwe word that meant "penis."

From a distance, the long, aspen-capped ridge looked like a naked giant lying supine upon the earth, and the solitary pinnacle unmistakably resembled an erect phallus. Ojibwe tradition held that the ridge was a reclining Nanaboozhoo, and they called the tall rock pillar Nanaboozhoo's Penis, though modern Shinnobs sometimes jokingly referred to it as Tricky's Dick. On official maps and in official nomenclature, it was called Trickster's Point.

They made their way across the lake, fighting a sudden cross-wind that had risen, and drew up to the shore. Stephen leaped from the bow and steadied the canoe for his father to disembark. They brought it fully out of the water and tipped it on the soft bed of needles beneath the pines that edged the shoreline, then started inland along a faint path that led toward the towering rock.

"Have you ever been here before, Stephen?" Cork asked.

"No, but there are some guys in school big into rock climbing. I've heard them talk about it. They say people have died climbing Trickster's Point."

"Only one that I know of, and that was a long time ago."

The trail meandered through pines that quickly gave way to birch, and then Trickster's Point loomed, a tower of slate gray stone sixty feet in diameter and more than a hundred and fifty feet high. Even in the cold air, the rock seemed to give off its own intense chill.

"Where did it happen?" Stephen asked.

"Follow me," Cork replied.

He led his son around the base of the formation to the north face. He stopped at a fold in the rock where, despite the sleet and drizzle that had fallen since Jubal Little died, the ground was still darkly stained.

"Here," he said.

Stephen stared at the place, nodded to himself, then asked, "What are we looking for?"

Cork's son was not a hunter. Stephen had never shown any interest, and although Cork had hunted since boyhood and would have been happy to pass down to his son the particular legacy of his knowledge, he'd never pushed the issue. Stephen's inclinations lay elsewhere, particularly in learning the way of the Mide, and Cork was fine with that. He was pleased that Henry Meloux had taken a special liking to Stephen.

Cork said, "Jubal went ahead of me and circled Trickster's Point from the south. The arrow entered his chest from the right, from the east. So from there." He pointed toward the rock ridge that was separated from the pinnacle by fifty yards and that formed the long mass which gave the impression of a giant lying on the earth. "The ground's been trampled by the sheriff's people. We probably won't find anything useful this side of those rocks."

"So we go up into the rocks?"

"Bingo," Cork said.

"People leave footprints on rocks?"

"Not necessarily, but they may leave other signs," Cork said.

"Didn't the sheriff's investigators look there?"

"They did. We're going to adjust our thinking and our eyes to look for what they didn't."

"Like what?"

"Let's go, and I'll show you."

Trickster's Point had once been a part of the long, upthrust ridge, but over millennia, the thousands of cycles of freeze and thaw had shattered the great stone wall and left a gap littered with talus. They crossed the rock-strewn ground, and at the base of the ridge, Cork paused. From there, the wall sloped upward in a ragged chest of boulders and ledges that topped out a couple of hundred feet above him.

"Even the best of bow hunters isn't effective much beyond fifty or sixty yards," he said. "So whoever sent that arrow into Jubal had to be somewhere within the first ten or fifteen yards of the bottom of this slope, hiding behind one of those boulders."

"So we're looking for the boulder he hid behind?"

"Yes, but even more, we're looking for an indication of how he came and how he left. By the time I got to Jubal, his killer was gone. I want to know where he went."

"What exactly are we looking for then?"

"Anything that strikes you as unnatural or out of place. With every step, take a moment, and don't just look with your eyes. Feel what's around you."

Stephen shot his father an easy grin. "You sound like Henry."

"Pay attention just like you would with Henry, okay?"

"You got it," Stephen said.

They separated from one another, a space of a dozen feet between them, then began slowly to make their way among the rocks and up the slope. Cork took his time, but Stephen seemed less careful and moved a little ahead of his father. Cork was about to caution him to be more observant when Stephen seemed to grow smaller before his eyes.

"Dad?"

"What is it?"

"Check this out."

Stephen had stepped down into a kind of box, a recessed area bounded on all four sides by tall rock. When Cork dropped into the box with him, Stephen pointed toward the stone surface that faced Trickster's Point.

"It looks like some kind of scraping, don't you think?"

Cork bent and eyed the mark, which stood out white against the charcoal-colored rock. "That's exactly what it is, Stephen. Maybe from a belt buckle where someone hugged that rock." Cork took a position and eyed the base of Trickster's Point where Jubal had fallen. "The logistics are right." He knelt and scrutinized the ground. "See this?" He put his index finger to a small line of stone particles and dirt pushed against the face of the rock wall opposite the scraped stone. "I'd bet that's from the shove of a boot as our killer positioned himself." He stood up and looked at his son with certainty. "Good work, Stephen. You found the place."

"Where'd he go from here?"

Cork scanned the wall right and left, then said, "Where would you go?"

Stephen studied their surroundings and shook his head. "We're pretty much blocked in here. Hard to move either way." He turned and scanned the slope behind them. "There's a kind of a natural trough up that way. I guess that's where I'd go."

"That's where I'd go, too. Let's see what we find."

Cork led the way, working slowly toward the top of the ridge, which was backed by the bare limbs of aspens and the gray overcast of the sky. He paused occasionally, pointing out to Stephen additional places where small rocks had clearly been displaced and, near the top of the ridge, a spot where a partial boot print had been left in a rare, thin layer of damp soil.

"Medium-size foot," Cork noted. He'd brought a camera that hung in a belt pouch, and he pulled it out. "Probably a common sole type, so it won't tell us much, but you never know."

Cork took some digital shots, then he and Stephen continued to the peak of the slope.

The line of trees that topped the ridge began a couple of dozen yards back from the edge. The stand was full of undergrowth that had caught and held many of the fallen aspen leaves, so that it presented itself as an impenetrable-looking wall of gold. Cork and Stephen scanned the area at the lip of the ridge, and Cork said, "Well?"

Stephen squinted at the ground. "Lots of trampling."

"Azevedo. One of Ed Larson's team. I saw him come up." Cork nodded far to the left of the trail that he and Stephen had followed up the slope. "He didn't find anything."

"The guy who was down there in the rocks came from somewhere."

"Exactly," Cork said. "So where?"

Stephen stood a moment, looking hard at the stand of trees. "There?" He pointed toward a place where the gold wall seemed to have been breached, where the leaves had been disturbed and had fallen to the ground.

"My guess, too," Cork said. "Let's go."

They entered the woods and slowly moved among the aspens.

The initial breach opened onto a trail that, because of the disturbance of the leaves among the undergrowth, wasn't particularly difficult to follow. They paralleled the edge of the ridge for about twenty yards and then came to a place where the trees opened onto a tiny clearing, which offered a broad vista of the lake and shoreline, dominated by Trickster's Point. As soon as they reached the clearing, they stopped abruptly. Both of them stood stone still, staring at the body splayed at their feet.

The man lay faceup, with an arrow shaft protruding from his left eye. A scoped deer rifle lay next to him, and his hunter's cap had been knocked from his head. Cork could see that the arrow had gone clear through his brain and out the back of his skull.

He knelt, and although he already knew the result, he nonetheless put his fingertips to the man's carotid artery to check for a pulse.

"Dead," he said. "And, from the looks of it, a day at least."

Stephen's face had gone ashen. When he spoke, his voice was barely a whisper. "So he was here when Mr. Little was shot?"

"He was here. I don't know if he was alive then, but he was here."

"Who is he?"

"No idea, Stephen."

"What should we do?"

"Did you bring your cell phone?"

"You said cell phones don't work up here, so I left it in the Land Rover."

"Me, too," Cork said. "No service there either. Okay, this is what you're going to do. Take the canoe back the way we came. Here are the keys to the Land Rover. Drive into Allouette or however far you have to go before you get a signal, then call the sheriff's office and report what we've found. Can you handle that?"

"Sure. But what about you?"

"I'll wait here until the sheriff's people arrive."

"Alone with the dead guy?"

"It won't be the first time," Cork told him.

"But why? It's not like he's going anywhere."

"I don't want the body disturbed by scavengers."

Stephen eyed the dead hunter a last time, with obvious revulsion, then gave his father a look Cork couldn't quite decipher. "I hope I never get to the point where sitting with a dead man doesn't bother me."

He turned and began to make his way out of the trees while Cork thought about his son's comment and decided that he hoped so, too.

CHAPTER 11

Cork stood at the edge of the ridge and watched his son paddle across the broad gray of the lake. It was like watching a small bird fly alone into a great threatening sky. He felt a deep sorrow in having to send Stephen on that lonely mission. No parent's child should have had to go through what Stephen, in his brief sixteen years, had already been asked to endure. Cork felt an abiding loneliness as well, but this was for himself, because the tone of his son's comment in parting hadn't escaped his notice. Corcoran O'Connor attracted death the way dogs attracted fleas, a phenomenon that his son clearly recognized and just as clearly disapproved of. Cork thought every man wanted to be understood by his children, but—he looked toward the dead man, the second he'd kept company with in as many days—how could anyone understand this?

He turned to a duty that, across the decades of his life, had become depressingly familiar: He investigated the corpse. He didn't touch anything, just looked the body over carefully.

The dead hunter was Caucasian, with a powerful build. He wore a full camouflage suit, insulated for cold weather, the kind of clothing worn when stalking rather than hunting from a blind. His boots were Danner, expensive but well worn. His rifle was a Marlin 336C, a common make, popular for hunting deer. It was scoped with a Leupold, which was what Cork, when rifle hunting, usually mounted on his own Remington. Cork bent close to the crusted eye socket and studied the entry wound. Probably the hunter had died instantly, or almost so. And, probably, he'd been caught by surprise, otherwise, considering the Marlin, he'd have had the advantage. Cork wished he knew if the hunter had been murdered before Jubal Little or after, and how the two killings were connected, because it was clear that they were. The fletching on the arrow that had killed the man was the same pattern Cork used on his own arrows, the same as on the arrow that had killed Jubal Little.

Cork would have loved to have been able to go through the hunter's pockets for a clue to his identity, but he knew better. He would have to wait, maybe hours, before the crime scene team from the Tamarack County Sheriff's Department made another visit to that remote location. He couldn't begin to imagine what Marsha Dross and Ed Larson and the BCA people would make of this. Hell, he had no idea what to make of it himself.

He was about to see if he could track the route of the hunter's approach, hoping that he might be able to determine if the killer had stalked him there, when movement at the base of Trickster's Point caught his eye. Cork knelt quickly to hide himself and watched as a figure slowly circled the great pinnacle. It was a man, he was pretty sure, although he couldn't be entirely certain because the head was down and the face hidden beneath the bill of a cap. The figure wore a blaze orange vest, a wise precaution during hunting season in order not to be mistaken for a deer. Every so often, he would pause and bend and scrutinize the ground, then move slowly on. He spent a good deal of time at the place where Jubal Little had breathed his last, then his eyes seemed to follow an invisible line that led to the base of the ridge. Cork laid himself fully on the ground and continued his vigil.

The man walked to the ridge and began to ascend, but gradually. He spent a while in the small natural box that Stephen had discovered and that Cork was certain Jubal Little's murderer had used. He continued to climb, pausing in the same places Cork had paused when he'd found the displaced stones and the boot print. He crested the ridge and studied the ground, just as Cork and Stephen had, then he eyed the aspens, went to the breach in the gold wall of captured leaves, and followed the trail. Cork finally stood up and moved to block his way before he entered the tiny clearing.

The man looked up, startled.

"Who are you?" Cork demanded.

"Officer John Berglund. U.S. Border Patrol." He reached inside his vest and brought out ID. "Who are you?"

"Cork O'Connor."

Berglund, who'd looked grim and official until then, smiled, as if the name was not unfamiliar to him. He appeared to be in his late fifties, medium height and weight, black-rimmed glasses, a friendly face. But there was something penetrating about his eyes, as if he knew things about you that you'd rather nobody knew. He offered his hand.

Cork hesitated in accepting the offer. "What are you doing here?"

"Sheriff Dross asked me to come out and look things over."

That explained a good deal. In law enforcement circles, the agents of the Border Patrol were legendary for their tracking ability. Cork finally shook the man's hand, but by then Berglund was more interested in the dead guy at Cork's back.

"What's going on?" the agent asked. It was a true question, no hint of an accusation.

"Found him here like this," Cork replied.

Berglund walked to the corpse, knelt, and while he studied it, said, "I saw evidence of several people climbing that ridge. I imagine you were one of them."

"And my son," Cork replied. "When we found the body, I sent him back to call the sheriff's department."

"This man's been dead quite a while. Think he came up the ridge, too?"

"My guess would be no."

"What, then? A hunter who found himself at the wrong place at the wrong time?"

"If he's a hunter," Cork said, "where's his blaze orange?"

Minnesota law required that anyone not hunting from a stand wear blaze orange clothing above the waist as a safety precaution.

Berglund thought a moment. "Maybe already got his limit and was poaching?"

"Maybe. What exactly did Sheriff Dross ask you to do?"

Berglund stood up and scanned the ground around him. "Pretty much the same thing you're probably here to do. She said she believed you weren't responsible for Little's death, and she wanted me to see if I could find any trace of someone else out here, someone you wouldn't necessarily have seen. She said she thought her people had done a good job with the crime scene itself, but she wanted me to look a little farther afield."

Marsha, God bless her, Cork thought.

Berglund began to walk slowly to the east, moving among the aspens, following the crown of the ridge, eyes sweeping earth covered with aspen leaves that had fallen in the weeks before and were soggy from the rain. He went out about fifty yards, then returned.

"Two men came in this way," he said. "Only one went back."

"Did they come together?"

"Can't tell."

"Think you can follow the trail far enough to figure out how they approached Trickster's Point?"

"As I understand it, there's just the one Forest Service trail, and that's the one I took from the trailhead back at the county road. Saw evidence of foot traffic along the way, but nothing that appeared recent. How'd you get here?"

"Canoed across the lake. It's the shortest route."

Berglund nodded. "We might be able to assume that this man and whoever killed him both approached the area in a way that assured they wouldn't be seen."

"Can you confirm it?"

Berglund considered. "I guess I can try. You want in on this?"

Cork shook his head. "I'm going to stay with the body, make sure it isn't disturbed."

Berglund shrugged as if to say "Whatever," turned his back, and began to move east along the ridge crown, his nose aimed toward the ground like that of a bloodhound.

Once again, Cork was left alone with the dead and in spitting distance of Trickster's Point.

The first time he'd been in that situation, he was just shy of seventeen. Not much older than Stephen was now.

It was early October, deep into football season. The Aurora High Wolves were at the top of their division that year, taken there mostly by the strong arm and reliable leadership of Jubal Little. Talk of a state title was on everyone's lips. But no team is built entirely on one man, and that year there were several fine players, among them Cork O'Connor, who was a junior and played end, and Donner Bigby—Bigs—in his senior year, at fullback. Between Jubal and Bigs there was no love lost. Since that first meeting in Grant Park when Jubal had stepped in to thwart Bigby's cruelty toward Willie Crane, there'd been a kind of charge building between them, like a summer storm you knew was on the way, inevitable, and even though it was still beyond the horizon, you could feel the buzz of the electricity everywhere around you. On the football field, Jubal was all business and didn't appear to let his own feelings toward Bigs get in the way of what was best for the team. Bigs wasn't so magnanimous; when a pass went awry or a play call was questionable, he was given to deriding his quarterback. If Donner Bigby hadn't been an unstoppable locomotive in the backfield, his mouth might have got him benched for much of the season.

The homecoming game that year was against the Virginia

High School Blue Devils, a team whose win record was only one game back of Aurora's. It was played in a downpour, on a field that was more mud than grass. The wet conditions seriously hampered both Jubal's accuracy in passing and his receivers' ability to hold on to the ball. So the game was played mostly on the ground and was dominated by the rhino charges of Donner Bigby. As the fourth quarter neared its end, the score was tied at 13–13. The Blue Devils had the ball and had pushed deep into Wolves territory. The drive stalled on the twenty-two-yard line, and the Blue Devils lined up for a field goal attempt. The kick went wide to the right. All that remained was for the Wolves to run out the clock—five or six running plays, or three and a good long punt—and the game would end in a tie, with Aurora's lead in the division secure.

In the huddle, Jubal Little called a fullback sweep right. The play was good for a short gain. He called a gut left. Bigs plowed ahead for four yards on that one. The team huddled. Their jerseys, once a glorious white and gold, were the color of pig slop and hung wet and heavy against their pads. Their bare legs and arms were so mud-crusted that you couldn't see the color of their skin or the bruising there. The air was chill, and their huffed breaths clouded the center of the circle that their bodies, shoulder pad against shoulder pad, had formed.

Jubal looked them over. His eyes were the color of his muddied uniform, and the whites of them, under the glare of the field lights, seemed to glow. He said, "You want to settle for a tie? Or do you want to beat these bastards?"

"I want to grind their nuts under my cleats," Bigs said without hesitation. "Just give me the ball."

"We all together on this?" Jubal asked his teammates.

"Yeah," they said and "You bet."

Jubal's eyes fell on Cork. "If I get it to you, can you hold on to it?"

"What are you doing?" Bigby said.

Cork's heart was stomping around in his chest, and he

couldn't swallow, nor could he speak. But he could still move, and he gave Jubal a decisive nod.

"Little, I'm telling you—" Bigs began.

"Ends, five and out. Quick right fake, on two," Jubal called. "Let's go."

They broke from the huddle. Cork saw the Blue Devils crowding the line of scrimmage, expecting a run, but their safeties were in a prevent formation, defending against the long pass. The area between, as Jubal had probably expected, was wide open. Cork set himself on the line, drier of mouth than he'd ever remembered. Jubal crouched under center and called out the count. The ball was snapped, and Cork gave a quick head fake to the end who guarded him, then broke toward the sideline. He looked back over his right shoulder, just in time to see the ball spiral toward him with a grace he would never forget. He opened his palms like cradles, and then it was in his hands, and he wrapped his arms around it and locked it against his chest and turned upfield. He saw the two safeties moving to intercept him and could sense, galloping hard at his back, the end who, for a fateful fraction of a second, had bought Cork's feint. Cork ran as he'd never run before. At midfield, the nearest safety angled toward him, and Cork veered straight at the kid. An instant before they collided, he danced right and spun and shed the arm tackle, and ran on. At the thirty-yard line, he heard a grunt as the end behind him launched himself in a last, desperate effort to grasp an ankle. Cork stumbled but didn't go down. He saw the goal line, twenty yards ahead, and the second safety running an arc that would cut him off well before he scored. There was no feeling left in his legs, no strength. He ran on wooden stumps that barely supported him and that had no trickery left in them at all. He would, he knew absolutely, come up short.

And then a figure flew past him, fleet as a deer or the dream of a deer, and a mud-covered body threw a block that toppled the Blue Devil safety, and Cork loped untouched across the goal line, and the game was theirs.

He turned in the end zone and watched Jubal Little disentangle himself from the safety and rise, exhausted. Across a ground as brutalized as a battlefield, their eyes met.

In his life so far, Cork had never known a finer moment. And in that moment, he thought that he would never know a better friend.

The trouble began at the homecoming dance on Saturday night.

The music for the dance was provided by a group who called themselves the Wild Savages. It was Willie Crane's idea and his energy that had brought the group together; Winona provided most of the vocals. Willie played lead guitar and Indian flute. Two other guys from the rez—Andy Desjarlais and Greg "Hoops" LeBeau, playing bass guitar and drums, respectively—completed the ensemble. They did covers of recent tunes—"Good Lovin'," "Hanky Panky," "Surfer Girl," "Hang on Sloopy"—but they also slipped in some of their own compositions, which tended to rely heavily on Willie's flute playing and the driving beat of Hoops's drums, so that an Ojibwe sensibility came through clearly. In the North Country of Minnesota, the Wild Savages had a following and had become a popular choice for school dances.

The dance was held in the high school gymnasium and was a pretty good affair, especially because praise continued to rain down on Cork for winning the game the night before. He knew it hadn't been just him; it was Jubal's calling of the play and it was Jubal's delivery of the ball that had made the difference. But Jubal was content to step aside and let Cork shine in the spotlight. Which was the kind of thing Jubal often did, and not just for Cork. He generously gave away the glory others desperately dreamed of having and shamefully coveted. The reason may have been that glory came to him so easily; but Cork chose to see something Ojibwe in his best friend's behavior. His generosity of spirit was the kind valued by Henry Meloux and Sam

Winter Moon, and Cork believed that, although Jubal wouldn't admit it, more and more he was acknowledging and embracing the Indian side of his heritage.

Donner Bigby came late to the dance and with the smell of alcohol on his breath. He brought a date, Gloria Agostino, who'd graduated a year before and worked in the office of the logging operation Bigby's father owned and who had always had a slightly tarnished reputation. At ten o'clock, the Wild Savages took a break and everyone left the dance floor and hit the long tables where there were cookies and punch. To the dance, Jubal had brought Judy Petermann, a cheerleader, a sweet girl with the kindest smile imaginable. She was clearly taken with him—what girl wouldn't be?—but Jubal, though polite, didn't seem especially interested. Girls fell all over him, yet Jubal didn't seem to notice anyone in particular. Cork had come to the dance stag. Lately, he'd been dating Winona Crane, something his mother wasn't particularly happy about. Winona had a reputation. But for Cork, who'd loved her forever, it was like finally reaching the promised land. He didn't delude himself. He understood Winona didn't feel about him the same way, but—he knew this was pathetic—he was willing to take whatever she offered him.

Jubal left Judy Petermann in the gymnasium talking with one of her friends and drinking punch while he and Cork went to the restroom. In an alcove off the hallway, they found Winona and Willie, cooling themselves in the breeze that blew from an opened exit door. Winona was just downing something from the palm of her hand, which she chased with a quick swig from a bottle of Coca-Cola. She smiled at them, her dark eyes incandescent.

"Great game yesterday," Willie told Cork, though it came from his mouth sounding more like *gray game yeday*.

Cork said, "Thanks, Willie."

"You were amazing," Winona said and gave his shoulder a gentle punch.

Which was a sisterly gesture from a young woman Cork

still hoped might someday see him differently. Since those days when he and Willie and Winona used to hit Sam's Place after school, Winona had changed a good deal. She'd grown more striking in her beauty, but she seemed more and more to be riding a self-destructive current, which was not unusual for Ojibwe youth raised on the rez. Cork was afraid for her, but he had no real way of influencing her differently. Even Willie, who despite all his own hardship, did his best to protect her, had told Cork he felt helpless most of the time. Winona did what Winona wanted to do. That's all there was to it.

Jubal leaned easily against the wall beside her, grinned, and said, "That's my man."

Winona glanced at Jubal, and then her gaze jumped away, as if she couldn't look long on that too handsome face. "You were pretty good yourself," she said to him, though her words seemed to be addressed to the floor.

It was the dance Jubal Little and Winona Crane had been doing for years. Those times they were together, the electricity between them crackled. Yet they both seemed intent on keeping their meetings to a minimum. To Cork, it appeared as if they were both terribly afraid—not of each other but of what might be created if they ever allowed themselves to touch. He loved Jubal and he loved Winona and he hated that attraction, which was so obvious between them.

"Fuck you" came another voice, this one from outside the open door. A moment later, Donner Bigby stepped in from the night. Behind him, but still in the dark beyond the door, stood Gloria. "Fuck you both. I was the one who got us there."

Jubal pushed from the wall and turned to Bigby, who held a small silver flask in his hand. "We got there as a team, Bigs."

"You got there on my back. Then O'Connor makes one play, and he's the big hero," Bigby responded. He gave Cork a killing look.

"You won," Winona said. "Isn't that what's important?"

"Who asked you, bitch?"

"Don't call her that," Willie said.

"*Doan caw her at*," Bigby mimicked.

"Just leave," Jubal suggested evenly.

"Fuck if I will."

Cork stepped next to Jubal, and together they filled the alcove as they faced Bigby. At that same moment, Mr. Hildebrandt passed along the main hallway. He taught English and was the assistant football coach and one of the chaperones at the dance. He was big and broad, a lot of power and authority contained in his frame. He glanced into the alcove, took in the body language of Cork and Jubal and Bigby, and must have understood immediately what was going on. He approached them.

"What're you drinking there, Donner?" he asked.

"Nothing," Bigby said and slipped the flask into his back pocket.

Hildebrandt nodded, considered all the young people in the alcove, then said, "Why don't you go on home, Donner?"

"I don't want to go," Bigby snapped.

In the face of the kid's anger, Hildebrandt brought out his coach's voice. "Go home, Donner," he ordered. "Go home now."

"Fuck you."

"What did you say? No, don't repeat it. Bigby, you're out of here. And don't bother suiting up for practice on Monday. Men like you I don't need playing for me."

Bigby looked as if he was contemplating taking a swing at his former coach. Then his eyes, burning through a thin alcoholic haze, passed over Cork and Jubal and Willie and finally Winona, and he didn't have to say what he was thinking. He turned and rejoined Gloria outside, and as they vanished into the night, Cork heard him say, "Let's blow this shithole."

When they were gone, Hildebrandt breathed deeply and nodded as if he'd simply finished a rational discussion in which a rational decision had been reached and said, as if nothing extraordinary had just transpired, "Winona, Willie, you guys are great up there. Love the music." He headed back to the gymnasium.

The alcove was silent for a long moment afterward, then Jubal shrugged. "Guess that's that."

"You think so?" Winona said. Her eyes were focused beyond the open door, as if she knew absolutely that the darkness there hid demons.

What happened later that night, Cork didn't learn about until the next morning. He was at the breakfast table in the kitchen, dressed for Mass at St. Agnes and working on a bowl of Wheaties, when a knock came at the front door. He found Deputy Cy Borkman standing on the porch, hat in hand.

"Your mom home, Cork?" the deputy asked.

"No, she's already gone to church, Cy. What is it?"

"Well, it's really you I want to see. Mind if I come in?"

They sat in the living room, and Borkman told him about Winona Crane. She and her brother had been packing up their equipment after the dance. By then, the only vehicles left in the school parking lot were the janitor's station wagon and the Cranes' old pickup. They had almost everything stowed in the bed of the truck when Willie remembered that he'd left his hat, a fine black Stetson with a band that Winona had braided for him and that was adorned with an eagle feather, an item sacred to the Anishinaabeg. He went back into the building. The hallways were mostly dark by then. Willie made his way to the gymnasium, but the lights were off, and he couldn't see well enough to locate his hat. He went in search of Mr. Guerrero, the janitor, whom he found in the basement, adjusting the furnace for the night. Together they returned to the gym and located the hat, which was under the bleachers and, to Willie's great dismay, had been stomped flat. The braided band had been ripped into pieces, and the eagle feather was gone. Mr. Guerrero was sympathetic but needed to close up, and he accompanied Willie to the school door. Ruined hat in hand, Willie crossed the parking lot to the truck where he'd left his sister. But Winona wasn't there.

Willie called for her and got no answer. He made his way back to the school as quickly as his awkward legs would carry him, and he pounded on the door until Mr. Guerrero opened up again. Then he explained his situation. Mr. Guerrero went to his station wagon and took a flashlight from the glove box, and together he and Willie began to search the grounds.

They found her lying on the torn and muddy football field, found her because they heard her crying. When Mr. Guerrero shone his light on her, they saw that she'd been beaten. They saw something else in that hard circle of light, something that Deputy Borkman refrained from mentioning but that Cork heard about later. Winona, that night, had dressed in a denim skirt whose hemline she'd embroidered herself with clan images: a bear, a crane, a loon, an eagle, and others. When her brother and Mr. Guerrero found her, she no longer wore the skirt.

"Did she see who did it?" Cork asked, his gut gone hard as a fist.

Borkman shook his head. "Too dark. And she was attacked from behind. Whoever did it hit her several times, and she doesn't remember much after that."

"You know who did it," Cork said.

"No, son, we don't. Do you?"

"Donner Bigby," Cork said.

"His name's been mentioned," Borkman acknowledged. "And that's what I wanted to talk to you about. We understand there was some kind of altercation at the dance last night and that you were involved."

"Nothing happened," Cork said. "Except Bigs got thrown out of the dance. You should talk to Mr. Hildebrandt about that."

"We have. You didn't see Donner Bigby come back to the dance?"

"No, but that doesn't mean he wasn't lurking around somewhere."

"Gloria Agostino says he wasn't. She says they left the school grounds and Donner was with her until well after one o'clock."

"She's lying."

"That's what we're trying to find out here, Cork."

"It was Bigs," Cork said angrily.

"Careful there," Borkman said. "We don't want to go accusing anyone without proof. After he left the dance, you didn't see Donner Bigby again last night?"

"No."

"Ken Hildebrandt told us that Winona Crane was involved in the altercation with Bigby. Is that correct?"

"Yeah."

"Did Bigby make any threats against her?"

"Not directly, but she was scared."

"Scared of what?"

"That he might do something."

"Because of something he said?"

"No, he's just that kind of guy."

"Did he make threats against anyone?"

Cork thought back and couldn't remember Bigs saying anything that was actually threatening. "He called Winona a bitch."

"But he didn't threaten her, or anyone else?"

Cork was forced to shake his head no.

Borkman stood up. "All right, Cork. Thanks for your help."

"What are you going to do now?"

"I've got a few more people I'm supposed to talk to. The sheriff's out interviewing people, too. We'll get to the bottom of this, I promise."

After the deputy left, Cork called Jubal's house. No answer. He ran upstairs, changed his clothes, wrote a note to his mother explaining that something had come up and he'd miss dinner and not to worry about him. He was just opening the front door when Jubal pulled up in his mother's rusted Pontiac. He got out and met Cork on the sidewalk.

"You hear?" he asked.

"Yeah. A deputy was just here."

"The sheriff himself came to my house," Jubal said. "I told him it was Donner. He said Donner had an alibi."

"Gloria Agostino."

"I told him she was lying," Jubal said.

"Did he believe you?"

"Who knows? But I'm not waiting. I'm going to find Bigby now."

"I'm going with you," Cork said.

They piled into the Pontiac and headed to Donner Bigby's house, which was a mile or so outside of town on the Old Soudan Road. It was a big place, perched on a slight hill, surrounded by woods. There were a couple of ceramic deer in the front yard and a nice flower bed that had already been cleared down to the topsoil in preparation for winter. Bigby's mother opened the door. She was older than the mothers of most of Cork's friends. She looked frail and worried and wary.

Jubal took the lead and lied his ass off, telling the woman that they were Donner's friends from school, and they were trying to put together a game of touch football at Grant Park that afternoon. She seemed relieved and told him that Donner was gone.

"Rock climbing," she said.

"That's right." Jubal nodded as if he should have known. "He's a Crag Rat." That was an organization in Aurora made up of guys who liked to climb. Bigs aside, they were an okay bunch.

"You don't happen to know where he's climbing," Jubal said, smooth as ice cream.

"Someplace that sounds like . . ." She thought a moment. "Tracker's Point, I think."

"Trickster's Point?" Cork said.

"Yes, that's it."

"Thank you, ma'am," Jubal said with a parting smile.

They went back to the Pontiac, and Cork said, "She didn't seem so bad. Bigs must've got all his asshole genes from his old man."

The day was sunny and warm, and the air was heavy with moisture that still lingered from the storm two days earlier. They went in the long way, hiking five miles on the trail off the county road. There was only one car parked at the trailhead, and they both recognized the silver Karmann Ghia that Bigby had been driving since he got it as a present on his sixteenth birthday. They double-timed it along the trail, where Cork saw boot prints that had been left not long before. They arrived at Trickster's Point to find Bigby already halfway up the formation, working without the aid of ropes or pitons, in the full light of the sun, which had climbed nearly straight overhead. They had to shade their eyes against the glare when they looked up at him and hollered his name.

Bigby secured his position with both feet and the firm grip of his right hand, then hung out a bit from the rock and looked down at them with a shit-eating grin.

"What do you know? It's Chip and Dale. Looking for acorns?"

"Looking for you, you son of a bitch," Cork spit out.

Bigby shrugged. "Found me. Now what?"

"Now you come down, and we talk about Winona."

"Winona? The squaw girl? Why talk about her?"

"You know why," Cork said. "Come on down. Or is it just girls you like to beat on?"

"Whoa, O'Connor. How about you come up here and we talk."

"All right."

Cork started for the rock, but Jubal held him back.

"You ever climb before?" he asked Cork.

"No."

"Then I'm going up."

"Do you know how to climb?"

"No. But I'm better at it than you."

Which was probably true. Jubal was better at everything. Still, it stung.

"You stay here," Jubal said.

"And do what?"

"If I chase him down off there, I don't want him running away." He looked up, as if contemplating the difficulty of the task ahead. "And if I fall, you think he's going to go get help? I need you down here."

Without waiting to confer further, Jubal stepped up to the rugged face of Trickster's Point and began to climb after Donner Bigby.

CHAPTER 12

Jubal was a spider, nimble on the rock. He climbed with a swiftness that astonished Cork, and Bigby was clearly alarmed. The big kid turned back to his own task and continued up the face of Trickster's Point, heading for the top, which was still a good seventy feet above him. Jubal relentlessly closed the gap between them, and by the time Bigby had topped the monolith, fifteen minutes later, Jubal was only a dozen feet below him. Bigby stood and caught the full light of the sun, and bright yellow flickered all over his body as if he were electric or on fire. He bent over the edge of the rock and called down to Jubal, "Gee, Little, it'd be a shame if you lost your grip and fell."

"You let him come up there," Cork hollered.

Bigby laughed. "Or what?"

Cork shielded his eyes against the midday sun and watched helplessly as Jubal approached the top with Bigby towering above him, showing his teeth in a kind of hungry grin. Cork was truly afraid that when Jubal's hands made their final reach, Bigby would stomp on them and send Jubal plummeting. He was furious with himself for not going up along with his best friend or going up in his stead. He felt twisted and helpless watching from the ground as the drama played out a hundred and fifty feet above him.

Bigby finally stepped back and disappeared from Cork's view.

Jubal crawled onto the flat crown of Trickster's Point unimpeded, and he, too, was lost from sight. Cork became aware again of the oppressive humidity of the day. Each breath felt heavy in his lungs, and his nostrils seemed clogged with the dank smell of wet earth. He realized that a deep stillness had fallen over the area. There wasn't a whisper of wind or the call of a single bird, and above him came no sound from the two kids facing off atop the great pillar.

"Jubal! Bigs! What's going on?"

The minutes passed, and Cork's concern grew. He remembered advice Sam Winter Moon had given him about hunting. "The most important skill of all, and the most difficult to master, is patience." Why hadn't they been patient? They could simply have waited on the ground, because Donner Bigby would have had to come down sometime. Cork knew the answer. Anger. It had clouded all their thinking. He looked up, unable to swallow and barely able to breathe.

That's when he heard the sound, one that made his blood turn to ice. From the top of Trickster's Point, but from the far side, came a brief, terrible scream. It hit the stillness like a rock might hit a big lake, with only a moment's impression, then it was gone and what was left was simply the vast stillness.

"Jubal?" Cork cried toward the sky. "Jubal?"

He received no answer. He thought for a second of climbing Trickster's Point but had no idea what good that would do. Instead, he ran around the base of the formation, toward the side from which the scream had come.

The body lay on its back, bent at an abnormally acute angle across a rock slab that had, ages ago, splintered from the flank of the pillar and toppled to the earth. The sight stopped Cork instantly. His legs, for a moment, refused to move him forward, and his brain refused to believe the image his eyes delivered to it. Slowly he lifted his gaze and saw, high above, a head and shoulders, silhouetted against the sun as they bent over the edge of the pillar's crown to face the scene on the ground below.

Cork finally willed himself forward.

Donner Bigby's eyes were wide open and his mouth, too, as if he was looking up at something that absolutely astonished him. Cork stared at the body, searching for any movement of those eyes, for any faint rise and fall of the massive chest, for any sign, no matter how feeble, that there might still be life in Donner Bigby. He knew he should touch Bigby, check for a pulse, speak to him, but he couldn't bring himself to do any of those things.

He glanced back up and saw that Jubal was easing his way over the lip at the top of Trickster's Point. Jubal moved more slowly, more carefully than he had when ascending. Cork figured that might have been because coming down was harder, but he also thought the reason could simply have been that Jubal was in no hurry to face what awaited him at the bottom. Knowing it would be quite a while before Jubal joined him, Cork finally forced himself to do what duty demanded.

He leaned close, and his shadow fell over the kid's face. "Donner? Can you hear me?" He gingerly touched Bigby's neck with his fingertips, feeling for even a ghost of a pulse. He laid his ear against Bigby's chest. Nothing came to him, except the smell of Bigby's emptied bowels. Cork stood and moved far enough away that he couldn't smell the stench of death.

The full weight of the situation fell on him, and his legs would no longer hold him up. He dropped into a sitting position on the wet ground and went, for a little while, into a kind of daze.

"Cork?" It was Jubal's voice cutting through the haze.

Cork snapped back to the terrible reality of the moment.

"You okay?" Jubal asked.

"He's dead."

Jubal's face was ghost white, and he sat down heavily beside Cork. "I know."

"What happened?"

Jubal was quiet a long time, and the voice that finally spoke was smaller than Cork had ever heard from his friend. "He stumbled. He just stumbled and fell."

Cork tried to look into Jubal's eyes, to find some clue there about the truth of that explanation, but Jubal averted his face.

"I want to know everything," Cork said.

"There's nothing to know," Jubal insisted, almost desperately. "I accused him of what happened to Winona. He didn't deny it, just told me to go fuck myself."

"And then he . . . just fell?"

"He swung at me. He started it. So I swung at him. Next thing I know, he's stumbling back and falling. It was an accident, I swear. Cork, we've got to figure out what we're going to say about this."

"What do you mean?"

"We both have to tell the same story."

"It was an accident. We just tell them that."

Jubal shook his head furiously. "We can't tell anyone I went up there with him. Who's going to believe that I didn't intentionally push him?"

"You didn't, did you?"

"Of course not. But nobody's going to believe me. I'm an Indian. That'll come out now. Think white people are going to take an Indian's side in something like this?"

"You're Jubal Little," Cork said, amazed that his friend had no idea how much weight that carried.

"Jubal Littlewolf. With a father in prison for manslaughter. Like father, like son. That's how they'll play it." He took Cork by the shoulders and leaned toward him until their faces were only inches apart. "You're my brother. I'm counting on you."

A breeze had finally come up, cooling against his face. Cork was suddenly deeply aware of how much he loved his friend. He had a choice. He could believe Jubal or not. If he believed him, there was only one thing he could do.

"What do we tell them?" he said.

CHAPTER 13

Phillip Holter, the agent in charge of the BCA team that had been sent to help with the investigation of Jubal Little's death, was a tall, good-looking guy somewhere in his forties. He had a build that made it clear he and a barbell were intimate friends. His hair was black and thick and held in place with a shellacking of mousse. He wore stylish glasses that had no framing around the lenses, so there was nothing to detract from one's view and appreciation of his deep baby blues. His gaze was studied; he seemed never to blink. There was a crispness in his actions and in the way he spoke that suggested he was a man who knew his abilities and was pretty sure others appreciated them as much as he did. Cork took an immediate dislike to him, a rare experience in all his own years as a cop, but he figured he'd take a dislike to anyone who eyed him as if he were the Son of Sam.

They interviewed Cork and Stephen separately. Holter took the father, and Ed Larson questioned the son. Under the circumstances, Cork couldn't very well insist that he be with Stephen while Larson conducted that interview, but he wasn't greatly concerned. The truth that Stephen would tell—and that Cork told as well—didn't incriminate either of them. This most recent body, they'd simply stumbled upon. When Holter pointed out that the arrow was identical to the one that had killed Jubal Little and also to the arrows Cork had carried in his own quiver, Cork simply replied, "If they are my arrows, then it would be just as easy to steal two as one. Same thing would be true if someone decided to manufacture an arrow identical to mine."

Cork and Stephen stood well out of the way while the crime scene techs—deputies whom Larson had sent to the BCA for special training—did their jobs. The dead man's wallet had yielded a driver's license bearing the name William Graham Chester, a resident of Red Wing, Minnesota. When he was asked, Cork replied that the name meant nothing to him and reiterated that he'd never seen the man before. A search of the area offered no other immediate evidence, except for the tracks that the officer from the Border Patrol had been following when he left.

After a while, among the bare aspen trees, Holter convened a conference with Sheriff Dross and Captain Ed Larson. In the time since her discussion with Cork that morning, Dross had changed into her uniform, over which she wore a yellow down vest. Though the day continued to threaten precipitation, she sported no hat on her short hair, which was the brown of otter fur.

"What do you think they're talking about?" Stephen asked.

"They're probably trying to figure what all this has to do with Jubal Little's killing."

"Are the two definitely related?"

"What do you think?" Cork asked. It wasn't rhetorical.

Stephen said, "That's what I was thinking about all the way to Allouette. It could have been that, whoever he was, he was just at the wrong place at the wrong time. But the more I thought about that, it just seemed too big a coincidence."

"I think you're right."

"So if they're related, how?"

Cork had been watching the three cops in discussion. Holter had said something that caused Larson to look in Cork's direction and furiously shake his head.

"Any speculation?" Cork asked his son.

Stephen seemed surprised to be asked, and he furrowed his brow for a while before he answered.

"It might make sense that they were in on it together and something went bad between them up here."

"In on it together?"

"Like, well, they wanted to be sure that Mr. Little was dead, and they meant to do it in a way that would throw the blame on you. So the arrow. But you've always talked about how hard it is to hit a moving target, especially from a distance, so they brought the rifle along, too, as sort of backup. If the arrow missed, they were going to shoot Mr. Little with the rifle."

Cork smiled at the beauty of the logic, which was different from his own, and better. He'd been thinking that it was two separate men with two separate agendas, but he couldn't quite put it together in an understandable way. Stephen's scenario, on the other hand, made good sense.

Stephen was almost as tall as his father, and he looked almost directly into his father's eyes as he went on. "But if the first plan didn't work, and they couldn't pin the murder on you, then . . ." He faltered. Traditionally, the Ojibwe were a people who ably hid their emotions behind a stolid mask, and Stephen was the O'Connor in whom the Ojibwe blood was most apparent. But he didn't bother to try to hide his horror. "If they hadn't killed Mr. Little with the arrow and had to shoot him, they'd probably have to get rid of the only witness. So you'd be dead, too."

Cork put a reassuring hand on his son's shoulder. "But I'm not dead." He nodded toward the great stone monolith that stood dark against the gray sky. "Nanaboozhoo, that old trickster, must have something else in mind for me."

"It's not funny, Dad."

"I wasn't trying to be funny, Stephen. I've always believed that things happen for a reason, and the reason is always part of some greater design. And so the question here is, What's the big picture?"

"You sound like Henry Meloux."

"I'll take that as a compliment. And the question still stands."

Cork spotted a lone figure threading his way among the

aspens on the crown of the ridge, and he quickly recognized John Berglund. Dross saw the officer, too, said something to Holter and Larson, and they all turned to watch him come.

Cork said to Stephen, "Let's mosey over and see what he has to say."

No one tried to stop them as they crossed the ridgetop, and they reached the sheriff and other officers just as Berglund arrived.

"Agent Berglund, I'm Agent Holter, BCA." Holter extended his hand. "This is Captain Ed Larson. Sheriff Dross, of course, you know. She's already filled us in."

Berglund shook hands around and gave Cork a nod in acknowledgment. Then he asked Holter, "Any idea who he is?"

"Driver's license says he's William Graham Chester, from Red Wing," Holter replied. "That's all we know at the moment."

"What did you find, John?" Dross asked.

"Two sets of tracks. They came from different directions, but their paths joined about a mile from here. One came from the lake, the other from an old logging road farther north. It's barely a road anymore, so overgrown you'd have trouble identifying it as such, and I couldn't find it on any of my maps. But a vehicle's parked there. My guess is that you'll find the keys to it somewhere on your dead man. When your people are ready, I'll be happy to show them where it is."

"Thank you," Larson said.

"One came from the lake?" Cork said. "Any sign of a canoe?"

"Gone, but I found where he'd beached it."

"So two came in, but only one left," Dross said.

They stood a moment, digesting the information.

Into that meditative silence Cork offered, "He looks like a hunter, but if he is, where's his blaze orange? Stephen believes he wasn't a hunter and that the guys were working together. The plan was to kill Jubal and make it look like I'd done it. But killing someone with a bow is pretty risky, so our guy on the ground over there was backup. If the arrow failed, Jubal Little would have been shot to death. And probably me along with him, to eliminate the witness."

Holter chewed on that a bit, then asked, "Okay. If they were in on it together, why is one of them lying there dead?"

"They had a falling-out," Stephen offered, but not boldly, clearly not prepared to defend his thesis.

Dross nodded, as if giving Stephen's speculation due consideration. Then she said, "Maybe there's another possibility, Stephen. What's the best way for two people to keep a secret?"

The young man thought a moment, then the light dawned. "If one of them is dead."

"Exactly," Dross said. "Maybe our killer simply eliminated the only man who could finger him."

"But who were they, and why would they want Mr. Little dead?"

"That's for us to figure out," Holter said, tersely drawing the discussion to a close. "Mr. O'Connor, I think your usefulness here, and that of your son, is at an end. You're free to go. I'm sure we'll have further questions, however, so please make yourself available."

Ed Larson had been staring at Trickster's Point, as if the great pillar held him hypnotized. Before either Cork or Stephen could move to leave, he asked, "Who chose this site for your hunting outing?" His voice was a little distant, as if he was daydreaming or maybe just very deep in thought.

Cork said, "Jubal did."

"Did anyone else know you were coming here?"

As if it should have been dismally obvious, Holter said, "Anyone who reads a newspaper knew that Little planned to go hunting here with O'Connor."

Larson shook his head. "I spent last night reading the major newspaper stories following the election. They all reported Jubal Little's intention to come north to hunt with Cork, but nowhere in any of the stories was Trickster's Point mentioned specifically."

For a brief instant, Holter looked like a kid who'd blown his homework assignment, then he swung his unblinking blue eyes to Cork and said, as in accusation, "Well?"

"At the Broiler yesterday morning, a lot of folks drifted over to wish him luck and tell him they were going to vote for him," Cork said. "Jubal mentioned to a few of them where we'd be hunting."

"What about before that?" Larson said. "Because if the killing was planned, they probably had to know in advance where they would do it."

"I told my kids," Cork said. "Did you mention it to anyone, Stephen?"

"I told people you were going hunting with Mr. Little. I don't remember if I said where."

"I'll ask Jenny when I get back to Aurora," Cork promised.

"What about Jubal?" Larson asked. "Who did he tell?"

Cork shook his head. "No idea."

Larson again eyed the great monolith and asked, as if genuinely mystified, "Why Trickster's Point?"

"I don't know," Cork said, maybe too quickly.

"Do you always hunt here?" Holter asked.

"We never have before."

"Why not?"

"It's a risky choice," Cork replied.

"Risky? Why?"

So Cork explained to the BCA agent about Trickster's Point.

Long before white men came, the Ojibwe told stories about the strangenesses of the place. They believed it was full of prize bucks, because Nanaboozhoo protected them here. He caused hunters to become confused. Around Trickster's Point, the Ojibwe couldn't necessarily believe what their senses told them. They would get mixed up about directions and become hopelessly lost. Or worse. Ojibwe lore was rife with tales of hunters who swore they'd let an arrow fly at a huge buck only to discover that what they'd felled was one of their own, another hunter.

"The best trophy deer I've ever seen have come from around Lake Nanaboozhoo," Cork said. "But within my own lifetime, it's also been the site of several fatal hunting accidents. Without exception, the hunters involved—those who came forward and admitted their guilt—maintained that they were absolutely certain what they were shooting at was an enormous buck."

"Those who came forward?" Holter said.

Cork held out a hand toward Larson, who explained, "On two occasions within the last decade, a worried wife has reported that a husband had gone hunting around Trickster's Point and hadn't returned. Both times, we instituted a search operation, and both times we found the missing man lying somewhere in the woods out here. In both cases, the men were dead from gunshot wounds. No one admitted responsibility for those deaths."

"Compasses behave weird out here, and cell phones don't work either," Stephen offered.

Holter frowned. "Is that so?"

"People around here know the stories, and most of them who hunt opt to do it somewhere else," Cork said.

"Which brings me back to my original question," Larson said. "Why Trickster's Point? I'm guessing Little knew this area's reputation."

"I don't think he took the stories seriously," Cork said, knowing he wasn't really answering Larson's question.

"A modern Indian," Holter replied sensibly. "He didn't believe the mumbo jumbo."

"Mumbo jumbo?" Cork said.

"You know what I mean."

With every minute that passed, Cork was liking this man less and less.

"One thing I still don't understand," Holter went on. "Why did no one discover this body until you just happened to stumble over it?" Although he'd directed the question at Cork, his eyes shifted in an accusing way toward Captain Ed Larson, whose crime scene team had been responsible for what had—and in this case, hadn't—been found at Trickster's Point the day before.

Cork said, "This is way beyond the range of any bow hunter. There was no real reason to look up here."

"And yet you did," Holter said suggestively.

"I saw the trail; Ed's people didn't. But they're not trained in tracking."

Holter flashed a smile, entirely disingenuous. "You must be pretty good."

"I'm okay. There are others much better than me. Jubal Little, for one."

"Do I detect a little envy?"

"I discovered a long time ago that it was useless to be envious of Jubal. He was better than everyone at everything."

Holter studied him, and Cork wondered if the BCA agent was going to ask him a lot of questions about what had happened the day before, cover the same territory that had already been well covered by Larson and Dross. In the end, Holter simply said, "I think that's enough here. Mr. O'Connor, I'd appreciate it if you wouldn't discuss any of this with anyone. Either of you." He gave Stephen a good, stern look.

Cork could tell that his son was disappointed at being sent away, and probably a little upset by Holter's dismissive treatment of them. They made their way down the ridge slope to the base of Trickster's Point, where the vehicles from the sheriff's department were gathered, and where Stephen had parked the Land Rover.

"Mind driving us out?" Cork asked.

"Okay," Stephen said without enthusiasm.

The trail to Trickster's Point had been created for hikers and was narrow, so the going was slow. Bare tree branches and the branches of underbrush scraped the sides of the Land Rover with little screeches, as if protesting the presence of metal and rubber where only the passage of flesh and blood were allowed. Stephen was sullen and quiet. Cork wasn't sure if it was the general effect of all that had happened that day or if it was something more specific.

"Still pissed at Holter?" he finally asked his son.

"Not really. He doesn't know you. But I don't understand why the sheriff and Mr. Larson didn't stand up for you more. I mean, they're your friends."

"It's because of our friendship, Stephen. They don't want me to be arrested for Jubal's death any more than you do. And if they clear me, they've got to make absolutely certain that there are no questions about the integrity of their work or their team's work. Do you see?"

"I suppose," Stephen allowed, but he seemed to do it grudgingly.

They continued the rest of the way in silence, and Cork lost himself in thinking about the question Stephen had asked on the ridgetop but to which he'd received no answer: Who would want Jubal Little dead?

To Cork, the most obvious answer was Indians.

Minnesota, like most states, was in the midst of economic chaos. The budget was a mess of red ink. No one wanted new or higher taxes, but neither was anyone willing to sacrifice their sacred programs or projects. One of Jubal Little's proposals during his campaign was to build six state-run casinos in order to generate revenue that would be dedicated solely to public projects designed to put Minnesota's multitude of unemployed back to work. The populace was largely in favor of the idea; the Indians, of course, were not, and it was clear that they considered Jubal Little, née Littlewolf, half Blackfeet by blood, to be a traitor. He'd received threats but had defended his proposal as one approach whose benefit was broad and egalitarian, and whose ultimate purpose—which was not just about income and employment but also about funding a desperately needed upgrade of the state's entire crumbling infrastructure—was forward-looking. With regard to the Indian casinos, he maintained that the profits benefited only a small portion of the entire Native population and that, ultimately, state-run casinos would benefit everyone, including the Ojibwe, Lakota, and Dakota, because the income would generate thousands of public works jobs and the standard of living statewide would be raised. He'd laid it out with graphs and charts, but mostly he'd sold it with his oratory and his down-to-earth charm. Sold it to all but the Indians, who'd spent a good deal of money trying to ensure that Jubal Little wasn't elected, and who were prepared to spend a good deal more to see that his plan was never implemented. It would be far cheaper, Cork thought, simply to eliminate Jubal Little before he had a chance to get that particular ball rolling.

There were others who probably wouldn't mourn Jubal's passing. He'd run as an independent, so neither side of the political aisle would shed a tear. He'd pledged to tax the very rich, so they'd probably popped a champagne cork when they heard the news of his death. He'd indicated he was in favor of opening some of the wilderness areas of northern Minnesota to additional mineral exploration, a stand that had pissed off environmentalists but had won the hearts of many people on the Iron Range who'd seen nothing but economic hardship since the great mines there began shutting down operation years earlier.

The people Jubal scared he scared a lot, but they were a decided minority. He appealed to the masses, as populist a candidate as the state had ever seen. Cork's own feelings about his old friend had, over the years, become terribly mixed. But one thing seemed certain to him as he and his son negotiated the trail away from Trickster's Point. If Stephen was right and the dead hunter had been there to kill both men if the arrow failed to hit its mark, then Jubal Little, in dying, had saved Cork's life.

CHAPTER 14

They avoided the house on Gooseberry Lane and went straight to Sam's Place. Because it was Sunday and the weather was gray and the season was late, the parking lot was almost empty. Jenny's Subaru was parked beside Judy Madsen's Focus. The only other vehicle was a silver Escalade with tinted windows. A couple of kids in hooded sweatshirts were at one of the serving windows, but the coast looked clear of reporters. Stephen parked, and they got out and started toward the Quonset hut.

The door of the Escalade opened, and a tall, well-dressed black man built like a wedge of granite stepped out and moved to cut them off.

"Mr. O'Connor," he called in a deep, melodious voice.

Even if the guy turned out to be a reporter—though Cork had never seen reporters dressed so well or so well muscled or driving such an expensive set of wheels—Cork decided that, because there was only one, he'd talk to him, if only to say "No comment."

"Kenny Yates," the man said as he approached.

Which was a name Cork knew.

Yates offered a hand that greatly dwarfed Cork's. Although the grip was restrained, Cork sensed the immense power behind it.

"My son, Stephen," Cork said.

"How do you do?" Yates shook Stephen's hand politely, then

said to Cork, "Mrs. Little would like to see you. Her brothers are with her."

"At the lake house?"

"Yes."

"Give me a few minutes inside."

"Fine, I'll wait."

"No need. I know the way."

"I've been instructed to run interference for you, if necessary."

"The media?"

"Yes."

"All right. Hungry?"

The tall man studied the wooden placard on the side of Sam's Place that displayed the offerings. "Is the Sam's Super any good?"

"The best burger in the North Country," Stephen replied.

"I'll take two. And a chocolate shake."

Yates reached to the inside of his black leather jacket, probably for his wallet, and Cork said, "It's on me."

"Thanks." Yates's enormous hand dropped back to his side. "I'll wait here."

As they continued to the door, Stephen leaned to his father and whispered, "That guy looks like a football player."

"Used to be," Cork said. "Hit some hard times, I heard, and Jubal hired him for the personal security of his family a few years ago. This is the first I've ever met him in person."

Inside, they found everything quiet. Judy was playing with Waaboo, rolling a big plastic ball to him, which he rolled back with great delight. Madsen was a widow in her early sixties, a retired school administrator whom Cork had hired a couple of years earlier to help manage Sam's Place. She was smart and plain and good-natured, and did a fine job supervising the teenagers Cork employed every season. She opened Sam's Place every day except for weekends, but she almost never closed. She didn't like to be out late at night, so closing fell to Cork or Jenny or, in a pinch, to Stephen.

As soon as they walked in, Jenny came through the door from the serving area, and her worry was obvious on her face.

"We heard," she said. "Another body."

"Yeah." Although it was his daughter to whom he replied, it was his grandson who had Cork's eye.

"Hey, big man," Cork said and opened his arms.

"Baa-baa," Waaboo cried and ran to him.

Cork swept up the little body and nuzzled Waaboo's neck so that his grandson giggled wildly.

"Who was it?" Jenny asked.

"They're not sure yet," Stephen replied. "But we think he was partnered up with Mr. Little's killer."

"Partnered up?" Cork said.

"Well, you know what I mean."

Jenny looked at her father. "They don't think you did it, right?"

"I'm still the only game in town," Cork said. "And the agent in charge of the BCA team is on the ambitious side. Before this whole thing is finished, he may end up blaming me for the Lindbergh kidnapping, too."

"Dad, it's not funny."

"I know," he said. "Don't worry. At least for the moment."

Jenny gave her brother a motherly look of concern. "And you're okay?"

"It all feels pretty weird, but, yeah, I'm okay."

"Any trouble here?" Cork asked.

"Nothing we couldn't handle," Judy replied. With some effort, she pulled herself up from the floor, where she'd been sitting, and tucked the plastic ball under her arm. "A couple of persistent reporters. I told them to go screw themselves."

"And then," Jenny said, smiling, "she convinced them to buy burger baskets before they left. They didn't get any interviews, but they didn't go away hungry."

"I'll give Leon Papakee a call," Cork said to Jenny. "Ask him to run interference for us with the media. Any questions you get or any more persistent reporters, just direct them to Leon. If you'd like, I'll see if he can hang out with you today."

"No," Jenny said. "We'll be fine."

"I have to leave again." He kissed his grandson's cheek and handed him over to his mother. "I'm going to see Camilla Little."

"I wondered when she'd show up," Jenny said. "So you'll be a while?"

"Probably."

"Have you eaten lately?" Judy asked.

"Not since breakfast."

"How about a patty melt and some onion rings before you go?"

"Thanks. And we've got a customer out there needs a couple Sam's Supers and a chocolate shake."

"I'm on it." She turned to head to the grill.

"I'd kill for a cheeseburger," Stephen said. He suddenly looked stricken. "Sorry. I didn't mean that."

"It's still okay to have a sense of humor, buddy." Cork turned toward the door. "I'm going out to keep our guest company. Don't wait up for me."

Although he never stayed long when he came, Jubal Little still listed Tamarack County as his official place of residence. He had a home on Iron Lake. It stood on the shore of a small cove just north of Aurora, and had once been a nice log lodge and restaurant called The Wander Inn, where his mother had been employed when Jubal was a kid. In the long economic downturn that had beset the Iron Range as the mines closed, the place had struggled and finally closed, and the structure had become a derelict. Twenty years ago, Jubal had bought it and had it completely renovated and expanded into a log mansion, gorgeous but huge beyond any sensibility. In front was a circular drive paved with crushed limestone. When Cork pulled up, the drive was nearly full of vehicles. Cork parked in back of the last in line. Yates's Escalade drew up behind him, and Yates got out.

"Wake?" Cork asked, nodding toward the cars.

Yates shook his head. "Jubal's media people and campaign folks. They're all scrambling."

"Give me a minute," Cork said.

"Shouldn't be a problem. The Jaegers will want to speak with you alone anyway. I'll let them know you're here." Yates went ahead into the house.

Though it was not quite evening, the overcast had brought on an early, oppressive dark. Instead of going inside the huge home, Cork walked around to the back and down a long flagstone path across the lawn to the dock. The air was breathless, and the surface of the lake lay absolutely still and flat. The water was a deep gray stretching toward a dark horizon, and the effect of all this made Cork think of the lake as if it had somehow been set afire and had burned and all that was left was a great basin full of ash.

"Remembering all the times you spent with him here?"

Cork turned and watched Camilla Little cross the last of the flagstones and step onto the dock. She stood next to him, smelling of a subtle, expensive cologne and looking where he'd been looking. She was in her early forties, almost as tall as Jubal had been, a statuesque beauty with long blond hair, eyes the color of fresh mint leaves, and a flawless complexion. At the moment, however, her whole aspect was drawn and gray, her lovely face hollowed from grieving.

"I'm sorry about Jubal, Camilla."

"Really? I heard it was you who killed him."

"You don't believe that."

"No," she said. "Like everyone else, you loved him too much."

He couldn't tell if she was offering him sincerity or sarcasm.

"I'm sorry for your loss," Cork said, trying his best for honesty.

"Loss? The truth, and we both know it, is that he was never really mine."

"I'm sorry, Camilla." He sounded like a pathetic, broken record, but he was sorry, sorry for the whole damn mess.

"We'd have done a lot of good," she said.

We, Cork thought and knew this was the key to understanding the marriage of a woman whose husband was never
really hers. In her way, she was as politically ambitious as
Jubal. They'd met while he was still quarterbacking, met at
a celebrity fund-raiser for cancer research. It was common
knowledge that Camilla couldn't have children; ovarian cancer in her twenties had ensured that. She'd become an outspoken advocate for cancer research and prevention, only two of
the many causes she championed. For a couple of years, she was
Jubal's most frequent and visible escort at social affairs. Jubal
was nearly forty when he ended his football career. Within a
year, he went from the playing field to the marriage altar and
finally to the political arena. Camilla, beautiful, intelligent,
and when the occasion required, eloquent, was at his side in
all his political appearances. She stated often and publicly that
both her life and her marriage were dedicated to public service
and to the greater good. In all this, she proved a perfect mate
for him.

"A lot of good," she reiterated. "Even for the Ojibwe. But
now they've killed him."

"Why do you think it was my people?"

"Why do you do that?" she said, suddenly irritated.

"What?"

"Identify yourself as Ojibwe. You're only a small part
Ojibwe. Less than Jubal was Blackfeet, and he only called himself Indian when it was to his political advantage."

"If I only identified myself as Ojibwe when it was advanta-
geous to do so, I probably never would. And you didn't answer
my question. Why do you think it was a Shinnob?"

She was wearing a knitted shawl whose color, in the faint
evening light, was hard to tell exactly. She pulled it more tightly
around her.

"Because Jubal had to sacrifice someone for the greater
good," she said, rather coldly, "and it was your people he chose

for that honor. He's always received threats, but lately they've been more vicious and more specific about the casino issue."

"I'm sorry," Cork said.

"No reason to be." She eyed him pointedly. "Unless you made them."

He decided it was time to cover other territory. "Camilla, before he died, Jubal told me—"

From the great house, someone called, "Camilla?"

"Just a minute, Alex," she called back, then returned her attention to Cork. "Jubal told you what?"

"Now," Alex said in a voice that clearly meant business.

Camilla frowned toward the house. "We'd better go. He's eager to talk to you."

She turned and began ahead of Cork up the flagstones. He watched her walk away, appreciating the natural grace that had been part of what had caught Jubal's eye long ago and knowing, at the same time, that all her graces and all her money would never have been enough to make up for the one thing she could not be: an Ojibwe woman named Winona Crane.

CHAPTER 15

From his days as a premier NFL quarterback and the investments he'd made then, Jubal Little had money, but not enough to mount a significant political campaign. He didn't have that kind of cash until he married Camilla Jaeger, of the meatpacking Jaegers. Great-great-grandfather Jaeger had been a German immigrant from Düsseldorf, an astute and ruthless businessman who'd built an empire slaughtering midwestern hogs. His son had amassed a second fortune as the result of an innovative process for grinding, compressing, and canning all the unsavory animal parts so that they could easily be shipped or stored, creating a product packed in revolting gelatin that he called Pork'm, which was a mash-up of the words *pork* and *ham*. In modern times, the name had become a joke, but the product itself continued to enjoy an inexplicable worldwide popularity.

The family no longer had a stake in the company, which had been sold years before to a faceless conglomerate, and the current generation of Jaegers were free to pursue interests that had nothing to do with slaughtering hogs. Mostly, their interest was politics, where generally the only slaughter involved the truth.

Camilla Jaeger's father had been a senator and had twice made a pretty good run at his party's presidential nomination. He was an old-school midwestern progressive, a man of good intentions and powerful ego. At the age of seventy, he'd died as the result of a stroke suffered on the floor of the U.S. Senate while delivering an impassioned defense of a bill he'd introduced that was intended to create a system of free day care for low-income women who wanted to work. His sacrifice made no difference. The bill was soundly defeated.

Senator Jaeger had three children. In addition to his daughter, Camilla, there were two sons: Alexander and Nicholas. When Cork accompanied Jubal Little's wife inside, he found the two brothers waiting in the large den. They were alone. The media team and campaign people had made themselves scarce. The room was comfortably furnished in plush brown leather and smelled of the cherrywood burning in the great fieldstone fireplace. Alex Jaeger stood near the bar, with a drink in his hand. Nick Jaeger leaned against the fireplace mantel. He also held a filled liquor glass. Cork had met the brothers before, but only briefly, when as sheriff of Tamarack County, he'd been involved in coordinating security for Jubal's appearances there. From what Jubal had told him, Cork had gathered that drinking was another major interest the Jaegers had taken up since they left off killing pigs.

Without a word of greeting or any other normal cordiality, Alex said, "Another body up there, we've heard."

In his mid-forties, Alex was the eldest of the Jaeger progeny. He'd graduated from the Naval Academy near the top of his class and had served a number of years before being assigned to the USS *Cole*. He'd been aboard ship the day it was torn apart while refueling in the port of Aden, and he was among the severely injured. He'd spent months recuperating and had finally been sent home with a face that would have made a suitable model for a Halloween mask. He'd undergone a number of reconstructive surgeries since, with limited success. His was still a face that, in a crowd, drew the curious eye. Cork knew that Senator Jaeger had hoped Alex might, at some point, follow in his political footsteps, but in a day when being photogenic was a more significant requirement for political office than being astute, Alex Jaeger didn't have a prayer. That hadn't stopped him from entering the political arena, but in another way. He'd worked for his father behind the scenes in Washington and at home in Minnesota. He'd become adept at negotiating treacherous political terrain and forging impossible alliances. He could be charming and ruthless in the same moment, and the power you felt when standing in his presence was undeniable. He'd managed the campaigns that had put Jubal Little in Washington as a U.S. representative and kept him there through several terms while he established his political credentials and acumen, and then had run the campaign that had promised to make Jubal governor.

"Yes," Cork replied. "Another body."

"New?"

"I'm not sure what you mean by that, but he was probably there when Jubal died."

"Why didn't the police find him yesterday?"

"No reason to look where the body was found."

"But you had a reason?"

"I saw some things they didn't."

Nick Jaeger drank from his glass and nodded. "That's right. You still-stalk. Whenever I hunted with Jubal, he was always going on about what a great goddamn tracker his friend Cork O'Connor was."

Nicholas was the youngest of the Jaegers, in his late thirties. Cork had the sense that he was an adrenaline junkie. Nick was always off somewhere exotic, doing something dangerous—climbing difficult mountains, hunting big game, enterprises generally reserved for the very rich.

"Who was he, the new dead man?" Alex said in a steel voice. "And what did he have to do with Jubal's murder?"

"I don't really know. And that goes for both questions."

Alex finished the liquor in his glass and studied the ice. "Don't the police think it's odd, your connection with both killings?"

"I'm sure they do. Hell, I think it's odd."

"A coincidence?" Camilla asked.

She'd seated herself in one of the big leather chairs, and Nick brought her a drink. He said, "I'll bet our Mr. O'Connor doesn't believe in coincidence. Am I right?"

Cork shrugged. "It happens sometimes."

"So. Is that what happened up there?" Alex asked. "Coincidence?"

Cork said, "We'll all know more when they've finished their investigation."

Alex gave him an unflinching stare, and the room was quiet except for the crackle of the cherrywood in the fireplace.

"Three hours, Cork." Alex finally said what was really on his mind. "You waited three hours before you went to get help."

Cork was getting tired of explaining that he hadn't gone for help at all, so this time he didn't. He simply said, "Jubal asked me to stay."

"He didn't want to be alone?" Camilla looked as if she was on the verge of tears.

"That's right."

"Was he in great pain, Cork?" Her voice was small and fearful, as if she wasn't at all certain that she wanted to know the truth.

And the truth was yes, Jubal had suffered. But what good would it do her to know? So Cork told her, "Not as much as you might expect. He was able to talk much of the time."

"What did he talk about?"

"You, for one."

"Me?" Camilla seemed surprised and happy. "What did he say?"

"He asked me to tell you something. He said he had a lot of regrets, and one of his greatest was that he didn't treat you better. He asked me to tell you that, although he didn't show it or tell you often enough, he loved you very much."

Which was the absolute truth of what Jubal had said.

Cork left it to Camilla to decide the truth of the statements themselves.

Camilla covered her face with her hands, and the tears came in a flood against her palms. Nick leaned down and put his arm around her shoulders.

"Did he talk about anything else?" Alex asked as he poured himself another drink from a bottle of Johnnie Walker Blue.

"He did a lot of reminiscing. Life-flashing-before-his-eyes kind of thing. And he talked about dying."

Camilla looked up and wiped at her eyes. "Was he afraid?"

"No."

"The greatest adventure of all," Nick said and lifted his glass as if in a toast.

"Oh, shut up," Camilla snapped.

Her younger brother smiled indulgently. "Do you have any idea how many times I've thought I was on the verge of dying?"

"Do you have any idea how little I care at this moment?"

"What I'm getting at, Camilla, is that, when you look death in the eye, I mean when it's right there in front of you, breathing into your face, it's an extraordinary experience. Did he laugh, Cork?"

"As a matter of fact, yes."

Nick nodded, as if that was exactly what he'd expected. "When you're about to let go for good, there are moments of euphoria," he said grandly. "I've seen it before."

Alex didn't seem to be paying any attention to what his brother was saying. He shook his head and muttered to himself, "What a waste."

Cork found it interesting that Alex Jaeger hadn't characterized Jubal's death as tragic or devastating or any number of things that might have signaled a deep personal feeling about a terrible loss. He'd said "waste" instead, as if Jubal Little had been nothing to him but a highly valuable commodity.

"Is there anything else?" Cork asked, more than ready to go, because he was tired—of the day, the circumstances, and especially these people.

Alex put his drink on the liquor cabinet, crossed the room, and positioned himself threateningly near Cork. He said, "You didn't kill Jubal?"

"Why would I?"

"We all have secrets. Some of them are probably worth killing for."

Cork had had enough. "It's been a rough day," he said curtly. "I'm tired. I'm going home."

"I'll walk you to your car," Camilla offered.

She stood and took his arm as if he was her escort at a ball, and they left the room. Behind him, Cork heard the sound of ice being dropped into a glass.

Outside, in the charcoal light of that dismal evening, they found Yates standing on the crushed limestone, looking up at the overcast. "Smells like winter," he said. Then he said, "I miss Texas." And finally he said, "Do you need me for anything else, Camilla?"

She shook her head. "Thank you, Kenny."

He turned his big, dark face toward Cork, sizing him up, the way he might have appraised an opponent on the gridiron. He looked as if he wanted to say something. Instead, all he said was "Good night," and left them alone and returned to the house.

From somewhere above the lake, but too deep in the approach of night to be seen, came the call of geese heading south. It was a sound Cork had heard a thousand times in his life, but at the moment, it struck him as profoundly sad, like the call of someone hopelessly lost and afraid.

"Camilla, does the name Rhiannon mean anything to you?"

She thought a moment. "No. Why?"

"When he was dying, Jubal mentioned it."

She shook her head. "The only name that seemed important to him was . . . hers." She leaned against the driver's door of his Land Rover, so that Cork couldn't have left immediately even if he'd wanted to. "Have you talked to her?"

Cork knew who she meant. "No."

"Do me a favor?"

"Sure."

"When you see her, tell her . . ."

Cork waited. Even in the gathering gloom, the tears that rolled down her cheeks were obvious and the hurt in her eyes unmistakable.

"Tell her I'm planning an elaborate funeral for Jubal. Everyone will be there. Everyone except her. Tell her that I'm not going to bury him up here either. I'm going to bury him in Saint Paul, next to the plot reserved for me. Tell her that she may have had him in this life, but he'll be at my side for eternity."

CHAPTER 16

Camilla's parting comment put Cork in mind of burials, and as he drove away from Jubal Little's home on Iron Lake, he recalled an incident at Donner Bigby's funeral.

After Donner's death, Cork told the investigators as much of the truth as he could. That he and Jubal had arrived after Bigby was well into his climb up Trickster's Point. That Bigby had reached the top. That from below they'd watched him disappear from view. That the next thing Cork had heard was Bigby's scream as he fell. That he didn't see the fall or what might have caused it. That when they reached him, Bigby was already dead.

When Cy Borkman asked Cork what they were doing at Trickster's Point in the first place, Cork told him that they'd come to confront Bigby about what had happened to Winona Crane, but Bigby had fallen before they had a chance to talk to him. Which was mostly true.

Jubal told the same story. It was uncomplicated, easy for them to stand by, and involved only one outright lie—that they both had stayed on the ground.

The whole sheriff's department knew Cork well. His father had led them as sheriff, and they'd watched Cork grow from a baby. Aurora was a small community, and everyone knew Jubal, or at least knew his reputation as a fine athlete and natural leader. And everyone knew the kind of kid Donner Bigby had been, and most folks suspected that he was responsible for the brutal attack on Winona Crane. When it came down to scraping the bedrock of people's belief, Cork and Jubal were good kids, and providence alone had delivered to Donner Bigby his just deserts.

Bigby's father felt differently. Buzz Bigby was a man as huge as the trees he felled, and anyone who'd had occasion to run afoul of him knew there was a good deal in him to fear. Which was exactly the experience Cork had at Donner Bigby's funeral.

He didn't want to go, but his mother insisted. "He was your classmate," she told him. "And I've known his mother all my life. I don't care what he might have done when he was alive. That's in God's hands now."

The service was well attended, which surprised Cork. In his mind, the whole world had disliked Donner Bigby. Afterward, those in attendance gathered in the community room in the basement of Zion Lutheran Church for a meal. The room had been set up with a big poster on which were glued photos of Bigby taken as he grew up, and Cork was yet again surprised when he saw visual proof that Donner Bigby might once have been something besides big and mean.

He recognized Mrs. Bigby from that fateful morning when he and Jubal had come knocking at her door, and as he stood with his mother in the basement, holding a plate of potato salad and sliced ham and black olives, he saw the woman look his way and then maneuver toward him through the large gathering.

"Hello, Alice," Cork's mother greeted her. "I'm so sorry about Donner."

"Thank you, Colleen," Mrs. Bigby said, then her eyes, blue and fragile as butterflies, settled on Cork. "I understand you stayed with Donner while your friend went for help."

"Yes, ma'am," Cork replied.

"Thank you. It's a comfort knowing that he wasn't alone."

He was dead, Cork thought. *Beyond alone. Or maybe as alone as you could ever get.*

She hesitated, then asked, "He didn't suffer?"

"No, ma'am, he couldn't have. The fall killed him instantly."

She nodded and looked down. "He was so often . . . unhappy." She raised her head and stared at her husband on the other side of the big room, where he dominated in the way a redwood might stand out above all other trees. "He believed he had a lot to live up to."

Beside Buzz Bigby stood Donner's kid brother, Lester. He was maybe ten years old, dressed in a dark suit and tie. It was clear he would never be big, not in the way Donner had been. He seemed to have inherited more of his mother's genes. Cork was glad to see him, to know that the woman had another son. Another chance, maybe.

Bigby's father caught sight of his wife and then—Cork's heart dropped—seemed to recognize Cork. He'd been talking to the Lutheran minister, but he cut off the conversation abruptly. He crossed the room, and the gathering made way before him. Lester trailed behind him like a leaf caught in a strong draft.

"You," Mr. Bigby said in a loud voice. "What are you doing here?"

"I asked him to come with me, Clarence," Cork's mother said.

Alice Bigby put a hand on her husband's arm and cautioned, "Buzz."

He shook her off and drilled Cork with accusing eyes. "There's something not right about what went on out there. My kid was like a mountain goat. I watched him climb. I don't understand how he could just fall."

"Leave him alone, Buzz," Alice Bigby said in a low, cold voice.

Cork looked up into Mr. Bigby's face. The funeral, the comforting scripture and the kind things that had been said, the poster with so many pictures of Bigs as a child, they'd all worked to haze over Cork's feelings about the unpleasant kid he'd known Donner Bigby to be. But staring up into that angry, bullying face, Cork saw the Donner Bigby he'd always feared and hated.

"I don't understand it either, sir," Cork managed to reply. "I just know that he did."

"You were out there to pick a fight with him, weren't you?"

"Not necessarily."

"What the hell does that mean?"

"Buzz, please," Mrs. Bigby pleaded.

"I'm going to keep at this kid and the other one," Bigby snapped at his wife, "until I know the truth."

"Clarence," Cork's mother said evenly, "I know you're upset, and so I'm going to overlook your tone and your accusation, but I don't want you bothering my son about this. Cork's told everything he knows, and that's that." She gave Mrs. Bigby a nod in parting and said, "Alice, I think we'd best be going."

Cork glanced at Lester, who was staring up fearfully at the towering figure of his father, and he felt an immeasurable sadness for all the Bigbys, alive and dead.

They left the church basement, which had grown crypt quiet during Buzz Bigby's outburst, and went upstairs and out into the bright October afternoon. Cork looked up, and the sunlight blinded him in much the way it had at Trickster's Point when he'd tried to see what was happening on top of the monolith. He felt sad to the point of tears, although he didn't actually cry, thinking especially about Donner's mother, whose suffering seemed great and was not just about the loss of her son. He felt his own mother's arm around his shoulders, and she said, "He's always been an angry man, Cork. And now he's hurting as well. I think you just do your best to forgive him, and leave the rest to God."

Although he'd told the Jaegers he was headed home, that wasn't true exactly. Cork had a stop to make first. He headed to the Iron Lake Reservation. As he approached Allouette, he turned west off the main road onto a narrow dirt lane that ran between poplars to a modest house on the lakeshore. He pulled to a stop, got out, and climbed the steps to the porch. Although the house was completely dark and appeared empty, he knocked anyway, waited, then called out, "Winona? It's Cork O'Connor."

He left the porch and walked around to the back, down a worn path to a small dock, where an aluminum boat fitted with an old outboard was moored. Across the lake, which in the growing dark and under the heavy cloud cover had taken on the look of a deep, empty hole, he could see the lights of town. Normally, the glimmer would have warmed his heart because it was a reminder of home, but that night it seemed like a kind of watch fire built against some nebulous threat.

In Allouette, which felt mostly deserted, he pulled up before an old wooden storefront that had been refurbished. The gray, flaking wood had been sanded and slapped with coats of white paint, and the broken windows had been replaced with new plate glass. Above the door hung a brightly lettered sign: IRON LAKE CENTER FOR NATIVE ART. It was an enterprise owned and operated by Winona and Willie Crane. Like the house Cork had just visited, the center was dark and empty.

When he drove past the Mocha Moose, however, he saw that he was in luck. At the counter inside the coffee shop, two men stood talking with Sarah LeDuc. One of the men was Isaiah Broom, a member of the Tribal Council and a Shinnob with a long history of activism on behalf of the Native community. His was also a name on the list that Henry Meloux had given Cork, the list of those whom Sam Winter Moon had taught to hunt in the old way. The other man was Winona's brother, Willie Crane. Cork parked at the curb and killed the engine.

He didn't go in immediately but sat for a couple of minutes watching. Sarah LeDuc was the widow of George LeDuc, who'd been an old and good friend to Cork before he was killed by the same people responsible for the death of Cork's wife. Cork sometimes dropped by the Mocha Moose, and he and Sarah talked in the way of people who shared an understanding others did not. Isaiah Broom, an enormous Shinnob, towered over her. He was nearing fifty and wore his hair in two long braids that hung down his chest. Beside him, Willie Crane seemed fragile. Willie had grown into a tall man, but slender and with a softness in his face and his voice. He still walked with the awkward gait that was one of the legacies of his cerebral palsy, and when he spoke, he spoke carefully in order to be clearly understood. In addition to running the Iron Lake Center for Native Art, he was a well-known wildlife photographer and nature writer.

The conversation the three friends were involved in was clearly a lively one. Broom's mouth worked in an exaggerated way, and he threw his arms about dramatically. Sarah put her hands close together, as if framing a picture she was trying to make Broom see. Willie just seemed to listen intently.

Cork got out of the Land Rover and went inside. The talk stopped immediately, and three faces with shaded skin turned his way.

"*Boozhoo*, Dead-eye," Isaiah Broom said.

"Not funny, Isaiah." Cork crossed the floor, where the old wood boards creaked under his weight.

"Not meant to be. It was spoken with respect."

"I didn't kill Jubal Little."

"Of course you didn't."

"Don't mind him, Cork," Sarah said. "How are you?"

"I've been better. It's been a tough couple of days."

"We were just talking about that," Sarah said. "I'm sorry. Being with Jubal Little while he died, that had to be awful."

"Another body up there, we heard," Willie said. Although he spoke it carefully, it still sounded something like *Nother bauee up ere, weeard*.

"Yeah," Cork said.

Sarah pulled a mug from a stack back of the counter, filled it from one of the big urns, and handed it to Cork, who said "*Migwech*."

"Do you know who it was?" she asked.

"They ID'd the guy. Nobody I know. His driver's license says he's from Red Wing. Maybe just a hunter. They were still working the scene when I left."

"Heard Stephen was there with you," Broom said. "Grisly sight for a kid to see, I imagine." There wasn't much real concern in his voice.

"He'll be okay," Cork said.

"You must be used to dead bodies by now," Broom said. "Two in as many days."

"Leave him be, Isaiah," Sarah said.

"That's okay." Cork gave Broom a long, steady look. "Where were you yesterday morning, Isaiah?"

Broom shrugged. "At home."

"Witnesses?"

"Why would I need witnesses?"

"Because a long time ago, Sam Winter Moon taught you how to hunt in the old way. I'm thinking that Jubal Little was killed by someone who knew the old way. And it's clear that you're not unhappy he's dead."

"Personally, I don't care one way or the other," Broom said. "But as a Shinnob, I'm relieved. He might've tried to pass himself off as Blackfeet, but that man was no friend to the Native community."

"So if I were to mention your name to the sheriff's investigators as someone who has both the ability and motive, and maybe even had the opportunity, to kill Jubal, you'd have no problem?"

"Oh, the *chimooks* would just love that," Broom said, using unkind Ojibwe slang for whites. "Indians pointing fingers at each other."

"Rainy Bisonette told me it was you who brought the news to her and Meloux out on Crow Point. How'd you hear about it?"

"Maybe the wind told me," Broom said with an enigmatic grin.

Sarah said, "Smiley Black's got a police radio scanner. He came roaring into town spouting the news to everyone in earshot.

By the time you and the sheriff's people got back to Trickster's Point, pretty much the whole rez knew."

"Why are you here?" Willie asked. *Whyouere?*

"Actually, I came looking for you, Willie. Mind if we talk a minute? Alone?"

Cork carried his mug, and they stepped outside. He walked slowly to accommodate Willie's laborious locomotion. They stood in the light that fell through the window of the Mocha Moose.

"I just stopped by Winona's house," Cork said. "She's not there. I need to talk to her."

"Why?"

"You know that list I mentioned, the one with names of Shinnobs who Sam Winter Moon had taught how to bow-hunt? Winona's name was on it."

"She didn't kill Jubal," Willie said with great care. "God knows she had reason to, but she didn't do it."

"Where is she?"

"When she's ready, she'll let you know."

"Is she hiding, Willie?"

"She's grieving. Just let her be."

"Will you tell her something for me?"

"Sure."

"Tell her that Jubal gave me a message for her."

"What message?"

"It's for Winona."

In the drizzle of light on the empty sidewalk, Willie Crane's face became unreadable, stolid in the practiced way of the An- ishinaabeg. At the Food 'N Fuel down the street, an old pickup pulled away, its bad muffler roaring like a wild beast. When the sound had faded into the night, Willie said, "Dead, and he still can't leave her alone." Then he said, in a voice vacant of all emo- tion, "I'll tell her."

CHAPTER 17

When Cork arrived home, Waaboo was already asleep in his crib. Cork wasn't surprised—it was well past the little guy's bedtime—but he was disappointed. He enjoyed those evenings when Jenny let him put Waaboo down. There was an old rocker in the bedroom that had become the nursery where Cork loved to sit with his grandson on his lap, and he would read to Waaboo from one of the many picture books—*Goodnight Moon* or *The Very Hungry Caterpillar* or *Chicka Chicka Boom Boom*—until those little eyelids drifted closed, and then he would sit for a while longer with that small, warm body nestled against him, and there was nothing he could think of that made him feel more content.

That night he would have appreciated a moment of contentedness.

Cork had come through the backyard, as he had earlier that day, to avoid any media who might still be lying in wait. Stephen and Jenny were at the kitchen table, and when he walked in, it was clear they'd been talking. Stephen was drinking from a glass of chocolate milk he'd made with Hershey's syrup. Jenny had a mug in front of her. They were both eating chocolate chip cookies that Cork knew had come from the cookie jar shaped like *Sesame Street*'s Ernie, which sat on the kitchen counter. The jar had been a baby shower gift when Jo O'Connor was pregnant with Jenny, and the cookies that had filled it had sustained the O'Connors through more crises than Cork could remember.

"There's coffee," Jenny said.

"No thanks." Cork went to the refrigerator and took out a bottle of Leinenkugel's beer. He lifted Ernie's head, pulled a cookie from the jar, and sat at the table with his children. "How're you doing, buddy?" he asked his son.

Stephen thought it over. "Okay, I guess. I just . . ."

"What?" Cork asked.

Stephen's face tightened. "I just don't understand why death seems to circle this family like some kind of, I don't know, vulture."

Cork said, "I don't either. When I quit law enforcement, you guys were part of the reason. I saw the toll it was taking, and I wasn't happy about it. I thought I could just step away, and that was that. I was wrong, I guess."

Jenny lifted her coffee but didn't drink. She said, "You're a windbreak."

"A what?"

"That's what Mom told me once. She said trouble's like this wind that blows and blows and there have to be windbreaks to keep it from sweeping everything away. She told me you're one of the windbreaks. It didn't make her happy, but it's who you are."

Cork said, "I don't look for trouble."

"*Ogichidaa*," Stephen said.

"*Ogichidaa?*" Cork repeated the Ojibwe word, whose meaning he knew well. It was often misused, or misinterpreted, to mean "warrior." Its true meaning, however, was "someone who stood between his people and bad things."

"That's what Henry told me once when we were talking about you," Stephen explained. "He said you didn't have a choice, that you were chosen. He said that when we come into the world we're given responsibilities by Kitchimanidoo. Yours was to be *ogichidaa*."

"I'd give it back if I could." Cork took a bite of his cookie. "These are good."

"Stephen made them," Jenny said.

"Did Meloux say your responsibility is baking?" Cork smiled.

"*Nanaandawi*," Stephen said seriously. "Healing."

"What about me?" Jenny asked.

"*Nakomis*," Stephen said.

"A grandmother?" Jenny didn't look pleased. "Like my skin's wrinkled and my boobs are saggy? I need to have a talk with Henry."

"He meant that your spirit is old and wise and nurturing, like Grandmother Earth."

"I still think I'd better have a talk with him," she said with a wry smile. She sipped her coffee and asked, "How's Mrs. Little?"

"Distraught. But all things considered, she's doing all right. She has her family around her for support."

"Dad, how come she never came up here with Mr. Little?" Stephen asked.

"She did sometimes."

"Not much. Whenever you got together with him, he was alone."

"I think Camilla isn't fond of the North Country, not like Jubal was. This was his home." Then, to cut off this particular line of conversation, Cork said, "School tomorrow. You have homework?"

"A little math," Stephen replied. "And an essay on Manifest Destiny. But I can do that in one word: Bullshit."

A gentle knocking came from the dining room, from the door that opened onto the backyard patio. They all looked at one another with surprise and then irritation. Cork set his beer down and scooted his chair away from the table.

"No, Dad, let me," Jenny said. "If it's a reporter, I'll say you're not here."

"And then tell him if he trespasses again, we'll have him arrested," Cork growled.

Jenny left and came back a few moments later. "It's Mr. Crane."

"At the patio door?" Then Cork understood. Willie had probably parked on Willow Street, just as Cork had, and come through the backyard to avoid any reporters who might still be lurking out front. He left the kitchen table and met his visitor on the patio.

Without preamble, Willie said, "She wants to see you." *Shewanseeyou.*

"Where is she?"

"I'll take you."

Because he couldn't trust his left leg to do what most people's legs did naturally, Willie drove a Jeep Wrangler modified with hand controls for braking. Because he used it often to get himself into remote areas of the backcountry where he shot the photographs that had built his reputation, the outside of the Wrangler was layered with caked mud. Willie Crane was one of the most admirable men Cork knew. Despite his cerebral palsy—or maybe because of it, Cork sometimes thought—Willie had a long list of remarkable accomplishments to his credit. He'd written articles and provided photographs for *National Geographic*, *Audubon*, *National Wildlife*, *Outside*, and dozens of other periodicals. He'd produced several collections of his own essays with accompanying photographs. He had a small gallery in downtown Saint Paul, which, like the Iron Lake Center for Native Art, featured not only his own work but the work of many Indian artists. He was painfully aware of his speech difficulty and never spoke in public, but through his writings, he'd become a strong and respected voice for habitat preservation and wildlife conservation.

They headed toward Allouette, but half a mile outside town, Willie turned onto a narrow gravel road, and Cork knew they were going to his cabin. Years before, Willie had built a little place on the far eastern edge of the reservation, nestled against a small lake. The cabin was simple, built of logs and surrounded on three sides by aspens. When they pulled up, Winona's Ford Ranger was parked in front, and light poured from the interior of the cabin. They got out, and Cork followed Willie inside. It was a cozy place, an open area that doubled as living room and kitchen, with a closed door off either end of the room. The place smelled of spiced tea and, more faintly, of photographic chemicals. When the photography world turned digital, Willie had stayed with film. He did his own processing in a darkroom behind one of the closed doors. Because Cork had been here before, he knew that the other closed door led to Willie's bedroom.

"Nona?" Willie called. He received no answer and started toward the bedroom door. He said to Cork, "Wait here." *Waiere.*

Willie kept the cabin neat, and he'd decorated the walls with framed prints of some of his award-winning photographs. Many were landscape shots that captured beautifully the dramatic interplay of light and wilderness. Others were of wildlife—moose and deer and bears and eagles and osprey and lynx and foxes— all caught unawares and in such a natural state and so clearly that Cork had the sense he was looking at them through a window and they were just on the other side of the glass, breathing.

Willie returned. "She's not here."

"Her truck's here," Cork pointed out.

"The fire ring, maybe," Willie said.

They went out the way they'd come in and around to the back of the cabin. Because of the overcast, there were no stars, no moon, and the night was pitch black. But in the faint light that fell through the cabin windows, Cork saw a narrow path. He followed Willie's clumsy feet along the path to the lakeshore. From there, he could see the fire, a small dance of light in the lee of a rock that stood a dozen feet back from the water and was as big as a buffalo.

When they reached the fire ring, only a few flames were still licking at the night air. A blanket that looked of Navajo design lay rumpled on the ground next to the ring, as if thrown there in haste. Winona was nowhere to be seen.

"Nona!" Willie called toward the woods. Then he turned and cried toward the lake, "Nona! It's Willie." He waited and finally turned to Cork. "She's afraid."

"Of what?"

"Of whoever it was that killed Jubal Little."

"Why?"

"She knows things, things about a lot of powerful people."

Of course she did. No one was closer to Jubal Little than Winona Crane. They'd been lovers forever. He told her everything.

"She's not afraid of me, is she?" Cork asked.

"When she gets like this, she's afraid of everyone. Nona!" Willie shook his head. "I'm sorry, Cork. I don't know where she's gone."

"That's okay. Mind if I stay a little while, just in case she comes back?"

"Okay, I guess. But when she gets like this . . ." Willie gave a shrug. "I'll wait at my cabin."

As the sound of Willie's awkward feet retreated, Cork turned and scanned the lake that, in the inky dark of the starless night, appeared to be nothing but a black hole. Although he couldn't see it, he knew the far shoreline was unbroken forest, and not far beyond that began the Boundary Waters Canoe Area Wilderness. For a hundred miles north, there was nothing but thick woods and clear water.

He didn't believe Willie Crane, didn't believe that Willie had no idea where Winona might be hiding. The real question was, Why had Winona fled? What was she really afraid of? It might well have been, as Willie said, that she knew things that made her dangerous to powerful people. But it also might have been because she'd finally grown tired of the way Jubal treated her, and she'd used an arrow to free herself from the prison of that relationship forever.

Cork circled to the far side of the fire, sat, fed a few sticks of wood to the dying flames, and thought about Winona. She was fifty, old by some standards, but a more handsome woman he'd never seen. Her hair was long and black and, in sunlight, shone like obsidian. Her face was finely boned and ageless. Her skin was a soft caramel color. Her eyes were light almond, and whenever she'd looked at him, there was a gentle intensity so compelling that, even if he'd wanted to, he couldn't look away. She gazed at people as if she saw their souls and understood everything, good and bad, about them.

The truth was that he'd known Winona Crane all his life, and he had never not been in love with her, just a little.

CHAPTER 18

What happened the night of the homecoming dance changed Winona Crane.

She'd always been outgoing and clearly not afraid to take a walk on the wild side. After the attack, however, she withdrew from the world. For a while, she simply disappeared. She didn't come to school or to Sam's Place or into Aurora at all. Cork knew she was still on the rez; Willie Crane told him that, but it was all Willie would say. Cork's mother, who had relatives in Allouette, told him a bit more. Winona had become deathly afraid. She didn't want to see anyone, yet the idea of being left alone terrorized her.

"Is she getting help?" Cork asked, trying desperately to think of something, anything, he might be able to do for her.

"Henry Meloux," his mother replied.

Two days later, Cork borrowed his mother's car, picked up Jubal Little, and they drove north out of Aurora until they came to the double-trunk birch that marked the beginning of the path to Crow Point.

Jubal had changed, too. The death of Donner Bigby had done that. He was still remarkable in all the ways people in Tamarack County had come to expect, yet Cork, who was his closest friend, recognized a difference. It was as if, when he climbed down from the top of Trickster's Point, Jubal had simply kept going and climbed right into himself. When he and Cork were together,

Jubal was often silent. Cork had no trouble with silence—it was an Ojibwe virtue he admired—and he didn't push his friend.

The day was sunny but cool. The forest floor was covered with fallen aspen leaves, and it seemed to Cork as if they were walking on a carpet of gold. It was Saturday, and the night before they'd won another football game and he should have felt like a million dollars, but all he could think about was how, yet again, death had changed his world. Jubal walked with his shoulders hunched and his eyes on the aspen leaves underfoot and said not a word the whole way.

They broke from the trees and crossed the meadow where the wildflowers were gone and the tall grass had turned yellow, dead from the frost that came now in the nights. Smoke rose up from behind the rocks west of the cabin, where Meloux had the fire ring he often used in his healing ceremonies. Cork headed toward the rocks, but as they passed Meloux's cabin, the door opened, and Willie Crane stepped outside.

"Don't go there," he said. *Dongoere.*

"He's with Winona?" Cork asked.

Willie nodded.

In the cool, still morning air, Cork could hear the faint chant of the Mide.

"Is it okay if we wait?" Jubal asked. "Please."

Willie thought about it and nodded once again.

Cork sat on the ground, and Jubal did the same, then Willie. The day warmed, and the sun reached its zenith, and still the Mide chanted beyond the rocks, and the air was redolent with the cleansing scent of burning sage and cedar.

An hour past noon, Cork saw Henry coming from the rocks with Winona at his side. Henry Meloux was nearly sixty then, tall and strong, and he walked regally and erect, with his long hair like a flow of white water over his shoulders. Winona was tall, too, but the way she carried herself made Cork think of her as a creature small and afraid. Henry didn't seem surprised in the least to see his two new visitors.

"Come inside," he said to them. "We will eat."

Winona looked at them as if they were not old friends but strangers who deserved her suspicion.

They ate stew that Meloux heated on his old cast-iron stove. And then they sat in the sun outside and smoked tobacco, and in all this time not more than a dozen words passed between them.

Finally Meloux said, "Come with me, Corcoran O'Connor."

The Mide led him away on the path through the meadow. At the edge of the forest he said, "It is time for you to go."

Cork looked back at the cabin, where Jubal still sat with Winona and Willie. "But I want to stay."

The Mide shook his head.

"What about Jubal?"

"Sometimes, Corcoran O'Connor, you can see the ropes that tie people together. When I look at Winona Crane and Jubal Little, I see ropes. Go home now. There's nothing more for you here today, and I have work to do."

Cork was crestfallen, but he knew it was useless to argue. He turned and headed alone back along the path toward the double-trunk birch.

Although it didn't please him, it also didn't surprise Cork that, when Winona Crane returned to the world, Jubal Little was almost always at her side. It wasn't like dating or going steady or anything Cork had a name for. They were together because of something powerful between them that seemed to have no name. It was like love but not love. It was necessity but not needing. It was the right hand to the left. It was nothing Jubal or Winona cared to explain to Cork, and it was something Willie claimed he couldn't. Whatever it was, it excluded Cork in a way that pained him deeply. He'd always been in love with Winona Crane, at least a bit. And he'd never had a better friend than Jubal Little. Now he was on the outside of some inexplicable intimacy between them, and he felt abandoned and a little betrayed.

In the spring, Jubal was accepted to the University of Northern Iowa, in Cedar Falls, and offered a full athletic scholarship. All that summer when they worked together at Sam's Place, Jubal confided in Cork that he was seriously thinking of not going. He didn't want to leave Aurora, which Cork understood really meant that he didn't want to leave Winona. Cork argued with him, pointed out that it was the kind of opportunity most guys would give their left nut for, and if he passed it up, God alone knew whether something like it might come again. But as the end of August drew nearer, Jubal only became more fixed in his determination. Cork figured there was nothing more he could do.

It was Jubal's mother who convinced him to try again. She came one evening to the house on Gooseberry Lane, and sat with Cork and his mother in the kitchen, and cried. She had such great dreams for her son, she told Cork. Jubal would be the first in the entire family who'd ever gone to college. Did Cork have any idea what that meant? When she left, she went with Cork's promise that he would do what he could to change Jubal's mind, and he knew the only person who could do that was Winona.

He found her at the community center in Allouette practicing with the jingle dancers for a powwow at Cass Lake a couple of weeks away. When the dancers were finished, she sat with him in the bleachers of the empty gymnasium and listened as he talked. Her face was beautiful and sad, and it hurt him to say the things he did, but they had to be said.

"I know," she admitted when he'd finished. "Jubal needs to go."

"Tell him that."

"He won't listen to me. He's made up his mind."

"He's going to throw his life away, Winona." Cork realized immediately how awful that sounded and added, "I mean he should at least give it a try."

She looked across the big, empty space of the gym, a look that went beyond the walls. "As long as I'm here, he won't go."

"Because you need him?"

She shook her head and said, "Because we need each other." Her sad eyes rested on Cork's face now, and his heart nearly broke seeing the pain there. "Henry Meloux told us that we both were healing and that we had to help each other but that we had to be careful because we might end up like skin that grows together over a wound. I guess we weren't careful." She stood up, and her dress gave a tinny jingle. "I'll make him go," she promised. And Cork saw tears trail down the fine bones of her cheeks.

Two days later, Winona Crane ran away. She stuffed a backpack with clothing and disappeared in the middle of the night. She left a note for Willie explaining that she had to go and that she would stay in touch and not to worry about her.

The news gutted Jubal. Cork had never seen him so desolate, so lost. "Why?" he kept saying and looked to Cork as if for an answer. After days of this, Cork couldn't stand it anymore, couldn't take Jubal's unrelenting despondency, and couldn't shoulder the guilt he felt because of his own part in Winona's sudden departure. He told Jubal the truth.

They were in Grant Park, late on a Thursday afternoon, standing on an empty fishing dock, staring at the lake, where a warm breeze rocked the blue water and the sun made it sparkle. Jubal glared at him for a long, painful moment, and then Jubal hit him. He drove his fist into Cork's midsection. The blow threw Cork onto the weathered dock boards, knocked all the air out of him, so that for a minute he couldn't breathe. When he finally got his wind back and his vision cleared, he found Jubal standing above him, huffing like a steam engine, his big hands fisted and ready to do more damage.

"You son of a bitch," Jubal said through clenched teeth.

"I didn't know she'd run away, Jubal."

"Why the hell did you have to interfere?"

"Your mom asked me to."

"You're my friend, or you're supposed to be. You should have stood up for me and for Winona."

"I'm sorry, Jubal. I swear to God I'm sorry."

The glare finally left his eyes, and Jubal slowly relaxed. His fists became hands again, and he shoved them into the pockets of his jeans.

"I want to get drunk," he said.

"All right." Cork stood up, carefully because of the pain just below his ribs. "I know a place."

There was a bar a few miles outside town, the Black Duck, popular with loggers. From listening to the talk of his father and his father's deputies, Cork knew it was a place where the bartender didn't mind serving someone who hadn't quite hit the legal drinking age. He drove Jubal there, and they went inside, sat in the dim light, drank beer, and listened to Waylon Jennings on the jukebox. Jubal talked about Winona, and for the first time in their history together, Cork saw his big friend cry.

They were both into their third bottles of beer when the door opened and Buzz Bigby walked in. He strode up to the bar and told the guy behind it—he called him Dwight in a tone that said they knew each other well—that he needed a bottle of Jim Beam to go, and he swung his eyes left and saw Jubal and Cork.

"Jesus Christ," he said. "This is a moment I been waiting for a long time."

Dwight looked at Bigby, then at Cork and Jubal, and two and two came together. "Take it outside, boys," he warned.

Bigby nodded toward the door. "Let's talk."

"I don't think—" Cork began.

But Jubal cut him off. "Sure thing," he said and slid from his barstool.

Cork put a hand on his friend's arm. "Jubal."

"Mr. Bigby wants to talk," Jubal said, pulling away. "I'm going to talk."

He took the lead, and Bigby followed. Cork said to the barkeep, "You might want to call the cops."

The barkeep said, "You might want to go fuck yourself, kid."

The bar was a ramshackle affair at the crossing of two back roads in the woods west of Aurora. Evening had settled. The sky was a soft blue, and the air was calm and quiet. There were half a dozen vehicles—dusty pickup trucks, mostly—parked in the dirt that served as a lot. In one of the trucks, Cork saw a kid staring out the window of the cab, and he recognized Lester, Donner Bigby's little brother.

Jubal walked ahead, Buzz Bigby immediately at his back, and Cork, because he'd talked to the bartender, a few steps behind them both. No sooner was Jubal out the door than Bigby swung a fist hard as a wrecking ball into Jubal's kidneys. Jubal arched and cried out and fell forward onto his knees. Bigby swung a steel-toed boot into Jubal's ribs, and Jubal went down onto the dirt of the parking lot. Bigby delivered another kick, this one to Jubal's head, and Jubal's neck snapped sideways as if broken.

It all happened in the blink of an eye, executed by a man who'd probably been in more fights than Cork had toes or fingers to count.

Bigby wasn't even breathing hard. He stared down at Jubal and said, "I want the fucking truth, boy."

Jubal tried to speak but could barely raise his head from the dirt.

Buzz Bigby set himself to swing his steel-toed boot again.

And that's when Cork went berserk. In the few seconds it had taken Bigby to bring Jubal down, Cork had stood paralyzed, stunned by both the swiftness of the attack and its brutality. But when he saw Bigby set to kick Jubal again, he snapped into action and launched himself blindly. Without thinking, he threw himself onto Bigby's broad, muscled back. He wrapped his right arm around the man's thick neck. With his left hand, he grasped his right wrist and put all his strength into keeping the bone of his forearm pressed against Bigby's throat. Bigby stumbled back. He grunted but couldn't speak. He grasped at Cork's arms and tried to break the grip, but adrenaline poured into every cell of Cork's body, and his arms were like the steel of a vise. Bigby swung his own body left, then right, trying to shake Cork loose. For Cork, it was like riding a raging buffalo, but he held on.

Bigby stumbled across the bare dirt of the lot and slammed Cork into the door of his pickup. Cork held. He could feel the man's strength ebbing, and he pressed harder against his throat. He wanted Bigby dead. He wanted to kill him with his bare hands.

Buzz Bigby leaned forward, away from the truck, preparing to go down like one of those great pines he'd made his living felling. He stumbled again and turned, legs all wobbly. And Cork suddenly found himself almost face-to-face with little Lester Bigby, who was staring through the glass of the driver's-side window, wearing a look of horror.

Cork came back to his senses. He released his grip on Bigby's neck and slid from the man's back. Relieved of the weight, Bigby lurched, fell into the dirt, rolled to his back, blinked rapidly at the evening sky, and gasped for breath.

Jubal was at Cork's side. Even though his face was smeared with his own blood and he grunted in pain when he moved, Jubal put his arm around Cork's shoulders firmly and urged him away from where Bigby lay sprawled on the ground.

"That's enough," he said to Cork hoarsely. "Let's go home."

At the end of August, Jubal Little left on a Greyhound bus for Cedar Falls, Iowa. Cork, along with Jubal's mother, saw him off at Pflugleman's Rexall Drugstore, which doubled as the bus depot. He stood watching as the bus drove away in a smelly cloud of diesel vapor. They'd sworn to each other that they'd stay in touch. Even so, it felt to Cork as if the best friend he'd ever known was heading out of his life forever.

He would discover later, and not without regret, that nothing except death was forever.

CHAPTER 19

The night grew cold, and the fire died to embers, and Winona Crane had not returned. Cork finally went back to the cabin, where he found Willie drinking hot spiced tea from a white ceramic mug.

Willie asked, "Did you talk to her?" *Diyoutatoher?*

"She didn't show."

"She's there. Watching. She'll come back when you're gone. You said you had a message from Jubal. I can give it to her."

"In a minute. There are some things I want to ask first, Willie. I'd have asked Winona if she'd shown herself."

"All right. Ask."

"Did Jubal talk to you or Winona about threats on his life?"

"Winona said he got threats all the time."

"Did he talk to her about any specific threat?"

"If he did, she didn't say."

"Did he take the threats seriously?"

"He wasn't afraid for himself. He was more concerned about his wife."

"What about Winona? Was he afraid for Winona?"

A sad smile warped Willie's lips. "No one knew about him and Winona."

"Not true," Cork said. "I knew. And Camilla knew. And, I suspect, her brothers knew as well."

"Her brothers?" Willie spoke as if the mention of them had brought something forgotten to his mind. "Jubal was concerned about something, but not a threat necessarily, or at least the kind of threat you're thinking of. He was concerned about his brother-in-law."

"Which one?"

"Nicholas. I guess he's always been a little on the unpredictable side. There was some trouble that Jubal was afraid might reflect badly on the family and, as a result, on his own candidacy."

"Did he tell Winona what the trouble was?"

"Yes, but she was vague about it when she talked to me. From the things she did say, I think it had to do with a hunt he and Jubal had done together in the Arctic wilderness in northern Canada last year. I had a sense that, whatever it was, it must have been pretty bad. Maybe even as bad as someone getting killed. One of the Native people, maybe. All covered up, of course. She did tell me Jubal thought that in the future it might prove to be a way to rein in the worst of Nicholas's excesses. Sounded to me like blackmail."

Cork gave a dry, humorless laugh. "Jubal told me once that in politics it's not called blackmail. It's called 'leverage.' Did Camilla and Alex Jaeger know about this . . . whatever it was?"

"I don't know. Like I said, Winona was vague."

Something came to Cork now, the sudden realization of a possible connection. "Willie, this incident in Canada, did Winona mention the name Rhiannon in connection with it?"

"Rhiannon?" Willie frowned and thought hard. "She never said that name to me. Are you going to tell me Jubal's message now?"

"Just a couple more questions. When we were kids, Sam Winter Moon taught Jubal and me how to hunt in the old way."

"I know."

"Sam also taught Winona."

Willie seemed surprised that Cork knew. "What of it?"

"Does she still hunt in the old way?"

"Not in years."

"Why did Sam teach her?"

"She asked. It was something she wanted to learn. I think because Jubal knew how, she wanted to know how, too."

"Where was Winona on Saturday, Willie?"

His dark eyes, which had held a kind of soft mournfulness, grew hard, and he stared at Cork, wordless for a very long time. "You think Winona killed Jubal?"

"I just want to know where she was."

"You want to know because you're wondering if she put an arrow in Jubal's heart."

Cork said, "It's a very small wonder, but it's there."

"She won't talk to you because she's afraid. And she ought to be afraid. Of everyone." Willie spit it out with such anger that Cork could barely understand the words. "We're done here."

"Don't you want to know the message Jubal left for your sister?"

A different kind of spark came into Willie's eyes, a deep, burning interest.

"He said that if only Kitchimanidoo had allowed it, he would have spent his life with Winona, and he would have been happy."

Willie's look changed again, this time to bitter disbelief. Cork wasn't sure if Willie didn't believe what Jubal had said or didn't believe what Cork had told him. He stepped into the kitchen, set his mug of tea on the counter, and said, "It's time I took you home."

"There's one more thing, Willie. Camilla asked me to pass along some information to Winona."

"What?"

"She's planning to bury Jubal in Saint Paul."

That wasn't exactly the message; it didn't carry the venom.

Willie considered it, then said, "Good," and headed out the cabin door.

They were nearing Aurora when Cork's cell phone rang. He checked the number. Out of Area. He answered, "O'Connor."

"Rhiannon."

"Who is this?"

"Drop it."

"Why?"

"She's got nothing to do with Little's death."

"Who is she?"

"Let it go, O'Connor."

"I don't think so."

"Understand this: If the name Rhiannon comes out of your mouth again, it'll be the last thing that ever does. And something else to keep in mind. You mention this conversation to anyone, especially the sheriff or her people, someone near and dear to you will pay the price. That's a promise."

"Listen—" Cork began, but the caller was gone.

Willie glanced across at him. "You look like you just talked to the Devil himself."

Cork thought about the warning he'd just received. It was a stupid call, of course, because now there was no way in hell he wouldn't pursue the mystery of Rhiannon. But it was effective in one respect. He would not mention the name again, not until he'd found the answer.

"It was no one, Willie," he said. "No one important."

CHAPTER 20

The house was quiet when he got home, everyone in bed, asleep. Cork went straight to his office, turned on his computer. He meant to do a search for anything related to Jubal Little and Rhiannon but saw that his daughter Anne had sent him a Skype message. It said, "Call me when you have a chance. Worried."

Anne was his middle child. On graduation from high school, she'd left Aurora and followed a path intended to lead her to the altar as a Bride of Christ. She was doing her best to join the Sisters of Notre Dame de Namur, an order well known for its social activism. That was Annie, by God. She was currently in Thoreau, New Mexico, working at a school and mission, preparing for her vocation. Cork shot her back a message saying everything was fine. No need to worry. And he promised to call.

He Googled Jubal Little and Rhiannon together, a search that yielded just over two hundred thousand hits. He scanned the first twenty pages of sites and realized it was getting him nowhere. He tried the name Rhiannon alone. He was pretty sure he'd get the Fleetwood Mac hit, and he did. He went through the lyrics—all about a Welsh witch, a woman taken by the wind—looking for a clue to the identity of Jubal's Rhiannon, but nothing leaped out at him. He searched a bit more and found the derivation of the name. According to Wikipedia, it was Celtic, the name of a great queen in Welsh mythology. Not much help, but he was fishing for anything. He checked the White Pages and found that there were seventy-two people in Minnesota with that first name. Because of Jubal's long ties with Washington, D.C., it was entirely possible that Rhiannon, whoever she was, was connected somehow with Jubal's activities there.

Cork sat back and thought about the phone call itself. The voice was unfamiliar, but he understood that it had been disguised. It was definitely male, low and graveled and obviously unreal. Willie had said he looked as if he'd just spoken to the Devil himself, and that was what the voice had, indeed, sounded like. Cork brought up the number on his cell phone. Out of Area. Calling card, most probably. Tough, if not impossible to trace. And even if he were able, he was pretty sure that he'd find it had come from a public phone. A dead end.

He tried to remember everyone to whom he'd spoken the name Rhiannon. He recalled only Rainy, Camilla Little, Marsha Dross, and Willie Crane. But maybe there was someone he'd forgotten. Or perhaps—probably, in fact—they'd mentioned the name to others. Though that couldn't have been true of Willie, who was with Cork when the call had come.

He looked at the clock. It was almost two a.m. He was tired, his brain all mushy, his thinking going fuzzy. He turned off his computer, but he sat for a long moment in the silence of his office, thinking one final thought. Whoever Rhiannon was, the real issue was what did she have to do with Jubal's death? Maybe nothing, exactly as the caller had said. And if so, maybe the call had been meant to tantalize him with this bait, to distract him from his pursuit of the truth about Jubal's murder, to lure him onto a different path, a blind alley. It had been a ridiculous kind of call, really, the kind from bad movies.

In the end, there was one consideration that overrode all the others. The caller had made a threat directed at someone Cork cared about. It might have been just theater, just a bluff, but he couldn't take that chance. Where Rhiannon was concerned, he would proceed with great caution.

He turned out the lamp on his desk, left his office, and slowly climbed the stairs toward bed, hoping he could sleep.

He didn't, not much. After a few hours of restless napping, he rose in the dark, showered, dressed, left a note for his children, and headed out. He pulled up to the curb in front of Johnny's Pinewood Broiler at 5:30, which was half an hour before the front door was unlocked and the place was officially open for business. On the other side of the big plate-glass windows, the restaurant was only dimly lit, but he could see Heidi Steger moving fast back and forth behind the counter. Heidi was somewhere in her thirties and three times married. No children though. She was always doing something to look younger. Her hair, for example. At the moment, it was a neon green that made her look a little like a Chia Pet. It was also on the wild side that morning, and Cork figured she'd overslept and was frantically trying to get the place ready for customers. He slid from the Land Rover, went to the Broiler door, and knocked on the glass. Heidi turned toward him, looked bewildered, pointed at her wristwatch, and shook her head. Cork beckoned her to him. He could tell she wasn't happy to be interrupted, but she came and unlocked anyway.

"I don't care how hungry you are," she said, "I'm not putting in any orders before six."

"This isn't about eating, Heidi."

"No? What's it about then? And make it quick, Cork. I'm running late as it is."

"The day before yesterday, the day Jubal Little was killed, when we came for breakfast, do you remember who else was here that morning?"

"Oh, Jesus. That was Saturday. You have any idea how many people come here for breakfast on a Saturday? You think I'm going to remember them all?"

"Just take a moment, Heidi. Relax and think. This was very early Saturday, first thing after you opened. Anybody come to mind?"

"Cork, I've got so much—"

"Please. It's important."

She took a breath and closed her eyes. Then she squeezed them together, as if it hurt her to think deeply. At last she said, "Gus Sorenson and Davey Klein and Mack McKenzie were at the counter. Two Greek omelets and one short stack with a side of link sausage. Cora Hubik was at table six. Eggs over easy and a waffle. Lester Bigby in booth three, right behind you and Jubal Little. Oatmeal and raisins. Jasper Davis in booth five. His usual—"

"Lester Bigby? He was here?"

"I just said he was. In the booth right behind you."

"I don't remember him."

"You probably didn't see his face. He's usually got it hid behind a newspaper."

"Bigby," Cork said.

She mentioned two more names, but they weren't anybody Cork had reason to be concerned about, especially after he'd learned that Lester Bigby had been there. He thanked Heidi and started away.

"Be back for breakfast?" she asked.

"I'll probably have something at home."

"Give that grandson of yours a big hug for me. And bring him in for a cinnamon roll sometime. On me, okay?"

"Will do, Heidi."

Cork didn't, in fact, go home. He drove north out of Aurora, along the lakeshore and back roads until he reached the double-trunk birch. Soft blue morning light was sifting through the tree branches as he set out along the path to Crow Point, and he realized the cloud cover that had hung heavy for days was gone, and the sun would break against a clear heaven. That idea alone lifted his spirits.

The sky had turned the color of a peach when he stepped from the trees and entered the meadow at the end of the point. He saw no smoke rising from the stovepipe on either of the cabins. He walked to Rainy's door, knocked lightly, and opened it.

"Rainy?" he called softly.

"Cork?" She rose in bed, propped herself on an elbow, and gave him a quizzical look.

"Would you like some company?"

She smiled and lifted the blanket for him. "I'd love some."

Later, they lay together, a braiding of arms and legs and moist flesh.

"I don't know what brought this on, but I'm glad it did," Rainy said in a breathless whisper.

"I spoke with Camilla Little last night, and then tried to see Winona Crane. They both seem to me to be crippled women. It's helped me realize how lucky I am to have you in my life, and I just wanted you to know that I know that."

In reply, she kissed his shoulder gently.

He said, "Some people, love just seems to sweep them up like a big wave, and then leave them stranded. I think that's the way it was with Winona and Camilla where Jubal was concerned."

"What about you?" Rainy said. "From what you've told me, Jubal left you kind of stranded, too."

Cork rolled onto his back and stared up at the boards of the ceiling. Rainy put her hand on his chest over his heart.

"He wasn't always like that," Cork said. "It wasn't always all about Jubal."

After Jubal left for college, Cork didn't see him for several years. Summers, Jubal worked in Cedar Falls at jobs arranged for him by the Athletic Department. They communicated occasionally through letters, but neither of them was particularly responsible in that way. It wasn't difficult for Cork to keep track of Jubal's football career, however. The University of Northern Iowa's team *was* Jubal. He became the starting quarterback in his freshman year, and in every year thereafter, he set new school records and new conference records. Although he played for a small school in a midwestern state that most of America associated with dumb cows and tall corn, Jubal's exploits excited national attention. Because of his Minnesota roots, he was often featured in the sports columns of the newspapers in the Twin Cities. His senior year warranted a full two-page article in *Sports Illustrated*, and that same year, he was profiled in *Time*. Part of it, of course, was his incredible athletic ability, but part of it was his unique history. The summer before his senior year, Jubal's father died, stabbed to death in the prison yard at Deer Lodge. Because of who Jubal was, the incident became a national story. By then, the sentiment in America had changed and being Indian was a unique, even honorable thing. Once the truth was known, Jubal seemed to embrace his heritage. On the football field that final year— and in the pros afterward, for a while—he took to calling himself the Wild Warrior and let his hair grow long. Off the football field, he often wore a beaded headband and sometimes a feather. He didn't return to Aurora until the following spring, when his mother died, and by then Cork was long gone, off to Chicago, training to wear the blue uniform of a cop. Cork didn't learn about Jubal's mother until later. When he did, he sent a letter of condolence, which Jubal never answered. Cork understood. Gradually over the years, he and Jubal, like most high school friends, had eased into their adult lives and had drifted apart.

It was Willie Crane who brought them together again. It happened in the spring.

Cork worked third-shift patrol, the late shift, and had just arrived home at eight a.m., ready to get some shut-eye, when his telephone rang.

"O'Connor," he answered.

"Hello, Cork. It's Willie Crane." *LoCor. IsWillieCrane.*

"Willie? My God, it's been forever. How are you?"

"Okay. I'm in Chicago. I was wondering if I could see you."

It had been a long time since Cork had heard his voice, but in the interim, Willie had improved his speech a little, and Cork had no trouble understanding the words.

"Sure, Willie. How long are you in town?"

"Not long, I hope. It kind of depends on you."

"Why?"

"When we talk, you'll understand. It's important. It's about Winona."

"What about her?"

"I'd rather talk in person."

"All right. How about breakfast right now?"

Willie was staying at the Congress Hotel on Michigan Avenue, and Cork met him there. He still walked with the shuffling gait Cork remembered well, but even that seemed to have improved a little. They sat at a table near a window that looked east toward Grant Park. Cork hadn't seen Willie in almost six years. Winona's brother had grown tall and lean and handsome. Cork had heard that Willie was making a name for himself as a wildlife photographer and a nature writer. Anyone looking at Willie who didn't know him would have been surprised. But from very early, Cork had seen the strength that was at the heart of Willie Crane.

"I hear you're doing well," Cork told him. Willie looked surprised, and Cork explained, "The rez telegraph reaches all the way to Chicago."

"I've worked hard. And I love what I do. You, too, I bet. I'm not surprised at all that you're a cop. Just that you're a cop here."

"My father's family are all from Chicago, Willie, and a lot of them are cops. It's not Aurora, but it feels comfortable to me."

"I hear you've met someone."

Willie was talking about Jo McKenzie, a law student at the University of Chicago, whom Cork had met on a routine burglary call and had fallen for. It was serious, although they weren't talking marriage yet. He was amazed that Willie knew.

Willie apparently saw his surprise and grinned. "The rez telegraph."

"What about Winona?" Cork finally said.

Willie's aspect turned grave. "She's in trouble."

"What kind of trouble?"

"Serious. She's in Oregon, hooked up with some people who aren't good people, and I need to get her away from them."

"What do you mean 'not good people'?"

"For one thing, the man she's with abuses her."

"Beats her?"

"That. And other things, I'm sure."

"Why doesn't she leave him?" Which was a natural question, although Cork had been on plenty of domestic disturbance calls in which the woman, clearly abused, refused to leave her abuser.

"At this point, I believe that, even if she wanted to, she couldn't. He won't let her."

"She's being held against her will? That's kidnapping. The Oregon authorities should be involved, Willie."

"It would be hard to prove, and there's another reason the authorities shouldn't be involved. These people she's with, they grow marijuana for a living. It's a pretty big operation."

"And you're afraid of what might happen to her because of her part in that?"

"It would just be better if we could get her away on our own."

"Ah," Cork said, suddenly getting it. "You want me to help you rescue Winona."

"I can't do it alone," Willie said.

"Just you and me? My guess is that, if those people are involved in drug trafficking, they're armed. And even if we got to her, there's no guarantee she'd leave with us."

"Jubal Little," Willie replied.

"What?"

"She would leave if Jubal asked her to."

"Jubal and her, that was a long time ago, Willie."

"Henry Meloux told me once that they're like two halves of a broken stone," Willie said. "The last time I saw her, all she talked about was Jubal. To her, it's like yesterday."

"I don't know."

"Please."

"I haven't spoken to him in years."

Out of college, Jubal Little had been drafted by the Los Angeles Rams. He was on their roster for two seasons, but his style, which network commentators tended to characterize as "undisciplined," relied enormously on his ability to scramble and make something out of a broken play. He had trouble working within the rigid professional system, and he'd been cut. He was picked up by the Denver Broncos but lasted only a season. The Kansas City Chiefs gave him a shot, but there, too, he'd proved a disappointment, and after two years of mostly sitting on the bench, he'd been let go. No one had shown any interest in him since. Cork wasn't even certain where Jubal was living at the moment.

"I don't know what else to do, who else to ask," Willie said.

Cork looked at his watch. "Tell you what. Hang tight in your hotel room today. I'll see if I can track down a telephone number for Jubal, and if I'm lucky, we'll give him a call."

Willie looked relieved and grateful. He reached out and took Cork's hand. "Henry Meloux asked me to tell you something. He said, 'Remind Corcoran O'Connor that I named him well.' I don't know what that means."

"Henry gave me my Ojibwe name," Cork said. "Mikiinak."

"Snapping turtle?"

Cork shrugged. "Tenacious, I think, is his point."

Willie thought about it. "And dangerous. A big snapper can take your finger right off. Thank you, Cork."

He didn't exactly go by the book, but Cork got the private telephone number for Jubal Little, who was living in Durango, Colorado. The La Plata County deputy Cork connected with told him Jubal worked for a company that custom-built expensive log homes.

"Yeah, this is Jube."

Jube? Cork wondered. *When did that happen?*

"Jubal, this is Cork O'Connor."

There was a long pause, then, "You've got to be shitting me."

"God's truth. It's Cork."

"Well, son of a gun. Where are you? Chicago still? Last we talked, you were going to try to get yourself into a cop's uniform."

"Yeah, still in Chicago. And, yeah, I got the uniform."

"No kidding. I could've told you fifteen years ago that's exactly what you'd end up doing. You always were the poster child for truth, justice, and the American way." Jubal laughed and asked, "What's this about?"

Cork explained the situation, and Jubal said nothing the whole time. For a while after he'd finished, Cork heard only the hiss of the static across the long distance.

Then Jubal said, "When do we leave?"

CHAPTER 21

Although Cork had often watched Jubal Little play football on the television screen, in the flesh, his old friend was startling to behold. Jubal had grown. Not just in height but also in mass. His football career had dictated that he create a body that could take brutal beatings week after week, pounding from men as big as rodeo bulls. And a magnificent body it was, broad and towering. But there was something that diminished his presence, an air of uncertainty, of defeat that Cork had never seen in him when they were kids. In high school in Aurora, when Jubal walked the halls between classes, the sea of bodies would part for him. It was subtle, but now Cork thought he saw in Jubal's eyes a look of desperation, the look of the lost.

They used Willie's American Express Gold Card and rented a Jeep at the Portland airport, then drove east down the Columbia River Gorge. It was early April, and Cork had never seen air so gray or mist so viscous. He had a sense of mountains rising up almost from the roadside, but a hundred yards above him, everything was swallowed by cloud and drizzle. The great river on their left looked as cold as water could get without becoming ice. On their right, waterfall after waterfall unspooled long, loose threads of liquid that hung down the face of wet black rock. It seemed like a world in which moss and rot reigned.

They passed through Hood River, a dismal-looking little

town squatting among the hills. They had breakfast, and Jubal flirted with the waitress, a pleasant woman who easily told him her name was Johanna Sisu. He asked, "So, Johanna, when will we see the sun?"

She laughed, didn't bother to look at her watch, but simply nodded instead toward the calendar on the wall. " 'Nother month, give or take a week."

Cork and Willie tipped her well. Jubal left her with only the golden memory of his smile.

Twenty miles later, they hit The Dalles and turned south into great hills that were soft and green with winter wheat. At Madras, they veered east again and eventually entered a desolate area of plateaus and canyons carved out of thick layers of old lava flow.

"The Great Oregon Desert," Willie said. *ThGreOrgnDeser.*

"You came out here alone?" Jubal asked, clearly astonished.

"I go everywhere alone."

There was no resentment in Willie's voice, but the statement saddened Cork. As kids, Willie and Winona had been inseparable, and her leaving must have been a terrible blow.

"What have you been up to, Willie?" Jubal asked.

"School mostly. I got my B.A. from the U of M in the Twin Cities, then did graduate work at Yale."

"Yale?" Jubal said. "You went to Yale?"

"For a while. I missed the North Country and came home after a year. I have a studio near Allouette now, but I go all over doing shoots for magazines."

"Willie's work has been in *National Geographic*," Cork said. He was driving, with Jubal riding shotgun. Willie was in back.

"*National Geographic*? I'll be a son of a bitch," Jubal said. "My hat's off to you, Willie."

"I've been lucky."

Cork knew there was more than luck involved. There was something at the heart of Willie Crane immeasurably strong and immensely admirable. He'd seen it sometimes, great adversity shaping great character. It could work the other way as well, killing everything in the human spirit. What made the difference, maybe only Kitchimanidoo or God alone knew.

"You've done pretty good, too," Willie said to Jubal. "I've watched you play on television. But you didn't play last year."

"I couldn't find an offense where I felt I fit in," Jubal said, with a note of defensiveness. "I'm in talks with the Dallas organization. I expect to hear from the Cowboys any day now."

"What are you doing in the meantime?"

"A friend of mine, guy I know from my days with the Broncos, he and I build luxury mountain homes."

Which, as Cork understood it from his discussion with the La Plata deputy, was an exaggeration at best. But he said nothing.

They reached a river called the John Day and then drove through a small town called Furlough, which wasn't much more than a grid of a dozen streets lined with cottonwoods, a grocery store, two bars, and a gas station, everything dusty-looking. A few miles beyond, they turned onto a dirt road that followed a rocky creek, and they began to climb in altitude. After five miles or so, Willie said, "Stop at the crest of this hill ahead."

Cork did as he'd been instructed. Beyond the rise lay a little valley, and beyond the valley rose blue mountains capped with snow. A stream ran the length of the valley, and on both sides of the stream grew orchards. In the middle of the orchards was a big white house and outbuildings.

They got out of the Jeep, stood on the dirt road, and studied the scene below them. A cool wind blew at their backs. In that high desert place, the air smelled of fresh sage.

"A man named Spenser McMurphy started this as a sheep ranch in the eighteen hundreds," Willie said. "A couple of generations later, it became what they refer to out here as a fruit ranch. It's owned by the McMurphys, three brothers. The oldest is Crandall. He's maybe forty, a bachelor, unattached. Middle brother is Caleb. Late thirties, married, has one son, a teenager named Beckett. Youngest brother is Cole. He's a few years older than Winona, and he's the one she's with. They all live communally in that one big house."

"Crandall McMurphy?" Cork asked. "Isn't that the guy in *One Flew Over the Cuckoo's Nest*?"

"That's Randle," Willie said. "But McMurphy went to college with Kesey and they were both wrestlers. Folks in Furlough are positive that Kesey based the character in his book on Crandall. Both of them, I guess, are sly and more than a little crazy. From what I understand, they're all a rough bunch."

"You told me they were heavily involved in drugs," Cork said.

Willie nodded. "The orchard's just a cover. They have several marijuana grows along the creek down the valley."

"You learned this just by asking around?" Cork was frankly amazed.

"No. I tracked them when I was here last week. It's planting season, and they've been busy getting the grows ready."

"How long has Winona been with them?" Jubal asked.

"She came here a little over a year ago."

"Came from where?"

"San Francisco. She was living on the streets."

"Homeless?" Jubal said, obviously dismayed.

"She preferred to be called a free spirit."

"You've seen her since she left Aurora?" Cork asked.

"Only once, a few years ago. She agreed to meet me when I flew to the Bay Area for an exhibit of my photographs."

Cork said, "How'd it go? The meeting, I mean."

"Awful. She was so lost. I begged her to come home, but she refused. I think she felt ashamed of what she'd become. She was into drugs, panhandling on the streets. Maybe worse. The one thing she agreed to was to let me send her money. Which I did. It was never much, but she wrote me that it helped, and she was grateful. Then she wrote me that she'd hooked up with a guy named Cole McMurphy and was moving to Furlough. I haven't heard from her since."

"Did you still send letters and money?"

"Yes, but I don't know if she got them."

"Have you tried to talk to her here?"

"I never got the chance. I had to ask around in Furlough to even find this place, and word got back pretty fast to the Mc-Murphy brothers. Crandall and Cole came looking for me. If I didn't talk so funny or walk so badly, they might have got physical with me. Folks tend to write me off. All they did was warn me not to try to see Winona."

"And if you did?" Jubal asked.

"It wouldn't go well for me, or for Winona. They weren't bluffing. When I was here last week, I spent three full days just watching that place down there. I saw how Winona gets treated. The other woman, too. It's not good."

Darkness swept over Jubal. He turned his back to the valley and slammed his fist on the hood of the Jeep. "My fault," he said. "Goddamn it, it's all my fault. She'd never have left Tamarack County except for me."

Willie didn't argue, but Cork said, "Blame gets us nowhere, Jubal. We've got to figure out how to get her away from there."

"We just go in and take her," Jubal declared.

Willie shook his head. "We would be trespassing, and it would be kidnapping. They have guns, and folks around here are pretty isolated and tight. I'm guessing the local authorities have some idea of what the McMurphys are up to but don't care, or maybe they're being paid off. If push came to shove, we'd be taking the bigger risk. Besides, I have another idea."

Jubal drew himself up, huge and angry, and said, "Let's hear it."

At dusk Cork and Jubal went to the store in Furlough. They left Willie behind because he didn't want to take a chance on being recognized in town. They bought cold cuts, cheese, bread, and soft drinks. They also bought a big thermos and filled it with hot coffee. When they came back, Willie directed them to a jumble of rocks a mile from the orchards, but still high in the hills above the valley. They parked the Jeep where it couldn't be seen from the road and hunkered down to wait for morning.

The sky was clear and the night was cold. The moon rose late, full and ice white over the valley. Cork slept fitfully in the front passenger seat of the Jeep. Willie dozed behind the wheel, and Jubal took up the whole of the backseat. Cork woke often and several times heard the cry of coyotes in the hills around them. Near morning, he woke again and couldn't go back to sleep. He took the thermos, slipped away, and climbed up to the flat top of one of the rocks that hid the Jeep. Below him, the orchards formed an irregular darkness against the moonlit wild grass that filled the valley. It reminded him of a huge bruise on a patch of pale skin. The white house, iridescent in the brilliant moonlight, dominated the middle of all that darkness. Somewhere inside, Winona slept. He poured coffee into the thermos cup and, while he sipped the tepid brew, tried to imagine what she was like now after all she'd been through. He thought about Stockholm syndrome, and wondered if, despite all they would be risking for her, Winona would actually agree to let them take her away. If she refused, what could they do?

He heard the scrape of a belt buckle across the rock at his back. Jubal crawled up beside him and stared a long time into the valley, saying not a word.

"You ever want to go back, Cork?"

"Back?"

"To when everything wasn't so complicated."

"Moot issue, Jubal. You can't go back. As far as I know, in life there's only forward."

Jubal was silent again. In the hills above them and to the left, a coyote howled. It seemed a forlorn sound, although Cork knew that under other circumstances he might have heard it differently.

"Back in Chicago, is there anyone special?" Jubal asked.

"Yeah. A woman named Jo."

"Is it serious?"

"It's headed that way."

"Me, I've had more women than I can remember. They all kind of blend together." Jubal's eyes fixed on the white house at the center of the darkness. "Except for one." He turned back and glanced at the Jeep. "That Willie. Man, he's amazing."

"He always has been," Cork said.

"He's getting famous. And you, you're doing exactly what you always wanted to do. It's funny."

"What's funny?"

"Don't take this the wrong way, but I always figured I was the one most likely to succeed."

"You've failed?"

"Hell," Jubal said. "I'm a washed-up football player. I've got no prospects at all on the horizon. That stuff I told you about, talking to the Dallas Cowboys, that's bullshit. Nobody's interested in me. You want to know the truth? Right now, I'm just a construction worker. A big, dumb ladder monkey."

Cork didn't know what to say to that, so he just looked at the moon. Jubal looked there, too.

"Winona had a vision once," he said. "She saw me on a mountaintop, holding the moon and the sun in my hands, the stars singing around my head. She told me I was destined for greatness." Jubal stood and reached skyward as if to take all the heavens in his hands. Then he held them out, empty, and shook his head. "So much for visions."

They heard the Jeep door close, and in another minute, Willie joined them atop the rock.

"Sun's up in an hour," he said. *Sunsupinour.*

"Any coffee left in that thermos, Cork?" Jubal asked.

They shared coffee from the same cup and listened to the birds that had begun to chatter, and watched the eastern sky above the distant mountains turn amethyst then amber, and waited for signs of life to come from the ranch house in the valley so that Willie's plan could be set in motion.

This was what Willie had proposed.

Every morning the McMurphys rose around six. They had breakfast. Then the three brothers headed south down the valley to tend to their marijuana grows. They would come back around noon, have lunch, and work the orchards the rest of the day. When the McMurphy brothers left after breakfast, Beckett, who was a freshman in high school, would ride an ATV to the main road, where a bus picked him up and took him to school in John Day. Which left only the two women at the house. And that, Willie had suggested, was when they would make their move.

Lights began to wink on in the house a few minutes after six. The sun was still below the mountains to the east, and the valley lay in the blue of their shadow. Cork took turns with his companions, staring through a pair of field glasses that Willie had brought, watching the fruit ranch for activity.

By seven, the sun was above the mountains and the valley was beginning to warm. Willie had the field glasses, and he said, "They're leaving."

Cork squinted and could just barely make out small figures moving in the yard between the house and what looked to be the barn. They went to a brown pickup, got in, and a moment later, across the mile of dry, high desert that separated them, Cork heard the distant sound of an engine growling to life. The pickup pulled out of the yard and down a lane that ran between the trees of the orchard. Outside the orchard, where the lane met the dirt road that came in over the hills from the main highway, they turned south. The pickup kicked up a little rooster tail of dust as it went, and Cork finally lost sight of it as it disappeared behind the broad chest of the hills where he and the others lay watching.

"How long before the kid takes off?" Jubal asked.

"Beckett should be leaving any time now," Willie replied.

But Beckett didn't leave. They waited nearly an hour, and there was no more movement at the fruit ranch below.

"What the hell's going on?" Jubal finally asked, tense and impatient. "Where's the kid?"

Cork said, "Sick maybe. Or maybe it's spring break for schools in Oregon. Or maybe he's just playing hooky. Whatever it is, we need to rethink our plan."

"Hell," Jubal said. "It's just the kid and his mother with Winona now. We can't handle a kid and a woman, we're in trouble."

Cork said, "If there's a rifle in that house and he's been taught how to use it, he can give us plenty of trouble. I don't want any blood shed over this."

Willie said, "What should we do?"

"If we drive down, they'll see us coming for sure. I'd rather catch them by surprise." Cork looked at Willie. "Can you handle the Jeep?"

"Yes."

"Okay, then Jubal and I are going to hoof it down there, sneak through the orchards to the house. When you reconnoitered here last week, Willie, did you see a dog?"

"Yes, but he always went with the men."

"Let's hope he went with them today."

"We get down there, then what?" Jubal said.

"We find Winona and talk to her. And then we bring her out. Willie, you keep those field glasses glued to your eyes. When you see us leave the house with Winona, you come down there fast."

"And if that kid goes for a rifle?" Jubal said.

"We talk to him."

"You got a lot of faith in talk."

"Talk doesn't kill people, Jubal."

Jubal eyed him a long moment, then laughed. "Shoot, we got nothing to lose. Let's find Winona."

CHAPTER 22

Cork and Jubal left the rocks and followed the road, which dropped into the valley in a series of lazy switchbacks. All those curves worried Cork. He hoped Willie's assurance that he could handle the Jeep hadn't been just cavalier or wishful thinking.

There was a white rail fence around the orchards, badly in need of whitewash, rotted in many places, completely collapsed in others. Cork and Jubal stepped over a fallen section and slipped among the rows of fruit trees. There were buds but no blossoms yet, and Cork couldn't tell what kind of fruit they might bear. He and Jubal moved quickly until they came to the place where the trees gave way to the yard. They paused, and Cork studied the house. It was a classic, old ranch house, two stories, with a long front porch and a widow's walk. White curtains framed the windows, but beyond that, the interior was invisible. Cork thought it would be best to slip in through the back door. He tapped Jubal's arm and signaled that way, but Jubal's eyes weren't on Cork. They were riveted to the front of the house. When Cork looked there, he saw what had captured his friend's attention. Winona was crossing the porch and descending the front steps.

There was no mistaking her. Her hair was shorter, and she seemed thinner, but even from fifty yards away, it was easy to see that she was every bit as graceful and lovely as Cork remembered.

She crossed the yard and entered the barn.

Without waiting for Cork, Jubal began to lope among the trees, following a course that would circle to the back of the barn. Cork was right on his heels. When the barn was between them and the house, they broke from cover. They raced to a back door, which had an old latch. Jubal lifted the latch, and when he swung the door wide, a bright corridor of sunlight cut through the dark of the barn's interior. Jubal stepped into that sunlit corridor, and his shadow, huge and black and menacing, fell on the dirt before him.

"Oh!" came a small cry from inside.

And then Cork was in the barn, too, standing next to Jubal and looking into the beautiful, stupefied face of Winona Crane.

Even after all the years, Cork found himself responding much as he had when he was a kid. Something melted in him, then formed into a solid longing. Winona Crane was the first girl he'd ever really loved, and although what he felt now was different, shaped by his age and experience, it was also very familiar.

But Winona wasn't even looking at Cork. She stared at Jubal, stared with an open mouth, stared as if she were seeing a ghost, or a dream, something that had to be unreal. Her eyes were almond-colored with a glint of fire from the sun. Her hair was black, but dull-looking, in need of a wash. She wore an old flannel shirt with the sleeves rolled to her elbows and jeans so faded they were colored with only the memory of blue, and she had on dirty tennis shoes.

What was most noticeable to Cork, however, was a discoloration along her left jawline just below her ear, the pale yellow of an old bruise.

Jubal spoke first. "Hello, Winona." There was something like reverence in his voice.

"It . . . how . . . you . . ." she stammered.

Jubal took a tentative step toward her, but she retreated and looked away. "You can't be here," she said.

"I am here." Jubal took another step. "And I'm not leaving without you."

"If they come back . . ." she began.

Cork said, "We'll be gone before they come back."

Winona finally seemed to notice him. "How did you find me?"

"Willie," Cork said.

"Willie? He's here?"

"He's waiting for us in the hills. Winona, we have to go."

But she didn't move. Her eyes settled again on Jubal, and a sad smile crossed her lips. "I've thought about you every day."

Jubal walked to her carefully, as if approaching a skittish wild animal, and slowly reached out and took her hand. "Nothing's felt right since you left me. Nothing's worked out the way I thought it would. I need you, Winona. And you need me. Remember what Henry Meloux said about us?"

"Two halves of a broken stone," she answered.

Jubal put his arms around her, huge arms bulked by pressing iron, and held her gently.

"We need to go," Cork said.

Winona eased from Jubal's embrace. "I can't."

"You're coming," Jubal said.

"My life's . . . different, Jubal. You don't know me."

"My life's different, too, Winona. No moon, no stars like you promised. No mountaintop. Just emptiness. Just wanting."

"Look at me." There were tears in her eyes. "I wouldn't be any good for you now."

"Without you, I won't be good for anything. Please, Winona. Come with me."

The barn door opened at Winona's back, and two figures stepped inside, a woman and the kid Cork figured was Beckett. Beckett held the rifle Cork had hoped would not come into play.

"What's going on?" It was the woman who spoke. "Who are these men, Nona?"

Winona turned. "Friends, Petra. Just old friends."

The woman was tall and painfully thin, with blond hair full of wild curls. She wore an old print dress, the kind people then called a "granny." Her feet were bare. She was, Cork guessed, in her late thirties. Beckett, a boy nearly as tall as she, with hair that was the color of wet creek sand and that hung nearly to his shoulders, stood beside her. He held the rifle with the barrel pointed in the direction of Jubal and Winona. He worried Cork, not because he looked menacing but because he looked scared. A scared kid with a loaded rifle was pretty much the circumstance Cork had feared most.

"What are they doing here?" Petra demanded.

"They want me to go with them."

Petra looked horrified at that thought. "You can't go." She sounded as desperate in her desire to have Winona stay as Jubal in his desire to have her leave. "What'll I do if you go?"

"Go with me," Winona said.

"She's not going nowhere," Beckett said. His voice broke as he stammered. "And neither is Nona. You all just get out of here. Just go." He waved the barrel toward the door.

"We're not leaving without Winona," Jubal said. He spoke with a firmness, a certainty Cork hadn't heard since they'd reconnected. It was the voice of the old Jubal.

"Me and this rifle say different."

Cork's eyes shifted between Jubal's face and the face of the kid. He saw fearlessness in one and nothing but fear in the other, and between them nothing but disaster. "Corcoran O'Connor," he said stepping forward. "Chicago Police Department. Son, I want you to put that rifle down. Put it down now."

"Chicago? What are you doing here?" Beckett asked.

"We came to bring our friend home, that's all. If you try to stop us, it will be kidnapping. There'll be cops all over this place. Is that what you want?"

Beckett looked at Winona, looked at her like a kid with no clue. "Do you want to go?"

Winona thought for a moment, then nodded. "Yes, Beckett. Yes, I do."

His eyes jumped from Cork to Jubal and back. "I think we need to talk to Uncle Cole about this."

Jubal said, "I'm going out through that door right now, and

I'm taking my friend. You can shoot me, or you can move aside and let me pass."

Jubal stepped in front of Winona and Cork and began to walk forward. The kid's eyes grew wide, owl-like, and he leveled the barrel at Jubal's chest. Cork knew this was not the way to play it, but Jubal had made his move, and anything Cork did would only confuse the kid more and maybe push him over the line.

Beckett retreated a step, then another. And then, more by accident than by design, stood with his back against the frame of the barn door, his body blocking their way. He could no longer simply step aside and let them pass. Unless he folded completely now, they would have to go through him. Blood pounded in Cork's temples, and his gut seemed to empty and then draw taut as he readied for the chaos of what he was afraid was about to come.

Suddenly Winona stepped from behind the shield of Jubal's body and put a hand on his arm to hold him back.

"Beck," she said gently. "These are my friends, and all they want is to take me home. That's all I want, too. Just to go home. Please."

She walked ahead, slowly, and to Cork she became a being of enigmatic contradiction. Her body seemed such a frail thing, slender and delicate, yet there was an unquestionable power in her spirit, in her measured step, even in the very gentleness of her voice. She closed the gap between herself and the end of the rifle, and her eyes never left the face of the boy in the doorway.

"Please, Beck," she said, reaching out as she neared him. "Let me go home." She put her fingers against the rifle barrel and eased it aside.

The moment the rifle was no longer pointed at them, Jubal sprang. In three long strides, done in the blink of an eye, he was on the kid, yanking the firearm from his hands and shoving him roughly out the door. Petra screamed, and Winona said, "Oh, Jubal, you didn't have to do that."

Through the open door, Cork saw the kid scramble to his feet and take off at a run. A moment later, he heard the sound of a small engine kick over and come to life. The ATV, he figured. And he knew the kid was going for his father and his uncles.

Jubal lifted the rifle to his shoulder.

Cork raced forward and tried to yank the firearm from Jubal's grip. "Let him go, Jubal," he barked.

Jubal shoved him away as the ATV shot down the lane between the trees and was gone. He turned on Cork, his face gone red with rage, and there was murder in his eyes. When they were kids, such a look would have shriveled Cork's heart. But he'd patrolled the streets of South Side Chicago long enough to have been glared at by men bigger and meaner and more heartless than Jubal Little could ever be. Still, Jubal was the one with the rifle, and Cork took a step back.

Winona came between them. "We need to go," she said. "Now." She turned to the other woman. "Oh, Petra, come with us."

"I can't," Petra said, her abject misery obvious. "Go. Go before they come back."

Winona hugged her briefly, kissed her cheek, and turned to Jubal. "Let's go."

They ran, following the lane between the trees where the ATV had gone. They neared the edge of the orchard with its broken-down white fence, and Cork saw the dust raised by the Jeep as Willie drove it out of the hills.

They kept running, and the Jeep hit the flat of the valley floor and bore down on them. As Willie pulled up to them and stopped, Cork cried out, "Let me drive."

Willie slid from his seat. While he shuffled around to the passenger side, Jubal and Winona piled in back. Cork turned the Jeep in a tight arc, and they shot toward the safety of the hills. In the rearview mirror, through the cloud kicked up behind them, he caught sight of another storm of dust rising far down the valley. The approaching McMurphys. He leaned more heavily on the accelerator.

They hit the switchbacks and began to climb. Cork took the turns hard and fast, and the tires slid precariously across the dirt roadbed. Below them, the brown pickup swung into the lane that led between the trees to the ranch house.

They hit the crest of the hill and, on the other side, followed the creek with its cottonwoods as it wound its way toward the main road into Furlough. Cork's eyes swung between the empty road ahead and the veil of dust behind him that was all he could see in the mirror now. After several miles, it became clear that the McMurphys had opted not to follow, and Cork slowed to a more reasonable speed.

"Could you stop?" Winona asked.

"I'd prefer to keep going," Cork said. "At least until I can see civilization."

"She asked you to stop," Jubal said.

Cork had heard watch commanders deliver orders in that same voice, and it rankled him. But he pulled to the side of the road and killed the engine.

Winona spoke again. "Could I get out, just for a minute?"

They all left the Jeep and gathered at the side of the road. Winona held herself as if she was cold.

"Are you all right?" Willie asked. *Arouaureye?*

"Everything's happened so fast, I just need to center a little." She looked at her brother and seemed for the first time to notice him. "Oh, Willie, this was your doing, wasn't it?" She threw her arms around him and held him for a long time, and her shoulders shook as she wept.

"It's okay, Nona." Willie spoke softly, with his cheek against her boyish hair.

She let go of her brother and turned to Cork.

"Is it really you?"

"Yeah," Cork said.

She wiped tears from her cheeks. "You look so . . . manly."

"I shave and everything," Cork said.

She smiled, and her eyes went to Jubal, and what was in

them was the same look that had been there the first time she'd seen him in Grant Park, when they were all hardly more than children. "It's been a long time."

She might as well have been a magnet, and his eyes two steel balls, because he couldn't look away from her face. When he finally spoke, he sounded like a man in a trance. "It's been forever."

In the next instant she was in his arms, with her face against his massive chest. She wept and murmured, "I don't deserve this."

He stroked her hair and said, "No, no. It was all those years of crap you didn't deserve. And that was my fault. All my fault. But I'm here now, and I'm taking you back where you belong."

"Home," she said and put her hand to her mouth as if in utter amazement.

"We should be going," Cork said. "Just in case they change their minds about following. There'll be time for reunions later."

"Yes," Winona said and stepped away from Jubal, and looked shyly down.

Willie helped her into the Jeep. Jubal held back and leaned to Cork and said in a low voice, "About that rifle."

"What about it?"

Jubal gave him another withering look and said, "Don't ever try to take anything from me again." He quit Cork and joined Winona in the backseat of the Jeep.

In the months that followed, the lives of Jubal and Winona shifted dramatically. Winona returned to the rez, where she became a kind of recluse. Jubal spent that spring and summer in Aurora, mostly in the company of Winona. He changed or, more accurately, changed back. It was as if he found something in his own being that had been lost, and he became whole again. He negotiated a tryout with the Minnesota Vikings and secured a spot on their roster that fall. By midseason, he'd become their starting quarterback, a position he would hold for the next ten years. In that time, he would create for himself a lasting place in the hearts of most Minnesotans.

Cork returned to Chicago, married Nancy Jo McKenzie, and a few years later, brought his family home to Aurora.

When Cork finished his story, Rainy laid her head on his bare chest. Her breath ghosted over his skin, warm and familiar. "So the old Jubal came back," she said.

"Not the old Jubal, although some of him was still there. He grew into someone else, the man he always believed he was meant to be, a guy destined for something great. And greatness takes up a lot of space. There wasn't room for anyone near him who might challenge him."

"That would be you?"

"Turned out that way. Jubal and I still had some good years ahead of us, good moments that felt like the old days. When Winona came back, he had reason to come back to Aurora, too. He spent winters here, used it as his official place of residence. Once in a great while, the old Jubal would slip out, and it would feel like it did in the old days."

Cork stroked Rainy's hair and finally asked the question that had been, in large part, the reason he'd come.

"Rainy, the day Jubal was killed, when I came here to talk to you and Henry, I asked if the name Rhiannon meant anything to you. Do you remember?"

"Sure. It was Jubal's Rosebud. The name on his lips as he died. Hard to forget."

"Did you talk to anyone about Rhiannon?"

"I asked Uncle Henry. The name meant nothing to him."

"You spoke to no one else?"

"I'm pretty sure not. Why?"

"Do me a favor," Cork said. "Promise me you won't mention the name to anyone."

Rainy eyed him with a mix of suspicion and concern. "What's going on, Cork?"

He thought of just trying to elicit a promise without an

explanation, but he knew Rainy wouldn't let it go at that. So he told her about the threatening phone call he'd received the night before.

"No idea who it was?"

"Male, that's all I can say."

"Maybe the same person who set you up in Jubal's murder?"

"Maybe. But I don't see the connection yet. Could be it's the other shoe I've been expecting to fall any minute. I just don't know. At the moment, nothing makes much sense to me. Until it does, promise me that Rhiannon goes no farther than us."

"It will give you peace of mind?"

"It will."

"Consider it done," she said and kissed him.

His cell phone beckoned from the pocket of his jacket, which hung on the back of one of Rainy's chairs. He said, "I'd better take that." He left the bed and, naked, danced across the cold cabin floor. He checked caller ID. The call was coming from his house on Gooseberry Lane. It turned out to be Jenny.

"You better come home, Dad."

"What's up?"

"The sheriff's people are here. They have a warrant to search our house."

CHAPTER 23

It was early enough that the media hadn't yet roused themselves for the day, and when Cork turned onto Gooseberry Lane, he saw no television vans or reporters. A few of his neighbors were out, standing on their lawns, watching the sheriff's people and agents of the BCA moving in and out of his house. The driveway was blocked by a Tamarack County Sheriff's Department cruiser and a dark blue sedan with state plates, and the garage door had been raised. Jenny's Subaru, which normally would have been in the garage, was parked on the street. Cork pulled up behind it and got out. Agent Phillip Holter and Captain Ed Larson came from the house and met him on the porch steps.

"What's going on?" Cork asked, keeping his voice low, though he wanted to scream the question. The sun was up, the sky clear and bright, but the morning was still cold enough that his breath huffed out visibly, like blasts of steam.

"The arrow that killed Jubal Little," Holter replied. "Your prints are all over it. And only your prints."

"I put my hand around that arrow, Agent Holter. Jubal insisted that I see if it might easily be pushed through or pulled out."

"When the sheriff's people got there, the arrow was still in him," Holter said.

"Of course it was. I had no intention of actually moving it. It was a hunting arrow, for Christ's sake. You have any idea how badly I would have torn him up if I'd tried? And what's with the search warrant? If you wanted to go looking through my house, I'd have been happy to let you in."

Larson said quietly, reasonably, "We need to go by the book, Cork. For your sake as well as ours."

Holter said, "Mind coming with me to the garage?"

Cork followed him through the wide opening where the garage door had been lifted. It was a two-car structure, which Cork kept clean and well organized. On the north wall hung all his lawn and gardening tools. On the south, he'd mounted large hooks where the O'Connors hung their bicycles when not in use. Along the east wall, he'd created a work area, with a bench and long table and good, bright shop light. Hand tools hung from Peg-Board above the table, and to the right stood a shelving unit where he kept his power tools and supplies.

At the moment, one of the agent's team was boxing some materials from the shelves, but he paused when Cork and the others entered.

Holter said, "Take a break, Greg," and nodded for him to leave.

Holter walked to the worktable and picked up a section of what looked to be a long, slender dowel. He rolled it between his fingers, then held it up for Cork to look at.

"The beginning of an arrow?" he said.

"I make my own. But you already know that."

"Do you make them all the same? With the same pattern of fletching?"

"Yes. It's a way to identify my arrow from others that might be shot during a hunt."

"The arrow that killed Jubal Little was exactly like all the arrows in the hip quiver you wore that day. The same fletching."

"What of it?"

"One of yours?"

"Like one of mine," Cork said.

"Exactly like one of yours," Holter said. "Yet when Captain Larson here talked with you at the department immediately following Jubal Little's death, you never mentioned that fact."

"I knew Ed was smart enough to figure it out eventually."

"The arrow that killed the man identified as William Graham Chester, that was exactly like one of your arrows, too. Tell me, O'Connor, how is it that someone else could have shot an arrow you made? Or one exactly like it."

"My guess is that someone stole it. Or they made it in exactly the way I make mine."

"Stole it? Just came in and took it? You don't lock your doors?"

"Agent Holter, I don't know anyone in Aurora who locks their doors. Could I see that warrant? What exactly is it that you're looking for?"

"I'd like to see that warrant, too." A tall man with a long ponytail and dressed in a jean jacket and white shirt and blue jeans walked into the garage. He had eyes the color of chocolate brownies and a voice that spoke its words as slow and rich as maple syrup. This was Leon Papakee, Cork's attorney. Like Cork, he was what Indians sometimes called a "blood," a man of mixed heritage. Leon's Indian heritage was Meskwaki, out of Iowa.

"Thanks for coming, Leon," Cork said.

"Captain Larson, Agent Holter," Papakee greeted the officers. "Could I see the warrant, please? And where's Sheriff Dross?"

"Inside," Larson replied, nodding toward the house. "I'll get the warrant." He left the garage through the side door and headed to the house.

"I haven't seen you in a while, Phil," Papakee said casually. "How have you been?"

"Busy, Leon," Holter replied, just as easily.

"You two know each other?" Cork asked.

"We crossed swords once before," Papakee said. "The Louis Santee case, down in Granite Falls, couple of years ago. So, is the miscreant business booming, Phil?"

"Economy's down, Leon. Always drives the crime rate up."

"Think Jubal Little was killed because of the poor economy?"

"At this point, Leon, your speculation is as good as mine."

"My speculation is that my client had nothing to do with the recent deaths at Trickster's Point, and that your presence here is entirely unnecessary."

Before Holter could reply, Larson returned with the warrant and handed it to Papakee, who read it carefully.

"I'd like to talk with my client in private. All right?"

"Sure," Holter said with a magnanimous air.

They walked out of the garage and into the backyard. Trixie, the O'Connors' mutt, was lying in the sun near her doghouse. She roused herself when she saw the two men and trotted toward Cork, her tail wagging like a crazy metronome. She came between the men, and both Cork and Papakee leaned down to pet her.

"What do you know about Holter?" Cork asked.

"Ambitious as they come. By the book, but if he's got it in for you, he's like a bronc rider, and he'll stay on you till you break. The warrant's pretty specific," Papakee said. "They're taking any tools and materials that might relate to the making of arrows. That's understandable. But they're also taking your computers and printers. And they're looking for some flyers advertising your P.I. business. Any idea why?"

"Not a clue, Leon. I had those flyers printed several years ago, when I first started the business. I still print a few on my own now and then, but I can't imagine what they could possibly want with them."

"Do you have any left?"

"A few maybe, somewhere around my office. The document's still on my computer, too."

"Okay. Let's see if we can get to the bottom of this."

They headed back inside, and as soon as they rejoined the officers, Holter said, "I'd like you to come down to the sheriff's department, O'Connor. I have a few questions I want to ask you."

"Mind if I check in with my family first?"

"No, go right ahead." Holter glanced at Papakee. "You'll be accompanying your client, I imagine."

"From here on, consider us joined at the hip, Phil."

Holter gave a nod, almost dapper, as if welcoming the challenge of Papakee in the mix. He signaled to the agent who'd been standing in the driveway, and the man returned to his boxing of potential evidence.

Ed Larson said to Cork and Papakee, "We'll see you down at the department, gentlemen," then he and Holter left.

Inside the house, Cork found Jenny, Stephen, and Waaboo in the kitchen with Sheriff Marsha Dross. Dross had Waaboo on her lap. When Cork walked in, she looked up, and the smile that had been there dropped away.

"Hello, Cork," she said.

Beyond the doorway that opened onto the rest of the house, Cork saw uniforms moving in the hallway that led to his office, and up the stairs that led to the bedrooms.

"Morning, Marsha."

He worked at keeping his voice neutral. It was her job, he told himself, the job he'd once done and that he'd taught her to do. In her shoes, he'd have been forced to carry out the lawful search warrant. He might even have sat with the suspect's grandchild on his lap. Still, the whole thing stuck in his craw.

"Everyone cooperating?" His eyes went to Jenny and Stephen.

"Everything's fine, Dad." Jenny smiled, pretty reasonably given the circumstances.

"Yeah," Stephen agreed, though he didn't really sound agreeable at all. "Except we still don't know what they're looking for or why they're taking all our computer stuff."

"They must have good reason, Stephen, or Judge Eide wouldn't have signed the search warrant," Cork told him.

"You mean like evidence that you had something to do with killing Mr. Little?"

"Is that it, Marsha?" Cork asked.

Dross handed Waaboo back to Jenny, scooted her chair from the table, and stood up. She spoke carefully. "I'm sure your father has told you that a lot of police investigation is done in order to eliminate possibilities. Nothing would please me more, Stephen, than to eliminate the possibility that your father was involved."

"So that's what you're doing? Trying to prove he's innocent?"

"What we're doing is gathering evidence. It won't be for us to determine anyone's guilt or innocence. That's what juries are for."

Stephen looked as if he was about to argue, but Cork cut him off. "I need to go down to the sheriff's department for a little while. You guys do everything you're asked, okay?"

"Sure," Stephen said, but it was clear he had his reservations.

Cork sat in the interview room where Larson had questioned him following Jubal Little's death. Larson was there again, but this time it was Agent Phil Holter asking the questions, while Larson sat silent in a corner. Leon Papakee was there as well. Holter had stalled awhile in the beginning, and Cork wondered if Larson had insisted that he hold off until Dross returned from the house on Gooseberry Lane and could observe from the adjoining room where the proceedings were being recorded.

"So," Holter continued, pressing Cork about the man he and Stephen had found dead on the ridge above Trickster's Point, "you'd never seen that man before you stumbled on his body?"

"That's right."

"But you've seen this before."

From an evidence envelope, Holter pulled a familiar flyer that had the name of Cork's one-man security firm. It contained a listing of the kinds of jobs he would do. And contact information. In the lower right-hand corner there was a photograph of Cork that made him look like the kind of guy who not only would be able to see to your investigative needs but also could be relied on to keep to himself the secrets he might learn about you in the process. Cork had been pretty happy with that particular shot.

"Sure. I had those printed years ago, when I first hung out my shingle as a P.I."

"What about this?"

Holter turned the flyer over. Printed on the other side was a contour map of the area around Trickster's Point, taken from a U.S. Forest Service website. Below the map were instructions on how to find the logging road where the man ID'd as William Graham Chester had parked his vehicle, and the easiest route from there to the ridge overlooking Trickster's Point.

"We found this in the glove box of Chester's rental. It has your fingerprints, Chester's fingerprints, and a set of prints we haven't identified yet."

"I put those flyers up all over Tamarack County. In every bar and Laundromat and grocery store with a bulletin board. Anybody could have got hold of this."

Holter returned the flyer to the evidence envelope and frowned a moment, deep in thought. "You've told us that you and Little canoed from that landing on the eastern end of Lake Nanaboozhoo to Trickster's Point. Is that still your story?"

"Agent Holter, we're not happy with that particular phrasing. The word *story* suggests invention. What my client has told you is the truth."

"I'm just wondering, Counselor, if maybe your client didn't drop Little at Trickster's Point and then paddle down the shoreline a mile or so."

Cork said, "You mean to the landing spot Officer Berglund from the Border Patrol found, where someone walked in and joined the dead man? That wasn't me, Holter. Jubal and I landed together."

"And then split up? Was that a usual procedure when you hunted together?"

"Sometimes we'd separate because it gave us a better chance of coming across a deer trail to follow. Once we'd found something, we'd hook back up and hunt together. But on Saturday, we didn't really split up. Jubal just went ahead of me while I stowed the paddles with the canoe." Cork shifted in his chair and looked toward Larson, who'd been silent so far. "Have you followed up on this William Chester? Do you know anything about him?"

Larson spoke toward the ceiling light that masked the recording equipment. "Would you turn everything off, please."

Dross's voice came disembodied into the room. "You want us to stop recording?"

"Yes." Then Larson said quietly to Papakee, "Counselor, I'd like to speak with your client for a few minutes, alone and off the record."

"I don't think—" Papakee began.

Cork cut him off. "I'm okay with it, Leon."

"Hell, I'm not," Holter blurted.

"You can lodge a complaint with Sheriff Dross if you'd like, Phil, but I'm going to talk with Cork, and I'm going to talk with him alone."

Papakee gave Cork a clear look of warning, then shrugged and said, "I'll be outside."

Holter said, "You rural guys, you fuck everything up."

Larson said, "Out, Agent Holter. I'll let you know when you can come back in."

When they were alone, Larson said, "William Graham Chester is a phony name. The driver's license was a fake. Our guy's still a John Doe."

"What about the registration on the vehicle he drove out there?" Cork asked.

"A rental. He used a bogus credit card. We've run his fingerprints through AFIS. Nothing. This guy seems professional, and good enough that he's been able to stay below the legal radar." Larson shook his head. "Off the record, I think you're being set up, Cork. But there may be some hope. We got prints off the arrow that killed the John Doe. They're not yours."

"But you don't have a match on those either?"

"Not yet. They definitely don't belong to anyone we're currently looking at." Larson took off his glasses, leaned to Cork confidentially, and said in a low voice, "Do you have any idea who would want Jubal dead and who would want you to take the fall for it?"

"Jubal received a lot of threats."

"A lot of politicians, especially controversial ones, get threats. Very few get murdered. Who was crazy enough, or angry enough, to go through with the threat? And of those possibilities, who has something against you as well?"

"I don't know, Ed. I'll need to think about that."

"Don't think too long, Cork. The way this is playing out, I get the feeling that someone's gone through a lot of trouble to set you up. The trap hasn't sprung yet, but that doesn't mean it won't. If it does, I'd hate to see you caught in it."

Cork managed a smile and said, "You and me both."

CHAPTER 24

Whenever Cork lied, he was usually able to convince himself that it was for the best of reasons. In the interview room of the Tamarack County Sheriff's Department, he'd lied to Ed Larson. Larson had asked him if he knew who might want Jubal Little dead and also have enough of a grudge against Cork to want him to suffer in the bargain. Cork had said he'd have to think about it. In truth, however, two pretty solid possibilities had readily come to mind. He held back from telling Larson his suspicions because he knew that in Tamarack County word could spread quickly, and before he was responsible for the shadow of suspicion falling across other innocent folks, he wanted to do a little investigating on his own. At least, that's what he told himself.

He hadn't eaten at all that day and was famished. He grabbed a breakfast sandwich—biscuit, egg, sausage, cheese—and a cup of coffee from a convenience store on his way out of town and headed toward Yellow Lake, a community a few miles south of Aurora. Just outside that small town, he pulled off the road and parked in front of a long, ramshackle structure built of corrugated metal and that was decorated with signage crying out archery supplies, bow-hunting equipment, targets, decoys, and a fully equipped indoor practice range. Above the entrance loomed a huge, handcrafted placard that read: STRAIGHT ARROW, INC.

Cork opened the door, and a little bell tinkled, a fragile and incongruous sound considering what was represented by the merchandise inside. The place seemed empty, except for the presence of a cat that lay on the countertop next to the register. It was a Chinchilla Persian, an old feline with long fur the color of campfire smoke.

"Hey, Mattie." Cork spoke softly to the cat. "Where's the old man?"

"Old man?" The voice, indignant, came from the back room. A moment later, a guy with a square build and silver hair appeared, wearing a Hawaiian shirt and jeans. "This old man'll be happy to kick your butt, you don't speak more respectfully."

"Morning, Dale," Cork said.

Dale Basham came to the counter and stroked Mattie's fur. "Wasn't sure if I'd be seeing you again this season."

"Why's that?"

Basham shrugged. "Accident like the one up at Trickster's Point with Jubal Little, I figured you might be thinking of hanging your bow up for good. I tell guys all the time, don't shoot at the first thing that moves. You? I figured you knew better. Trained by Sam Winter Moon and all."

"What exactly have you heard?"

Basham picked up the cat, who began to purr.

Basham and Mattie were an interesting pair. Basham was Oklahoma born, had been a pilot during the war in Vietnam, then flown for Northwest Airlines. When he'd retired as a commercial pilot, he'd moved north to open the Straight Arrow. He'd brought along Mattie, a cat that was now more than two decades old and famously loved by Dale Basham. In the last few years, Mattie's heart had stopped five times, and Basham, using gentle CPR, had brought her back to life each time. On the surface, he might have appeared gruff—they'd called him Bash when he was in the service—but Cork figured any guy willing to do mouth-to-mouth on a feline couldn't be all badass. Strange maybe, but certainly good-hearted.

"What have I heard?" Basham put the cat back on the counter, and Mattie sprawled out—loose limbed and eyes closed—in a way that made Cork think the animal had suffered another heart attack, and maybe he'd see Basham in action. But the cat's purr box kept running. "Heard Jubal Little took an arrow in the heart. Hunting accident. Sheriff's Department claims they're still uncertain about some of the details. Got all that from the television and radio. Also heard, by way of the grapevine, that you were alone up there with him, and it was you who shot him."

"That's what folks are saying?"

"Enough of 'em that it got to me. Also heard they found some other fella dead up there, yeah? What's that all about?"

"You want to know the truth, Dale, that's what I'm trying to figure out. And maybe you can help me."

"Me?"

"You're the only retailer of archery equipment in these parts, so I figure most of us bow hunters buy from you."

"Or the Internet. Christ, I hate to tell you how much business those damn online stores have cost me."

"You know most of the good bow hunters in the area?"

"Lot of 'em."

"Lester Bigby bow-hunts, doesn't he?"

"Sure. Don't know if he's any good, but he buys here."

"Buys materials to make his own arrows?"

"Nah. He usually buys RedHead carbons. He's got himself a Bear Carnage, a top-of-the-line compound bow."

"Thought you said you didn't know if he was any good."

"Having a big dick doesn't guarantee a guy knows how to score. Got a lot of hunters come in, spend a shitload of money thinking the gear alone'll do the trick. You shop garage sales a year later and you can pick that stuff of theirs up for a dime."

"Have you seen Lester recently?"

"Came in just before season opener, bought that Bear Carnage I told you about."

"What about Isaiah Broom?"

Basham shook his head. "Makes all his own gear. Arrows,

bow, quiver. Hell, heard he fashions his bowstring out of elk sinew. Christ, I don't know anybody who gets that into it. He's good, I hear. Real good. Leastways, I never heard of *him* shooting anybody by accident."

By accident. That was the key phrase. Jubal Little's death had been no accident.

Cork decided not to try to change Basham's understanding of what had occurred at Trickster's Point. Until he knew who the real killer was, it would be useless to argue. And when the truth was finally known, argument would be unnecessary.

CHAPTER 25

Lester Bigby was a wealthy man. When he was twenty-two and just out of college, he'd taken over his father's logging operation, which had, by then, fallen on hard times, mostly because Buzz Bigby had come to prefer drinking to running his business. Lester turned the situation around and, when things were looking good again, sold the operation and invested the money in stocks. He chose wisely and did well, and then began doing the same for other people in the Arrowhead region of Minnesota. He'd established a good reputation as an investment counselor and had built a solid clientele. A couple of years earlier, he'd created the Crown Lake Development Company and had purchased a very large tract of land southwest of Aurora that included its own pristine lake, one of the very few in the area without any cabin homes already on the shoreline. Last spring, he'd begun construction of a luxury resort, but building had been halted in midsummer. Jubal Little was a large part of the reason.

Lester had built himself an ostentatious house on North Point Road, just outside the town limits. If there hadn't already been a number of outrageously ostentatious places on the point, his would have stood out magnificently. As it was, it became just another in a line of homes that, in Cork's opinion, had no place in what should have been the natural and simple beauty of the shoreline of Iron Lake.

He pulled into the drive, a ribbon of blacktop that curved through a lot of lawn and landscaped garden and stopped at the portico in front. Noon wasn't far off. The sky was clear blue, and the sun was bright, and the grass sparkled with the wetness of the last few days. Cork got out and was about to ring the bell when the door opened suddenly. Lester Bigby's wife, Emily, stood there, clearly startled to find Cork blocking her way.

"Oh!" she said and took a step back.

"Sorry, Emily," Cork said. "I didn't mean to scare you. I was just about to punch the doorbell."

She put a hand to her breast, as if stilling a wildly beating heart. "It's all right," she said. "I just . . . It's all right."

Like her husband, she was small, in her late thirties or early forties, attractive, with dark brown hair, long and nicely styled. She dressed well, expensively but not showy, and because Jo, who'd served with her for several years on the library board, had spoken well of her, Cork was inclined to like her.

"I'm looking for Lester. I tried his office in town, but he's not there. I was just wondering if he might be home."

"No, he's not," she said, still a little breathy from the fright.

"Know where I might find him?"

She glanced at her watch. "Have you tried the Broiler? He likes to lunch there."

The garage door opened, and a black Mercedes backed out. Cork saw the Bigbys' son, Lance, at the wheel of the sedan. He was Stephen's age, a big kid who reminded Cork uncomfortably of Donner. The genetic linkage to his dead uncle was clear in the massive build of his upper body, and whenever Cork looked at the kid's face, he saw the face of another kid, dead for more than thirty years. But Lance's resemblance to Donner ended there. He wasn't an athlete; he was a musician. Violin. And Stephen liked him. That said a lot.

"I read in the *Sentinel* that Lance played with All-State Orchestra in the Twin Cities last Saturday," Cork said casually. "How'd it go?"

"Fine," she said. "They were wonderful."

"So, you were there?"

"Of course."

"Was Lester with you?"

"No."

"Oh? Why not?"

"He told me he wanted to spend the day with his father." She'd answered immediately and without guile, but her face suddenly clouded. "Why do you ask?"

Instead of answering, Cork glanced at the Mercedes. "I'm keeping you."

"I really do have to go," she said. "Lance has a doctor's appointment."

Cork smiled in parting. "I'll pull out so I'm not blocking your way."

He stopped at Johnny's Pinewood Broiler. Lester Bigby wasn't there, and so far, Johnny Papp hadn't seen him that day. But it was still early, so maybe Cork wanted to wait? Cork thanked Johnny and said he might be back.

His next stop was The Greenbrier, an assisted-living facility in a newer section on the north side of town. It was a two-story redbrick building of recent construction, with nicely landscaped grounds full of squat evergreens and some young willows. There was also a little man-made pond, the kind that in summer might hold goldfish. In anticipation of winter, the pond had been drained, and the bottom was lined with the dark residue of rotting leaves. Because it was a secure building, Cork had to buzz for the door to be opened to him.

The Greenbrier was warm and quiet inside. Just beyond the front door was a large open area, carpeted, where four ladies, grown thin and fragile with age but dressed almost formally, sat facing one another in the armchairs that had been placed about.

Cork couldn't tell if they'd been talking and had stopped to observe him when he came in or if they'd simply been sitting in silence for a while, waiting for something—anything—to happen. Above cheeks rosy with rouge and softened with powder, their eyes followed him keenly. The attendant at the front desk was young, maybe twenty, fresh-faced, and pretty. Her face lost some of its freshness as soon as Cork inquired after Clarence Bigby.

"Buzz? You'll find him in the community room. He's always there after lunch."

"Is he alone?"

"Whenever Mr. Bigby's in the community room, he has it to himself."

Cork got her meaning. Some people mellowed with age. Not Buzz Bigby.

Cork was about to walk away when the attendant said, "You'll need to sign in."

She nodded toward a register book at one end of the desk. It was open, and a pen was attached by a thin chain. Cork signed and jotted down the time, noting that there hadn't been many visitors before him that day. But it was Monday. Weekends were probably more likely times for families to come calling.

The big flat-panel television was on, tuned to ESPN, the volume turned up loud. Bigby sat slouched in an easy chair, facing the screen but not really looking at it. His eyes seemed to be focused on something well above the television. Next to Bigby's easy chair sat a small oxygen tank on rollers, feeding him through a tube that hung over his ears and plugged into his nose. He was dressed in a flannel shirt and wrinkled khakis, and wore slippers on his feet. His white hair was wild, as if windblown, though there wasn't even a whisper of a breeze in the room. When Cork was a kid, Bigby had been a great pillar of muscle and bone. Now he seemed only a huddle of wrinkled flesh.

"Buzz?"

Bigby's eyes moved but not his head, as if Cork wasn't worth the effort of his full attention. "What do you want?" He spoke in a wheeze.

"To talk."

"I got nothing to say to you."

The remote control for the television was on a coffee table within reach of Bigby. Cork walked to the table, picked up the remote, and hit the Mute button. The room dropped into quiet. Cork grabbed an empty armchair and positioned it so that he sat between Bigby and the television. "You were always a son of a bitch, Buzz, and pretty proud of it."

"So?"

"You carry a grudge better than any man I ever knew. And one thing I know about you absolutely is that you hated Jubal Little."

Bigby made a sound that might have been meant as a laugh but came out like air from a punctured tire. "I feel that way about a lot of people, you included."

"Never pull any punches, do you? Tell me, Buzz, does Lester visit you here very often?"

"That boy don't come to see me like he should. Ungrateful little bastard."

"Did he visit you last Saturday?"

"Hell, no." Bigby's steel blue eyes suddenly went wary, and he said, "What's it to you?"

"Did you hear what happened to Jubal Little?"

"Dead. Dumb-ass hunting accident."

"I was with him. Some folks think I might have had a hand in his death."

"You were the dumb-ass that shot him?" A vicious little smile crept across his lips. "There's a God in heaven."

An old woman came into the room, using a walker. Her face held a look of happy anticipation, but when she saw Buzz Bigby in the easy chair, she stopped abruptly, and the happy look died. She carefully maneuvered her walker in a U-turn and left.

"You were the one who taught Lester to bow-hunt, right?" Cork asked.

"Tried. Christ, he couldn't draw a bowstring to save his soul. Spindly little arms of his."

"He's got himself a new compound bow now. A Bear Carnage, top of the line. You didn't know that?"

"Like I said, that boy don't visit me like he should. Little snot."

"I thought he was here on Saturday."

"I told you not two minutes ago he wasn't." Bigby shifted and sat up. It wasn't only his eyes that seemed on the alert now. His whole body, collapsed as it was, had tensed. "Or maybe he was. That was a couple of days ago. Sometimes I forget things."

Forget the slight of an ungrateful son? Cork thought not.

He stood and said, "Thanks for your time, Buzz."

"And you, thanks for nothing. Give me that remote before you go."

On his way out, Cork stopped at the front desk to sign out. He used the opportunity to check the register pages where visitors had logged in and out over the weekend. He didn't see Lester Bigby's name there at all.

The young attendant was on the phone. Cork hung around until she'd finished her call, then he asked, "Does everyone sign in and out?"

"Not always. Sometimes family who visit a lot just go to their relative's room without stopping here."

"Does Buzz Bigby's family visit often?"

"Oh yeah. Especially his son."

"Do you know if he visited on Saturday?"

"I didn't work this weekend, so I couldn't say."

"Anybody here who might be able to say?"

"I really don't know." She said it in such a way that Cork understood she probably did but was not going to tell him. A professional thing, he figured, resident privacy or something. He didn't push it.

As he left, the eyes of the ladies in the open area followed him, as if they were watching the passage of an exotic bird.

* * *

Cork pulled up to the curb in front of Johnny's Pinewood Broiler and parked behind the car that Lester Bigby often drove, a mint-condition 1965 Karmann Ghia. He found it interesting that Bigby preferred the same kind of vehicle his brother, Donner, had driven before he died.

Inside, Cork found Bigby sitting in the same booth that, according to Heidi Steger, he'd occupied when Cork and Jubal breakfasted there on the day Jubal died. There was an empty plate in front of him, and he was reading a newspaper, *The Wall Street Journal*. Compared to both his father and his brother, Lester Bigby was small and, in his face, more resembled the fine-boned features that, Cork recalled, had made Mrs. Bigby so lovely and yet so sad. In his mid-forties, he was mostly bald, with only a narrow strip of dull brown hair circling his skull like a dead laurel wreath. He didn't notice Cork approaching.

"Mind if I join you?" Cork said.

Bigby looked up from his paper. "I prefer to eat alone."

"Looks to me like you've finished eating." Cork slid into the seat on the other side of the booth.

Bigby carefully folded his paper and set it aside.

Cork laid his arms on the table and leaned forward. "We've never liked each other, Lester."

"That's not something I lose any sleep over."

"In a town like Aurora, it's hard to avoid folks, but somehow we seem to do a pretty good job of it."

"Believe me, I don't go out of my way, O'Connor."

"I think I can truthfully say the same. But there it is. I've been wondering why."

"You looked me up just to tell me that?"

"That's not the reason. It's just something that came to me."

"What's the reason then?"

"I've been thinking about your resort on Crown Lake."

"What about it?"

"You're pretty heavily invested in it, I imagine. All that land, the cost of construction."

"So?"

"Sulfide mining," Cork said. And he saw from the look in Bigby's eyes that he'd struck home.

Cork had grown up in the Arrowhead of Minnesota, the northeasternmost section of the state, where some of the most beautiful wilderness in the entire nation lay next to the richest ore deposits imaginable. Historically, this unfortunate positioning had resulted in the decimation of a great deal of the pristine Northwoods by iron mining. The sacrifice of that land had made possible the industrial growth of the rest of the United States in the late 1800s and well into the twentieth century, but the deep open-pit mines of the Iron Range were wounds that would never heal.

The mines had begun closing in the late 1960s, and the Arrowhead suffered one economic blow after another. Businesses folded. Range towns became ghost towns. But in recent years, there'd been a great deal of renewed interest in the mineral resources of the area. The demand for the raw materials to make steel in China and India had spurred a resurgence of mining in the open pits. Perhaps more important, there was intense interest in creating additional operations that would mine the deposits of base metals—copper-nickel and platinum. These precious ores had been discovered long ago in the Arrowhead but, until recently, were too difficult and costly to get at. New advances in mining technology, however, promised cheaper, better methods of extraction, and global mining concerns were clamoring for a shot at the riches that still lay beneath the wilderness of the Arrowhead. The proposals for these new mines had set factions in the North Country at war.

Because the metals were contained in sulfide ore, the technique for extracting them was called sulfide mining. Environmentalists claimed the mining of this ore would create mountains of sulfide tailings that were exposed to the elements. When sulfide mixes with air and water, the result is sulfuric acid, which would inevitably leach into the groundwater, polluting the pristine lakes and streams of the region. This had already been the case in other areas where sulfide mining had been allowed, and a lot of folks in the Arrowhead believed that looming on the horizon was yet another instance of the earth suffering horribly for the benefit of industry.

On the other side of the coin, the new mines represented the possibility of a rebound in the depressed economy of the region. This meant jobs in an area where, for too long, they'd been far too rare, and also much-needed tax revenues for the state as a whole. Because the mining companies were full of assurances that the new technologies would allow safe, nonpolluting extraction—they had all kinds of reports and charts to prove it—a great many people in the Arrowhead, and in Minnesota in general, welcomed the prospect.

In his gubernatorial campaign, Jubal Little had talked about the need for sacrifice in order to make Minnesota self-sustaining. He'd strongly supported opening the North Country to additional mining. He never spoke of this as sacrifice but couched it in terms of responsibility and risk. It would be his responsibility as governor to ensure that mine companies kept their promises. And what small risk there might be to the Arrowhead was outweighed by the great benefit to the state as a whole. This was in direct contrast to the position of the incumbent, a man of liberal leanings who'd made environmental protection one of his top priorities but who'd been ineffectual in all his efforts to revitalize the state's stagnating economy.

Jubal's argument about exploiting Minnesota's mineral potential was the same kind of argument he'd made about the casinos. Responsibility and risk.

Politically, Jubal characterized himself as socially progressive and fiscally conservative. But his politics had mattered a good deal less than his image. He was tall and good-looking. Confident, charming, self-assured. He could be winningly self-effacing. But more than anything else, he offered the image of a man who, like a great frontier scout, knew the way ahead was fraught with danger, but if you followed him, he'd absolutely get you to the promised land. In all the darkness of economic uncertainty, he offered voters the hope of light, and they flew to him like moths.

Not Cork. And not the Ojibwe. And not, he knew, Lester Bigby.

"As I understand it, Lester, construction of that resort of yours ground to a halt last summer. All because Jubal Little pledged to open the area to sulfide mining if he was elected. Crown Lake is just a few miles downstream from the site where that Canadian company intends to begin mining as soon as they get approval, which Jubal's election would pretty much have assured. You stood to lose a lot of money."

"I've lost money before," Bigby said.

"This would have been on a huge scale. And probably a lot of other folks you talked into investing in your company stood to lose their shirts, too."

"And your point is?"

"Somebody killed Jubal Little, killed him before he had a chance to make good on his campaign promises. I'm just thinking you had a lot of reason to want him dead."

Bigby seemed actually amused at this thought. He smiled and said, "Jesus, you think I killed Little?"

"You bow-hunt. You've got yourself a good Bear Carnage as I understand it."

Bigby saw that Cork wasn't joking, and the smile dropped from his lips. "You really think I killed Jubal Little."

"I think you had good reason to want him dead."

"Wanting somebody dead and killing him are at two different ends of the stick, O'Connor. Are you saying that everybody you want dead you've killed?"

"Where were you on Saturday, Lester?"

Bigby opened his mouth to answer, then stopped. "Hell, I don't have to tell you."

"You'll have to tell the sheriff."

"Why?"

"Because you're a hunter with a fine new compound bow, and you have a pretty good reason to have wanted Little dead, and your wife believes you were visiting your father, and your father says you weren't. At the very least, you have some explaining to do. And if the sheriff questions you about all this, word is going to spread, and whether you like it or not, people are going to start talking about you and wondering. I just thought I might be able to save you and your family some embarrassment."

"You talked to my wife and my father?" Bigby's fine-featured face took on a stern look that was somehow still delicate.

"I spent some time with both of them earlier today."

"You drag my family into this, O'Connor, and I'll destroy you."

"Your family doesn't have to be dragged in, Lester. All you have to do is tell me where you were on Saturday."

"Who the hell are you to be asking me questions?" He'd raised his voice above the general hubbub of the Broiler, and other voices grew quiet; eyes swung his way. Bigby noticed and spoke more softly. "You're not the law around here anymore. Just who the hell do you think you are?"

"I'm the guy somebody's trying to frame for Jubal Little's death, and I'm not just going to sit around and let that happen, Lester. Where were you Saturday?"

"You don't know me at all, O'Connor. I'd never kill anybody over money."

Cork leaned closer and said, "Maybe it wasn't just about money."

Bigby's eyes once again gave him away, and Cork knew he'd touched a nerve. Bigby sat up a little straighter and brought out a confused look, but he was a beat too late. "I don't know what you're talking about."

"Your father's always blamed Jubal and me for your brother's death."

"That was a long time ago."

"In some people, that kind of wound never heals. You know, when I was sheriff, I never encountered your father without him making some comment about how I couldn't hide behind a badge forever. We both knew exactly what he was talking about."

"And yet here you are," Bigby said. "Alive and well."

"Yeah, here I am the prime suspect in Jubal Little's death. Exactly the kind of situation that would warm the cockles of your father's heart." Cork sat back. "You love your father, Lester?"

"I'm not going to answer that, or any more of your questions."

"See, I think he would be a hard man to love. But I also think that one thing we seek most as men is the approval of our fathers. It seems to me that goes a long way to explaining everything from why Alexander the Great felt compelled to conquer the world to why George W. Bush led us into Iraq. And maybe it even explains why the son of Buzz Bigby would kill Jubal Little."

"That's such bullshit."

"Is it? Easy enough to disprove. Just tell me where you were on Saturday."

"Fuck you."

Cork made ready to leave. "I'll give you a while to think about it, Lester. But if I haven't heard from you by the end of the day, next time you're questioned, it'll be by the badges investigating Jubal Little's death."

Cork walked away. But he couldn't help feeling a tingle in his back, as if the point of an arrow was about to bury itself there.

CHAPTER 26

When Cork left Lester Bigby, he drove directly to the Iron Lake Reservation. The afternoon had turned remarkably warm, especially considering the spitting snow and sleet of only a couple of days earlier. The sky was the soft blue of a baby blanket, and the sun, already well past its zenith, put a fire to everything so that the forest and the lake and even the pavement of the road itself seemed to pulsate with electric vitality.

He pulled into Allouette and saw Isaiah Broom's pickup parked next to Willie Crane's Jeep in front of the Iron Lake Center for Native Art. The door to the establishment was just opening, and both men were coming out. Cork drove past them and watched as they ambled down to the Mocha Moose and went inside. He made a U-turn and parked on the street across from the coffee shop. Broom and Crane stood at the counter while Sarah LeDuc made them something to drink, then they sat at a table near the front window, leaned toward each other, and appeared to talk in the way of intimate friends.

The roads that led to friendship were, Cork knew, as numerous as those in a Rand McNally atlas, but the underlying construct was always the same: a true sharing of self with another, a deep and vulnerable trusting. In the case of Isaiah Broom and Willie Crane, the friendship had begun in childhood, a connection between two boys painfully awkward in their own ways and filled with a terrible sense of isolation. Willie's situation was obvious, his difficult gait and tortured speech. Isaiah Broom's problems were less so but, in their way, just as challenging. His father had never been around, and his mother had dropped out of the picture when Isaiah was still a small child. Like Willie and Winona Crane, he'd been taken care of by a laundry list of relatives. He was a big kid, but unlike Jubal Little, whose size and physical ability were proportionally equal, Isaiah Broom was hopelessly uncoordinated. He lived in a body that seemed beyond his control, and perhaps even his comprehension. Cork had seen him sit for long periods of time staring at his big, meaty limbs as if they totally confounded him. Willie Crane, on the other hand, seemed determined to rise above the limitations of the body he'd been given, and although every word he spoke was a struggle and every step he took a battle, he faced the challenge of his life with the heart of a warrior. Probably more than anyone else on the Iron Lake Reservation, he understood what the clumsy, bearish Isaiah Broom was up against.

But maybe most important in their relationship was the fact that, when they were kids, Willie Crane had saved Isaiah Broom's life. It had happened this way.

It was early summer. They were fishing on Iron Lake, in an old aluminum rowboat Broom had borrowed from one of his uncles. They'd rowed out a good half mile from shore and cast their lines off an island called Gull, where legend had it, a monster muskie dubbed Old Flint liked to feed. They were eleven years old. Broom had the bulk of a kid several years older. Willie was small and slender, but strong because he exercised constantly to compensate for his weak, sometimes spastic, left side. They'd been out maybe an hour when the storm came up. It blew in from nowhere, a huge, angry bluster, wind and rain and lightning that shoved the lake into a rage of whitecaps. They tried to make it back to the old dock in Allouette, each boy bent over an oar, pulling for dear life, but the boat began taking on water, wave after wave, and the vessel grew more sluggish and their arms more tired as the waterline crept toward the tops of the gunwales.

They were still fifty yards out when the boat swamped completely, and they took to the water. They swam for shore. That is, Willie swam for shore. Broom didn't know how to swim. He flailed, arms like great tree limbs beating the water, throwing up sprays of desperate white in the troughs between the waves. Willie went back for him. Broom reached out, grasping wildly in his panic, but Willie stayed away. The oars from the boat had lifted from their locks and were easily riding the wild undulations of the lake. Willie latched on to one of them and shoved it toward his friend. Broom grabbed it, and Willie shouted for him to hold on. He swam them both near enough to shore that his feet found bottom, but by then Broom had taken in so much water and was so exhausted that the oar slipped from his hands and his body slid below the surface. Willie dived after him, wrapped his hands around fistfuls of Broom's T-shirt, and dragged him to solid ground. He dropped him in the wash of the waves and saw that the boy's chest had ceased to rise and fall. He cocked Broom's head back, locked his lips against Broom's blue lips, and breathed life back into his friend.

It was a remarkable story, but when the *Aurora Sentinel* reported the incident, a lot of white folks in Tamarack County refused to believe it, refused to accept that the Indian kid they sometimes spotted limping down Center Street, and who was incomprehensible when he tried to talk, could have performed such a physical feat. But Cork believed it. He believed it because he knew the heart within Willie Crane, and he believed it because he knew that friendship, true friendship, was the stuff of miracles.

Cork got out of his Land Rover and headed into the Mocha Moose. Except for Broom and Crane and Sarah LeDuc, the coffee shop was empty. There was music playing over the sound system, and Cork recognized the flute work of Bill Miller. Sarah smiled from behind the counter and greeted Cork with *"Boozhoo."*

"*Boozhoo*, Sarah. Quiet today," he said.

"Monday afternoon. Always quiet. Can I get you something?"

"A small dark roast."

"Regular or decaf?"

"Regular. Never understood the point of drinking coffee without caffeine in it. Like drinking nonalcoholic beer."

Broom and Crane had been talking before he came in, but with his appearance, they'd lapsed into a watchful silence.

Cork got his coffee and paid. Then he strolled to the table where the two men sat. "I was just on my way over to your place, Isaiah. Mind if I sit down?"

"Heard the cops tossed your house this morning," Broom said.

Though uninvited, Cork pulled a chair from another table and joined the men. "They were respectful," he said.

"Find what they were looking for?"

"You'll have to ask them, Isaiah. I left before they finished."

"You okay?" Willie asked. *U-k?*

"I feel like I'm in a vise at the moment, Willie, and the jaws are closing. Thanks for asking."

Willie said, "I should get back to the business. Unless you want to talk to me, too."

"No, it's Isaiah I came to see."

"All right." He nodded to Broom. "Seven?"

"I'll be there," Broom said.

Willie scooted his chair from the table. He got up and limped out, the sound of his gait like uneven drumbeats on the old wooden floorboards.

"Seven?" Cork asked.

"Tribal Council's holding a meeting to talk about this sulfide mining thing," Broom replied. "Some guy from that mining company is gonna try to convince us they'll tear up the earth safely. Kinda like Custer saying all he really wanted to do was have tea with Sitting Bull. What did you want to see me about?" He lifted his mug, sipped his coffee, and his dark eyes watched Cork closely.

"I asked you yesterday where you were on Saturday. You treated it like a joke. It's no joke, Isaiah. Where were you?"

"Why do you want to know?"

"Sam Winter Moon taught me how to hunt in the old way. He taught a lot of Shinnobs, including you. He also taught me how to make my own arrows, which is something I still do. I know that you do, too."

"Yeah, what of it?"

"Do you splice your fletches?"

"Yeah."

"And the pattern?"

"What are you getting at?"

"Sam made his arrows using two different colors of fletching, red and green. They were round-back, with a left-wing offset. When I asked him why he used that pattern, he told me it was out of respect for the man who'd taught him. Cat-Eye Jimmy LeClair. When Cat-Eye died, Sam began using his pattern as a sign of respect and to preserve his memory. When Sam died, I began making my arrows using Sam's pattern, for the same reason. Respect and memory. I'm just wondering if you might have done the same thing. What fletching pattern do you use?"

"What difference does it make?"

"Humor me and just answer the question."

"I feel like a rabbit looking at a snare here, O'Connor, so I think I'm going to keep that information to myself." Broom glanced at the clock on the wall. "And we're finished talking here. I've got to see somebody in Yellow Lake about a tree they want me to carve." He stood up and turned away to drop his mug off with Sarah as he left.

Cork watched him go.

Broom was a good Shinnob in every way. Unlike Lester Bigby, whose emotions were tattooed all over his face, Broom gave away nothing. But all that meant to Cork was that he'd have to keep digging.

* * *

After he left Allouette, Cork drove east on a road that wound for nearly two miles through a mix of marsh and popple. He came to a dirt track that split off to the right and that was marked with a sign, beautifully carved and lacquered, and into which were wood-burned the words CHAINSAW ART. He drove a short stretch, into a clearing, and pulled to a stop in front of the home of Isaiah Broom. It was a cabin of Broom's own design and construct, not large but sturdy, built of honey-colored pine. Next to it stood another structure, almost as large but of flat-board construction, which, Cork knew, served Broom as both garage and studio.

Over the years, Isaiah Broom had tried his hand at a lot of occupations, mostly associated with heavy labor. He'd logged timber in his early years, worked on road crews laying down steaming asphalt in summer, when the days were straight out of a pressure cooker, mopped hospital floors, and finally settled on tree and stump removal. Mostly, he'd eked out a living, and what was left after he'd fed and clothed himself (never very well) he'd spent in advocacy on behalf of his people. He was known on the rez as a rabble-rouser. He considered himself a skin's skin. He could quote at length Russell Means and Dennis Banks and Clyde Bellecourt, Chief Joseph and Black Elk, James Welch and Sherman Alexie. He'd been on the Trail of Broken Treaties in 1972, which had culminated in the taking of the BIA office in Washington, D.C. He'd twice marched across the continent in support of the sovereign rights of indigenous people, first in 1978, on what the American Indian Movement called the Longest Walk, and again thirty years later, on the Longest Walk 2. Whatever else he might think of Isaiah Broom, Cork respected the man's dedication to the principles he advocated.

Isaiah Broom's star was on the rise because of his ability to find, in a great chunk of wood, the spirit inside it that sought form. That was Broom's explanation for his art, anyway, which amounted to taking large sections of tree trunk and, using mostly a chain saw, creating remarkable sculptures. He'd begun this art because his tree and stump removal business gave him easy access to the raw material, and he'd never married and so had a lot of time on his hands. Even after he'd made a name for himself, he still cut trees, but he did so only for those who wanted a part of the tree left standing and hewn into an image. On the front lawns of a number of the finer homes in Tamarack County what had once been an oak or elm or linden tree a hundred feet tall was now a ten-foot bear or an Ojibwe maiden or eagles standing guard over an aerie or a winged serpent, courtesy of the skilled hands of Isaiah Broom.

Willie Crane was pretty much directly responsible for the recent widening recognition of Broom's art. He showed the sculptures at the Iron Lake Center for Native Art, and also at the gallery he owned in Saint Paul, and he'd introduced Broom to influential patrons. Thanks to Willie, those hands and arms, which most of his life had so confounded Isaiah Broom, had become not only the way he expressed what was deepest in him but also the manner in which he earned his living.

Cork walked across a patch of ground covered with wood chips and sawdust where, in the summer, Broom plied his art. He knocked at the front door of the cabin, but no one answered. He went to the other building and peered in a window. The space where Broom's Explorer would have been parked stood empty. Through the panes, Cork could see the area that, in winter, Broom used for his carving. He looked around to be sure he was still alone, then went to the door and tried the knob. It was unlocked—not surprising; on the rez, no one locked their doors—and he stepped inside.

The place was a jumble of smells, all battling for dominance. There was the sweet aroma of cut pine; the sharp petroleum bite of lacquers and mineral spirits and gasoline; the heavy, metallic smell of cutting oil and engine oil; and the underlying mustiness of the dirt floor. A workbench ran along most of the length of the back wall, and it was a mess of tools—chisels, hammers, hacksaws, coping saws, planes, knives with straight blades and knives whose blades curved oddly, rasps, sandpaper, and utensils with points so delicate-looking that they reminded Cork of a dentist's picks. Broom's chain saws, three of them of varying size and horsepower, sat side by side at the far end of the bench.

There was a smaller worktable against the far wall. On it, Cork saw all the tools necessary for arrow making—fletching stripper and jig, arrow saw, nocking pliers. He walked to the table, where several dark gray commercial carbon arrows lay next to the tools. He picked up a can of white paint that was also on the table, and he was pretty certain he knew who'd fired the arrow into the door of Rainy's cabin, though the why of it was still a mystery. On the upper corner of the table sat a handmade pine box. When he lifted the lid, Cork found feathers that would be used for fletching. They were turkey feathers in two colors, red and green, the same colors he used for his own arrows. Above the table, hung on hooks screwed into the wall, were the items that had drawn him into the structure in the first place: a recurve hunting bow and a belt quiver full of arrows. He drew out an arrow. It was tipped with a Braxe broadhead, the same kind Cork used. But that mattered less than the fletching. The pattern of red and green spliced turkey feathers, round-back and with a left-wing offset, matched exactly what Cork used. It was the same pattern that had been on the arrows that killed both Jubal Little and the John Doe.

CHAPTER 27

Cork didn't like it. He didn't like the feel of the idea that Isaiah Broom was deeply involved in the cold-blooded killing of another human being—maybe two. He wasn't fond of the man, but he didn't think of him as a murderer. On the other hand, there were certainly good reasons to suspect Broom. First of all, on the gaming issue, Jubal Little had sold out the Native population of Minnesota; second, and maybe even more important, with Jubal Little dead, Broom might yet have a shot at winning the heart of Winona Crane; finally, whoever had given the map to the dead man on the ridge knew the back ways and old logging roads that ran through the reservation. It was someone who'd spent time in that neck of the woods. Like most Shinnobs on the rez, Isaiah Broom knew the area well.

Still, given Broom's distaste for and distrust of white people in general, it was odd that he would have brought in a *chimook* to back him up in a plan to kill Jubal Little. If that, in fact, was the role the dead man on the ridge had been meant to play. It was much more likely that one white man would trust another, which brought Cork back to Lester Bigby. In the days when Bigby's family logged timber, they'd cut trees from a lot of leased tracts north of the rez in the area of Trickster's Point, so Lester Bigby was no stranger to that territory. But was either money or a son's hopeless desire for his father's love enough motivation for

murder? Maybe neither one separately, but what about both together, each feeding the dark, depthless hunger of the other?

Cork was driving south from the Iron Lake Reservation,
along County 16, which shadowed the lakeshore. The road had
been built in the 1930s by state highway engineers to replace
the old, meandering dirt track to the rez that ran well east of the
lake through a lot of sloppy bogland. For the new road, sections
of great rock outcrops had to be blasted away and then evened
into sheer walls. In two places, bridges spanned narrow gorges,
through which streams ran in tumbles of white water. The sun
was sliding down the southwestern sky and was a blinding glare
against Cork's windshield as he approached the second bridge,
which crossed the gorge over Ahsayma Creek.

He was thinking about the nature of human beings, the
darker nature. Which was the part of the human spirit involved
in killing, wasn't it? Cork had killed. He'd killed for what, in his
own mind, were the best of reasons, but he'd still had to give
himself over to a side of his nature that scared him, that spoke to
him mostly in his nightmares, that was the reason for laws, political and religious, and that made wars, just or otherwise, possible. Henry Meloux had told him once that in every human being
two wolves battled, one dark and one light, and in the end, the
victor was always the one you chose to feed.

Cork understood and accepted that both Broom and Bigby
were capable of killing Jubal Little, but, given the right circumstances, so was every other human being who walked the earth.

Not much help, he told himself.

The bullet, when it hit his windshield, drilled a small hole
with a spiderweb of hairline cracks around it. It made a sound
like a rock hitting the glass and, at almost the same instant, another sound like someone giving an angry thump to the headrest on the passenger side. Cork slammed his foot on the brake
pedal and swerved, and as he left the pavement, the shadows
of the red pines that lined the road made a pattern of dark and
light stripes across his vision. The chasm crossed by the bridge

rushed at him, and he spun the steering wheel hard to the right. The nose of the Land Rover swung away from the precipice, but the rear wheels slid across the soft bed of pine needles, the left tire hit thin air, and for a brief moment, Cork felt the vehicle tilt backward in a drop toward the white water below. The other three tires grabbed and held, and the Land Rover skidded back onto solid ground. He finally came to a stop a foot shy of the trunk of a great pine, and he thanked God for the guy who invented four-wheel drive.

He jerked the door handle and rolled free from the Land Rover, then crouched in the lee of its body. In his mind, he re-created the moment the bullet had hit the windshield and smacked beside him into the headrest. The bullet hole was well above eye level and to his left. The round had followed a downward trajectory to the headrest. He peered around the front end of the Land Rover toward a bare ridge on the far side of the little gorge where the stream ran. There were a dozen places along the top of the ridge that would have provided both a good view of the road approaching the bridge and ample cover from which to shoot.

The shot had missed its mark, but was the shooter still there?

Cork had long ago given up carrying a firearm, but that didn't mean he didn't miss the comfort it might have offered in just this kind of situation. He tried to come up with a plan for what he would do if the shooter came off the ridge to hunt him in the open. He couldn't run. A good hunter with a decent scope would bring him down easily. Maybe he could make it to the gorge, climb down, and hide among the rocks. The shooter would have to come down to him, and that proximity might even the odds a little.

Cork didn't like having to expose himself to keep an eye on the ridge, and he went flat on his belly and slithered under the Land Rover. In the shadow there, with the left front wheel masking him, he kept a sharp eye to the far side of the bridge.

He lay that way for a good ten minutes and saw no movement

on the ridge. He'd just about decided that the shooter had fled when he heard a vehicle approaching on the road. A few moments later, a dusty white pickup swung into view, coming from the south. It crossed the bridge, slowed, pulled onto the shoulder, and stopped. A Shinnob, Hooty Nelson, got out and walked toward where Cork lay. He looked startled when Cork slithered from beneath the Land Rover.

"Car trouble?" Hooty asked.

He was tall and lean and wore his hair in a crew cut. There were deep creases at the corners of his mouth, because he smiled a lot. But the thing that anyone who dealt with Hooty noticed most was his left eye, which was lazy. Sometimes, because of that wandering eye, it seemed as if Hooty was talking to someone over your right shoulder. He was a mechanic at the Tomahawk Truckstop on Highway 1 and must have been heading home from work. He wore oil-spotted Carhartt coveralls, and although his hands were clean, under every fingernail lay a crescent of black engine grease.

"Not exactly. Take a look at that windshield," Cork said.

Hooty eyed the bullet hole and whistled. "You okay?"

"Yeah."

Hooty looked at the place under the Land Rover where Cork had lain for protection, and he said, "Checking the oil pan to see if it got hit, too?" He grinned, an expression that came and went quickly, and he ended with a philosophic shake of his head. "Hunting season. Them damn hunters from the Cities, they'll shoot anything that moves. Last year, my cousin Glory, she was just sittin' in her trailer watchin' TV. Damn bullet comes through the wall, whizzes right past her, not a foot from her nose, goes out the other side of the trailer. She's more mad than scared, and she goes outside and spots three white guys in brand-new blaze orange outfits runnin' off into the trees like kids scared cuz they broke a window or something. Come huntin' season, I don't let my kids outta my sight."3

Cork chose not to disabuse Hooty of the notion that it was an accident. He thanked the man for stopping, and both went their separate ways.

Sheriff Marsha Dross looked at the slug Cork had put in the palm of her hand.

"I dug that out of my backseat," he told her.

"You think somebody was actually shooting at you?" she asked.

He sat in her office at the Tamarack County Sheriff's Department. Agent Phil Holter was there, too, and Ed Larson. Dross and the BCA agent had given a press conference shortly after noon. To avoid any lingering reporters, Cork had parked a block from the building and had managed to slip inside unseen.

"Or was it just a stray hunter's round, as your friend on the rez suggested?" Holter said.

"A huge coincidence that somebody would be shooting at a buck and almost hit me instead, don't you think?"

Holter took off his rimless glasses, pulled a clean handkerchief from his back pocket, huffed a breath onto each lens, and began to wipe. "Why would somebody be shooting at you, O'Connor?"

Rhiannon was what he thought, but what he said was "Maybe because I'm asking questions."

"Questions we should be asking?"

"Not necessarily."

"But important enough, apparently, that somebody wants you to stop asking them."

Dross entered the questioning. "What were you doing on the reservation, Cork?"

"I wanted to talk to Isaiah Broom."

"About what?"

"Bow hunting."

"Is he a bow hunter?"

Cork nodded. "He hunts like Jubal and I did, still-stalking."

"You think he had something to do with Jubal Little's death?" Dross continued.

"It was a possibility I wanted to check out."

"What did you find?"

"In his hunting, he uses arrows identical to mine."

"Meaning the arrow that killed Jubal Little might have come from him? Why would Isaiah Broom want Jubal Little dead?"

"Casinos." It was Ed Larson who answered. He was wearing one of his tweed sport coats with suede elbow patches, and he'd been sitting quietly in a corner, tugging on a loose thread hanging from the sleeve. He'd seemed to be paying very little attention, but Cork knew that brain of his was working at light speed. "Jubal Little's proposal for six state-run casinos. That's a political hot potato none of the other candidates would touch. Little could because he was Indian. Take him out of the election and the problem goes away."

"Thin," Holter said.

"But worth checking," Larson insisted.

"There's another possibility you might want to look into," Cork said. "Talk to Lester Bigby."

"Bigby?" Dross looked bewildered. "What's the connection?"

"Lester bow-hunts, too, and he has a long-standing personal grudge against Jubal. Tie that to the fact that Bigby's heavily invested in preserving the environmental status quo of our area, while Jubal Little's on the bandwagon for new mining operations, and I think you've got a couple of good reasons for him to want Jubal dead. If you talk to him, ask him where he was on the day Jubal was killed."

"Why?"

"Because when I talked to him, he danced all around that question."

"You've talked to him already?" Holter had put his glasses back on, and from behind those clear lenses his eyes shot fire at Cork. "Jesus, this is our investigation, O'Connor, and I don't appreciate you mucking around in it."

"Last time I looked, Agent Holter, it was a free country. A man can still ask questions."

The office was filled with afternoon sunlight that came through the window facing west. Where the direct rays hit the floor, the old oak boards looked as if they were made of crystallized honey. That same window overlooked the department's parking lot. In the stillness that followed Cork's retort, he could hear the grumble of an engine from one of the media trucks leaving. He heard a reporter shout an unintelligible question, to whom, he couldn't say.

"Okay," Holter said, shifting his body as if squaring off against Cork. "Let me tell you what I think about this slug of yours. Seems to me there are three possibilities."

"Love to hear them," Cork said.

"One: Someone did try to shoot you and missed. Two: The slug was a stray from a hunter, as your Ojibwe friend suggested. And three: The slug was fired to make it look as if someone was trying to shoot you."

"A phony attempt on my life, is that what you're saying?"

"That's exactly what I'm saying."

"Why would someone do that?" Dross asked the agent.

"To make O'Connor here look less guilty," Holter replied.

"Someone risked blowing my head off just to make me look innocent?" Cork actually laughed.

"Not someone," Holter said and pointedly eyed Cork.

"Me? You think I shot that slug through my window?" Cork glanced at Dross and Larson to see if they were reacting with the same disbelief, but their faces gave away nothing of what they were thinking. "That's just ridiculous."

"We'll follow up on the leads you've given us, Cork," Larson promised. "In the meantime, it would be best if you stepped back and let us handle the investigation. For your own sake."

Anger made everything inside him burn. Cork wanted to hit someone, Holter especially. But he held himself in check. "One question before I leave. Have you got anything more on the dead man on the ridge?"

Larson replied, "We're still looking into it. Let me walk you to your car, Cork."

They went out a side door and made their way unnoticed to Cork's Land Rover, parked a block away. Neither man had spoken, but at the vehicle Larson said, "In an hour, can you be at the spot where you say the shot was fired?"

"Why? You want to take a shot at me, too?"

Larson smiled. "Not easy being on your side of all this, I'm sure. But it's not easy on our side either, Cork. We're trying to be thorough and impartial. It's best if you can refrain from taking this investigation personally."

"You realize how moronic that sounds, Ed?"

"Yeah." Larson gave a boyish kind of shrug. "But keep it in mind. So, an hour?"

"I'll be there," Cork said.

CHAPTER 28

He drove through Aurora, a town he knew so well he could have walked it blind and not been lost for a moment, a town he loved as much as he loved anything outside his family. But he drove angry. He was pissed at Jubal Little. Pissed at Jubal for dying, pissed at Jubal for the way he'd died, and pissed at what, with his final breaths, Jubal had left behind, a mystery that threatened Cork and his family: Rhiannon.

"Who are you? What am I supposed to know?" he shouted at the hole in his windshield. He slammed the palm of his hand against the steering wheel. "Goddamn you, Jubal. Why couldn't you keep your goddamn trap shut, just this once."

He headed to Sam's Place and was relieved to see the parking lot empty but for Jenny's Subaru. He was just about to go inside when his daughter came out with Waaboo toddling beside her. His grandson smiled, and Cork's mood changed instantly. Anger drained away; love flooded in; but with it came rushing back his fear for the safety of his family.

Jenny let Waaboo run, if you could call it that, to Cork, who swept him up. The little boy's black hair smelled of French fries.

"You timed it well," Jenny said to him. "The last reporter got discouraged an hour ago and left. Ever since word got out about the search of our house this morning, we've been fighting them off like mosquitoes."

"Sorry," Cork said. "Did you call Leon Papakee?"

"Yes. He said he'd see what he could do."

"Good." That, at least, was a little relief. "Is Stephen inside?"

"Yeah. He and Judy are holding down the fort, such as it is." She swept her hand across the empty lot. "The good thing about all the reporters, we sold a lot of burgers this afternoon."

Waaboo squirmed in his arms, wanting to get down, and Cork released him. Waaboo toddled toward the lakeshore, but Jenny caught him before he'd gone far and picked him up. "Are you sticking around?"

"No. I'm meeting Ed Larson out on County Sixteen."

"Anything in particular?"

"Yeah, take a look at this." He walked her to the front of the Land Rover.

"Is that a bullet hole?" she asked, horrified.

"From a deer slug."

"Somebody tried to shoot you?"

"Not necessarily, according to Agent Phil Holter. I may have shot my own windshield."

"Why would he think that?"

"Because he's covering all the possibilities, which include me being responsible for Jubal Little's death and trying to make it look like I'm not."

"He can't believe that."

Waaboo was straining to get free and making unhappy noises.

"I honestly don't know what he believes. Look, Jenny, I want you to close up Sam's Place. Close it up now, and go home. Shut the curtains and don't open the door for anyone."

She looked at the windshield. "Because one of those may come our way?"

"I don't think so, but I'm not taking any chances. And I'm going to give Cy Borkman a call, have him come over and hang out with you guys."

Borkman had retired from the sheriff's department a couple

of years earlier, but he still moonlighted in private security. Cork was pretty sure that, when Cy knew the gravity of the situation, he'd give a hand in a heartbeat.

"Do you really think we're in danger?"

Cork nodded toward Waaboo. "Do you want to take a chance?"

Jenny had been in that kind of danger before. Only a year earlier, she'd risked her life, faced down a cadre of crazy religious zealots armed to the teeth, in order to save the life of the child in her arms. In a sad way, it had armored her against just the sort of brutal potential that Cork was afraid she might be facing again. Her look went hard, and she put her cheek against her son's head. "I understand."

"I may be home late tonight, so don't worry about me."

Again, she eyed the hole left by the slug. "That's probably not possible."

Larson was at the bridge ahead of him, and he wasn't alone. John Berglund, from the Border Patrol, was there, too. Both men stood at the base of the ridge from which Cork believed the shot through his windshield had been fired.

Cork shook Berglund's hand and said, "Seeing a lot of you these days."

"Back at you."

"Is this what you do on your time off?"

Berglund smiled. "Been doing this pretty much since I was a Boy Scout. Lot of years now. Not much I like better than reading trail."

"You guys ready?" Larson said.

"For what?" Cork asked.

Larson lifted a hand toward the top of the ridge. "Let's see about that shooter."

It was late afternoon. The sun was an emptying orange balloon caught in the branches of the trees. The temperature was dropping noticeably.

Berglund hesitated, eyeing the ridge, the sun, and finally the far side of the bridge Cork had been approaching when the shot was fired.

"How long ago did it happen?" he asked.

"A little over two hours," Cork said.

"The sun would have been about there in the sky?" Berglund pointed to a spot about sixty degrees west of zenith.

"About," Cork agreed.

"Glare on your windshield?"

"Yeah. Tough to see clearly."

Berglund considered the ridge again. "Probably a blessing. You couldn't see the shooter because of it, but the reflection off the windshield probably also made it tough for the shooter to see you clearly. Missed by a hair, Ed told me."

"A little more than that, but close enough it scared the hell out of me."

Berglund seemed satisfied. "All right, let's go."

They climbed the ridge, which was bare rock until very near the top, where scrub undergrowth had taken root among the crags. Above that, a stand of tenacious poplar saplings capped the rock outcrop. The men separated by a dozen feet and began to go over the ground carefully. The light was fading quickly, and Cork wasn't sure they'd be able to see anything.

It was Berglund who said, "Over here."

Cork and Larson joined him, and he pointed to a spot behind one of the larger saplings where there was an indentation in the thin topsoil.

"From a knee," he said. "Somebody knelt here, probably in a firing position." He walked away, toward the back of the ridge, his eyes reading the ground. "He left this way."

Cork had always considered himself to be a pretty good tracker, but whatever the signs Berglund saw Cork was blind to.

He and Larson followed the Border Patrol agent down the

backside of the ridge, where Ahsayma Creek ran. In the language of the Anishinaabeg, *ahsayma* meant "tobacco." The creek was named for the color of the water, a tobacco-spit brown, the result of bog seepage, from which much of the flow had come. They trekked through a gully heavily lined with popple, and Cork finally saw tracks pressed into the leaves underfoot. The trail led back to the road, to a pull-off a quarter mile south of the bridge. In the soft earth there, they found tire indentations.

"You might want to get people out here to get impressions, Ed. You got good tire tracks, and look here." Berglund crouched and put his finger to the ground where the perfect imprint of a boot sole had been left. "Not a common-looking pattern," he noted. "Might not be too hard to identify the brand." He gazed back in the direction of the bridge. "This guy picked a pretty good spot to take a shot at you, and it was probably only the angle of the sun and the reflection off your windshield that saved you. If, in fact, he was trying to take you out. So he's somebody who has a sense of what it takes to hunt. What do you think, Ed?"

"I think that's a lot of conjecture, John, but I've got nothing better to offer. When we get these tire impressions evaluated and that boot imprint, we'll know a hell of a lot more. And, Cork? I'll tell Phil Holter he can let go of thinking you might have done this yourself. I'm looking forward to seeing the disappointed expression on his face."

Cork filled his tank at the Food 'N Fuel in Allouette. It was getting late and he was hungry, so he grabbed a bowl of chicken wild rice soup and a cup of coffee at the Mocha Moose. He glanced at the headline on that day's copy of the *Duluth News Tribune*, which had been left on one of the tables. The dam collapse was the lead. The death toll in Colorado was rising dramatically. The pictures of the towns in the canyon below the dam were devastating, all rubble and mud. Jubal Little was still front-page news, but his death, which was still officially being called a hunting accident, had taken a backseat to the greater loss. Cork wondered how Jubal would have felt about that.

He called home and talked with Jenny and then with Cy Borkman, who was breathing hard from wrestling with little Waaboo. "It's under control here, Cork," Cy told him, wheezing a bit. "No reporters. No visible threats. But I'm not leaving until I see you walk in the door."

"Thanks, Cy. I owe you."

"It's what friends do," Cy said.

A simple understanding, Cork thought, but one that Jubal Little had forgotten long ago.

He left the Mocha Moose. It was dark outside. The moon was up in the eastern sky, and the air was cool and damp enough that he could see the silver clouds his breath made when he exhaled. As he opened the door of his Land Rover, his cell phone rang.

"Hello, Cork. This is Camilla Little. I need your help. I want to talk to Winona Crane."

CHAPTER 29

The Escalade was parked in front of the Tamarack County courthouse. When Cork pulled up behind it, Kenny Yates stepped from the driver's side to meet him. The man was dressed in black and, under the streetlamp, looked like the kind of huge form that might emerge from the closet in a child's nightmare.

"Couldn't do this at Jubal's place?" Cork asked.

"I just drive," Yates said. "I don't ask."

He opened the back door, Camilla Little swung her long legs into the light on the street, and Yates offered his hand to help her out. She seemed unsteady, maybe a little drunk.

"Thank you, Kenny."

"No problem." Yates spoke in a voice that was gentle and assuring.

Cork walked her to the passenger side of his Land Rover and helped her in. As he came back around, he saw that Yates had moved forward to study the hole in the windshield.

"We heard about this," Yates said.

Cork didn't ask how they'd heard. He figured the Jaegers were probably keyed in to every aspect of the investigation, through one of Holter's people or someone in the sheriff's department. There weren't many doors that money and political power couldn't open.

"I told Mrs. Little that I'm real uncomfortable with this," Yates said. "I'd like to follow you, if that's all right."

Cork shook his head. "Where we're going, I'd rather go alone."

Yates reached inside his leather jacket and drew out a small handgun, a Beretta Tomcat. He held it out toward Cork. "Jubal told me you don't carry. I'd rather you did on this trip."

Once again Cork gave his head a shake. "We'll be fine."

The pupils of Yates's eyes were as dark as bullet holes. "Anything happens to her, I'll hold you personally responsible."

"That'll make two of us," Cork said.

"I'll be waiting right here," Yates told him.

"We may be a while."

"I said I'll be waiting."

Cork got into his Land Rover and drove away.

Camilla stared ahead, offering him mostly profile, lit by streetlamps, in light, then in shadow. Her hands lay clasped on her lap in a way that made it clear to Cork how pensive she was. That and her silence. Which he didn't mind. It was, after all, Winona Crane to whom she wanted to speak.

In his own mind, he remarked again on what a lovely woman she was, in a grand and stately way. She'd been raised in the political arena, trained in the etiquette of diplomacy and the nuance of statesmanship. She'd attended National Cathedral School in Washington, D.C., along with the daughters of presidents and diplomats. For college she'd chosen Mills, and law school at Stanford, specializing in environmental issues. She'd been an attorney for the Nature Conservancy when she met Jubal Little at that cancer fund-raiser in Saint Paul. She had, as Jubal once told Cork, a brain, a body, and a beautifully broad view of the world. Which meant, apparently, that she understood about Winona Crane.

Jubal had also told Cork, on more than one occasion, that it was she who'd chosen him. Or more likely the Jaeger family who'd chosen him for her. He was big. He was handsome. He was articulate. He was Indian. And he was beloved. He was made to run for politics.

And the Jaegers were just the family to groom him for it.

Senator Arnold Jaeger desperately wanted a son to follow in his political footsteps. Except for the unfortunate legacy of his time aboard the USS *Cole*—a face that could have scared a badger—Alex Jaeger, with his military credentials, his political savvy, and his deep hunger to be a player in that world, would have been the perfect choice. His brother, Nick, wasn't an option. He'd rather have been hunting polar bear or musk ox in Canada's Northwest Territories than beating the bushes for votes in a congressional district. And Camilla, for all her intelligence, beauty, and legal knowledge, lacked an element that her father considered essential in being ultimately successful in the national political arena: a penis. Jubal had told Cork that Jaeger was fond of saying, "There will never be, in my lifetime, a woman elected to the White House. It's unfair, yes, but it's the truth. No matter how liberal they say they are, most voters, in the end, believe it takes balls to run this country." So when his daughter began to be seen with Jubal Little, Senator Jaeger put a bull's-eye on Jubal's back and, in the end, bagged the man who would carry forward the Jaeger political flag.

Jubal won his first election—U.S. representative from the district that included Tamarack County, in which he maintained his official residence—by a landslide. He bought a luxurious town house in Georgetown. Camilla was usually in D.C., where she had a huge circle of friends from her childhood, or in the Twin Cities, where she had family. When Jubal came north to Tamarack County, unless he was campaigning, he came alone. It was always put out officially that he was up north to relax, to fish, to hunt, to enjoy the solitude of the great Northwoods. The truth, which Cork and very few others knew, was that, more often than not, he came because of Winona Crane.

"Does she know I'm coming?" Camilla asked.

"I called her brother. He relayed the message. Sure you want to do this?"

She looked ahead, into the dark of the long road to the rez. "I have to do this."

* * *

Willie Crane's cabin was lit from inside. Cork parked, the cabin door opened, and Willie stood silhouetted against the light. When Cork escorted Camilla to him, Willie said, with as much graciousness as his twisted speech would allow, "*Boozhoo*, Mrs. Little." *Bz'yooMizLil*.

"*Boozhoo*," she replied naturally. "Thank you for allowing me to come."

Willie stepped back and let them in.

Every time Cork visited Willie Crane he was struck nearly dumb with wonder at the beauty of the photographs that hung on the walls. The wildlife shots were particularly amazing. Willie, with his clumsy gait, had somehow managed to photograph animals who spooked if you were within a mile of them and you breathed too hard. He caught them in poses so relaxed and so integrally a part of their surroundings that they might have existed in a world where humans or other predators never intruded. And maybe, in a way, that was true, at least as far as humans were concerned, because Willie Crane went deep in the Northwoods, far from any roads, to do much of his shooting. Cork figured that, in order to move such a distance and to do it quietly enough that he didn't scare away the animal life, Willie had to walk agonizingly slow. But he also figured that, if Willie's life had taught him anything, it was probably the virtue of patience.

Camilla scanned the cabin, and Cork could tell she was uncomfortable. Or maybe just nervous at the prospect of finally meeting the woman her husband had loved all his life.

"Is she here?" Camilla asked.

"No."

"But she's coming?"

"I told her," Willie replied. "She said she would think about it."

"What do we do?"

"We wait." He went toward the refrigerator. "Can I offer you something to drink?"

"No, thank you."

"Beer, Cork?"

"Sure, thanks."

Willie took out two bottles of Leinie's Original, unscrewed the caps, and handed a bottle to Cork.

"*Migwech*," Cork said.

"I heard your windshield took a bullet," Willie said.

"A deer slug actually."

"Careless hunter?"

"Yeah." Cork let it go at that.

Willie clearly wasn't interested in pursuing the topic. He looked at Camilla Little with great interest and said, "I always knew this day would come. And I guess I knew that Jubal would have to be dead first."

Which was Cork's sentiment exactly.

The week before his wedding, Jubal Little came north. He came quietly, and Cork might not have even known he was in town except for Willie Crane.

When Winona returned to the reservation after her rescue from the McMurphys, she kept mostly to herself. Whenever he encountered her, Cork found a woman who'd grown beautiful in a distant way and who eyed him as if he were on the far side of some secret knowledge that was hers alone and who spoke to him as if he were very young in his understanding of the world and she very old. The Shinnobs on the rez talked about her as if she were some kind of witch.

Because Jubal came north a lot, Cork often saw his old friend, although they didn't connect in the former way. The powerful friendship of youth was mostly memory, but a good one still, and one they both respectfully acknowledged.

The powerful connection between Jubal and Winona did not diminish over the years, but it was a relationship kept deep in the shadows. A small town and the rez, especially, were difficult places to keep secrets. Even so, if Cork hadn't already known the whole history of Jubal and Winona—two halves of a broken stone—he'd have suspected nothing. When he heard about Jubal's engagement, it made him wonder. It also made him a little angry: What about Winona? But it was, after all, none of his business. Until early one summer morning when he received a desperate call from Willie Crane.

He was a deputy with the Tamarack County Sheriff's Department. He'd worked late the night before, a fatal accident on Highway 1 because of an unusually thick fog, and then the paperwork after. He was groggy but woke up quickly when Willie explained the situation.

"I'll be there as soon as I can," he promised.

It wasn't yet dawn, just the promise of morning in a faint evanescence above the tree line to the east. He drove fast, and the whole way, Willie's words kept echoing in his head: *Jubal's going to kill Winona.*

The sky was peach-colored by the time he reached Winona Crane's little house outside Allouette. Her truck was parked in the dirt drive, alongside her brother's modified Jeep, but Jubal's vehicle was nowhere to be seen. *In the garage,* Cork thought, looking toward the small structure so rickety a strong wind might blow it down. If Jubal and Winona didn't want anyone to know he was there, that was the place for him to park.

As Cork approached, Willie opened the front door. From inside came Jubal's voice, drunk and angry.

"Why, goddamn it? Give me one good reason."

Winona's voice in reply was measured. "I've given you several, Jubal. You just won't hear them. That's always been a problem for you. You hear only what you want to hear."

"And what I want to hear now is one word. Yes. That's all. Just yes."

"No."

Something broke—smashed against a wall.

"He has a gun," Willie told Cork. *E-as-agun.*

Cork entered carefully. Winona sat at the Formica-topped table in the tiny dining room. Her hair was a little wild, but it was a look that seemed to be more from sleep than anything else. She wore a kimono, an odd dressing gown, Cork thought, for a Shinnob on the Iron Lake Reservation. He'd never been inside the house, and he was surprised by what he saw. The walls and shelves and every available flat surface held images and icons and sculptures, things that he associated with a variety of religious traditions: a fat ceramic Buddha; a Celtic cross; a clay plate kiln-fired and painted with Navajo symbols; a figure with an elongated neck, African-looking and carved from what might have been ebony; little finger cymbals of the kind he'd seen in photos of Tibetan monks. It felt clean but cluttered, like a mind in search of truth and stuffed with too many ideas of what that was.

Jubal Little towered over Winona, his back to Cork. He wore boxer shorts, nothing else. His broad back was thickly muscled and his skin deeply tanned. On the speckled Formica of the tabletop stood a bottle of Maker's Mark Kentucky bourbon, the red seal broken, but no glass that Cork could see. He did see, as Jubal waved his hands, the gun that Willie had warned him about.

The house lay mostly in the gloom of a day not yet arrived. Only one light was on, a little lamp on a table in the corner behind Winona, a lamp with a tan shade decorated with images of dream catchers.

"Then there's nothing to be done," Jubal said with a despair that didn't quite ring true. "I'll kill us both."

Winona's eyes shifted from Jubal to where Cork and Willie stood. Jubal must have seen, because he turned to face them.

"Well, what do you know? Dick Tracy's here."

"Morning, Jubal," Cork said.

"Is it?" His eyes, bloodshot, swung toward a window. "The dawning of a new day. Fuck."

Cork looked at the firearm in Jubal's hand, a small-caliber stainless-steel handgun with a rosewood grip. An expensive boutique weapon, he thought, but it could do damage. "Jubal, that gun has me a little nervous. Mind putting it down?"

"I like the feel of it in my hand. This is one thing I can control." He threw a disappointed glance in Winona's direction.

"I understand," Cork said. "It's just easier to talk—for you, Winona, me—if the gun's not a part of our conversation. And I don't know what you're upset about, but I can absolutely guarantee you that Winona's more likely to be amenable if you're not threatening her with a gun. True, Winona?"

Winona Crane's face was as implacable as the face on her ceramic Buddha. "He'll get the same answer from me, gun or no."

That wasn't the help Cork was looking for. But he said, as if it was exactly the answer he'd expected, "There, you see, Jubal. The gun's of no use here. Put it down and we can talk this out."

Jubal studied Cork. He swayed a bit as he stood there, a skyscraper in a mild earthquake. He said, "You took a gun from me once. I told you never to try it again. Remember?"

"I remember. And, Jubal, I won't try to take it from you. I just want you to put it down so that we can talk."

"I'm done talking." He turned the barrel of the gun toward Cork, his face a stone mask as he pulled the trigger.

Cork's heart gave a kick, but that was all that happened. The gun didn't fire.

"Not loaded," Jubal said and laid the firearm on the table.

Cork walked straight at Jubal and, when he was within distance, dropped him with a right cross that Jubal, if he saw it coming, did nothing to stop.

Cork breathed fast and angry. He eyed Winona, who hadn't moved, hadn't shown any surprise in anything that had occurred, as if she didn't care in the least or maybe had known all along how it would play out.

"What's this all about?" he said.

"Jubal wants me to marry him," she replied.

Cork looked down to where Jubal lay, his eyes glazed from the blow and the alcohol. "But you won't?"

"I can't," Winona said.

"Why not?"

"He has a different destiny, a great one, and he needs a different kind of wife for that."

"A great destiny?" Cork said.

"He's going to stand on the mountaintop. He's going to shape nations," Winona replied.

"And you're not good enough to be there with him?" Willie said. He was angry, and Cork couldn't tell if his ire was directed at Winona or Jubal.

She smiled indulgently at her brother and explained, as if to a child, "I was a wild kid. A runaway. Raped at sixteen. Living on the streets of San Francisco at seventeen, doing whatever I had to do for drugs, food, a place to crash. And let's not forget the whole McMurphy enterprise. And, as any Shinnob on the rez will tell you, I'm now a witch. What kind of wife is that for a man on his way to the mountaintop?"

"What you did isn't who you are," Willie fired back, but the meaning was so twisted in his speech that Cork had to spend a moment untangling the garble.

Willie seemed to give up on the argument, his anger quickly spent. He walked to his sister, put his arm around her shoulders, leaned to her, and kissed her hair. "I was afraid he really might kill you."

"He wouldn't," she said. "I knew that. As his wife, I'm no use to him. To go where he's going, he'll have to rid himself of me. He doesn't understand it now, but someday he will. That day will be his beginning," she said with a sad glance at the man prone and miserable on the floor, "and my end."

Later, Cork sat with Jubal on the porch steps in the full light of the morning sun. They each had a cup of the coffee Winona had brewed. She and Willie had gone for a swim in Iron Lake and left the two men together to talk.

"She's always insisted on being so damn discreet," Jubal said. "I come across on the lake or come at night and park in her garage so no one'll see. She never comes to my place. She insists on absolute secrecy. For my sake, she says. She still believes I'm destined for great things, and she'll only hold me back. She's seen my future, and she's not in it. She says when I marry Camilla we're through. Finished. It's not anger or jealousy, she says. It was just always meant to be this way. Bullshit, we're through," he finished angrily.

A dragonfly darted in front of them, held a moment, vibrating in the sunlight, then was gone.

"Let me ask you something, Jubal. Camilla Jaeger, do you love her?"

Jubal stared at the sun, stared without blinking. "I suppose. But she's not Winona. Nobody's Winona."

Then, maybe it was because of the booze that still flooded his system, or the intimacy of the history he shared with Cork, or an unguarded impulse that would become rare for Jubal after he stepped into the political arena, or maybe the result of all of these things together, he confessed, "I killed for her, Cork. I killed for her, but she still won't marry me."

"Killed for her?" Cork lowered the cup he was just about to sip from. "Who did you kill?"

Jubal took his eyes from the sun, and his pupils had become black pinpoints. "You were there."

It took Cork a couple of seconds to put it together. Although decades had passed, he felt an electric jolt, as if the whole incident had only just happened, or had just happened again. "Donner Bigby?" he said. "But I thought—"

"Jesus, Cork. You always knew. You just didn't want to see."

That wasn't true. Was it? He'd believed the story Jubal had told him about what happened on top of Trickster's Point. Hadn't he?

"You killed him? In cold blood?"

"I knew the moment I started climbing Trickster's Point that only one of us would come down. That's why I went up and not you. You couldn't have done what needed doing."

"What needed doing? Jubal, we didn't go out there to kill Donner Bigby."

"Didn't we? Then why were we there? You wanted him dead as much as I did. We both wanted him dead for what he did to Winona. Don't go all sanctimonious on me. I just did what I knew you couldn't."

Long before the sun had risen, the birds had begun to sing, but it seemed to Cork that he was only just now hearing their songs. In the early light, there'd been clouds the color of fuzzy peaches, but he saw that they'd evaporated or moved on, and the sky was a clear blue. *An innocent blue,* he thought. The smell of the coffee in his cup rose up, a good aroma that filled his senses every time he breathed. This was life, he understood. This was life, and this was what, according to Jubal, he'd had a hand in taking from Donner Bigby.

But was Jubal right? When they'd stood together at the bottom of Trickster's Point, Cork had wanted to be the one to climb up after Bigby. He remembered that. And he remembered the rage that had filled his heart. But was it a rage so intense that it was murderous? Had the real reason he wanted to climb up after Bigby been to ensure that the brute never came back down? And, as had so often been the case in those days, had it simply fallen to Jubal to do what Cork could not?

Finally Jubal said, "Winona's always known what's in my heart, Cork. And I've always known what's in yours."

Cork let a moment pass, a moment of further dark consideration, then said simply, "Bullshit."

He put his cup down hard, and coffee sloshed on the porch boards, and he left Jubal sitting alone in the sunlight and he didn't look back.

CHAPTER 30

Camilla Little stood looking at one of the framed photographs on the wall of Willie Crane's cabin, a shot of a lynx alert in an arrow of gold light in the middle of a stand of winter birch. The shaft of sunlight, the animal's thick coat and great paws, the soft snow, the pillars of birch, all of the elements were lustrous, as if imbued with some holy spirit. Willie was at the front window, staring into the dark, watching for Winona to arrive.

"These photographs are stunning," Camilla said. "How do you . . . ?" She stopped herself.

"How do I shoot them with this twisted body of mine?" Willie said without turning.

"That's not what I was going to say."

"It was what you were thinking." Willie finally turned and spoke to her directly. He didn't seem bothered in the least by what he assumed she thought. "Do you know the story 'The Bound Man'?"

"No."

"By Ilse Aichinger, an Austrian writer. A man is set on by thieves. They beat him, rob him, bind him with rope, leave him for dead. When he wakes, he finds that the rope isn't tight enough to keep him from moving, just tight enough that he can't move like a normal person. He discovers that, if he accepts the limitations imposed by the rope, he can do things that amaze people. He becomes a circus performer. The Bound Man. He's famous. One day he's attacked by a wolf, and because he understands his own predicament so well, understands the capabilities of his body, even bound, he defeats the animal. No one believes him, so he enters the circus ring, tied up in his rope, to fight another wolf. But a woman who loves him and is afraid for him cuts him loose. The Bound Man is forced to shoot the wolf. His circumstances become normal again, and he does everything like everyone else. He's no longer special."

Camilla listened politely and, when Willie had finished, said, "That's a lovely story, and I understand, honestly. But really what I was wondering was how it is that you're able to capture on film the soul of nature."

"The soul of nature?" Willie laughed easily, as if genuinely and pleasantly surprised. "The spirit of the Great Mystery is how I think of it. It's something we can't name or even comprehend. We can only allow ourselves to be a part of it and, in that way, know it. I'm never so happy as when I'm out on a shoot. It's just me and the woods and the Great Mystery. John Muir said, 'In every walk with nature one receives far more than he seeks.' That's how I've always felt." Willie held his hand toward the dark window glass. "When I die, I want to be left out there in the woods, not buried in a grave or cremated. I want the forest to consume me completely, so that I can give back something in return for all that I've received."

Cork finished his beer. "It's been a long wait, Willie. Maybe she isn't coming."

"Let me call her," Willie said.

They were in an area where cell phone coverage was iffy at best. For his business, Willie Crane had long ago had a landline strung to his cabin. He went to the phone that hung on the wall in the kitchen area, punched in a number, and waited.

"Nona," he said. "It's me. They're here. Are you coming?"

He closed his eyes and listened.

"No," he said. Then, "It's safe, I promise."

He shook his head at whatever his sister was saying.

"She deserves answers," he said.

His shoulders dropped, and Cork could tell that Willie had failed to convince her.

"It's all right," Willie said, as if soothing a child. "It's all right, Nona. I'll explain."

He hung up the phone and faced them.

"She's afraid."

"Of me?" Camilla asked.

"Of everything. She gets this way."

It was true. Cork had seen it, especially whenever Jubal had been with her and then left. Sometimes Winona would disappear for weeks, and Willie was the only one who saw her. In those times, Willie took care of her completely.

"I'm sorry," Willie said to Camilla. "A wasted trip."

With great admiration, Camilla looked at the photographs on the cabin walls and offered Willie Crane the most cordial of smiles. "I don't think so. And thank you for trying."

Willie stood in the doorway as they left, silhouetted alone against the light inside the cabin in exactly the way he'd been when they arrived.

"Well," Camilla said quietly, when they were in the Land Rover, "I guess that's that."

"Not necessarily." Cork started the engine.

She turned to him, her face a dim, sickly green from the illumination of the dash lights. "What do you mean?"

"We came to see Winona Crane. We're going to see Winona Crane."

He pulled away from the cabin and offered her no further explanation.

Winona lived in the house that had been her grandmother's. It was a small thing of weathered gray clapboard, one story, which

Cork had been in only once in all those years, and that was on the day Jubal had threatened to kill her. By the time Winona returned from the outside world, her grandmother was dead, and Winona lived in the house alone. Willie had offered to live there with her for company, but she preferred her privacy. Cork figured that her lifelong consort with Jubal Little was probably a major factor.

As he threaded his way among the trees along the drive off the main road, Cork could see already that the house was dark. He'd hoped to find a light on, a sign that Winona was in hiding there.

"What is this place?" Camilla asked when Cork parked and killed the engine.

"Winona's house."

She studied it a long time. In the starless night and without any ambient light, Cork couldn't see her face but could imagine her reaction. This was where her husband, time and again, had slept with another woman.

"No one's home," she said.

"It looks that way, doesn't it?" Cork opened his door.

"Where are you going?"

"No one locks their doors on the rez."

"You're just going to walk inside?"

"I'll knock first. It's the polite thing to do."

He reached across Camilla to the glove box, popped it open, and pulled a flashlight from inside. He got out, and after a moment, Camilla followed. They climbed the steps, and Cork knocked, then knocked again. He tried the knob and swung the door open.

"This doesn't feel right," Camilla said, holding back.

"After you've done it a few times, you get used to it," Cork said.

Camilla gave him a puzzled, and not very pleasant, look.

Inside, the beam of the flashlight swept across the tiny living room, which looked pretty much the same as when Cork had seen it years before. Lots of icons and artifacts and images from other religious traditions. Framed photographs on the walls, all clearly shot by her brother. Simple, comfortable furniture. He continued through the small dining area to the kitchen.

"What are you looking for?" Camilla asked.

"I was hoping for Winona. But I'll take anything that might give me a clue to where she's hiding."

"And that would be?"

"I'm hoping I'll know when I see it."

"Why don't you just turn on a light?"

"Might bring someone from the road. I'd rather nobody caught us in here like this."

"Duh," Camilla said.

It was so pedestrian a response from so grand a lady that it made Cork laugh. He ran the light over the floor, the table, the counters, the walls.

Camilla said, "Wait. There."

Her hand entered the beam, and a bright, white finger with a dark red nail pointed at a piece of stationery framed and hanging on the wall. She reached for the frame, a thin construction of honey-colored pine with a clear glass covering the paper, and pulled it from the hook where it hung. On the paper inside was a poem, handwritten. Camilla read it silently and said, "That son of a bitch."

"May I?" Cork took the frame from her. It held a love poem titled simply "To Winona." Cork read it. Although his own knowledge of poetry didn't extend much beyond Robert Frost, he thought it was a little sentimental and not very original. But he supposed a woman might be flattered to be the subject of a poem, even a bad one.

"He gave that poem to me on our wedding night," Camilla said bitterly. "Only it was my name at the top of the page. Christ, he couldn't even give that little bit of himself just to me."

She grabbed the frame from Cork and threw it to the floor, where the glass covering shattered.

"I'm leaving," she announced.

"Hold on, Camilla. There are a couple more rooms I want to check."

"I'll wait for you in the car." She spun away and took a step.

"There might be animals out there."

She stopped. "You're just trying to scare me."

"Just alerting you. On the rez, bears and coyotes and even wolves aren't uncommon. Just make sure you go straight to my Land Rover and lock the doors."

She hesitated, clearly weighing her options, and finally decided in favor of what might threaten her outside over what she might have to face if she stayed inside with Cork. She disappeared, stomping away in the direction they'd come. Cork heard the front door open and slam closed. He figured it was probably for the best, because the next room he wanted to check was Winona's bedroom, and God alone knew how Camilla might react at the sight of the bed where so much infidelity had taken place.

He found the bed unmade, the sheets a rumpled mess. Each of the two pillows still held a clear indentation where a head had lain. Otherwise, the room was clean and neat. Cork discovered nothing of interest there and continued on to the final room of the house, the bathroom.

Although Winona tended to clutter her home with religious and spiritual knickknacks, she was essentially a good housekeeper. The bathroom, like the other rooms, was spotless. Cork swung the flashlight across the top of the small vanity, opened the cabinet, checked the shelves where the towels and washcloths lay neatly folded. On a small, low table next to the tub sat a big candle, a compact CD player, and a single plastic CD case. He remembered how his wife, Jo, used to love to relax at the end of a long day with a bath, a candle, and soft music. There was a wicker hamper next to the door. He lifted the lid. What was inside surprised him. Several towels lay thrown there, all of them deeply stained red. He touched the topmost towel. The red was crusted. He turned and ran the beam of the flashlight more carefully over the small room. When the light fell on the floor beneath the claw-footed bathtub, Cork caught another glimpse of crimson.

He knelt and looked more closely. It was a thin rivulet, a few inches long. He touched it and confirmed that it had long ago dried. He swept the whole area under the tub with the light but could see nothing more. He went down on his hands and knees and carefully examined the rest of the bathroom floor, which was hardwood. In a tiny seam where the old wood had shrunk and separated, he found another gathering of what appeared to him to be dried blood.

He stood up and considered, and what he thought was that someone had bled here, bled quite a lot, and then someone—a different someone?—had tried to clean up all that blood. Whether for the sake of cleanliness or to get rid of evidence he didn't know.

A scream came from outside, and Cork spun, thinking, in that instant, that he'd warned Camilla against the wrong kinds of animals. He ran through the house, out the door, and found Camilla in the Land Rover with the doors locked. When she saw him, she lowered her window.

"Someone," she said. "There." She pointed to the side of the garage, and Cork shot the beam of his flashlight in that direction. It illuminated the garbage bin, and a fat raccoon with his little paws full of fish bones. His eyes glittered in the light, and he stared at them as if they, not he, were the intruders.

"Sorry," Camilla said.

"That's all right." Cork decided his visit to the house was at an end for the moment. He slid into the driver's seat.

Camilla asked, "Well?"

He considered telling her what he'd found but, because he didn't know yet what it meant, decided discretion was best.

"Nothing," he replied.

* * *

When they arrived back at the courthouse, the Escalade wasn't the only vehicle waiting for them. A gray Mercedes SUV had parked behind it. Cork pulled to the curb under the streetlamp in front of the Escalade and got out. As he walked to the passenger side to open the door for Camilla, Yates left his vehicle, and two figures emerged from the Mercedes. They all converged on Cork.

Nick Jaeger held back a discreet distance, but Alex thrust his face to within inches of Cork's. "Jesus Christ, O'Connor, what the hell do you think you're doing?"

Before Cork had a chance to respond, Camilla Little stepped out and said, "I asked him to do me a favor, Alex. He was just honoring my request."

Yates, who stood very near to her, said, "Sorry, Mrs. Little. They just showed up."

"That's okay, Kenny."

Alex forgot about being upset for a moment. "You saw her?"

"No," Camilla replied. Then added, "I'd rather not talk about it."

"We'll discuss it, but not here." He turned his attention to Cork again. In the harsh light of the streetlamp, the scar lines on his face were like worms embedded under the skin. "After what happened to you this afternoon, I can't believe you'd put my sister at risk this way. And you"—to Yates—"you're supposed to protect her."

"I'm also supposed to respect her wishes."

"In this situation, that kind of respect could have got her killed."

"She's your sister. You try arguing with her."

"And you try finding a job after I fire you."

"With all due respect, I work for the Littles."

Alex ignored the remark and addressed his sister once again: "You're coming with us. We have things to talk about."

He tried to take hold of Camilla, but Yates clamped a huge and powerful hand on his arm, cutting short the man's reach.

"Is that what you want, Mrs. Little?" Yates said.

"It's fine, Kenny."

Yates released his grip on Alex Jaeger's arm but with reluctance, it was clear. He stood beside Cork, watching silently as Camilla Little was taken away by her brothers. Cork glanced at his face and saw concern there. And something more, maybe?

"She'll be okay," Cork said. "They're family."

Yates seemed unimpressed. "Jubal hired me to protect her from the crazies out there. You ask me, what she most needs protecting from is that family of hers. Crazy as peach orchard pigs."

"Peach orchard pigs? What's that mean, Kenny?"

"I don't know exactly. Just something we say in Texas."

"Jubal married into that family with his eyes wide open."

"Yeah, I asked him once why he put up with their smug white liberalism and their relentless political maneuvering. He told me that when he played professional ball, even though he didn't particularly like some of his teammates, he understood that the only way he'd ever make it to the Super Bowl was playing on a team."

"The Super Bowl?"

"A metaphor," Yates said and looked at Cork as if he were an idiot. "For the presidency. Jubal had his sights set on the White House." Yates stared down the street, where the taillights of the Mercedes were like two eyes glaring at him from the dark. "She'd have made a hell of a First Lady," he said.

He arrived home in the late dark. The patio door was locked, so Cork used his key to come in through the side door. He crept into the kitchen, and Trixie got up from where she lay sleeping under the dining room table and came to greet him.

"Hey, girl," he said quietly and petted her with one hand while she licked his other.

The house was dark except for a single lamp in the living room, where he found Cy Borkman snoring on the sofa, a crocheted afghan thrown over him. He shook his friend gently, and Borkman awoke.

"I'll take the next watch, Cy," Cork said. "Thanks, buddy."

Borkman, a big man, particularly around his middle, yawned and stretched and eased himself up. "Everything go okay?"

"Yeah, Cy. Just fine. And it helped not worrying about my family."

"You need me again, you just call."

"I will, Cy. Thanks."

Borkman took his jacket from the coat tree near the front door and left.

Upstairs, a soft crying began. Cork heard steps in the hallway and then Jenny's voice gently offering comfort. In a minute, the house was quiet once more. He caught again the sound of Jenny's light tread in the hallway, but instead of entering her bedroom, she came downstairs.

"Hi, kiddo." Cork spoke softly so that he wouldn't startle her.

"I thought I heard you come in. Did Cy go home?"

"Yeah."

"He's a good man. Waaboo loves him."

"Waaboo loves everyone."

"Long day," she said. "Any luck?"

"Luck?"

"Clearing your name. Getting yourself out from under the cloud of suspicion."

Cork gave her a brief smile. "You sound like a writer of bad mystery stories. Let's go into the kitchen, and I'll fill you in."

He pulled the curtain over the sink and turned on the hood light above the stove, intentionally keeping the room dimly lit. He poured himself a glass of milk, took a couple of chocolate chip cookies from the cookie jar, and sat with his daughter at the kitchen table.

"Rainy called," she told him. "She and Henry heard about the deer slug through your windshield. She was worried. She tried your cell, but you didn't answer."

Cork pulled his phone from the holder on his belt. "Damn battery's dead. You told her I'm all right?"

"Yes, but she's still worried. We all are, Dad."

"It's too late to call her now. I'll check in with her in the morning."

"So," Jenny said. "Fill me in."

He did. Told her everything, including his suspicions concerning Bigby and Broom.

"Do you really think that either of those men could have killed Jubal Little?" she asked when he'd finished.

Cork took a long drink of his milk and, with the back of his hand, wiped the residue from his upper lip. "Remember when we found Waaboo? You were ready to kill to protect him. I think either Lester or Isaiah could have killed Jubal if what they wanted to protect was important enough to them."

"Isaiah and Indian casinos?"

"Couple that with a lifelong love of Winona Crane, and maybe so."

"And you really think Lester Bigby would kill to protect his investments?"

"Again, couple that with a deep desire to raise his esteem in his father's eyes, and maybe so. And one more thing to keep in mind about them both. Neither of them would shed a tear if I went to prison for the deed."

"I don't buy that," Jenny said. "I don't think either of them killed Jubal Little."

"You think I did it, then?"

"Don't joke about this."

He sat back and studied her. In the weak light, with her hair the color of a moonbeam on a dark lake and her eyes like chips of blue glacial ice, she reminded him of her mother. He'd often sat with Jo in just this way, discussing a case that had him puzzled. He still missed her, still felt the ache of her loss, but the current of life had carried him on to a new place, and he'd discovered that he could be happy there, too.

"I found blood at Winona Crane's house," he said.

"Somebody was hurt?"

"Looks like. Probably not Winona. She talked with Willie tonight and didn't say anything to him about it, at least while I was there."

"What do you think it means?"

"Maybe nothing. I don't know."

"So," Jenny said. "What now?"

"I've turned over all the rocks I can think of. Now, I guess, we wait."

"For what?"

"To see if anything crawls out."

"Coming from you, that sounds awfully passive."

"The truth is I don't know what else to do, except hope that tomorrow something breaks."

As it turned out, that's exactly what happened.

CHAPTER 31

He rose early, long before the media might arrive at his door, dressed, put a note on the kitchen table explaining things to Jenny and Stephen, and left the house. He didn't call Borkman; the guy needed his sleep. He hoped the early hour was reasonable protection for his family, and he planned to be back before it got too late.

Another November overcast had moved in, and Cork drove under a sky still inky from night and promising nothing better than a day capped with clouds the color of despair.

He'd awakened that morning with an uncomfortable thought, a thought about Winona Crane, and he needed to talk it over with Henry Meloux. The morning was cool, almost cold. Before starting down the path to Crow Point, he zipped his leather jacket up to his chin, pulled his gloves on, and settled a red stocking cap over his ears.

Half an hour later, he broke from the trees and saw, against the gray sky that backed the meadow, smoke vining upward from both Meloux's cabin and Rainy's. The meadow grass was long and dry, the color of apple cider. Against the walls of the two small cabins, cords of split wood lay stacked, banked in anticipation of a winter just over the horizon. The wood made the walls look unnaturally thick, and the image reminded Cork of those wild animals who, in the fall, grew their coats huge to protect them from the brutal cold that was to come. Behind the branches of the bare aspens along the shoreline, Iron Lake was a great slab of fractured gray slate. The only sound was the cry of the crows that perennially used the trees as a rookery and, in that way, had given the point its name.

He headed to Rainy's cabin first. He knocked; she didn't answer. He went on to Meloux's, where he found them both having breakfast. Rainy gave him a kiss, then gave him coffee and offered to fix him something to eat. He settled for a couple of hot biscuits with homemade blueberry jam.

When they'd finished their meal, Meloux sat back in his old birchwood chair. He appeared well rested and refreshed, something Cork envied.

"You look like an animal of burden, Corcoran O'Connor, given too much to carry."

"Are you going to tell us about the bullet through your windshield, Cork?" Although she tried to speak casually, there was a note of irritation in Rainy's voice.

"Jenny told me you called. Sorry, Rainy. The battery on my cell phone was dead."

"It could have been you instead of that battery," she replied.

"Niece," Meloux said gently. "He did not come for a scolding." His eyes, brown as old pennies, settled expectantly on Cork.

"Henry, I want to talk to you about Winona Crane and Jubal Little."

"Then talk."

"If I told you I thought that she might have killed Jubal Little, would you say I was crazy?"

"Crazy is trying to tickle a bull moose, Corcoran O'Connor. I would not say you are crazy."

"Winona loved Jubal, and I know Jubal loved her. But I'm wondering if it was the other side of love that might have made her kill him."

Rainy said, "You think that, in the end, she hated Jubal?"

Cork shook his head and nodded toward Meloux. "Your uncle once told me that the other side of love isn't hate but fear. Here's the deal, Henry. In those three hours I spent with him before he died, Jubal told me a lot of things he clearly wanted to get off his chest. Some of it I've told the sheriff's people, but some I've kept to myself. One of the things Jubal told me was that he came north this time to tell Winona good-bye for good. He said he'd made a decision never to see her again."

"Why?" Rainy asked.

"She'd become a liability to him."

"He was preparing to reach the mountaintop," Meloux said.

"You know about Winona's vision?" Cork asked.

"It came to her here, long ago."

"After Donner Bigby died, when you worked to heal her?"

"And Jubal Little. They both needed healing, but there was more to it than just that. There was something unusual about them. They were two pieces of the same broken stone. Winona had the vision then."

"What was the vision?" Rainy asked.

Cork said, "She saw Jubal alone on a mountaintop, holding the sun and moon in his hands, and the stars singing around his head."

"Did you tell her what the vision meant, Uncle Henry?"

Meloux shook his head. "It was her vision. She believed she knew what it meant. Who was I to say she was right or she was wrong?"

"What did she think it meant?"

"That Jubal Little was destined for greatness. That he would have to achieve it alone."

Cork said, "So when she ran away from Aurora right after that, she was somehow trying to fulfill the vision?"

"Maybe," Meloux allowed. "Or maybe it is simply a hard thing to accept that someone you love will someday abandon you."

"But her vision wasn't fulfilled," Rainy pointed out. "Jubal Little died before he reached the top."

The old man shrugged. "A vision is not necessarily what will be. It is more like a light showing the way toward what could be. And sometimes it is a warning."

Meloux's old dog, Walleye, got up from the corner of the cabin where he'd been lying with his head cradled on his paws. He came to the table, to Rainy, who scratched his head. Then she frowned at Cork. "What did you mean when you said that Winona had become a liability to Jubal?"

"He was going to be in the public eye in such a way that everything he did would be watched. His relationship with Winona would be too risky. If it's true that he had his eye ultimately on the presidency—and knowing Jubal, that's exactly where his ambition would push him—he had to make sure that he appeared to be squeaky clean."

Rainy didn't look convinced. "If all her life Winona's known that Jubal would have to abandon her, for the mountaintop, as you put it, why believe that she killed him just as he was poising himself to get there?"

On his fingers, Cork counted off the reasons. "One: Sam Winter Moon taught her to bow-hunt and still-stalk. Two: She knows the area around Trickster's Point well. And three: I tend to agree with the guy who said that hell has no fury like a woman scorned."

"I'm going to ignore for the moment the sexist nature of that last comment and repeat what Uncle Henry told you, that hate isn't the other side of love. That would be fear. So if Winona Crane killed Jubal Little, what was she afraid of?"

Cork shrugged. "I don't know. I'm really just thinking out loud."

Meloux put an old hand in the center of the table, his fingers spread like the points of a star. "Does your heart, Corcoran O'Connor, agree with the way your head is trying to lead you?"

"No," Cork had to admit. He sat back, feeling defeated again. "I'm flailing here, Henry."

"Did you come hoping for advice? Or did you come hoping for something else?"

"I was wondering if you might be willing to talk to Winona."

Meloux fell silent as he considered Cork's request. Walleye circled the table and nudged his old head under the Mide's right hand, and Meloux idly stroked the dog's yellow fur.

"If she comes to me, I will talk to her," he finally agreed. "But my purpose will be to help her spirit heal, if that is what she wants, not to help you put her in the hands of the police."

"Fair enough, Henry," Cork said, and he rose to leave. "*Migwech.*"

Rainy walked him across the meadow to where the trail entered the trees. Morning had arrived fully, but because clouds sealed the entire dome of the sky, there was no sun.

"Do you think you can convince Winona to talk to Uncle Henry?" she asked.

"If I can find her. She's gone into hiding again."

She smiled at him and reached out to touch his cheek. "Do you know what Uncle Henry says about you?"

"No, tell me."

"He says you're like a dog who can't remember where he's buried his bone. You just keep digging until you find it."

"Pretty pathetic, huh?"

"I don't think so at all."

She kissed him just as his cell phone began to ring. He pulled it from his belt holder and saw that it was Ed Larson calling.

"This is Cork. What's up, Ed?"

Larson said, "You might want to come down to the sheriff's department, Cork. We just brought in Isaiah Broom. Holter's insisting we arrest him for the murder of Jubal Little."

CHAPTER 32

"We showed up at his door," Holter said. "Captain Larson and myself. We wanted to get to him early, but just to talk to him. He took one look at us and said, 'I killed him.' It was that simple."

That simple, Cork thought. He wanted to say, *Come on, Holter, nothing's that simple*, but he held his tongue.

They sat in the office of Sheriff Marsha Dross. They all had mugs of coffee, and someone had put a plate of doughnut holes on Dross's desk. Nobody was eating them. Cork thought the feel in the room was different from the excitement that should have been there if they really believed they were going to be able to close the case.

"Have you questioned him yet?"

Larson shook his head. "He asked to have his attorney present."

Cork saw the dismal look on Holter's face. "Wouldn't happen to be Leon Papakee, would it, Agent Holter?" he asked.

"It is," the BCA agent replied coolly. "He's on his way. Should be here soon."

"So what do you think?" Cork asked of them all in general.

Dross said, "We're reserving judgment, but we'd be interested in what you think."

Cork lifted his mug. The smell of the coffee was good and

strong, and he figured Dross had made it herself. He sipped and considered the question, then replied, "I think Broom is the kind of man who could have done this kind of thing, but I don't think he's the kind of man who would hand himself over to you gift-wrapped."

Holter said, "Unless he plans to use this whole tragic situation as a political forum of some kind."

"I could see him doing that," Cork said. "What about Lester Bigby?"

Holter looked surprised at the apparent jump in topic. "What about him?"

"Did you talk to him?"

"Yes. He wasn't happy about it, but he was cooperative. He showed us his hunting bow, his arrows. Very nice, but very commercial. Nothing homemade. Nothing like the arrow that killed Jubal Little."

"As I explained to you once before, Agent Holter, I don't lock my doors. I still think he could have taken one of mine."

"You don't really believe that, do you?"

"Did you get his fingerprints to match against the ones on the arrow that killed your John Doe on the ridge?"

"I didn't believe it to be necessary at this point."

"Did you at least ask him where he was last Saturday?"

"We did. He was out all day, at that resort property of his on Crown Lake."

"Interesting. He told his wife he was going to spend the day with his father."

"Time enough for both, I suppose."

"His father says he wasn't there at all."

"Look, what difference does it make? We have in custody the man who admits to the murder."

"Yeah, a guy who normally wouldn't say boo to the cops, and without even being prompted insists, 'Cuff me.' You really buy that, Holter?"

"Jesus, O'Connor. You were the one who suggested we take

a good look at Broom. Now you're saying we made a mistake? Give me a break."

Larson intervened evenly. "For now, it's the best lead we have, Cork. We're not going to send an innocent man to jail, you know that."

"Do I? I was looking pretty good to you there for a while."

"Maybe you still are," Larson said. "Go on home. We'll be in touch."

Cork stood up to leave. As he put his half-empty coffee mug on Dross's desk, the sheriff asked, "Just for the sake of argument, why would Broom lie about something like this?"

Love, Cork wanted to tell her. Instead he said, "Maybe it's like Holter says. Isaiah's got some political points to make, and he just wants the spotlight."

"Risky," Dross said.

"If you're born Indian, your whole life is about risk," Cork replied, and he left.

As he'd been doing for some time now, he'd parked his Land Rover a couple of blocks away so that he could slip into and out of the sheriff's department without the media spotting him. When he got there this time, however, he saw that he'd been found out. A silver Escalade was parked behind the Land Rover, and as Cork approached, Kenny Yates stepped out. He wore a sanded calfskin leather jacket and leather gloves. Although it was overcast, he had on an expensive pair of shades.

"The Jaegers would like to see you," he said, blocking Cork's way.

"Fine, but I have a couple of things I need to do first."

"They would prefer that you come right now."

"They would, huh?" He looked up into the big man's face, into his own reflection in the lenses of the sunglasses. "I was under the impression that you didn't work for the Jaegers. You work for the Littles."

"Consider it a request from Mrs. Little then. But the Jaegers'll be there, too."

"All right. I'll follow you."

"I'd prefer you rode along with me." Yates finally took the sunglasses off, and Cork saw that his eyes were troubled. "Got something I want to say to you."

"All right. Let me call home first."

He checked in with Jenny. Everyone was up, and everything was fine, and Cy Borkman, God bless him, had shown up of his own accord and was having a plate of pancakes and eggs at the kitchen table even as they spoke. Jenny relayed a message from him to Cork: Do what you have to. The home front is secured.

Yates drove, but not a direct route to Jubal Little's place on Iron Lake. Cork waited for him to say what was on his mind, but it was clear that Yates had to work up to it. Cork figured it must be something pretty hard, considering all the posturing and now all the delay.

They came to a stoplight, one of only three in Aurora, and Yates said, "It's like this. No matter how it turns out, Camilla's going to be hurt."

So it's Camilla now, Cork thought. What he said was, "Jubal's dead. What could hurt her more than that?"

Yates shot him a cold look. "It's going to all come out about Jubal and that Indian woman, isn't it?"

"I'm not sure I know what you're talking about, Kenny."

"Don't play stupid, Cork. I'd hate to see Camilla have to go through the public shit bath that would result if the press found out why Jubal came north."

"Kenny, you have no idea why Jubal really came north."

"To fuck the Indian woman."

"The physical thing was part of it, I'm sure, but there was something else, something much deeper going on. In a way, I think Jubal was looking for wholeness of spirit. I think that's what he was really after."

"Doesn't matter what he was really after. Those reporters, if they get wind of this woman, won't be saying he visited her for wholeness, believe me."

"I'm going to do my best to keep anyone out of this who doesn't have to be a part of the public story. Once again, I'm giving you my word."

The light turned green, and Yates pulled ahead.

"Okay, something you maybe ought to know, Cork. That bullet hole through your windshield? You got a lead on the guy who fired it?"

"Not yet."

"Check this out. Yesterday afternoon Nick Jaeger leaves the house. He's carrying a piece, a rifle. Gets into his Mercedes and takes off. Doesn't come back for maybe three hours. Brings the rifle with him back into the house. This morning Camilla tells me he's heading down to the Twin Cities tomorrow. Not even sticking around to see the end of the investigation into Jubal's murder."

"A pressing appointment?" Cork asked.

"Right," Yates scoffed. "Him and Jubal used to hunt together. Black powder, muzzle-loaders, that antique gun shit. Jubal told me that Nick Jaeger was the second best shot he'd ever seen."

Cork said, "Let me guess. Jubal was the best."

"There's a gun case in Jubal's house," Yates went on. "It's locked or I would have checked to see if any of his rifles had been fired recently. Maybe it's something you ought to think about. That's all I'm saying."

"Why would Nick Jaeger try to kill me?"

Yates pulled into the drive of Jubal Little's lake home. "You're the P.I. You figure it out."

Jaeger's Mercedes SUV was parked in the drive, and Yates pulled up behind it. They got out, and Yates walked ahead. Cork saw a curtain in a front window drop into place. Yates opened the door for Cork and ushered him inside.

"In here," Alex Jaeger called from down the hallway.

"They're all yours," Yates said and bowed out.

Cork walked to the den, where he'd faced the Jaeger family the day after Jubal died. They'd scattered themselves about the room like throw pillows, Alex standing by the fireplace, Nick at the liquor cabinet, and Camilla sitting demurely on the brown leather divan. When he came in, they watched him like a caribou might track a nearby wolf.

"Thank you for coming," Alex said.

"With all due respect, Kenny didn't give me much choice."

"I'm sorry, Cork," Camilla said. "Kenny's . . . well, Kenny takes his job seriously. I don't know what I'd do without him."

A fire crackled away in the fireplace, and the room felt too warm.

"Mind if I take my coat off?" Cork asked.

"Be my guest," Alex said. He waited until Cork had slipped off his jacket and laid it over the back of one of the plush easy chairs, then he got down to brass tacks. "Is it true they've arrested the man who killed Jubal?"

Cork didn't answer immediately. He took a moment to study each of the Jaegers carefully. Alex stood erect, almost imperious, and Cork could see him commanding men in uniform, or standing before legislators and speaking to them in a way meant to bend them to his purpose. He was born to lead, or at least held himself as if that were the case. Nick dropped ice into a glass and poured in some Johnnie Walker Blue. He seemed more intent on his liquor than on what was occurring in the room, but it was, Cork thought, a studied gesture. And then there was Camilla, who sat lovely and attentive and with a lingering air of sadness about her, and who seemed to Cork to be somehow at the apex of this familial triangle.

"Why am I really here?" Cork said.

"I don't understand," Alex replied. "It was a simple question."

"And one you already know the answer to. You've been inside this investigation from the beginning. I don't know how, and I don't care, but everything I know about it, you know, too. So what is it that you really want to ask me?"

Nick glanced up from his glass of scotch and locked eyes

with his brother. Camilla looked down at her hands, which were folded in her lap.

"All right, here it is," Alex said. "How much will it cost us to make sure that you say nothing to the press about Jubal and this Indian woman?"

"Ah," Cork said. He thought a moment. "How much are you willing to pay?"

"I assume you have a number in mind."

"Make an offer."

"All right," Alex said. "Five hundred thousand dollars."

Cork smiled. "What is it you're trying to protect? Jubal's name? The Jaeger name?" His eyes swung toward Camilla. "Or just protective brothers trying to stand between their sister and the bullies of the world? I don't want your money."

Camilla spoke up immediately. "I told them you wouldn't accept something like this, Cork. They wouldn't believe me. And honestly, I don't care what people might say about Jubal and Winona Crane. I know the truth, and that's what's important to me."

Alex said, "The truth? Hell, Camilla, the truth is that the guy's been unfaithful to you for years with this woman."

"We had an understanding about her."

"Yeah, that Jubal could walk all over you and you wouldn't say boo to him."

"You wouldn't understand." Her anger was clearly mounting.

"Oh? I'd love to be enlightened. Because whenever I confronted Jubal with it, he just clammed up. Christ, the stink of guilt poured off him."

"It wasn't like that," Camilla shouted. "Jubal loved me."

"Then why was he fucking another woman?"

"Because," she said as the tears began, "I wasn't enough. And I understood that. And I wanted Jubal anyway. And she was the price." She wiped her cheeks with her knuckle.

Alex threw his arms up as if in disgust or surrender. "It doesn't matter. If the press gets wind of her, they'll fry him up and serve him to the public on a platter."

"He's dead," Camilla said. "It can't hurt him now."

Nick said, "But it'll hurt you, Camilla." This was the first he'd spoken since Cork arrived, and it was a tender offering. "The shadow of Jubal will follow you, and people will think all kinds of things about you. They don't know you."

She smiled at her brother. "You don't think I'm strong enough to endure that?"

"All these years, I've watched you take what Jubal offered you, and I couldn't understand why you accepted so little when you deserved so much more. It's not right that he should go on making your life miserable even after he's dead."

She stood up, walked to the liquor cabinet, put her hand against her brother's cheek, and said, "The life I had with him was the life I chose, Nickie."

"No, Dad and Alex chose it for you. You were the sacrifice on the altar of their political ambition."

"Is that what you've thought all these years?"

"When we hunted together," Nick said, "I sometimes put Jubal in my sights and thought about pulling the trigger, just to set you free."

Her hand slid from his cheek, and she took a half step away. "You didn't kill him, did you, Nickie?"

"Me?" He seemed genuinely surprised at the question. "No. But I won't lie to you. I'm not sorry he's dead."

"I don't want to hear that." Camilla turned from him and walked away.

He watched her go, then took a long swallow from his glass.

An uncomfortable silence had fallen over the room, and into it Cork dropped this: "Is that why you tried to kill me, Nick? To protect your sister from more hurt?"

"Tried to kill you?" Nick gave a short laugh. "What the hell are you talking about?"

"The slug through my windshield. I think you fired it."

"Whoa, O'Connor, hold on a minute," Alex said. "That's a hell of an accusation."

"Maybe so, but easily proven." Cork walked to a window of the den that overlooked the driveway. He pulled a curtain back, so that Nick Jaeger's Mercedes was visible on the drive. "Whoever it was who fired the shot left tire tracks at the scene. The sheriff's people took impressions. My guess is that if I told them to check the tires on your SUV, Nick, they'd get a match."

"There are lots of vehicles with those tires on them, I'm sure," Nick said.

"Maybe so. But they also got an impression from the sole of an expensive hiking boot. If they secured a search warrant, I'd be willing to bet they'd find that boot and its mate somewhere among your things. So, I'm going to ask you again, is that why you tried to kill me?"

Nick didn't flinch, didn't move at all. He was like one of the animals he hunted, frozen in crosshairs. "If I'd wanted to kill you," he finally said, "I would have shot you through the eye."

"Jesus, Nick, just shut up," Alex cried.

"You just wanted to scare me?" Cork said.

"Don't say another word, you dumb ox," Alex said.

"Fuck you, Alex. I'm not Jubal. I don't have to listen to you." To Cork, Nick said, "I didn't want you asking any more questions that might end up hurting Camilla. I just wanted you to butt out."

"No, Nickie, no," Camilla said. "You didn't."

"Yeah, I did," he told her. "Alex was just standing around doing nothing. I knew he didn't care about you."

"What the hell does that mean?" Alex fired at him.

"To you and Dad, all Camilla's been is a way to get the Jaeger name firmly imprinted on American politics. You never cared if she was happy."

"Oh, Nickie, I wasn't unhappy."

He gave her a look that Cork thought was full of a lifetime of love and concern. "I wanted more for you than that. You deserved more."

"Oh, God," Alex said and leaned against the mantel as if he needed support.

Camilla returned to her younger brother and stared deeply into his eyes. "You didn't kill Jubal. Promise me that you didn't kill Jubal."

"I didn't," Nick said. "I swear to you. I was having brunch and Bloody Marys at Hell's Kitchen in Minneapolis when Jubal was killed. I can prove that, if I need to."

Alex said, as if exhausted, "So what now, O'Connor?"

Camilla went to Cork and took his hands in hers. "Please, let it go. I know it was awful, but you weren't hurt. Please, if you ever cared about Jubal and me, let it go."

The green of her eyes reminded him of wet mint leaves. In her gaze, he saw desperation and hope and sincerity, and although it went against everything sensible and every instinct he'd ever acquired in his years as a cop, he said to her, "All right." To Nick, he said, "I want to talk to you. Alone."

Cork let Nick Jaeger go ahead. He picked up his jacket, slung it over his arm, and walked out the door, leaving in the room behind him a silence broken only by the crackle of the fire and the slide of ice in an emptied liquor glass.

In the hallway, at the front door, Nick stopped and turned to face him.

"Rhiannon," Cork said.

Nick looked at him blankly.

"Did you fire that shot because of Rhiannon?"

Nick seemed genuinely confused. "I don't know what you're talking about."

Cork had dealt with enough liars in his law enforcement career and in his life to know more often than not when he wasn't being given the truth. As disappointed as he was, he thought Jaeger was being straight with him.

"All right," he said. Then he leaned threateningly close. "I heard that you're thinking of leaving Tamarack County tomorrow. See that you do. By first light would be good, don't you think?"

Nick's eyes narrowed to slits, as if he was swallowing something bitter, and his hand squeezed the glass he still held as if choking the life from it.

"And I'd like it if I never saw you here again."

For a long moment, Nick didn't move. At last he gave a nod, barely perceptible.

"Good. One last question," Cork said. "How'd you know I'd be on the road and where to position yourself for that shot?"

Nick straightened himself, as if attempting to recover his dignity. "You're not the only one who knows how to stalk when he's hunting."

Cork let it go at that, stepped away from him, opened the door, and left the house.

Yates was waiting for him at the Escalade. "So?"

"One hell of a goofy family."

"Tell me about it." Yates made no move to get into the vehicle. "So?"

"Kenny, we'll probably never know who fired that shot at me. I'm thinking maybe it was just a dumb-ass hunter who didn't know what he was doing."

"That's the way it is, huh?"

"That's the way it is. Mind taking me back to my car now?"

Yates opened the door. "My pleasure."

CHAPTER 33

In November, a little over a year after he'd married Camilla Jaeger, Jubal Little came north to bow-hunt with Cork O'Connor. That's what he told Camilla anyway. Cork knew it was for a different reason, and he knew because Jubal had asked him to help in the deception. As a married man with children, he normally would have had no part in helping a man deceive his wife in order to be with another woman. But this was different.

When Jubal married Camilla, it was a union of purpose. It reminded Cork of the royal marriages of old Europe, mergers for the consolidation of power. The Jaegers had political savvy and their name had political cachet. Jubal had the bearing, the looks, the image, the ambition. But he told Cork, in a drunken phone conversation shortly after the wedding, that he felt like a big empty ship gone off course. He made it clear he wasn't fond of the Jaegers.

In that same drunken conversation, he told Cork, "All they want me to be is some kind of horse they can all ride to political glory on. They want it to be all about the Jaeger legacy. They want to pull the strings and have me do their dance."

"What about Winona's vision, you on the mountaintop?"

"Fuck her vision. And fuck the Jaegers. Fuck 'em all."

"Does that go for Camilla?"

Jubal was quiet a long time. "She deserves better than me," he finally said.

Better than Jubal Little? Cork thought, and he knew that his old friend was in trouble.

"Winona won't answer my calls. And Willie won't pass along my messages. I need to see her, Cork."

"What do you want from me, Jubal?"

"Talk to her. Tell her I've got to see her. Tell her I'm dying."

Coming from anyone else, that would have been hyperbole. But coming from the mouth of Jubal Little, it was serious.

"I'm not going to help you start something with her."

"I don't want to start anything, Cork. I want . . ." He'd fallen quiet again, but this time it was as if he'd lost his way.

"What do you want, Jubal?"

"Tell her I want to heal. Tell her I want to be strong again. Will you do that, Cork?"

And so Cork had been the intermediary, and Jubal Little had come north without his wife on the pretext of a bow hunt with his best friend from boyhood.

They had, in fact, gone bow hunting, for the first time since they'd parted ways after Jubal graduated from high school. Cork hunted every season, hunted in the old way Sam Winter Moon had taught him, often with Sam himself, who was still alive in those days. He was amazed at his old friend's ability. Not only was Jubal still able to find and follow the track of a deer but he was also, even after all the years away from the hunt, a better shot with an arrow than Cork could ever hope to be.

But the bow hunt was only the cover. Jubal's visit with Winona was the real point, and he sandwiched his time with Cork between his times with Winona. Cork had no idea what passed between them, though he could guess about part of it. In his own mind it was, as Henry Meloux had said long ago, that there were spiritual bonds connecting certain people, that they were two sides of the same leaf, two halves of a broken stone, and that it was not about love, as most people thought of that word, but about a wholeness that was there when the two parts came together.

Whatever it was, when Jubal headed south again, Cork could

see a healthy difference. It was shortly thereafter that Jubal entered the political arena. He returned to Tamarack County as frequently as possible, always without Camilla—unless he was campaigning—using the excuse of a fishing excursion or simply the need to reconnect with his North Country roots. Until the outing at Trickster's Point, which had its own purpose, Cork never again allowed Jubal to use a bow hunt as one of his excuses. He refused to be a party to a continuing lie. But whatever it was that Winona gave him in their time together, it was like an elixir that filled Jubal with vigor.

It was different for Winona. She often disappeared after Jubal left, and when Cork saw her next, she looked withered and drawn. Despite his marriage to a woman he loved deeply, Cork still had a special place in his heart for his first love. He sometimes despised Jubal for all he took from Winona.

Meloux had once told Cork this about healing: "Sometimes the connection runs one way. You pour your own energy into the sick one, and when it is done, you are empty. It is not always like that, but sometimes. So you have to be careful, because some spirits are so hungry they will devour you."

Cork understood only too well that Jubal Little was one of those spirits who, if you allowed him to, would consume you.

He thought about all this as he drove from his confrontation with the Jaegers directly to the Iron Lake Reservation. He stopped at Willie Crane's cabin, but no one was there. He headed toward Allouette and knocked at Winona's front door but received no answer. When he reached the town, he found the Iron Lake Center for Native Art open and Willie Crane inside.

Half of the center was devoted to showing the work of contemporary Indian artists. The other half, which Winona was largely responsible for, was a museum of Ojibwe cultural artifacts. There were beaded bandolier bags, cradleboards, flutes, drums, pipes, moose-hide moccasins, figures carved of wood, baskets woven of reeds or made from birch bark, the shells of snapping turtles used as war shields, ash bows, deer-hide quivers, arrows, and other ornate implements of warfare. Over the past twenty years, Winona had patiently accumulated a wealth of items that showcased Ojibwe ingenuity, spiritual sensibility, and artistic appreciation.

Willie was behind a display case of Ojibwe jewelry and smaller artifacts, and he looked up with surprise when Cork entered, as if, despite the Open sign on the door, he really wasn't prepared for visitors.

"What do you want?" he said. *Waouwan?*

"*Boozhoo* to you, too, Willie."

Cork crossed the old wood floor to the counter, which Willie stayed behind as if it were a protective wall.

"You heard about Isaiah?" he asked.

"Of course," Willie answered.

"You really think he killed Jubal?"

"Why would he say so if he didn't?"

"I can think of a lot of reasons, and your sister's at the top of the list."

Willie bent and rearranged two items in the case. "I don't understand."

"I think that, given the right set of circumstances, Isaiah could have killed Jubal Little, but I don't think he did. I think he's covering for Winona."

"You're crazy," Willie said, still fiddling in the case. The words of his denial had no energy.

Cork said, "Know what Jubal and your sister talked about their last night together, Willie?"

"How would I know something like that?"

"Because I think Winona told you everything. For want of a better word, I think you've always been her confessor."

Willie finally stood up straight. His face was tawny and tight, and reminded Cork of deer hide stretched for drying.

"Cork, if you ever cared about Winona and Jubal, you'll stop asking questions."

"What I care about most right now is the truth."

"You talk like it's something you could just wrap your hand around." Willie's eyes were hard and dark and shiny and tired. But they weren't empty. Something flickered in them, and Cork couldn't tell whether it was fear or anger. "You know the story of the blind men and the elephant? I think that's the reality of truth. What you understand depends mostly on the perspective you bring to it."

"How about you tell me your own perspective, and we'll see what I understand?"

Willie shook his head. "It's not that easy."

"Okay, how about I tell you something I believe to be the truth, and then you can give me your perspective? One of the things Jubal confessed to me when he was dying was that he'd said good-bye to Winona forever. He told her it was their last night together. He was cutting her loose."

"You see," Willie said. "Right there. You're holding only a small part of the elephant."

"Jubal kissed her off, after all these years and all she'd done for him. She was pissed. Anybody would be. But the question is, was she pissed enough to kill him?"

"Hurt isn't always followed by anger, Cork."

"No? What followed Winona's hurt?"

"Acceptance."

"How very understanding of her."

"Jubal was going on the path he was born to, and she always knew that he would have to go alone."

"But he wasn't going to be alone, Willie. His wife was going to be there beside him. Not your sister. In the eyes of the world, Camilla Little would always be the woman behind the great man. A bitter pill to have to swallow."

Willie's jaw worked in a way that made Cork wonder if he was trying to get words out of his twisted mouth or struggling to keep them in.

"Jubal used people, Willie. He used me, and he used Camilla and the Jaegers, and he used the Ojibwe. I don't claim to understand the whole dynamic of what was between Winona and him, but what I saw was your sister giving and Jubal taking, and so I can't help but believe that, in the end, he just used her, too."

"She believed that helping Jubal was the path she was born to."

To Cork, it sounded as if Willie was trying to defend the indefensible.

"It wasn't the one I was born to," Cork said, "or anyone else, but Jubal sure as hell thought it was so. He walked on all of us to get to that mountaintop of his."

Willie seemed to fold, all the strength of his objections crumbling away.

"So," Cork went on, "the part of the elephant I'm holding on to right now, Willie, is that Winona had finally had enough of being stepped on, and she went out to Trickster's Point to put an arrow in Jubal's heart. And now she's gone into hiding, and I think you know where."

Willie didn't deny it.

"Do her and yourself a favor. Tell her that I want to talk to her. But if she won't, tell her to see Henry Meloux. Will you do that?"

Willie thought it over and nodded. But he said, as if he knew it was absolutely the truth, the whole elephant, "She didn't kill Jubal."

"I'd love to hear that coming directly from her."

"I'll see what I can do," Willie promised.

Cork got into his Land Rover, which was parked outside the center, and sat a moment, thinking. He wasn't sure if he'd ever actually believed Winona had killed Jubal, but from all his years in law enforcement, one of the things he understood was that most investigations primarily involved eliminating possibilities. Although he had nothing concrete to go on, he was having difficulty buying her guilt. For one thing, there was Willie's absolute belief in her innocence, which had seemed sincere. Although Willie loved his sister and would probably say or do anything to protect her, there were a couple of other considerations that seemed to Cork to bolster Willie's position. The first was the dead man on the ridge. He couldn't see Winona in league with a *chimook*, nor did he see her as capable of that kind of cold-blooded killing. The other was Meloux's assertion that the other side of love wasn't hate, it was fear. Winona might have killed Jubal out of hate or anger, but fear? The only thing Winona Crane had to be afraid of was a life without Jubal Little in it.

So, unless something new arose to change his mind, Cork was willing to take her off his list of suspects. For the time being.

Which left two possibilities: Isaiah Broom, who'd already copped to the crimes, and Lester Bigby, who'd done nothing but blow smoke in response to all of Cork's questions. If Broom hadn't so willingly given himself over to the sheriff's people, Cork would have suspected him more, odd as that seemed. But he tended to agree with Phil Holter that Broom had a hidden agenda. Maybe he was looking for a public forum, risky as that was. Or maybe he believed that Winona had killed Jubal and the John Doe on the ridge, and love compelled him to the sacrifice of himself. At any rate, Broom didn't top Cork's list. That slot was still reserved for Lester Bigby.

CHAPTER 34

Cork was deep in thought when he was startled back into the moment by a knock on the window of his door. He turned, surprised but very pleased to see Rainy Bisonette smiling at him through the glass. He rolled the window down.

"I called to you," she said. "You seemed to be in another world."

"A lot on my mind," he apologized.

"I just came into town to do a little shopping at LeDuc's store. Do you have time for some coffee at the Mocha Moose?"

"For you, I'll make time."

He got out, and together they walked to the little shop. There were a couple of other Shinnobs at tables drinking coffee and eating some of Sarah LeDuc's locally famous cowboy cookies. Sarah, who was full-blood Ojibwe, appreciated the irony of that situation, and she was fond of saying that, when she made the cookie batter, she just wished John Wayne was still alive so he could see an Indian woman beating cowboys. Cork greeted the other customers with a raised hand and said *"Boozhoo"* to Sarah, and he and Rainy got their coffee and a cookie to split and sat at a table near the window.

"So, is it true?" Rainy asked. "Isaiah Broom confessed to killing Jubal Little?"

"Yes."

"Is that what you're thinking about so deeply?"

"No."

"Because you believe he did it? Case closed?"

"I don't think he killed Jubal. I think he's covering for Winona Crane."

"You believe Winona killed Jubal?" She seemed utterly amazed.

He explained to her briefly the history of Winona Crane and Jubal Little, two sides of the same leaf, a complicated connection that included an abiding love and, in the end, rejection and hurt. "The wrath of a woman scorned," Cork finished.

"What a load of crap," Rainy said and took a bite of the cookie.

"Yeah, that's what I've decided, too. But I think Isaiah Broom believes it. He's been in love with Winona since we were all kids. I think maybe he believes this is his chance to prove his love for her, a love greater than anything Jubal ever gave to her."

"Love," she said, picking up on the word. "After you left this morning, Uncle Henry and I talked about Jubal Little's killing. He says he believes you'll discover that Little was killed because of love."

"I thought so, too, but like I said, I don't think Winona did it, or Isaiah."

"Not romantic love, necessarily. Love of money, love of power, love of territory, love of people. Uncle Henry says that more often than not we kill to protect the things we love. We kill to hold on to them." She drank her coffee and looked at Cork over the cup rim, her dark eyes gently probing his face. "So, who has something to protect?"

Only one name came to Cork at the moment. The last guy left on his short list of suspects. Lester Bigby.

"Do you really think Bigby could have killed Jubal Little?" she asked, after he'd explained.

"The question of the day," he said. "He certainly has something to protect. That resort development. It's clear he's lied about where he was the day Jubal was killed. And I've been thinking about the John Doe on the ridge. A white guy. I don't see Isaiah Broom or Winona Crane throwing in with a *chimook*. But Lester Bigby might."

"Or one of his investors," Rainy offered.

Cork didn't want to think about that. It opened up a whole new list of suspects. And he still had no idea who Rhiannon was or what part she played in all this and why she was important and threatening enough to put Cork and everyone he loved in imminent danger.

Rainy said, "You told me that a lot of what you do is just turn over rocks to see what's there. What rocks are left to turn over, Cork?"

"What I really ought to do is track down Winona. It would be best if I could talk to her in person. But I keep hoping she'll come out of hiding on her own. Even if she doesn't talk to me, maybe she'll go to Henry."

"And then you'll pump my uncle for answers." It was a statement, not a judgment.

"Henry?" Cork laughed. "I could put your uncle on the rack and tear his arms out of their sockets, and he still wouldn't tell me something he didn't want me to know."

They left together, and he walked Rainy to her Jeep. She would drive back toward Crow Point, park on an old logging road that ended a couple of miles from her cabin, and walk the rest of the way from there, a Duluth pack full of supplies on her back.

"I'd love to have you come home with me," she told him as they stood together under the heavy overcast.

He shook his head. "Miles to go before I sleep."

She put her hand to his face. Her palm was warm against his cold cheek. "You could use a vacation."

"What I need is a good long lie-down in your arms. And a few more answers."

He kissed her and stood watching as she drove away.

Then he turned back to all the miles still ahead of him before he slept.

CHAPTER 35

The bullet hole in his windshield reminded Cork of a spider with a dozen legs too many, and as he drove back toward Aurora the wind blew through, cold and with an eerie whistle. He thought about the shot Nick Jaeger had fired at him. To protect his sister, Nick had said. To protect something he loved.

What was it that the person who'd murdered Jubal had been protecting? What was it they loved enough to kill for, twice? What did Lester Bigby love that much? His investment? His father? Or was it his brother, an old love whose loss had lain festering in his heart for decades and then exploded in a tragic mess? Or maybe it wasn't just one of these things but all of them together, braided in a thick rope of confused emotions that bound him to an inevitable end.

An inevitable end. The phrase sounded familiar to Cork, but why? Then he remembered. He realized those had been Jubal's words, or nearly, spoken on the day that Cork had put in place the final stone in the wall that had been building between them for years. They'd been said in the late spring, just after Jubal had publicly announced his intention to run for governor and put forward his platform.

Politics, from the beginning, had agreed with Jubal Little. He was a natural leader, and even men and women who'd been in the political arena far longer than he found themselves falling in behind him. The mix of his message—fiscal conservatism and social responsibility—found a following in Washington, among centrists on both sides of the aisle, not just because Jubal spoke his platform so well but because of the way he conducted himself, with a Teddy Roosevelt kind of diplomacy. He was charming as hell, but in his eyes, his voice, his bearing, he carried a club, the threat of someone who knew how to wield power, the understanding that he was not a man to be crossed.

From the isolation of the deep woods that surrounded Aurora, Minnesota, Cork had watched his friend's rise. And although from the outside Jubal seemed unchanged, something on the inside, Cork knew, was being transformed. The seed for what Jubal was becoming had always been there, but it had been nourished by circumstance, and the vision and tending of Winona Crane, and the money and ambition of the Jaegers. Cork wasn't certain that Jubal really believed in any ideals, believed in anything he'd have sacrificed his life for. What Jubal believed in was the rightness of his own being. He believed himself to be the chosen one, and nobody and nothing could stand in the way of his destiny.

But Cork had tried to do just that. In spring, when he'd heard Jubal's gubernatorial platform and, like many Ojibwe and residents of the Arrowhead, had felt stunned and betrayed, he'd summoned his friend north with a cryptic threat. They'd gone fishing, an excuse for them to be alone because Cork had insisted on it, in order to get away from the reporters and the photographers. Jubal's people had spun it as an outing with the candidate's oldest friend. Cork had thought, *Whatever.*

On Iron Lake, far from the eyes and ears of the public, Cork had laid it out.

"I don't understand what you're doing, Jubal. You're selling out the Ojibwe. You're selling out the North Country."

"No, I'm buying back Minnesota," Jubal replied, casting easily and watching his lure plop into the mirror that was the lake that day.

"Sulfide mining? That's part of the price tag? Jubal, are you crazy?"

"I've looked at the impact studies. It can be done safely."

"On paper maybe. Have you read the reports from the areas where it's been tried? Ecological disasters, Jubal."

"You got a nibble," Jubal said, nodding toward Cork's line.

"To hell with the fishing." Cork threw down his rod. It hit the bottom of the boat with a sound like a thin bone cracking. "And the casinos? You build those and it'll be just like in the old days when white men shot all the buffalo."

"The studies show that there's plenty of interest to support both state-run casinos and Indian gaming. Your vision is far too narrow, Cork," Jubal said, as if lecturing a schoolboy. "You think of Tamarack County, I think of all of Minnesota. Like so many shortsighted people, you want to have things but without sacrifice. You need someone like me to make the hard decisions, the ones you can't make on your own, the decisions about who gets what and how. What you need, and everyone like you, is someone who's willing to do what you can't bring yourself to do."

The sun was brilliant that day, and Jubal, against the sky, slowly reeling in his line, looked absolutely imperious.

"Christ," Cork said. "Who are you, Jubal? I don't know you anymore."

Jubal leveled on him a look that put ice water in Cork's blood. "Did you ever? Really?" He held Cork's gaze, a cobra mesmerizing his prey, then he said, "Why are we out here, Cork? What is it you have to say to me?"

"Politics have changed you, Jubal."

"Politics bring out both the best and the worst in people. And you want to know something? Sometimes they're the same thing."

"You have an answer for everything, don't you? Well how about this? I know your secrets."

Jubal visibly relaxed, as if, with everything in the open, he understood his enemy and was confident that he was equal to the challenge.

"Secrets? You mean me and Winona?"

"That's one."

Jubal shrugged. "It would be inconvenient if the media found out about my friendship with Winona, but not fatal to my campaign. Camilla's always known and understood. You said secrets. What else?"

Cork picked up the final stone and mortared it into place. "Trickster's Point."

Jubal didn't seem surprised. "A long time ago. And you have no proof."

"I don't need to prove anything. An accusation of murder would be enough in itself, I imagine."

"I could always say that you were the one who pushed Donner Bigby to his death."

"Of course you could. But then you'd be guilty of covering up a murder. Almost as horrific to voters, I imagine. Either way, it would kill you politically."

Jubal had gradually reeled in the last of his line. The lure came out of the lake, a walleye flicker shad, shiny in the sunlight, water falling from the barbs into a quiet so profound that Cork could hear the dull patter of the drops on the boat gunwale. Jubal carefully laid down his rod and said, "Blackmail?"

"You told me once that in politics it's called 'leverage.'"

Jubal looked toward the shore, toward the gathering of homes and shops and schools that formed Aurora. Sam's Place was visible, small against the broad scatter of the town. And Cork was wondering if Jubal might be thinking of Sam Winter Moon, who'd taught them both important lessons about stalking, and about killing deer, and ultimately, about what it was to be a decent man in a difficult world. Cork thought Sam might be disappointed that he'd stalked and attacked Jubal in such a cowardly way, but it was done, and he waited.

Jubal finally turned his gaze on Cork, who found himself startled by what he beheld. It was as if Jubal's size had grown suddenly even more remarkable, as if the shadow he cast had tripled and turned unfathomably dark and had swallowed Cork whole.

"I've warned you before," Jubal said. "Never try to take something from me. I won't warn you again. You can't beat me. You never could. If you try, I won't be responsible for what happens. Your end is your own doing."

"My end?"

"Your end is inevitable. One way or another, you yield."

"I'm not backing down, Jubal."

"In that case," Jubal said with a slight shrug, "I'll have to break you."

He stated it simply, as if it were a minor fact of life, as if he and Cork had no history, as if they'd never loved each other as brothers.

Cork, who'd always given in to Jubal, sometimes out of friendship and sometimes out of fear, stood his ground and said, "Bring it on."

Outside Allouette, after he'd left Rainy, Cork pulled into Winona's drive and parked at her house. Although he risked being seen, he wanted another look inside, this time in daylight and without Camilla Little distracting him with screams.

He disconnected his cell phone from the car charger and slipped it into the little holster on his belt. He got out and checked the garage. Empty. He knocked on the front door. No answer. He went inside, where the heat was on, but only enough to keep the cold at bay. He wandered to the kitchen and discovered that the broken glass from the frame Camilla had shattered the night before had been cleaned up. In the bedroom, he found the bed neatly made. In the bathroom, there were clean towels hanging on the rack and the bloodied towels in the hamper were gone. It was clear to him that Winona Crane had returned, but she wasn't there now. He wondered why she'd come back, and why she'd run again.

Then his eyes fell on the little table beside the claw-footed tub, with its candle and the portable CD player and the single CD case, all of which he'd seen the night before. Now he saw something he'd overlooked in the dark. He picked up the plastic CD case, which was empty. Along the edge, someone—Winona probably—had put a little strip of white tape and had written the title of the disc the case held: *Fleetwood Mac.* Cork lifted the top of the portable player. The CD was inside. He picked it up and read the label, the list of the tunes he remembered well: "Monday Morning," "Warm Ways," "Blue Letter." At the fourth song, he stopped scanning. "Rhiannon."

It was no coincidence. He was holding a key. He knew it absolutely. But he had no idea what door it opened. What was the connection between Rhiannon and Winona and Jubal? And why was it, apparently, such a deadly one?

He'd only just begun to consider this when his cell phone chirped. He pulled it from the little holster on his belt. Caller ID told him it was Lester Bigby.

"O'Connor, will you meet me?" Bigby asked as soon as Cork answered.

"Where?"

"At my resort complex. Something I want to say to you."

"You can't tell me over the phone?"

"You want to know who killed Jubal Little, you'll come."

"I'll be there in twenty minutes," Cork said.

Bigby hung up without a word of good-bye.

CHAPTER 36

The Crown Lake Resort was ten miles southwest of Aurora, nestled among rugged hills whose slopes were thick with pine trees and spruce and stands of aspens and birch. The shoreline was undeveloped because it had, for a very long time, belonged to the Arrowhead Mining Corporation. The mine, one of the smaller open pits on the Iron Range, had shut down operations more than a dozen years earlier, but Arrowhead Mining had held on to the property, until Lester Bigby made them an offer they couldn't refuse. The resort had the lake all to itself. Which would have been perfect, except that, within the last year, a Canadian corporation had purchased mineral rights to land two miles east, from which they hoped to be given permission to extract base ore—copper-nickel and platinum. Sulfide mining would be the extraction process. Several streams ran through the mine area and emptied into Crown Lake. If the environmental watchdogs were right, the mining would eventually turn the water of the lake to sulfuric acid.

Cork drove his Land Rover down the single paved road, which had been built at the behest and expense of Lester Bigby. The road ended near the lakeshore, where an area had been cleared and preliminary construction on some buildings had begun. There was no activity at the moment, had been none for some time, not since news of the possibility of nearby sulfide mining had become public.

Lester Bigby's Karmann Ghia was parked in tall, dead grass ten yards from the lake. Bigby sat on a big slab of gray rock that jutted into the lake. Cork parked next to the little car, got out, and walked onto the slab. Bigby had his back to Cork and was staring at the lake. Cork crossed the flat rock, which was tilted at a slight angle toward the water. As soon as he came abreast of Bigby, Cork saw the firearm in Bigby's right hand. *Ruger*, his mind told him without being prodded, *.22 caliber.*

"Beautiful, don't you think?" Bigby said.

"Lovely," Cork replied, not taking his eyes off the Ruger.

"You ski?"

"No."

"Me neither. But a lot of people in Minnesota do. That slope over there would have held one of the best runs in the state."

"Would have?"

"It's not going to happen. Ever." He nudged the barrel of the handgun in Cork's direction. "Sit down." An order, not an invitation.

Cork sat. The clouds hung heavy over the hills and the lake. There was a slight breeze across the water, a cool November wind that already presaged winter, and Cork felt the chill of it against his face. The other chill he felt came from the threat in Bigby's hand.

"What are you going to leave your kids, O'Connor?"

"A lot of good memories, and Sam's Place," he said without hesitation.

Bigby nodded. "Me, I was going to leave my son this. Do you know what I have to leave him now? Nothing. I've lost everything."

"Jubal's dead. The polls are saying our governor will be re-elected. Champion of the environment."

"As long as there's money to be made in the ground up here, the risk will always be there. If it wasn't Jubal Little, it would have been someone else. Those people, they always find a way to get what they want."

"I'm sorry."

"All my promised backers have pulled out. I put another mortgage on my house. The third. Sold all my stocks and bonds a while ago. Borrowed against my life insurance. None of it enough to save this dream. You want to know what I was doing on Saturday? I spent the day out here, planning for it to be my last day on earth. I was going to kill myself. I knew I couldn't do it at home and have Emily and Lance find me there. I couldn't do that to them. In the end, I couldn't do it at all. Coward. Just like my father always said."

"I don't think so," Cork offered.

"You don't know me," Bigby shot back with sudden viciousness.

"I know your father, and you're nothing like him."

"Is that so? You're ready to believe I killed Jubal Little." He looked at Cork with a kind of grim curiosity. "Why exactly do you think I would do that?"

"Because of the sulfide mining."

"I'd kill myself over that, not someone else."

"I also thought maybe it might have something to do with wanting your father's approval. For some sons, that would be important enough to kill for."

Bigby laughed, a bitter sound. "Christ, are you barking up the wrong tree. My father's a cruel man. He was cruel to my mother. He was cruel to me. And he was cruel to Donner. I grew up knowing what people thought of my brother, but I loved him. He stood up to my father, stood between Buzz and my mother, between Buzz and me. When Donner died, there was no one to stand up for us. Hell, if I killed anybody it would be my old man."

"I also thought maybe it was because of Donner."

Bigby looked confused. "I don't understand."

"Your father blamed Jubal for Donner's death."

"He blamed you, too."

"My point, more or less. By putting an arrow into Jubal Little and making it look like I did it, you'd kill two birds with one stone."

"You give me more credit for planning than I'm capable of."

"It's been a tough investigation. Any port in a storm," Cork said, putting a little smile on his face while still eyeing the barrel of the Ruger.

"You think it's funny? You sent cops to my house. My wife was there, and my son, and I had to explain to them why the police came into our home. My family looked at me as if they didn't know me. You have any idea how that feels?"

"Did you tell them about Saturday?"

"I haven't told them anything about this mess. I don't want my son thinking of me like I think of my father."

"I'm sure you don't have to worry about that, Lester."

"For a man who's clearly screwed up in his thinking, you seem awfully sure."

Cork decided it was time to take the bull by the horns. "You told me you knew who killed Jubal Little. Is that true, or was it just a way to get me here? Are you planning on shooting me?"

Bigby studied the gun. "I've thought about it. Still thinking about it. And still thinking maybe I'll shoot myself as well. Take us both out in a blaze of glory."

"Let me tell you something, Lester. I lost my father when I was thirteen. No matter what mistakes he might have made in his life, I'd have forgiven him anything to have him alive and with me again. Think about Lance. Do you want him to see you as your father does, just a coward? And worse, a murderer? Or do you want him to think of you as a man who failed in a resort enterprise but picked himself up and went on?"

"Just shut up," Bigby said.

He looked away, stared across the lake, which was long and narrow. At the far end, clouds darker than before had begun to mount over the trees that lined the shore. *Snow clouds*, Cork thought. A darkness that was the reflection of what was coming from the west slid toward them across the water as if it was something huge and alive and hungry.

"Fuck it," Bigby finally said and heaved the Ruger far out into the lake.

For a long time after that, he didn't move. Nor did Cork.

They both stared at the water, which rolled under the breeze, as if disturbed by the breath of what was coming, the cold exhalation of some great, invisible spirit.

Bigby spoke. "Now let me tell you something, O'Connor. I hate bow hunting. I always have. I hate the idea of killing a living thing just because I can."

"Why do you do it then?"

"It used to be because I had to. My father made me. Then it was because my friends bow-hunted. Now I do it sometimes with clients. But you want to know the real reason? Because from the time I was small, I had this wonderful fantasy. Every time I was out, I fantasized putting an arrow in my father's heart. When I go out now, I usually go alone because I love the quiet and the solitude. If you'd really done your homework, you'd know that I never come back with a deer. But I still have that fantasy about putting an arrow through Buzz Bigby's heart." He leveled a cold, dark look on Cork. "I remember watching you choke my father in the parking lot in front of the Black Duck. I was sitting in the truck. The cab smelled like spilled beer. It always did. I remember you suddenly stopped, otherwise you might have killed my old man that day."

Cork remembered, too.

Bigby got up from the rock. "Stand up," he said.

Cork rose and faced him. Without warning, Bigby swung. Cork turned instinctively, but not quickly enough to avoid the blow completely. Bigby's fist caught him squarely in the left ear, and Cork stumbled and fell back onto the rock. Bigby stood over him, rubbing the sore knuckles of his right hand.

"That's for bringing me and my family into all this crap. You have a knack, O'Connor, for doing what you think is right, but in the end, it's all wrong. My old man should've died that day, saved all of us a lot of grief. But you screwed up. You want to know who killed Jubal Little? I'll tell you. It was some guy who actually knew how to get things done right."

Bigby headed back to his Karmann Ghia. From where he sat on the rock with his ear ringing, Cork watched as the man pulled away, drove up the solitary road, and was lost in the trees.

CHAPTER 37

Aside from the cowboy cookie he'd had in Allouette, Cork had eaten nothing that day since the biscuits he'd shared in the morning with Rainy and Henry. It was a little after two o'clock when he drove away from Crown Lake, and he was famished. He was also sliding into a despondent place. He seemed no closer to understanding who'd killed Jubal than he'd been during those three long hours while he watched the man die. He still had no idea who the hell Rhiannon was or what she might have to do with Jubal's death. And he was kicking himself for having dragged Lester Bigby, an innocent man, into the mess. His ear ached from the blow Bigby had landed, but he figured it was a pain he deserved. The weather was no help. As he made his way toward Aurora, snow began to spit against his windshield. He thought after he got food in his stomach, he might rebound a little, so he headed home.

If he was looking for sympathy there, he didn't find it. He found Stephen in a rotten mood.

In the instructions he'd left on the kitchen table that morning, he'd given Stephen permission to stay home from school another day. He'd indicated they should all stay close to the house, and not open Sam's Place until he okayed it. When he pulled into the drive, he saw Stephen playing with Waaboo and Trixie in the backyard. His grandson didn't notice him; Waaboo was too busy trying to catch on his tongue the flakes drifting out of the sky, a precipitation not nearly heavy enough yet to be called a snowfall. But Stephen saw Cork and gave him a long, hard look.

Jenny was in the kitchen, working on her laptop.

"They should be inside," Cork snapped. "I left instructions."

Jenny slid the sheet he'd left across the table where he could see it. "Your instructions were to stay close to home. They're in the backyard. Can't get much closer to home."

"I meant—" Cork began.

"We're not mind readers," Jenny shot back.

"Sorry," Cork said. "Bad day. Where's Cy?"

"He went to Pflugleman's to get some NyQuil. He's coming down with a cold, he thinks. He promised to be right back."

From the refrigerator, Cork pulled a plate of cold fried chicken and a bottle of Leinie's. He grabbed a napkin from the holder on the counter and sat at the table with Jenny. "What are you working on?"

"Another short story."

"When are you going to start a novel?"

"When I'm ready."

"Sorry. Didn't mean to pry."

Jenny closed her laptop. "That's okay. Just a little testy. I feel like I'm caged in here. Any progress?"

"Not much." Cork took a bite of a chicken leg and through the window watched Waaboo and Stephen lick snowflakes from the air. "What's his story?" Cork asked. "When I drove up, he looked at me like I was a rat bringing the plague."

"He's pissed at you."

"Me? Why?"

Jenny shrugged. "Ask him."

Cork waited until he'd eaten before he went out to face his son. Jenny walked with him, scooped up Waaboo, and said, "We'll be inside, playing with a ball or something."

Waaboo tried to slither loose, calling "Baa-baa." He reached desperately toward his grandfather, but Jenny held him tightly and, though he protested with little cries, carried him into the house, calling after her, "Come on, Trixie. Come on inside, girl."

Cork stood with Stephen in the empty backyard. In the young man's stiffness and the shove of his hands deep in his jeans pockets and the way he averted his face, Cork could see his son's anger. He thought he could even feel the heat of it radiating across the space of cold air that lay between them. They didn't look at each other but stared at the sky as if the dull grayness was hypnotizing.

"Is there something you'd like to say to me?" Cork asked.

"Yeah, as a matter of fact."

"I'm listening."

"Just butt out of things."

"What do you mean?"

"Just stop doing what you do, Dad."

"What is it I do?"

Stephen turned to him, his dark eyes blazing. "You leave early. You come home late. In between, people shoot at you."

And sometimes hit me with a sucker punch, Cork thought, though there was no way he'd say that out loud. Not at that moment anyway.

"You like to hunt," Stephen said, his voice pitched and rasping with anger. "I don't get it, but I get that it's something important to you, so I let it slide."

When Stephen was young, Cork had hoped to share with him the experience of hunting, as his own father and Sam Winter Moon had shared it with him. But from early on, it was clear that Stephen had no interest. In fact, it was clear that Stephen abhorred the whole idea of killing something for the sport of it. Cork tried to explain that hunting played an important role in control of wild game populations and that, for him, there was a spiritual element to it, threaded far back in the culture of the Ojibwe and probably in the psyche of human beings, but Stephen never bought it. Cork hadn't forced his son to participate, and he and Stephen had reached the mutual understanding that it was a subject on which they would probably never see eye to eye.

Stephen continued his tirade. "But when you let yourself become the thing that's hunted, Jesus, I just don't get that."

"Let myself? Stephen, I had no idea someone was going to take a shot at me."

The fire in his son's eyes flared to brilliance, as if Cork had only added more fuel. "What about after that? You could have stayed home, where it's safe, like you ordered us to do. But no, there you are, running all over God knows where by yourself, still a target, and maybe next time whoever's shooting at you won't miss."

"Stephen, I know who shot at me."

That clearly caught him by surprise. "You do?"

"Yeah."

"Who?"

"I pretty much promised to keep that to myself. A deal I made with the guy who pulled the trigger. His side of the bargain was that he wouldn't do it again. And that he'd leave Tamarack County for good."

"You believed him?"

"Yeah, I believed him."

"Why'd he shoot at you?"

"To scare me. To protect someone he loves."

Stephen drilled his father with a penetrating glare. "There," he said. "That's the point. Someone he loves." He turned away, and Cork watched the snowflakes drift between them. "You should be thinking more about the people you love. At Trickster's Point, someone was ready to kill you, but that doesn't seem to matter to you. You just keep doing what you do. And me and Jenny, we're just sitting around waiting for the time we get a call and some stupid voice on the other end of the line tells us you're dead."

Which was pretty much how the news had been delivered when Stephen's mother was killed.

Cork didn't say anything for a while, simply stared where his son stared, upward at a sky as gray as a tombstone.

"I don't look for trouble, Stephen. Honest to God, I don't just go looking for it." He shrugged. "*Ogichidaa*. What can I say?"

Anyone else might have looked at Cork as if he were crazy or full of hubris, but Stephen's own perception of the world was very much colored by his love of what was Ojibwe in his blood and in his life, and rather than disbelief, he eyed his father with disappointment.

"But why you, Dad?"

"I don't know. I just know it's true. I know it here." Cork tapped his heart.

"So am I supposed to be, like, proud of you or something?"

"No. Well, yes, but not because of that. It's who I am, same as you were born a spirit meant to heal. I admire that in you. Me, I'm a guy who seems to step into the fire again and again, and it's not because I'm stupid or insensitive to the danger or to what it would mean to you if I got myself killed. It's just who I am. It's not something I'm proud of. It's simply something I accept."

Stephen didn't reply. He stood motionless as snowflakes settled on his shoulders, held a moment, and melted away. Then suddenly he turned to his father, and there were tears in his eyes. "I don't want you to die. I don't want you to leave me, ever."

And now there were tears in Cork's eyes as well. "I won't. I promise."

He took Stephen in his arms, his son who was on the edge of manhood, with all the weight and uncertainty and responsibility that meant, and held him, knowing there was no way he could make a promise like that but wishing, at the moment, with all his heart, that it was true.

As they turned together to head back into the house, a car pulled into the drive and parked next to Cork's Land Rover. Leon Papakee got out and watched Cork and Stephen come to greet him.

"*Boozhoo*," Papakee called.

"What's up, Leon?" Cork said.

"Hey, Stephen. Good to see you." Papakee shook Stephen's hand. "You're almost as tall as your old man now."

"And still growing," Cork said.

"I just left the sheriff's department," Papakee said. "They've finished interviewing Isaiah Broom, for the time being anyway."

"What do you think?"

"He couldn't give salient answers to half the questions. He's as guilty of killing Jubal Little as you or me."

"You're not on their list of suspects, Leon."

"It's clear that he's covering for somebody. Well, clear to me anyway. I don't have any idea who that might be. Holter's afraid he also wants a public platform to spout activist rhetoric. They'll probably cut him loose soon. And then, I'm guessing, our intrepid BCA investigator will turn his attention back to you. He's got to throw something more out there for the media to chew on, and at the moment, Cork, you're the only item on the menu."

"I think I'd better go have a talk with Agent Holter." Cork looked at Stephen. "Are you okay with that?"

Stephen thought it over seriously a moment, then said, "Just don't let him shoot you, okay?"

Cork waited until Cy Borkman returned. His friend looked a little under the weather, but he refused to be relieved of what he saw as his duty. Cork could have argued, but he was grateful and told his friend, "When this is over, I'm buying you the biggest steak the Pinewood Broiler can grill."

"When this is over," Cy said, putting his big mitt of a hand on Cork's shoulder, "I go back to boredom. So take all the time you need."

CHAPTER 38

The parking lot of the Tamarack County Sheriff's Department was still dotted with a few media vehicles, so Cork, as he'd been doing since Jubal was murdered, parked a couple of blocks away. When he approached the entrance, he saw that a podium had been set up on the front sidewalk in preparation for a news conference, or at least some kind of impending public update on the course of the investigation. Cork pulled the bill of his cap down low and turned up his coat collar and slipped inside without being recognized or accosted.

Deputy George Azevedo was on the contact desk, and he buzzed Cork through the security door. Inside, things were awfully quiet, the common area deserted.

"Where is everyone?" Cork asked Azevedo.

"Captain Larson's in his office. The sheriff and Agent Holter are in her office. Holter's people have all gone out for something to eat."

"Looks like things are set up for a press conference out front."

"Holter's going to update them in half an hour."

"Any idea what he's going to tell them?"

Azevedo smiled. "Yeah. That he ain't no Sherlock Holmes."

Larson's office door was open. The captain was at his desk, bent intently over some documents, his glasses low on his nose. Cork gave the door a light knock. Larson looked up.

"Broom's interview didn't go so well, I heard," Cork said.

Larson nudged the glasses up the bridge of his nose. "Depends on what you were looking for. If you just wanted someone to charge in Jubal Little's murder, then it was pretty much a washout. If you were looking for the truth of this whole thing, then it was helpful in its way. Took Broom out of the mix as far as I'm concerned. I'm pretty sure you were right. He's trying to cover for someone else. The question is who."

Cork could have offered up Winona Crane but didn't want to send the investigation down another blind alley that would just result in dragging more innocent people into the mess.

"Are Marsha and Holter in conference on what to tell the media?"

"Yeah. Holter let it slip that he'd turned from investigating a hunting accident to a homicide investigation, and that he had his man. Marsha was pissed, and now he's got to figure out how to make a strategic retreat."

"Any more word on the identity of the John Doe on the ridge?"

"Nothing." Larson sat back, clearly tired. "As far as legal radar is concerned, the guy seems to have always flown below it."

"What about whoever it was shot the arrows into him and Jubal?"

"We had almost nothing to begin with, and that's still all we've got. The only thing we really know about the shooter doesn't make a lot of sense to me."

"What's that?"

"He may have been a little drunk. Maybe had to find some courage in a bottle. But for somebody who'd been drinking, he had awfully good aim with those arrows. So, like I said, I'm not sure what sense to make of it."

"Drunk?" This was news to Cork. "How would you know that?"

"Something the Border Patrol agent, John Berglund, noted when he finished tracking that day."

"Did he write up a report?"

"Just some notes."

"Mind if I take a look?"

"Be my guest. But don't let Holter know I'm doing this."

Larson took one of the manila folders from a small stack on his desk, thumbed through some papers inside, and came up with three pages torn from a small wire-bound notebook. He handed them to Cork and said, "Take your coat off and have a seat."

It was late afternoon, darkening already from both the gloom of the overcast and the early sunsets that came with the season. Snowflakes kissed the windows of Larson's office and melted and formed trickles down the glass. Larson had his desk light on, and between that and the soft gray illumination that still sifted through the windowpanes, Cork could see well enough to read.

The words on the lined paper were in ink, ballpoint probably, written neatly. They indicated directions, distances, topography, ground conditions, weather. They elucidated the particulars of the signs that Berglund had found and followed. Cork read the description of the two sets of tracks, with special interest in the set made by what Berglund, in his notes, referred to as the "unsub," the unknown subject in the investigation, the killer, who'd come up from the lake, shadowed the John Doe to the ridge, and returned the same way when he finished what he'd come there for. Berglund had noted that often the footprints seemed askew, as if the person who'd made them was stumbling, unsteady in his gait, a little drunk perhaps.

Cork handed the notes back.

"Anything?" Larson asked.

"Nothing," Cork lied.

But in his head he was thinking, *Not drunk. Just someone trying to protect the things he loves.*

* * *

It was dark by the time Cork pulled up the drive to Winona Crane's place. Willie's modified Jeep was parked there. A dim light shone inside the house, and Cork saw a shadow cross a window. He parked his Land Rover, got out, climbed the front steps, and knocked at the door. A few moments later, Willie Crane stood in the open doorway, looking at him with surprise, then with irritation.

"What do you want now?" he asked. *Whayouwannow?*

"May I come in?"

"What for?"

"I've been looking for you. Went to your cabin and then to the Native Art center in Allouette. I'd like to talk to you and Winona."

"She's not here."

"I figured that. So I'd like to talk to you about where I think she is." He waited a moment, then added, "Please."

Willie relented and stepped back to let him pass. They stood in the living room, surrounded by all the evidence of Winona Crane's search for . . . what? Truth? Peace of mind? Love?

"I came to apologize," Cork said.

"What for?"

"For leaning on you so hard in a difficult time."

"Apology accepted." It was obvious that, for Willie, the matter was ended, and he was just fine with Cork leaving.

Cork's cell phone rang. Without looking at the incoming call, he turned the unit off. In what was ahead, he didn't want any disturbance.

He walked toward a framed photograph on the wall, a magnificent shot of a moose, standing in the shallows of a wilderness lake at sunset with red fingers of sunlight stretched across the sky above, as if the hand of God had reached out in benediction.

"You're a remarkable guy, Willie. I've always admired you. There's nothing the rest of us can do that you can't. I still remember when you saved Isaiah Broom from drowning. That was amazing." Cork idly scratched the back of his neck and turned casually toward Willie. "You sure proved Sam Winter Moon wrong."

Willie stood with his back to a wall where one of Winona's exotic icons hung, a ceramic mask, a grotesque-looking thing with a mouth stretched in a huge, ruby-lipped oval, a silent scream of pain or maybe terror. What god it represented or what religious sensibility Cork hadn't the faintest idea, but it eyed him wildly over Willie's left shoulder and made Cork even more uncomfortable with what lay ahead.

"What do you mean?" Willie asked.

"Sam taught me and Jubal and your sister to hunt in the old way, but not you. He must have figured you couldn't handle it."

"He offered to teach me, but I had no interest in killing anything."

"He must have taught you to track though. You sure know how to stalk an animal with a camera." Cork nodded toward the photograph of the moose at sunset.

"He taught me," Willie admitted.

"So. Was it Winona who taught you how to shoot an arrow? Or was that your good friend Isaiah Broom?"

Willie frowned at him but didn't reply.

"The man who killed the *chimook* on the ridge above Trickster's Point and then killed Jubal Little left an odd trail," Cork explained. "The tracks were a bit awkward. The official thinking in the investigation is that the killer had been drinking to build his courage. Maybe. But if you ask me, it would be awfully hard for a drunk man to stalk anything quietly. So I've been thinking about a different kind of man. About a man who's walked a little awkwardly all his life and who knows how to compensate. About a man who, despite all the challenges against him, can stalk wild animals and get close enough for remarkable photographs."

Willie was as speechless as the screaming mask at his back.

"I'm willing to bet that, when I tell the sheriff's investigators to compare your fingerprints with those on the arrow through the John Doe's eye, they'll get a match. I don't know how you acquired the skill, Willie, but I'm sure you can shoot a hunting arrow as well as I can. Hell, from what I've seen of you over all these years, I'm willing to bet you can probably shoot better."

"Why are you here?" Willie finally asked.

"Believe it or not," Cork replied, "it's love that brings me."

CHAPTER 39

Willie said, "I need to sit down." *Ineedasidon.* He dropped into an easy chair, collapsed there like an emptied sack.

Cork sat on the small sofa, facing him. "I have to ask you some questions, Willie."

"Ask," Willie said in a dead voice.

"I found blood in the bathroom. It's Winona's blood, isn't it?"

Willie looked at Cork a long time and finally nodded.

Cork said, "At first, I figured maybe she'd been hurt, but not too badly since you talked to her last night while Camilla Little and I were at your cabin, and she didn't say anything. But I've been thinking about that call. You made it. I heard only your end of the conversation. It could have been anybody on the other end of the line. Or nobody." Cork waited a couple of breaths, then said, "Winona tried to kill herself, didn't she, Willie? Cut her wrists, am I right?"

Willie made no response, neither spoke nor gestured, just sat like a stunned man, mute and staring.

"She's gone, just like after all the other times Jubal left her," Cork went on. "Only this time, Jubal left her for good. And I'm thinking, Willie, that this time Winona may be gone for good."

Willie didn't respond immediately. First he studied Cork, who summoned everything Ojibwe in him and did his best to present an unreadable face. Then Willie's eyes swept the room slowly, taking in all the odd things Winona had gathered over the years, all the exotic talismans. When his gaze finally returned to Cork, his expression was so full of grief that it was heartbreaking.

Willie's words were more tortured than Cork could ever recall, and he had to strain to understand them. "He never loved her. He only needed her. He took and never gave back. He took everything from her, and then he took her life. She cut her wrists in the bathtub, but it was Jubal Little who killed her just as sure as if he'd put the knife in her hand."

"You found her?"

"She called me. I'd never heard her so upset. I told her I'd be there. I told her I'd take care of her. But I was too late."

"I'm sorry," Cork said. And he was. He felt sorrow in every cell of his heart.

Willie stared at the floor. "I suppose I always knew this was how it would end. She always said Jubal would have to leave her someday. 'For the mountaintop,' she would say. As if that was all her life was about, sacrificing for Jubal Little."

"Where is she?"

Willie gestured vaguely toward the main road, beyond which the woods began and ran north almost unbroken to Canada. "I buried her in a beautiful place. She will become the flowers and wild grass and trees."

Cork sat forward, nearer to Willie, rested his arms on his knees, and said quietly, "I have to ask you about Jubal. Why the arrow? Was it to throw the blame on me?"

"An accident of circumstance," Willie said, shaking his head. "I stole Isaiah's bow and some of his arrows. He never locks his doors."

"Isaiah taught you to shoot?"

"Yes."

"So he knew it was you who killed Jubal Little. He was covering for you, not for Winona."

"All my life, he's been my friend. I would never have let them prosecute him for what I did."

"How did you know we'd be at Trickster's Point?"

"Winona. When she called me, she was rambling, all over the place, not making much sense, but it was one of the things she said."

"And you decided to kill him. Revenge?"

Again he shook his head. "Justice. He killed Winona. He was going to betray the Anishinaabeg and Mother Earth. I killed him before he could do these things."

We kill to protect what we love, Cork thought. *And sometimes in the name of justice.*

"Tell me about the man on the ridge," he said.

Willie seemed puzzled at that. "I went early to get there ahead of you. I found his trail when I came up the back of the ridge, and I followed it."

"Just a hunter in the wrong place at the wrong time?" Cork said. "So you killed him?"

"No. Not just a hunter. Or not a hunter of deer anyway. He was hunting you."

That made Cork sit up. "Me? How do you know that?"

"I came up the ridge quietly. God bless Sam Winter Moon and all he taught me. The hunter didn't see me. He was lying on the ground, sighting his rifle. You and Jubal had just landed your canoe. Jubal had walked away, but you were still on the shore. Easy for me to see that it wasn't Jubal the man was taking a bead on."

"Me?" Cork said, trying to make sense of it.

"I'd brought three arrows that Isaiah had made. I grabbed one, nocked it, and got ready to shoot if I had to. When I was maybe thirty feet away, I called to him. He was on his stomach, and he rolled to his back, sat up, and brought his rifle with him. He didn't pause, not for an instant. He jammed the rifle butt to his shoulder, and it was clear he was going to shoot me. So I let the arrow fly."

"You killed him instantly," Cork said. "A perfect shot."

"I didn't think of it that way. I thought of it as a necessary shot. And a tragic one." He looked sad and troubled. "I discovered that killing takes two lives. The moment it was done, my life, as I knew it, was gone." He took a breath and finished. "There was no turning back, so I went ahead with what I'd come there to do."

Willie closed his eyes and breathed deeply. When he looked again at Cork, he seemed resigned. "You're going to tell them the truth?"

"Yes, Willie. But I want to tell them the whole truth."

"The whole truth?"

"Rhiannon," Cork said.

Willie didn't look at all surprised, but he said nothing.

"When I asked you about the name Rhiannon, you lied. You knew all of Winona's secrets, and Rhiannon was one. I want the truth."

Willie sagged, as if what Cork asked had drained him of any strength that remained. "There was a child," he said at last.

"Winona and Jubal?"

"Yes."

"When?"

"A dozen years ago. Nona became pregnant just before Jubal left for his first term as a congressman."

"Did Jubal know?"

"Not at first. Nona didn't want him to. She said he had enough to worry about."

"They'd been lovers for years without a pregnancy. How did it happen?"

"Nona had always been careful in her timing. She knew her body. But Jubal didn't plan on coming back to Aurora for a very long time. He wanted to solidify his position in Washington, and she was sad and desperate and a little careless before he left. When she realized she was pregnant, she thought about aborting the child but couldn't bring herself to do it. She went full term."

"I don't remember any word of this on the rez."

"As soon as she began to show, she went into seclusion at my cabin. She was always disappearing, so no one thought anything of it."

"And she had the baby?"

"She delivered, yes."

"Where?"

"In my bedroom."

"What happened?"

"She didn't want a doctor. She didn't want anything official to be known about the child. So she planned on doing it on her own. She read everything she could and took care of herself. I don't think I ever saw her so happy. She had a name for the baby. Rhiannon." Willie smiled sadly. "She loved Stevie Nicks, and she loved that song."

"What happened to Rhiannon?"

"Before her time, Nona began to experience a lot of pain. She was almost forty, and I thought maybe it was because she was older than most women with their first pregnancy. I wanted her to see a doctor. She refused. I was worried. I finally called Jubal in Washington. He dropped everything and came out immediately. She went into labor before he got here. I was with her. I'd read the books, too. But things weren't going like in the books. By the time Jubal arrived it was over."

"She'd delivered Rhiannon?"

"Yes. But the baby was stillborn. I don't know why."

"Oh, Willie. I'm sorry."

"They grieved together. Hell, I grieved, too. Then we buried her."

"Where?"

"Out there." Willie again gestured toward the forests that ran to Canada. "In a beautiful spot where no one would ever find her. Three nights ago, I laid Nona beside her."

"Who else knew about Rhiannon?"

"No one. It was a well-kept secret, Cork. I don't know who else could know."

"Someone knows, Willie. He threatened me, anonymously."

"I swear, Cork, I don't know."

Cork felt the weight of that particular concern settle once more on his tired shoulders. "Okay, will you do me a favor? For the time being, when the sheriff's people question you, don't say anything about Rhiannon."

"All right, Cork. But will you do me a favor in return?"

"What is it?"

"Give me a little time before you turn me in. I need to get things in order."

"I can do that, Willie."

Cork took one final look around the house where Winona Crane had lived her life according to a purpose she'd accepted long ago but, judging from the evidence she'd left behind, had never fully understood, a life she had made sacrifices for that hadn't, as far as Cork could see, brought her any happiness. He'd loved her once, loved her with all the ardor and ache of a young man's heart, and because of that, he had, in a sense, loved her always. Yet, as he drove off, leaving Willie to mourn her alone, Cork was very glad his own life had gone a different way and without her.

CHAPTER 40

A mile after he left Winona's house, the headlights appeared in Cork's rearview mirror. He noted them, then went back to his thinking.

He considered Jubal Little. He'd loved Jubal once, loved him as a brother, but it had, in actuality, been so brief a time. Had he really known Jubal then? He thought not, because Jubal hadn't known himself, any more than Cork understood who he was. Their roads had diverged, and they'd gone in different directions, become different kinds of men. Cork had created a family. Jubal had created a following. Cork had lived pretty much in anonymity in the small world of Tamarack County, and had been happy there. Jubal had lived in the spotlight, but had he been happy? All the evidence indicated no. Jubal had spent a good deal of his life chasing greatness, that mountaintop Winona had seen in her vision so very long ago. And what had it brought him in the end except regret? When they were children, Cork had envied Jubal. But he envied him no more.

The headlights behind him had approached, coming dangerously near, casting a blinding glare in Cork's mirrors. The road was empty. It was never heavily trafficked and at night it was particularly abandoned. But it was winding, and Cork kept his speed steady, thinking the vehicle would pass on the next straightaway. When the opportunity came, the vehicle shot around his Land Rover, and Cork saw the Escalade that belonged to Kenny Yates pass in a blur of shiny silver metal. It pulled ahead and swerved back into the right-hand lane directly in front of Cork, way too close. The taillights immediately bloomed red, and the Escalade began to slow, forcing Cork to slow with it. What the hell was Yates up to? Cork had no idea, but he didn't like this aggressiveness. It felt threatening. Felt, he realized, much like the call he'd received from the voice of the Devil on that same stretch of road, a manufactured voice meant as disguise. Low, gravelly, male. It could easily have been Yates.

The Escalade slowed to a stop on the empty highway, and Cork brought the Land Rover to a halt behind it. A moment passed. The door of the Escalade opened, and Yates stepped out. He wore a black leather jacket. His hands were in his pockets. He stood still, as if waiting for Cork to meet him.

Cork thought, *Ah, hell*, and got out. He approached the big man, the football player turned bodyguard, and kept his eyes on the pockets that hid Yates's hands. He stopped ten feet away.

"What's with the road rage, Kenny?" he asked.

"Road rage?" In the glare of Cork's headlights, the big man's eyes were white orbs drilled at the centers with fathomless holes. "I just wanted a word with you before this whole thing goes any further."

"A word? You could have called me on my cell phone."

"Tried. Got nothing."

Which could have been true, because during his talk with Willie Crane, Cork had turned his cell phone off.

"How'd you know I was out here?"

"Tailed you from town."

"You wanted to talk to me, why didn't you do it before this?"

"Had to work myself up for it."

Which didn't sound encouraging to Cork. He thought that if Yates pulled a gun from his coat—maybe that Beretta he'd offered Cork earlier—he'd dash behind the Escalade and head for the darkness of the woods that lined the road. It wasn't a great plan, but it was something.

"Okay, you've got me now," Cork said. "What's the word?"

"Rhiannon," Yates said. Only he didn't say the word in a normal way. He used the voice of the Devil. He studied Cork and seemed confused at Cork's lack of surprise. "You knew it was me?"

Cork didn't answer that one. Instead he said simply, "Why, Kenny?"

"What do you know about Rhiannon?"

"Everything."

Yates nodded, as if what he already suspected had just been confirmed. His shoulders sagged, but his hands stayed in his pockets. "That night you first met with the Jaegers, after you left, I heard Camilla ask her brothers about the name. She said you'd run it by her. I panicked, thought you were onto Jubal's dirty little secret."

"You knew?"

"I've worked for the Littles for nearly five years. Each of those years, on the second day of October, Jubal got shitfaced. He'd have me drive him out into the country somewhere, always some isolated rural place, and he'd go off alone with a bottle of Kentucky bourbon and drink himself into a stupor. If he didn't go far enough, I'd hear him wailing something awful. Eventually I'd gather him up and bring him home."

"He told you about Rhiannon?"

"He confessed to me once, like I was a priest or something. Told me how he should have been there, how he should have made certain that little child had the right care, how he'd buried her in the woods, unbaptized, her grave unmarked. He asked me to pray for him."

"Did he remember telling you these things?"

"Never. Jubal liked his Kentucky bourbon, but I never saw him that drunk except on that one day every year. Jubal shouldered a shitload of guilt, but his little baby, she was more than he could bear."

"Why the threats, Kenny? Jubal's dead. The truth can't hurt him."

"Not him. Camilla. Folks, they'd understand a man having another woman on the side, forget about it eventually. Happens all the time. But what he did with that poor baby, nobody's going to forget or forgive. Jubal's gone, but Camilla'd have to live with the way people looked at her, married to a man like that."

We kill to protect the things we love, Cork thought.

"Why are you telling me this, Kenny?"

Yates slowly withdrew his hands from his pockets. Cork tensed, then was relieved to see that they were empty.

"Because I didn't know you before. What I know now is that you're a decent man, and I don't want you worrying about your family. I'm ashamed of what I did to you. So go on and do whatever you've got to do. Bring charges, tell Camilla the truth, it's up to you."

"I ought to just coldcock you."

"You go right ahead." Yates braced but made no move to protect himself.

Cork said, "But I guess I understand."

Yates relaxed. "Hoped you would. So, you going to tell her?"

"I don't know, Kenny. What good would it do? Jubal's dead. Winona's dead. Seems best to let that secret die with them."

"See? Knew I could trust you to do the right thing."

"I don't know that it's right. But it's something I can live with."

Yates walked across the distance that had separated them and put out his big hand. "Been a pleasure getting to know you."

Cork took the offered hand. "Likewise."

Yates nodded toward the Land Rover. "I'll let you get on with things now. I'm guessing you still have places to go. And me, I need to get back to Camilla."

When Yates left, Cork stood alone on the highway, relieved.

312 WILLIAM KENT KRUEGER

He called home, told Jenny that Cy's tour of duty was over, and that the danger was past. He didn't explain, just said, "I think we're nearing the end of the road on this one."

"Home late?"

"Probably."

"I'll leave a light on," she promised.

CHAPTER 41

Cork had seen optical illusions created in such a way that, when you looked at the image, at first you saw one thing, but if you stared at it long enough, or from a different angle, you saw another image entirely. After he left Kenny Yates, as he drove back into Aurora, he realized that's how it was with what had occurred at Trickster's Point.

He turned on his cell phone, called ahead to the Tamarack County Sheriff's Department, and made a suggestion to Ed Larson. When he arrived, he found Larson, Sheriff Marsha Dross, and BCA Agent Phil Holter gathered in Dross's office.

"Well?" he asked as he headed to the chair they'd left empty for him.

"You were right," Larson replied. "The other set of prints on the flyer we took from the John Doe's car belonged to Jubal Little. How did you know?"

Cork took off his leather jacket, hung it on the chair back, and sat down. "I realized we were all looking at the man on the ridge as if he and whoever murdered Jubal were connected. When Stephen first suggested that possibility, it seemed natural. The killer and his backup. To have two men up there with no relationship to each other seemed too enormous a coincidence. But coincidence it was. When I understood that, I understood things in a different way, although largely because I knew something no one else did."

"And that was?" Holter said, obviously wanting to be able to write off as nonsense whatever it was Cork was going to say.

"That when Jubal was eighteen, he murdered someone."

This clearly hit them all with shocking effect. Their stares went owl-eye huge, and they seemed dumbfounded. So Cork told them what had happened at Trickster's Point the day Donner Bigby died.

When Cork finished, Holter asked, "You knew all along Little had killed that kid?"

"Not when it happened. I bought the story Jubal told me. Years later, he told me the truth. And not long ago, I threatened to use what I knew against him." He turned to Dross. "You asked me what Jubal and I argued about the morning before he died. That was it. Jubal pretty much demanded to know if I still planned to use Donner Bigby against him. I told him that if he won the election and went ahead with the mining and the casinos, I would. He tried to argue me out of it. I wouldn't budge. He repeated something he'd said to me once before. My end was my own doing. I didn't understand then, but it's obvious to me now. He'd arranged to have me silenced."

"You really believe that?" Holter asked.

"Jubal died thinking I'd shot that arrow into his heart. He recognized my fletching pattern. He thought I'd done it deliberately. I didn't try to argue with him, what was the point? At the end, he told me, with a grudging kind of respect, that I'd finally bested him. Bested him in what way, I had no idea. Now I get it. He thought that somehow I knew he was planning to kill me, and I simply struck first. It was what he would have done in my place."

Holter said, "You're saying that he arranged for the John Doe to kill you and gave him your flyer so that the guy would know what you looked like? Is that it?"

"Jubal chose Trickster's Point. He told me he wanted to go back where it all began, to make our peace there, with each other and with the past. He said Winona had advised him it would be a good thing to do. Do you remember, Ed, when you interviewed me at the start of all this, and I told you that what I was hunting wasn't deer but Jubal Little?"

"I remember."

"I thought maybe if we made peace, I'd find the old Jubal, or what was left of him. But it had been a trap all along. Jubal figured, and rightly so, that we'd be alone out there. Even though I'd be hard to miss, I'm guessing that flyer with my picture on it was just Jubal making sure nothing got screwed up."

"A hell of a lot of speculation," Holter said dismissively. "No proof of anything."

"If we knew the true identity of our John Doe, we might be able to prove a connection," Dross offered.

"Do you have a photo of him?" Cork asked.

"Lots from the crime scene," Larson replied.

"I have an idea," Cork told them.

Holter gave him a dismal look. "Why does that not surprise me?"

When Kenny Yates showed Cork and Larson in, the Jaegers were gathered in the den. They all had drinks in their hands, and there was a nice fire crackling away in the fireplace. The room carried the pleasant, comforting scent of woodsmoke, yet the way the Jaegers eyed their visitors was anything but comfortable.

"Thank you, Kenny," Camilla said.

"You're welcome." Yates turned to leave.

"I'd like you to stick around, Kenny," Cork said. "I'm hoping you might be able to help me out here."

Yates looked surprised, then looked to Camilla Little, who nodded her assent.

Alex Jaeger said, "What exactly is it that you think we can do for you?"

Ed Larson stood next to the chair where Camilla sat. He said, "In most homicides, we find that the perpetrator and the victim are acquainted. The motive tends to be something personal between them. I'd like you all to take a look at the photograph of the man killed on the ridge above Trickster's Point the same day Mrs. Little's husband was killed. I'd like to know if you recognize him, if he might have been someone Mr. Little was acquainted with."

Larson handed the photo to Camilla first. She studied it and shook her head.

Alex was next, and he did the same. "Never saw him before."

Larson took the photograph to Nick, who was finishing off a glass of what looked like scotch on the rocks. He put the drink down, took the photograph, eyed it carefully, and said, "Son of a bitch."

"You know him?" Larson asked.

"He looks different dead, but I'd swear it's Chet Carlson."

"Carlson?" Yates said. "Let me see that picture." He crossed to where Larson stood with Nick Jaeger, took the photograph, glanced at it, and said, "That's him all right."

"Who was Chet Carlson?" Larson asked.

"A linebacker for Kansas City when Jubal quarterbacked for them," Yates explained. "He wasn't in the league very long. Mean mother. Some guys, they played for the love of the sport or maybe for the money. Carlson, he played to get his licks in. Loved doing damage on the field. I heard that after he left football he signed on with that mercenary company."

"Blackwater?"

"Blackwater. That's it. Didn't surprise me in the least that he'd go into a line of work where it's always open season on human beings."

"What about you?" Larson said to Nick. "How do you know him?"

"He used to hunt with Jubal and me sometimes. I didn't care for him at all. Like Kenny says, the guy was all about hurting things. I finally told Jubal I wouldn't go on any more hunts if Carlson was going to be a part of them."

"Good shot?" Cork asked.

"With the right equipment, anybody can be a good shot," Nick said. "He never joined any of the hunts when Jubal and I shot muzzle-loaders and black powder, so not a pure hunter. But with a Marlin and a good scope, he could put a bullet where it had to go for a kill shot."

"I don't understand," Camilla said. "Why would he be involved in killing Jubal?"

"He wasn't," Cork said. "He was supposed to kill me."

He explained his reasoning, and when he'd finished, the room was dead still.

"Doesn't make a lick of sense," Alex finally blustered. "How would Jubal have explained you getting shot?"

Cork shrugged. "Hunting accident, maybe, but not his doing. All he had with him was a bow and a few arrows. So a stray shot from some careless hunter, who either didn't know the damage he'd done or vanished because of it. Probably another reason Jubal chose Trickster's Point, all the incidents of accidental hunting deaths out there. He believed he could sell ice to Eskimos, so I'm sure he figured that whatever he said people would buy it."

"Carlson's a loose end," Larson pointed out. "And kind of a loose cannon, it sounds like. Seems to me a dangerous man for Little to bring into something like this and just hope he'd keep quiet."

Cork looked toward Nick. "If I were Jubal, I'd plan on another hunting accident, maybe somewhere in the wilds of Canada where there'd be no witnesses. Or maybe he'd just report that they got separated out there and lost and Carlson was never found. What do you think, Nick? Things like that happen, don't they?"

Nick's face clouded, and he said vaguely, "I've heard."

"It's all speculation, of course," Cork went on. "Jubal took the answers with him when he walked the Path of Souls."

Alex shook his head fiercely. "His fingerprints on a sheet of paper. That's all you have. Proves nothing."

"Not yet," Larson said. "But it's a beginning, Mr. Jaeger. And I'm going to make sure that we find out where it leads."

Camilla's hands lay folded in her lap, and her eyes rested there, as if holding them in place. She didn't look up when she spoke. "I'm sorry, Cork."

"Nothing to be sorry for, Camilla. Jubal always did what Jubal wanted. Not your fault."

"Hey," Nick said suddenly. "So who killed Chet Carlson? And who killed Jubal?"

Camilla finally lifted her eyes and looked at Cork. Everyone did.

CHAPTER 42

When Cork pulled into his driveway on Gooseberry Lane, the hour was late. The street was empty and the houses were dark. A light shone through his own kitchen window, and when he walked inside, the room was still redolent with the aroma of sweet baking. On the table sat a plate with chocolate chip cookies, and beside it lay a note.

Comfort food, Dad.

The handwriting was Stephen's.

He shed his coat and hung it on a peg near the door. He poured himself some milk, leaned against a counter, and drank slowly while he ate a couple of the cookies. He listened to the house, the beautiful quiet, and, for the first time in days, felt at ease.

Trixie wandered in, tail wagging in a slow, sleepy way, and put her nose against the hand he lowered.

"Hey, girl," he said. "Keeping the place safe?"

He rinsed out the glass in the sink and headed upstairs, where the kids had left the hallway light on for him. He stopped in the open doorway to his grandson's room and stood watching Waaboo asleep in his crib. The little guy was dressed in footie pajamas patterned with tiny moose. He lay splayed on the mattress, arms and legs all akimbo. Cork walked to the crib, lifted the twisted blanket, and gently covered his grandson. When he turned back to the door, he found his daughter smiling from the hallway.

"Within an hour, he'll have kicked that blanket off again," she whispered when he joined her.

"Always moving," Cork said. "Even in his sleep."

"You're one to talk. Late night."

"And not over yet."

"Oh?"

"I'll be getting a couple of visitors soon."

"Should I make coffee?"

"No. We'll leave right away."

"Anyone I know?"

"I'll tell you about it in the morning."

She studied his face. "You look . . . peaceful. A good day?"

"An enlightening day. Jenny, if you ever wonder what your life is all about, just pick up Waaboo and hold him. Everything you need to know, it's all right there."

"And right here," she said and leaned to him and kissed his cheek. Then she yawned.

"Go back to bed," he told her gently. "Everything's okay now."

The knock at the back door came just as he returned to the kitchen. When he opened up, Marsha Dross stood on the doorstep beside a hulking Isaiah Broom.

"Holter's pissed as hell," she said. "If he doesn't have answers from you by the time the sun comes up, he says he'll arrest you for obstruction."

"He'll know everything by the time he pours his first cup of morning coffee," Cork replied. "Promise."

"What the hell's going on?" Broom said.

"You're free, Isaiah." Cork reached to his leather jacket hanging on the peg beside the door. "And you're coming with me."

"Yeah?" Broom threw back, not happily. "Where?"

"You'll see."

The big Shinnob frowned, then lifted his broad nose. "Cookies?"

Cork went to the table where the plate still held half a dozen. He picked up a couple and returned to the door.

"For the road," he said to Dross and handed her one. The other he gave to Isaiah Broom. "Let's get going."

In the light that fell through the doorway, Cork saw Dross wince. She was taking a big chance, and he appreciated it. "I'll be at your office by first light," he promised.

She took a bite of the cookie he'd given her and said, "I'll be waiting."

He drove down the empty streets, through a town deep in its own dreaming. Snow spit from the sky, a few flakes, like moths fluttering in the headlights. For a long time, he drove in a silence that both he and Broom seemed comfortable with.

"Traitor," Cork said at last, breaking the silence.

"What?"

"That's what you wrote on the arrow you shot into the door of Rainy's cabin. *Traitor.* Why?"

"Why *traitor*, or why the arrow?"

"Both."

They'd left Aurora behind, and the dark had swallowed them. The only light came from the back splash of headlights and the glow of the dash. The big Shinnob sat silent and brooding in the night gloom, and was quiet for so long that Cork wasn't sure he'd get a reply at all.

"I made that arrow for Jubal Little," Broom finally said. "I meant to shoot it into his heart myself. When I heard it was you who killed him, I figured I'd let you know that I understood."

"You could've just told me. I admit I was more than a little confused by that message."

Broom stared ahead where the thin scatter of snowflakes drifted white against the black asphalt of the highway. "I was drunk. Celebrating his death, I thought, but later I decided maybe I was just relieved that I didn't have to go on hating him. I knew you'd be at Henry's." He swung his face toward Cork for an instant. "Rainy," he said. Then he shrugged. "The decisions you make when you're drunk usually aren't your best."

322 WILLIAM KENT KRUEGER

Cork didn't have to press him about the *traitor* part. That arrow had long ago been intended for Jubal Little. "When did you realize it was Willie who killed him?"

Cork felt the huge body on the other side of the Land Rover tense up.

"Don't know what you're talking about."

"Yeah, you do, Isaiah. That's why you gave yourself up. To protect Willie. He would never have let you take the blame, you know."

They'd negotiated the southern end of Iron Lake and had started up the shoreline toward the reservation. Broom was like one of those wooden statues he carved so adroitly, massive and silent.

Cork went on. "I talked with Willie earlier tonight. He's going to turn himself in."

Broom twisted quickly, facing Cork. "No." It was like a command.

"It has to be done, Isaiah. Willie understands that."

"There's no way he's going to spend his life in jail. I won't let him. And it'll kill Winona."

Cork drew to a stop at the side of the road. "Isaiah, there's something else you need to know. I wish . . ." He was suddenly at a loss for words. He'd delivered bad news, news of death, many times in his law enforcement career, and it had always knotted his gut. "Winona's dead, Isaiah. She killed herself. That's pretty much what drove Willie to kill Jubal."

Broom looked as if Cork had just done the same to him, put an arrow into his heart. He seemed stunned, deeply wounded, then he turned away, hid his face by staring out the window on his side of the Land Rover.

"We're going to see Willie," Cork told him. "I figured you might want to talk to him alone before he turns himself in. Everything'll get hard after that."

Broom kept his face to the window. "Drive," he said.

When they reached Willie Crane's cabin, there was a light

on inside and the Jeep was parked in front. They stood on the doorstep with snowflakes wetting their faces, but when Cork knocked, no one answered.

"Willie?" he called. He tried the knob and pushed the cabin door open. "Willie, it's Cork O'Connor. I've brought Isaiah with me."

"Was he expecting us?" Broom asked.

"Not exactly. He wanted some time to get things ready before he turned himself in. I figured he'd be here."

But the cabin was empty. On the table where Willie ate his meals lay a sheet of paper printed with text, and at the bottom was Willie Crane's signature. Cork picked it up and read it. A full explanation of the killing of Jubal Little. A signed confession. There was also a note to Cork on a separate sheet of paper. It said simply, "With Winona."

Broom read the confession and the note. He walked to one of the windows overlooking the lake that backed the cabin. "There's a fire on the shore," he said, and he turned and quickly went outside.

Cork followed, and they stumbled through the dark along the path where a couple of days earlier Willie had led Cork on a wild-goose chase in search of Winona. They came to the place in the lee of the great rock where the earlier fire had been kindled, and a more recent fire had also burned. The flames were slowly dying. Willie had been there but was gone.

Broom turned to the black hole that was the lake. "Willie!" he cried desperately. "Willie!"

Cork stood beside him, thinking how, long ago, Willie Crane had saved his good friend's life. Thinking how Isaiah Broom, in trying to take the blame for Jubal's murder, had done his best to repay that debt. Thinking, too, that, in their lives, Willie Crane and Isaiah Broom had been blessed by their great friendship. Thinking of Jubal Little, who'd done his best to have Cork killed. And thinking, finally, that for a big man with such huge ambition, Jubal had had a very small heart.

"He's gone, Isaiah," Cork said.

Broom turned to him, and the Shinnob's cheeks were cut by streams of tears that glistened in the light of the dying fire. "Where?"

"He told me that, when he died, he wanted to be left out there." Cork nodded toward the deep forest that began on the far side of the lake. "He wanted to become a part of all that beauty. Wherever he is, he's with Winona, and I doubt that we'll find them."

The snow had begun falling in earnest, thick as ash from some all-consuming fire.

"We should go," Cork said.

"I want to stay for a while."

"I have to leave, Isaiah."

"Then leave."

"Long walk home."

Isaiah Broom said, "I know."

EPILOGUE

Snow had fallen the night before, not deep, but enough to coat the ground. A hunter's snow. As they came across Lake Nanaboozhoo, the sun was just rising, and the eastern sky, clear now, was a deep russet, the color of oak leaves in the fall. Above the distant shoreline, the top of Trickster's Point caught the first light of day, and it reminded Cork of a finger dipped in old blood.

The air was cool. A low white mist lay on the water, and the canoes glided through as if touching nothing but air. Cork had the stern, Rainy the bow. In the stern of the other canoe, Stephen dug his paddle into the lake easily and almost without sound. Up front, despite his age, Meloux kept pace just as smoothly.

When they reached the far side, the whole upper half of Trickster's Point was lit with morning sunlight, which by now had turned gold, and the tops of the trees looked bathed in honey. They pulled the canoes onto shore and tipped them and laid the paddles against the upturned hulls. Without a word, they began to thread their way through the trees, following the same path, more or less, that Cork and Jubal Little had followed only a week before. They said nothing to one another as they walked, and the only sound was the soft crush of their boot soles on the thin crust of snow.

They broke from the trees, and Trickster's Point rose above

them, and for a moment, Cork's heart beat faster, as he remembered all the death he'd been a part of there. But all that death was, in fact, the reason they'd come.

Meloux had brought his bandolier bag, an ancient accoutrement made of ornately beaded deerskin. At the base of the great monolith, he slid the bag from his shoulder, opened it, and drew out a small leather pouch filled with tobacco.

"Stephen," he said and held the tobacco pouch toward Cork's son.

Stephen seemed surprised and pleased. He took it, loosened the drawstring, and dipped his thumb and index finger inside. He pulled out a pinch of tobacco and offered it to the East, the first of the four grandfathers. Then he turned clockwise and made an offering to each of the other grandfathers: South, West, and North. He let a pinch fall to the ground where he stood, as an offering to Mother Earth, and finally tossed a bit in the air as an offering to the Great Spirit above.

Meloux took back the pouch and returned it to his bandolier bag. Next he pulled out four sage bundles tied with hemp threads, which he'd prepared by lantern light that morning in his cabin while it was still dark outside. He gave a bundle to each of them and kept one for himself. From the bag, he took four shallow clay bowls painted with designs in ocher, and gave them out. After that, he carefully drew out four black turkey feathers, each quill wrapped in soft leather binding, and handed them around.

The old Mide sat down on the snow, and the others sat with him. He set his clay bowl on the ground, untied his small bundle, and mounded the dried sage in the center of the shallow cupping. He took a box of kitchen matches from his bandolier bag and put flame to the dried sage, which began to smolder. He held his hands in the smoke to cleanse them, then used his feather to blow smoke gently across his heart and his head. He wafted smoke across each of the others in turn.

He sang a prayer in Ojibwe, which Rainy and Stephen both

clearly understood, but Cork, whose own knowledge of the language remained rudimentary at best, heard only the rise and fall of the gentle invocation.

Then Meloux spoke in English. "All life is one weaving, one design by the hand of the Creator, the Great Mystery. All life is connected, thread by thread. When one thread is cut, the others weaken."

He lifted his bowl and, with his feather, encouraged the smoke across Cork.

"We are here to help this man heal."

He turned toward the towering monolith beside him, and the smoke that rose from the smoldering sage drifted against the face of the rock.

"We are here to help this place heal," Meloux said.

He nodded to the others, and they loosed their bundles into their own bowls. They lit the sage and stood with Meloux.

"Stephen, you come with me." The old Mide nodded to the north. "Rainy, you and Corcoran O'Connor go that way." He indicated south.

"And do what, Henry?" Cork asked.

"Pray."

"What prayer?"

"Whatever is in your heart. There are no right words, and there are no wrong words."

Rainy and Cork began to circle to the south. They used the feathers Meloux had given them to keep the sage embers burning and to draft the smoke against the gray stone and diffuse it into the air around them. They spoke quietly to themselves. Cork couldn't hear Rainy's words, but his own prayer was brief and sincere: "Give peace to this place and peace to my heart."

They all met halfway round and stood at the spot where, over the course of three hours, Jubal Little's life had trickled away. The sage had burned to ash. They tipped their clay bowls, and the ashes fell and lay like faint shadows on the white snow. Cork looked across the jumble of broken talus between

Trickster's Point and the ridge slope where Willie Crane had hidden himself and had fired the fatal arrow. Above it, among the aspens that capped the top of the ridge, was the place where Willie had killed the *chimook* and, in doing so, had saved Cork's life.

"Coincidence," Cork said. "I never believed in it much until now."

"Nanaboozhoo," Meloux told him, as if that explained everything.

"The trickster," Rainy said, "who delights in confounding our ambitions and expectations."

"When I was a kid, I envied Jubal everything he'd been given," Cork said.

"And now?" Rainy asked.

"Now?" Cork put his arm around her. "I feel like the richest of men."

The sun had risen fully, and the great stone tower was ablaze with the morning light, as if, in addition to the smudging, it was being purified with fire.

"Anything more?" Stephen asked Meloux.

"Yes," the old man replied. "You send us off from this place with a prayer."

Which clearly caught Stephen by surprise. But Cork's son composed himself and thought for a long moment. And this is what he said.

> *O Great Spirit, whose voice I hear in the winds*
> *And whose breath gives life to everyone,*
> *Hear me.*
> *I come to you as one of your many children;*
> *I am weak. I am small.*
> *I need your wisdom and your strength.*
> *Let me walk in beauty, and make my eyes ever*
> *Behold the red and purple sunsets.*
> *Make my hand respect the things you have made,*
> *And make my ears sharp so I may hear your voice.*

Make me wise, so that I may understand what you
Have taught my people and
The lessons you have hidden in each leaf and each rock.
I ask for wisdom and strength,
Not to be superior to my brothers, but to be able
To fight my greatest enemy, myself.
Make me ever ready to come before you with
Clean hands and a straight eye,
So as life fades away as a fading sunset,
My spirit may come to you without shame.

It was not an original prayer. Cork had heard it many times before, but he was impressed and pleased that his son knew it by heart.

Meloux smiled and nodded and said, "It is done."

He collected the clay bowls, returned them to his bandolier bag, and together they walked back toward the blue lake and the rising sun.

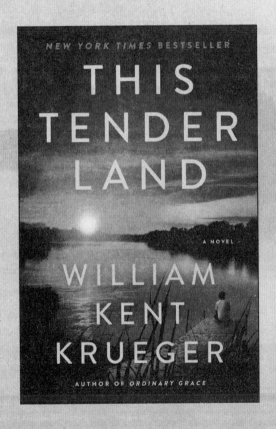